MICHAEL CRICHTON

ALSO BY MICHAEL CRICHTON

Fiction
The Andromeda Strain
The Great Train Robbery
Eaters of the Dead
A Case of Need
Sphere
Jurassic Park
Rising Sun
Disclosure

Non Fiction
Five Patients
Jasper Johns
Electronic Life
Travels

MICHAEL CRICHTON

CONGO

THE
TERMINAL MAN

CRESSET
EDITIONS

This edition first published by Cresset Editions in 1995
an imprint of the Random House Group
20 Vauxhall Bridge Road, London SW1V 2SA

Copyright © Michael Crichton 1995

The right of Michael Crichton to be identified as the author of
this work has been asserted by him in accordance with the Copyright,
Designs and Patents Act 1988

Congo copyright © Michael Crichton 1980
The Terminal Man copyright © Michael Crichton 1972

Papers used by Random House UK Limited are natural recyclable products made
from wood grown in sustainable forests. The manufacturing processes conform to
the environmental regulations of the country of origin.

A catalogue record for this book is available from the British Library

Printed and bound in Great Britain by
Mackays of Chatham PLC, Chatham, Kent

ISBN 07126-7620 1

CONGO

For Bob Gottlieb

The more experience and insight I obtain into human nature, the more convinced do I become that the greater portion of a man is purely animal.

—HENRY MORTON STANLEY, 1887

The large male [gorilla] held my attention. . . . He gave an impression of dignity and restrained power, of absolute certainty in his majestic appearance. I felt a desire to communicate with him. . . . Never before had I had this feeling on meeting an animal. As we watched each other across the valley, I wondered if he recognized the kinship that bound us.

—GEORGE B. SCHALLER, 1964

Contents

Introduction

ONLY PREJUDICE, AND A TRICK OF THE MERCATOR projection, prevents us from recognizing the enormity of the African continent. Covering nearly twelve million square miles, Africa is almost as large as North America and Europe combined. It is nearly twice the size of South America. As we mistake its dimensions, we also mistake its essential nature: the Dark Continent is mostly hot desert and open grassy plains.

In fact, Africa is called the Dark Continent for one reason only: the vast equatorial rain forests of its central region. This is the drainage basin of the Congo River, and one-tenth of the continent is given over to it—a million and a half square miles of silent, damp, dark forest, a single uniform geographical feature nearly half the size of the continental United States. This primeval forest has stood, unchanged and unchallenged, for more than sixty million years.

Even today, only half a million people inhabit the Congo Basin, and they are mostly clustered in villages along the banks of the slow muddy rivers that flow through the jungle. The great expanse of the forest remains inviolate, and to this day thousands of square miles are still unexplored.

This is true particularly of the northeastern corner of the Congo Basin, where the rain forest meets the Virunga volcanoes, at the edge of the Great Rift Valley. Lacking established trade routes or compelling features of interest, Virunga was never seen by Western eyes until less than a hundred years ago.

The race to make "the most important discovery of the 1980s" in the Congo took place during six weeks of 1979.

Introduction

This book recounts the thirteen days of the last American expedition to the Congo, in June, 1979—barely a hundred years after Henry Morton Stanley first explored the Congo in 1874–77. A comparison of the two expeditions reveals much about the changing—and unchanging—nature of African exploration in the intervening century.

Stanley is usually remembered as the newsman who found Livingstone in 1871, but his real importance lay in later exploits. Moorehead calls him "a new kind of man in Africa . . . a businessman-explorer. . . . Stanley was not in Africa to reform the people nor to build an empire, and he was not impelled by any real interest in such matters as anthropology, botany or geology. To put it bluntly, he was out to make a name for himself."

When Stanley set out again from Zanzibar in 1874, he was again handsomely financed by newspapers. And when he emerged from the jungle at the Atlantic Ocean 999 days later, having suffered incredible hardships and the loss of more than two-thirds of his original party, both he and his newspapers had one of the great stories of the century: Stanley had traveled the entire length of the Congo River.

But two years later, Stanley was back in Africa under very different circumstances. He traveled under an assumed name; he made diversionary excursions to throw spies off his trail; the few people who knew he was in Africa could only guess that he had in mind "some grand commercial scheme."

In fact, Stanley was financed by Leopold II of Belgium, who intended to acquire *personally* a large piece of Africa. "It is not a question of Belgian colonies," Leopold wrote Stanley. "It is a question of creating a new State, as big as possible. . . . The King, as a private person, wishes to possess properties in Africa. Belgium wants neither a colony nor territories. Mr. Stanley must therefore buy lands or get them conceded to him. . . ."

This incredible plan was carried out. By 1885, one American said that Leopold "possesses the Congo just as Rockefeller possesses Standard Oil." The comparison was apt in more ways than one, for African exploration had become dominated by business.

Introduction

It has remained so to this day. Stanley would have approved the 1979 American expedition, which was conducted in secrecy, with an emphasis on speed. But the differences would have astonished him. When Stanley passed near Virunga in 1875, it had taken him almost a year to get there; the Americans got their expedition on-site in just over a week. And Stanley, who traveled with a small army of four hundred, would have been amazed at an expedition of only twelve—and one of them an ape. The territories through which the Americans moved a century later were autonomous political states; the Congo was now Zaire, and the Congo River the Zaire River. In fact, by 1979 the word "Congo" technically referred only to the drainage basin of the Zaire River, although Congo was still used in geological circles as a matter of familiarity, and for its romantic connotations.

Despite these differences, the expeditions had remarkably similar outcomes. Like Stanley, the Americans lost two-thirds of their party, and emerged from the jungle as desperately as Stanley's men a century before. And like Stanley, they returned with incredible tales of cannibals and pygmies, ruined jungle civilizations, and fabulous lost treasures.

I would like to thank R. B. Travis, of Earth Resources Technology Services in Houston, for permission to use videotaped debriefings; Dr. Karen Ross, of ERTS, for further background on the expedition; Dr. Peter Elliot, of the Department of Zoology, University of California at Berkeley, and the Project Amy staff, including Amy herself; Dr. William Wens, of Kasai Mining & Manufacturing, Zaire; Dr. Smith Jefferson, of the Department of Medical Pathology, University of Nairobi, Kenya; and Captain Charles Munro, of Tangier, Morocco.

I am further indebted to Mark Warwick, of Nairobi, for his initial interest in this project; Alan Binks, of Nairobi, for graciously offering to take me into the Virunga region of Zaire; Joyce Small for arranging my transport, usually at short notice, to obscure parts of the world; and finally my special thanks to my assistant, Judith Lovejoy, whose untiring efforts through very difficult times were crucial to the completion of this book.

M.C.

Prologue:
The Place of Bones

DAWN CAME TO THE CONGO RAIN FOREST.
The pale sun burned away the morning chill and the clinging damp mist, revealing a gigantic silent world. Enormous
trees with trunks forty feet in diameter rose two hundred feet
overhead, where they spread their dense leafy canopy, blot-
ting out the sky and perpetually dripping water to the ground
below. Curtains of gray moss, and creepers and lianas, hung
down in a tangle from the trees; parasitic orchids sprouted
from the trunks. At ground level, huge ferns, gleaming with
moisture, grew higher than a man's chest and held the low
ground fog. Here and there was a spot of color: the red
acanthema blossoms, which were deadly poison, and the blue
dicindra vine, which only opened in early morning. But the
basic impression was of a vast, oversized, gray-green world—
an alien place, inhospitable to man.

Jan Kruger put aside his rifle and stretched his stiff muscles. Dawn came quickly at the equator; soon it was quite
light, although the mist remained. He glanced at the expedition campsite he had been guarding: eight bright orange
nylon tents, a blue mess tent, a supply tarp lashed over boxed
equipment in a vain attempt to keep them dry. He saw the
other guard, Misulu, sitting on a rock; Misulu waved sleep-
ily. Nearby was the transmitting equipment: a silver dish
antenna, the black transmitter box, the snaking coaxial cables running to the portable video camera mounted on the
collapsible tripod. The Americans used this equipment to
transmit daily reports by satellite to their home office in
Houston.

Kruger was the *bwana mukubwa*, hired to take the expe-

1

dition into the Congo. He had led expeditions before: oil companies, map-survey parties, timber-mining teams, and geological parties like this one. Companies sending teams into the field wanted someone who knew local customs and local dialects well enough to handle the porters and arrange the travel. Kruger was well suited for this job; he spoke Kiswahili as well as Bantu and a little Bagindi, and he had been to the Congo many times, although never to Virunga.

Kruger could not imagine why American geologists would want to go to the Virunga region of Zaire, in the northeast corner of the Congo rain forest. Zaire was the richest country in black Africa, in minerals—the world's largest producer of cobalt and industrial diamonds, the seventh largest producer of copper. In addition there were major deposits of gold, tin, zinc, tungsten and uranium. But most of the minerals were found in Shaba and Kasai, not in Virunga.

Kruger knew better than to ask why the Americans wanted to go to Virunga, and in any case he had his answer soon enough. Once the expedition passed Lake Kivu and entered the rain forest, the geologists began scouring rivers and streambeds. Searching placer deposits meant that they were looking for gold, or diamonds. It turned out to be diamonds.

But not just any diamonds. The geologists were after what they called Type IIb diamonds. Each new sample was immediately submitted to an electrical test. The resulting conversations were beyond Kruger—talk of dielectric gaps, lattice ions, resistivity. But he gathered that it was the electrical properties of the diamonds that mattered. Certainly the samples were useless as gemstones. Kruger had examined several, and they were all blue from impurities.

For ten days, the expedition had been tracing back placer deposits. This was standard procedure: if you found gold or diamonds in streambeds, you moved upstream toward the presumed erosive source of the minerals. The expedition had moved to higher ground along the western slopes of the Virgunga volcanic chain. It was all going routinely until one day around noon when the porters flatly refused to proceed further.

This part of Virunga, they said, was called *kanyamagufa*,

which meant "the place of bones." The porters insisted that any men foolish enough to go further would have their bones broken, particularly their skulls. They kept touching their cheekbones, and repeating that their skulls would be crushed.

The porters were Bantu-speaking Arawanis from the nearest large town, Kisangani. Like most town-dwelling natives, they had all sorts of superstitions about the Congo jungle. Kruger called for the headman.

"What tribes are here?" Kruger asked, pointing to the jungle ahead.

"No tribes," the headman said.

"No tribes at all? Not even Bambuti?" he asked, referring to the nearest group of pygmies.

"No men come here," the headman said. "This is *kanyamagufa*."

"Then what crushes the skulls?"

"*Dawa*," the headman said ominously, using the Bantu term for magical forces. "Strong *dawa* here. Men stay away."

Kruger sighed. Like many white men, he was thoroughly sick of hearing about *dawa*. *Dawa* was everywhere, in plants and rocks and storms and enemies of all kinds. But the belief in *dawa* was prevalent throughout much of Africa and strongly held in the Congo.

Kruger had been obliged to waste the rest of the day in tedious negotiation. In the end, he doubled their wages and promised them firearms when they returned to Kisangani, and they agreed to continue on. Kruger considered the incident an irritating native ploy. Porters could generally be counted on to invoke some local superstition to increase their wages, once an expedition was deep enough into the field to be dependent on them. He had budgeted for this eventuality and, having agreed to their demands, he thought no more about it.

Even when they came upon several areas littered with shattered fragments of bone—which the porters found frightening—Kruger was not concerned. Upon examination, he found the bones were not human but rather the small delicate bones of colobus monkeys, the beautiful shaggy black-and-white creatures that lived in the trees overhead. It was true that there were a lot of bones, and Kruger had no idea why they should be shattered, but he had been in Africa a long time, and he had seen many inexplicable things.

Nor was he any more impressed with the overgrown fragments of stone that suggested a city had once stood in this area. Kruger had come upon unexplored ruins before, too. In Zimbabwe, in Broken Hill, in Maniliwi, there were the remains of cities and temples that no twentieth-century scientist had ever seen and studied.

He camped the first night near the ruins.

The porters were panic-stricken, insisting that the evil forces would attack them during the night. Their fear was caught by the American geologists; to pacify them, Kruger had posted two guards that night, himself and the most trustworthy porter, Misulu. Kruger thought it was all a lot of rot, but it had seemed the politic thing to do.

And just as he expected, the night had passed quietly. Around midnight there had been some movement in the bush, and some low wheezing sounds, which he took to be a leopard. Big cats often had respiratory trouble, particularly in the jungle. Otherwise it was quiet, and now it was dawn: the night was over.

A soft beeping sound drew his attention. Misulu heard it too, and glanced questioningly at Kruger. On the transmitting equipment, a red light blinked. Kruger got up and crossed the campsite to the equipment. He knew how to operate it; the Americans had insisted that he learn, as an "emergency procedure." He crouched over the black transmitter box with its rectangular green LED.

He pressed buttons, and the screen printed TX HX, meaning a transmission from Houston. He pressed the response code, and the screen printed CAMLOK. That meant that Houston was asking for video camera transmission. He glanced over at the camera on its tripod and saw that the red light on the case had blinked on. He pressed the carrier button and the screen printed SATLOK, which meant that a satellite transmission was being locked in. There would now be a six-minute delay, the time required to lock the satellite-bounced signal.

He'd better go wake Driscoll, the head geologist, he thought. Driscoll would need a few minutes before the transmission came through. Kruger found it amusing the way the Americans always put on a fresh shirt and combed their hair before stepping in front of the camera. Just like television reporters.

Overhead, the colobus monkeys shrieked and screamed in the trees, shaking the branches. Kruger glanced upward, wondering what had set them going. But it was normal for colobus monkeys to fight in the morning.

Something struck him lightly in the chest. At first he thought it was an insect but, glancing down at his khaki shirt, he saw a spot of red, and a fleshy bit of red fruit rolled down his shirt to the muddy ground. The damned monkeys were throwing berries. He bent over to pick it up. And then he realized that it was not a piece of fruit at all. It was a human eyeball, crushed and slippery in his fingers, pinkish white with a shred of white optic nerve still attached at the back.

He swung his gun around and looked over to where Misulu was sitting on the rock. Misulu was not there.

Kruger moved across the campsite. Overhead, the colobus monkeys fell silent. He heard his boots squish in the mud as he moved past the tents of sleeping men. And then he heard the wheezing sound again. It was an odd, soft sound, carried on the swirling morning mist. Kruger wondered if he had been mistaken, if it was really a leopard.

And he saw Misulu. Misulu lay on his back, in a kind of halo of blood. His skull had been crushed from the sides, the facial bones shattered, the face narrowed and elongated, the mouth open in an obscene yawn, the one remaining eye wide and bulging. The other eye had exploded outward with the force of the impact.

Kruger felt his heart pounding as he bent to examine the body. He wondered what could have caused such an injury. And then he heard the soft wheezing sound again, and this time he felt quite sure it was not a leopard. Then the colobus monkeys began their shrieking, and Kruger leapt to his feet and screamed.

DAY 1: HOUSTON

June 13, 1979

1. ERTS Houston

TEN THOUSAND MILES AWAY, IN THE COLD, WIN-
dowless main data room of Earth Resources Technology Services, Inc., of Houston, Karen Ross sat hunched over a mug
of coffee in front of a computer terminal, reviewing the latest
Landsat images from Africa. Ross was the ERTS Congo Project Supervisor, and as she manipulated the satellite images
in artificial contrast colors, blue and purple and green, she
glanced at her watch impatiently. She was waiting for the
next field transmission from Africa.

It was now 10:15 P.M. Houston time, but there was no
indication of time or place in the room. Day or night, the
main data facility of ERTS remained the same. Beneath banks
of special kalon fluorescent lights, programming crews in
sweaters worked at long rows of quietly clicking computer
terminals, providing real-time inputs to the field parties that
ERTS maintained around the world. This timeless quality
was understood to be necessary for the computers, which
required a constant temperature of 60 degrees, dedicated
electrical lines, special color-corrected lights that did not
interfere with circuitry. It was an environment made for machines; the needs of people were secondary.

But there was another rationale for the main facility design. ERTS wanted programmers in Houston to identify with
the field parties, and if possible to live on their schedules.
Inputting baseball games and other local events was discouraged; there was no clock which showed Houston time, although on the far wall eight large digital clocks recorded
local time for the various field parties.

9

The clock marked CONGO FIELD PARTY read 06:15 A.M. when the overhead intercom said, "Dr. Ross, CCR bounce."

She left the console after punching in the digital password blocking codes. Every ERTS terminal had a password control, like a combination lock. It was part of an elaborate system to prevent outside sources tapping into their enormous data bank. ERTS dealt in information, and as R. B. Travis, the head of ERTS, was fond of saying, the easiest way to obtain information was to steal it.

She crossed the room with long strides. Karen Ross was nearly six feet tall, an attractive though ungainly girl. Only twenty-four years old, she was younger than most of the programmers, but despite her youth, she had a self-possession that most people found striking—even a little unsettling. Karen Ross was a genuine mathematical prodigy.

At the age of two, while accompanying her mother to the supermarket, she had worked out in her head whether a ten-ounce can at 19¢ was cheaper than a one-pound-twelve-ounce can at 79¢. At three, she startled her father by observing that, unlike other numbers, zero meant different things in different positions. By eight, she had mastered algebra and geometry; by ten, she had taught herself calculus; she entered M.I.T. at thirteen and proceeded to make a series of brilliant discoveries in abstract mathematics, culminating in a treatise, "Topological Prediction in n-Space," which was useful for decision matrices, critical path analyses, and multidimensional mapping. This interest had brought her to the attention of ERTS, where she was made the youngest field supervisor in the company.

Not everyone liked her. The years of isolation, of being the youngest person in any room, had left her aloof and rather distant. One co-worker described her as "logical to a fault." Her chilly demeanor had earned her the title "Ross Glacier," after the Antarctic formation.

And her youth still held her back—at least, age was Travis's excuse when he refused to let her lead the Congo expedition into the field, even though she had derived all the Congo database, and by rights should have been the onsite team leader. "I'm sorry," Travis had said, "but this contract's too big, and I just can't let you have it." She had pressed, reminding him of her successes leading teams the year before to Pahang and Zambia. Finally he had said, "Look, Karen, that site's ten thousand miles away, in four-plus terrain. We need more than a console hotdogger out there."

She bridled under the implication that that was all she was—a console hotdogger, fast at the keyboard, good at playing with Travis's toys. She wanted to prove herself in a four-plus field situation. And the next time she was determined to make Travis let her go.

Ross pressed the button for the third-floor elevator, marked "CX Access Only." She caught an envious glance from one of the programmers while she waited for the elevator to arrive. Within ERTS, status was not measured by salary, title, the size of one's office, or the other usual corporate indicators of power. Status at ERTS was purely a matter of access to information—and Karen Ross was one of eight people in the company who had access to the third floor at any time.

She stepped onto the third-floor elevator, glancing up at the scanner lens mounted over the door. At ERTS the elevators traveled only one floor, and all were equipped with passive scanners; it was one way that ERTS kept track of the movements of personnel while they were in the building. She said "Karen Ross" for the voice monitors, and turned in a full circle for the scanners. There was a soft electronic bleep, and the door slid open at the third floor.

She emerged into a small square room with a ceiling video monitor, and faced the unmarked outer door of the Communications Control Room. She repeated "Karen Ross," and inserted her electronic identicard in the slot, resting her fingers on the metallic edge of the card so the computer could record galvanic skin potentials. (This was a refinement instituted three months earlier, after Travis learned that Army experiments with vocal cord surgery had altered voice characteristics precisely enough to false-positive Voiceident programs.) After a cycling pause, the door buzzed open. She went inside.

With its red night lights, Communications Control was

like a soft, warm womb—an impression heightened by the cramped, almost claustrophobic quality of the room, packed with electronic equipment. From floor to ceiling, dozens of video monitors and LEDs flickered and glowed as the technicians spoke in hushed tones, setting dials and twisting knobs. The CCR was the electronic nerve center of ERTS: all communications from field parties around the world were routed through here. Everything in the CCR was recorded, not only incoming data but room voice responses, so the exact conversation on the night of June 13, 1979, is known.

One of the technicians said to her, "We'll have the transponders hooked in in a minute. You want coffee?"

"No," Ross said.

"You want to be out there, right?"

"I earned it," she said. She stared at the video screens, at the bewildering display of rotating and shifting forms as the technicians began the litany of locking in the bird bounce, a transmission from a satellite in orbit, 720 miles over their heads.

"Signal key."

"Signal key. Password mark."

"Password mark."

"Carrier fix."

"Carrier fix. We're rolling."

She paid hardly any attention to the familiar phrases. She watched as the screens displayed gray fields of crackling static.

"Did we open or did they open?" she asked.

"We initiated," a technician said. "We had it down on the call sheet to check them at dawn local time. So when they didn't initiate, we did."

"I wonder why they didn't initiate," Ross said. "Is something wrong?"

"I don't think so. We put out the initiation trigger and they picked it up and locked in within fifteen seconds, all the appropriate codes. Ah, here we go."

At 6:22 A.M. Congo time, the transmission came through: there was a final blur of gray static and then the screens cleared. They were looking at a part of the camp in the

Congo, apparently a view from a tripod-mounted video camera. They saw two tents, a low smoldering fire, the lingering wisps of a foggy dawn. There was no sign of activity, no people.

One of the technicians laughed. "We caught them still sleeping. Guess they do need you there." Ross was known for her insistence on formalities.

"Lock your remote," she said.

The technician punched in the remote override. The field camera, ten thousand miles away, came under their control in Houston.

"Pan scan," she said.

At the console, the technician used a joystick. They watched as the video images shifted to the left, and they saw more of the camp. The camp was destroyed: tents crushed and torn, supply tarp pulled away, equipment scattered in the mud. One tent burned brightly, sending up clouds of black smoke. They saw several dead bodies.

"Jesus," one technician said.

"Back scan," Ross said. "Spot resolve to six-six."

On the screens, the camera panned back across the camp. They looked at the jungle. They still saw no sign of life.

"Down pan. Reverse sweep."

Onscreen, the camera panned down to show the silver dish of the portable antenna, and the black box of the transmitter. Nearby was another body, one of the geologists, lying on his back.

"Jesus, that's Roger. . . ."

"Zoom and T-lock," Ross said. On the tape, her voice sounds cool, almost detached.

The camera zoomed in on the face. What they saw was grotesque, the head crushed and leaking blood from eyes and nose, mouth gaping toward the sky.

"What did *that*?"

At that moment, a shadow fell across the dead face onscreen. Ross jumped forward, grabbing the joystick and hitting the zoom control. The image widened swiftly; they could see the outline of the shadow now. It was a man. And he was moving.

"Somebody's there! Somebody's still alive!"

"He's limping. Looks wounded."

Ross stared at the shadow. It did not look to her like a limping man; something was wrong, she couldn't put her finger on what it was. . . .

"He's going to walk in front of the lens," she said. It was almost too much to hope for. "What's that audio static?"

They were hearing an odd sound, like a hissing or a sighing.

"It's not static, it's in the transmission."

"Resolve it," Ross said. The technicians punched buttons, altering the audio frequencies, but the sound remained peculiar and indistinct. And then the shadow moved, and the man stepped in front of the lens.

"Diopter," Ross said, but it was too late. The face had already appeared, very near the lens. It was too close to focus without a diopter. They saw a blurred, dark shape, nothing more. Before they could click in the diopter, it was gone.

"A native?"

"This region of the Congo is uninhabited," Ross said.

"*Something* inhabits it."

"Pan scan," Ross said. "See if you can get him onscreen again."

The camera continued to pan. She could imagine it sitting on its tripod in the jungle, motor whirring as the lens head swung around. Then suddenly the image tilted and fell sideways.

"He knocked it over."

"Damn!"

The video image crackled, shifting lines of static. It became very difficult to see.

"Resolve it! Resolve it!"

They had a final glimpse of a large face and a dark hand as the silver dish antenna was smashed. The image from the Congo shrank to a spot, and was gone.

2. Interference Signature

DURING JUNE OF 1979, EARTH RESOURCES TECH-
nology had field teams studying uranium deposits in Bolivia,
copper deposits in Pakistan, agricultural field utilization in
Kashmir, glacier advance in Iceland, timber resources in Malaysia, and diamond deposits in the Congo. This was not
unusual for ERTS; they generally had between six and eight
groups in the field at any time.

Since their teams were often in hazardous or politically
unstable regions, they were vigilant in watching for the first
signs of "interference signatures." (In remote-sensing terminology, a "signature" is the characteristic appearance of
an object or geological feature in a photograph or video image.) Most interference signatures were political. In 1977,
ERTS had airlifted a team out of Borneo during a local Communist uprising, and again from Nigeria in 1978 during a
military coup. Occasionally the signatures were geological;
they had pulled a team from Guatemala in 1976 after the
earthquake there.

In the opinion of R. B. Travis, called out of bed in the late
hours of June 13, 1979, the videotapes from the Congo were
"the worst interference signature ever," but the problem remained mysterious. All they knew was that the camp had
been destroyed in a mere six minutes—the time between the
signal initiation from Houston and the reception in the Congo.
The rapidity was frightening; Travis's first instruction to his
team was to figure out "what the hell happened out there."

A heavyset man of forty-eight, Travis was accustomed to
crises. By training he was an engineer with a background in
satellite construction for RCA and later Rockwell; in his thir-

ties he had shifted to management, becoming what aerospace engineers called a "rain dancer." Companies manufacturing satellites contracted eighteen to twenty-four months in advance for a launch rocket to put the satellite in orbit—and then hoped that the satellite, with its half-million working parts, would be ready on the assigned day. If it was not, the only alternative was to pray for bad weather delaying the launch, to dance for rain.

Travis had managed to keep a sense of humor after a decade of high-tech problems; his management philosophy was summarized by a large sign mounted behind his desk, which read "S.D.T.A.G.W." It stood for "Some Damn Thing Always Goes Wrong."

But Travis was not amused on the night of June 13. His entire expedition had been lost, all the ERTS party killed—eight of his people, and however many local porters were with them. The worst disaster in ERTS history, worse even than Nigeria in '78. Travis felt fatigued, mentally drained, as he thought of all the phone calls ahead of him. Not the calls he would make, but those he would receive. Would so-and-so be back in time for a daughter's graduation, a son's Little League playoff? Those calls would be routed to Travis, and he would have to listen to the bright expectation in the voices, the hopefulness, and his own careful answers—he wasn't sure, he understood the problem, he would do his best, of course, of course. . . . The coming deception exhausted him in advance.

Because Travis couldn't tell anyone what had happened for at least two weeks, perhaps a month. And then he would be making phone calls himself, and visits to the homes, and attending the memorial services where there would be no casket, a deadly blank space, a gap, and the inevitable questions from families and relatives that he couldn't answer while they scrutinized his face, looking for the least muscle twitch, or hesitation, or sign.

What could he tell them?

That was his only consolation—perhaps in a few weeks, Travis could tell them more. One thing was certain: if he were to make the dreadful calls tonight, he could tell the families nothing at all, for ERTS had no idea what had gone wrong. That fact added to Travis's sense of exhaustion. And there were details: Morris, the insurance auditor, came in and said, "What do you want to do about the terms?" ERTS took out term life insurance policies for every expedition member, and also for local porters. African porters received U.S. $15,000 each in insurance, which seemed trivial until one recognized that African per capita income averaged U.S. $180 per year. But Travis had always argued that local expedition people should share risk benefits—even if it meant paying widowed families a small fortune, in their terms. Even if it cost ERTS a small fortune for the insurance.

"Hold them," Travis said.

"Those policies are costing us *per day*—"

"Hold them," Travis said.

"For how long?"

"Thirty days," Travis said.

"Thirty *more* days?"

"That's right."

"But we know the holders are dead." Morris could not reconcile himself to the waste of money. His actuarial mind rebelled.

"That's right," Travis said. "But you'd better slip the porters' families some cash to keep them quiet."

"Jesus. How much are we talking about?"

"Five hundred dollars each."

"How do we account that?"

"Legal fees," Travis said. "Bury it in legal, local disposition."

"And the American team people that we've lost?"

"They have MasterCard," Travis said. "Stop worrying."

Roberts, the British-born ERTS press liaison, came into his office. "You want to open this can up?"

"No," Travis said. "I want to kill it."

"For how long?"

"Thirty days."

"Bloody hell. Your own staff will leak inside thirty days," Roberts said. "I promise you."

"If they do, you'll squash it," Travis said. "I need another thirty days to make this contract."

"Do we know what happened out there?"

"No," Travis said. "But we will."

"How?"

"From the tapes."

"Those tapes are a mess."

"So far," Travis said. And he called in the specialty teams of console hotdoggers. Travis had long since concluded that although ERTS could wake up political advisers around the world, they were most likely to get information in-house. "Everything we know from the Congo field expedition," he said, "is registered on that final videotape. I want a seven-band visual and audio salvage, starting right now. Because that tape is all we have."

The specialty teams went to work.

3. Recovery

ERTS REFERRED TO THE PROCESS AS "DATA RECOVery," or sometimes as "data salvage." The terms evoked images of deep-sea operations, and they were oddly appropriate.

To recover or salvage data meant that coherent meaning was pulled to the surface from the depths of massive electronic information storage. And, like salvage from the sea, it was a slow and delicate process, where a single false step meant the irretrievable loss of the very elements one was trying to bring up. ERTS had whole salvage crews skilled in the art of data recovery. One crew immediately went to work on the audio recovery, another on the visual recovery.

But Karen Ross was already engaged in a visual recovery.

The procedures she followed were highly sophisticated, and only possible at ERTS.

Earth Resources Technology was a relatively new company, formed in 1975 in response to the explosive growth of information on the Earth and its resources. The amount of material handled by ERTS was staggering: just the Landsat imagery alone amounted to more than five hundred thousand pictures, and sixteen new images were acquired every hour, around the clock. With the addition of conventional and draped aerial photography, infrared photography, and artificial aperture side-looking radar, the total information available to ERTS exceeded two million images, with new input on the order of thirty images an hour. All this information had to be catalogued, stored, and made available for instantaneous retrieval. ERTS was like a library which acquired seven hundred new books a day. It was not surprising that the librarians worked at fever pitch around the clock.

Visitors to ERTS never seemed to realize that even with computers, such data-handling capacity would have been impossible ten years earlier. Nor did visitors understand the basic nature of the ERTS information—they assumed that the pictures on the screens were photographic, although they were not.

Photography was a nineteenth-century chemical system for recording information using light-sensitive silver salts. ERTS utilized a twentieth-century electronic system for recording information, analogous to chemical photographs, but very different. Instead of cameras, ERTS used multi-spectral scanners; instead of film, they used CCTs—computer compatible tapes. In fact, ERTS did not bother with "pictures" as they were ordinarily understood from old-fashioned photographic technology. ERTS bought "data scans" which they converted to "data displays," as the need arose.

Since the ERTS images were just electrical signals recorded on magnetic tape, a great variety of electrical image manipulation was possible. ERTS had 837 computer programs to alter imagery: to enhance it, to eliminate unwanted elements, to bring out details. Ross used fourteen programs on the Congo videotape—particularly on the static-filled section in which the hand and face appeared, just before the antenna was smashed.

First she carried out what was called a "wash cycle," getting rid of the static. She identified the static lines as occurring at specific scan positions, and having a specific gray-scale value. She instructed the computer to cancel those lines.

The resulting image showed blank spaces where the static was removed. So she did "fill-in-the-blanks"—instructing the computer to introject imagery, according to what was around the blank spaces. In this operation the computer made a logical guess about what was missing.

She now had a static-free image, but it was muddy and indistinct, lacking definition. So she did a "high-priced spread"—intensifying the image by spreading the gray-scale values. But for some reason she also got a phase distortion that she had to cancel, and that released spiking glitches previously suppressed, and to get rid of the glitches she had to run three other programs. . . .

Technical details preoccupied her for an hour, until suddenly the image "popped," coming up bright and clean. She caught her breath as she saw it. The screen showed a dark, brooding face with heavy brows, watchful eyes, a flattened nose, prognathous lips.

Frozen on the video screen was the face of a male gorilla.

Travis walked toward her from across the room, shaking his head. "We finished the audio recovery on that hissing noise. The computer confirms it as human breathing, with at least four separate origins. But it's damned strange. According to the analysis, the sound is coming from inhalation, not exhalation, the way people usually make sounds."

"The computer is wrong," Ross said. "It's not human." She pointed to the screen, and the face of the gorilla.

Travis showed no surprise. "Artifact," he said.

"It's no artifact."

"You did fill-in-the-blanks, and you got an artifact. The tag team's been screwing around with the software at lunch again." The tag team—the young software programmers—had a tendency to convert data to play highly sophisticated versions of pinball games. Their games sometimes got sub-routed into other programs.

Ross herself had complained about it. "But this image is real," she insisted, pointing to the screen.

"Look," Travis said, "last week Harry did fill-in-the-blanks on the Karakorum Mountains and he got back a lunar landing game. You're supposed to land next to the McDonald's stand, all very amusing." He walked off. "You'd better meet the others in my office. We're setting advance times to get back in."

"I'm leading the next team."

Travis shook his head. "Out of the question."

"But what about this?" she said, pointing to the screen.

"I'm not buying that image," Travis said. "Gorillas don't behave that way. It's got to be an artifact." He glanced at his watch. "Right now, the only question I have is how fast we can put a team back in the Congo."

4. Return Expedition

TRAVIS HAD NEVER HAD ANY DOUBTS IN HIS MIND about going back in; from the first time he saw the videotapes from the Congo, the only question was how best to do it. He called in all the section heads: Accounts, Diplo, Remote, Geo, Logistics, Legal. They were all yawning and rubbing their eyes. Travis began by saying, "I want us back in the Congo in ninety-six hours."

Then he leaned back in his chair and let them tell him why it couldn't be done. There were plenty of reasons.

"We can't assemble the air cargo units for shipment in less than a hundred and sixty hours," Cameron, the logistics man said.

"We can postpone the Himalaya team, and use their units," Travis said.

"But that's a mountain expedition."

"You can modify the units in nine hours," Travis said.

"But we can't get equipment to fly it out," Lewis, the transport master, said.

"Korean Airlines has a 747 cargo jet available at SFX. They tell me it can be down here in nine hours."

"They have a plane just sitting there?" Lewis said, incredulous.

"I believe," Travis said, "that they had a last-minute cancellation from another customer."

Irwin, the accountant, groaned. "What'd that cost?"

"We can't get visas from the Zaire Embassy in Washington in time," Martin, the diplomatic man, said. "And there is serious doubt they'd issue them to us at all. As you know, the first set of Congo visas were based on our mineral exploration rights with the Zaire government, and our MERs are non-exclusive. We were granted permission to go in, and so were the Japanese, the Germans, and the Dutch, who've formed a mining consortium. The first ore-body strike takes the contract. If Zaire suspects that our expedition is in trouble, they'll just cancel us out and let the Euro-Japanese consortium try their luck. There are thirty Japanese trade officials in Kinshasa right now, spending yen like water."

"I think that's right," Travis said. "If it became known that our expedition is in trouble."

"It'll become known the minute we apply for visas."

"We won't apply for them. As far as anybody knows," Travis said, "we still have an expedition in Virunga. If we put a second small team into the field fast enough, nobody will ever know that it wasn't the original team."

"But what about the specific personnel visas to cross the borders, the manifests—"

"Details," Travis said. "That's what liquor is for," referring to bribes, which were often liquor. In many parts of the world, expedition teams went in with crates of liquor and boxes of those perennial favorites, transistor radios and Polaroid cameras.

"Details? How're you going to cross the border?"

"We'll need a good man for that. Maybe Munro."

"Munro? That's playing rough. The Zaire government hates Munro."

"He's resourceful, and he knows the area."

Martin, the diplomatic expert, cleared his throat and said, "I'm not sure I should be here for this discussion. It looks to me as if you are proposing to enter a sovereign state with an illegal party led by a former Congo mercenary soldier. . . ."

"Not at all," Travis said. "I'm obliged to put a support party into the field to assist my people already there. Happens all the time. I have no reason to think anybody is in trouble; just a routine support party. I haven't got time to go through official channels. I may not be showing the best judgment in whom I hire, but it's nothing more serious than that."

By 11:45 P.M. on the night of June 13, the main sequencing of the next ERTS expedition had been worked out and confirmed by the computer. A fully loaded 747 could leave Houston at 8 P.M. the following evening, June 14; the plane could be in Africa on June 15 to pick up Munro "or someone like him"; and the full team could be in place in the Congo on June 17.

In ninety-six hours.

From the main data room, Karen Ross could look through the glass walls into Travis's office and see the arguments taking place. In her logical way, she concluded that Travis had "Q'd" himself, meaning that he had drawn false conclusions from insufficient data, and had said Q.E.D. too soon. Ross felt there was no point in going back into the Congo until they knew what they were up against. She remained at her console, checking the image she had recovered.

Ross bought this image—but how could she make Travis buy it?

In the highly sophisticated data-processing world of ERTS,

there was a constant danger that extracted information would begin to "float"—that the images would cut loose from reality, like a ship cut loose from its moorings. This was true particularly when the database was put through multiple manipulations—when you were rotating 10^6 pixels in computer-generated hyperspace.

So ERTS evolved other ways to check the validity of images they got back from the computer. Ross ran two check programs against the gorilla image. The first was called APNF, for Animation Predicted Next Frame.

It was possible to treat videotape as if it were movie film, a succession of stills. She showed the computer several "stills" in succession, and then asked it to create the Predicted Next Frame. This PNF was then checked against the actual next frame.

She ran eight PNFs in a row, and they worked. If there was an error in the data handling, it was at least a consistent error.

Encouraged, she next ran a "fast and dirty three-space." Here the flat video image was assumed to have certain three-dimensional characteristics, based on gray-scale patterns. In essence, the computer decided that the shadow of a nose, or a mountain range, meant that the nose or mountain range protruded above the surrounding surface. Succeeding images could be checked against these assumptions. As the gorilla moved, the computer verified that the flat image was, indeed, three-dimensional and coherent.

This proved beyond a doubt that the image was real.

She went to see Travis.

"Let's say I buy this image," Travis said, frowning. "I still don't see why you should take the next expedition in."

Ross said, "What did the other team find?"

"The other team?" Travis asked innocently.

"You gave that tape to another salvage team to confirm my recovery," Ross said.

Travis glanced at his watch. "They haven't pulled anything out yet." And he added, "We all know you're fast with the database."

Ross smiled. "That's why you need me to take the expedition in," she said. "I know the database, because I generated the database. And if you intend to send another team in right away, before this gorilla thing is solved, the only hope you have is for the team leader to be fast onsite with the data. This time, you *need* a console hotdogger in the field. Or the next expedition will end up like the last one. Because you still don't know what happened to the last expedition."

Travis sat behind his desk, and stared at her for a long time. She recognized his hesitation as a sign that he was weakening.

"And I want to go outside," Ross said.

"To an outside expert?"

"Yes. Somebody on our grant list."

"Risky," Travis said. "I hate to involve outside people at this point. You know the consortium is breathing down our necks. You up the leak averages."

"It's important," Ross insisted.

Travis sighed. "Okay, if you think it's important." He sighed again. "Just don't delay your team."

Ross was already packing up her hard copy.

Alone, Travis frowned, turning over his decision in his mind. Even if they ran the next Congo expedition slambam, in and out in less than fifteen days, their fixed costs would still exceed three hundred thousand dollars. The Board was going to scream—sending an untried, twenty-four-year-old kid, a *girl*, into the field with this kind of responsibility. Especially on a project as important as this one, where the stakes were enormous, and where they had already fallen behind on every timeline and cost projection. And Ross was so cold, she was likely to prove a poor field leader, alienating the others in the team.

Yet Travis had a hunch about the Ross Glacier. His management philosophy, tempered in his rain-dancing days, was always to give the project to whoever had the most to gain from success—or the most to lose from failure.

He turned to face his console, mounted beside his desk. "Travis," he said, and the screen glowed.

"Psychograph file," he said.

The screen showed call prompts.

"Ross, Karen," Travis said.

The screen flashed THINKING A MOMENT. That was the programmed response which meant that information was being extracted. He waited.

Then the psychograph summary printed out across the screen. Every ERTS employee underwent three days of intensive psychological testing to determine not only skills but potential biases. The assessment of Ross would, he felt, be reassuring to the Board.

HIGHLY INTELLIGENT / LOGICAL / FLEXIBLE / RE-SOURCEFUL / DATA INTUITIVE / THOUGHT PRO-CESSES SUITED TO RAPIDLY CHANGING REALTIME CONTEXTS / DRIVEN TO SUCCEED AT DEFINED GOALS / CAPABLE SUSTAINED MENTAL EFFORT /

It looked like the perfect description of the next Congo team leader. He scanned down the screen, looking for the negatives. These were less reassuring.

YOUTHFUL-RUTHLESS / TENUOUS HUMAN RAPPORT / DOMINEERING / INTELLECTUALLY ARROGANT / IN-SENSITIVE / DRIVEN TO SUCCEED AT ANY COST /

And there was a final "flopover" notation. The very concept of personality flopover had been evolved through ERTS testing. It suggested that any dominant personality trait could be suddenly reversed under stress conditions: parental personalities could flop over and turn childishly petulant, hysterical personalities could become icy calm—or logical personalities could become illogical.

FLOPOVER MATRIX: DOMINANT (POSSIBLY UNDESIR-ABLE) OBJECTIVITY MAY BE LOST ONCE DESIRED GOAL

IS PERCEIVED CLOSE AT HAND / DESIRE FOR SUCCESS
MAY PROVOKE DANGEROUSLY ILLOGICAL RESPONSES /
PARENTAL FIGURES WILL BE ESPECIALLY DENI-
GRATED / SUBJECT MUST BE MONITORED IN LATE
STAGE GOAL-ORIENTED PROCEDURES /

Travis looked at the screen, and decided that such a circumstance was highly unlikely in the coming Congo expedition. He turned the computer off.

Karen Ross was exhilarated by her new authority. Shortly
before midnight, she called up the grant lists on her office
terminal. ERTS had animal experts in various areas whom
they supported with nominal grants from a non-profit foun-
dation called the Earth Resources Wildlife Fund. The grant
lists were arranged taxonomically. Under "Primates" she
found fourteen names, including several in Borneo, Malaysia, and Africa as well as the United States. In the United
States there was only one gorilla researcher available, a primatologist named Dr. Peter Elliot, at the University of California at Berkeley.

The file onscreen indicated that Elliot was twenty-nine
years old, unmarried, an associate professor without tenure
in the Department of Zoology. Principal Research Interest
was listed as "Primate Communications (Gorilla)." Funding was made to something called Project Amy.

She checked her watch. It was just midnight in Houston,
10 P.M. in California. She dialed the home number on the
screen.

"Hello," a wary male voice said.

"Dr. Peter Elliot?"

"Yes . . ." The voice was still cautious, hesitant. "Are
you a reporter?"

"No," she said. "This is Dr. Karen Ross in Houston; I'm
associated with the Earth Resources Wildlife Fund, which
supports your research."

"Oh, yes . . ." The voice remained cautious. "You're
sure you're not a reporter? It's only fair to tell you I'm

recording this telephone call as a potential legal document."

Karen Ross hesitated. The last thing she needed was some paranoid academic recording ERTS developments. She said nothing.

"You're American?" he said.

"Of course."

Karen Ross stared at the computer screens, which flashed VOICE IDENTIFICATION CONFIRMED: ELLIOT, PETER, 29 YEARS.

"State your business," Elliot said.

"Well, we're about to send an expedition into the Virunga region of the Congo, and—"

"Really? When are you going?" The voice suddenly sounded excited, boyish.

"Well, as a matter of fact we're leaving in two days, and—"

"I want to go," Elliot said.

Ross was so surprised she hardly knew what to say. "Well, Dr. Elliot, that's not why I'm calling you, as a matter of fact—"

"I'm planning to go there anyway," Elliot said. "With Amy."

"Who's Amy?"

"Amy is a gorilla," Peter Elliot said.

DAY 2: SAN FRANCISCO

June 14, 1979

1. Project Amy

IT IS UNFAIR TO SUGGEST, AS SOME PRIMATOLOGISTS later did, that Peter Elliot had to "get out of town" in June, 1979. His motives, and the planning behind the decision to go to the Congo, are a matter of record. Professor Elliot and his staff had decided on an African trip at least two days before Ross called him.

But it is certainly true that Peter Elliot was under attack: from outside groups, the press, academic colleagues, and even members of his own department at Berkeley. Toward the end, Elliot was accused of being a "Nazi criminal" engaged in the "torture of dumb *[sic]* animals." It is no exaggeration to say that Elliot had found himself, in the spring of 1979, fighting for his professional life.

Yet his research had begun quietly, almost accidentally. Peter Elliot was a twenty-three-year-old graduate student in the Department of Anthropology at Berkeley when he first read about a year-old gorilla with amoebic dysentery who had been brought from the Minneapolis zoo to the San Francisco School of Veterinary Medicine for treatment. That was in 1973, in the exciting early days of primate language research.

The idea that primates might be taught language was very old. In 1661, Samuel Pepys saw a chimpanzee in London and wrote in his diary that it was "so much like a man in most things that . . . I do believe that it already understands much English, and I am of the mind it might be taught to speak or make signs." Another seventeenth-century writer went further, saying, "Apes and Baboons . . . can speak but will not for fear they should be imployed, and set to work."

31

Yet for the next three hundred years attempts to teach apes to talk were notably unsuccessful. They culminated in an ambitious effort by a Florida couple, Keith and Kathy Hayes, who for six years in the early 1950s raised a chimpanzee named Vicki as if she were a human infant. During that time, Vicki learned four words—"mama," "papa," "cup," and "up." But her pronunciation was labored and her progress slow. Her difficulties seemed to support the growing conviction among scientists that man was the only animal capable of language. Typical was the pronouncement of George Gaylord Simpson: "Language is . . . the most diagnostic single trait of man: all normal men have language; no other now living organisms do."

This seemed so self-evident that for the next fifteen years nobody bothered to try teaching language to an ape. Then in 1966, a Reno, Nevada, couple named Beatrice and Allen Gardner reviewed movies of Vicki speaking. It seemed to them that Vicki was not so much incapable of language as incapable of speech. They noticed that while her lip movements were awkward, her hand gestures were fluid and expressive. The obvious conclusion was to try sign language.

In June, 1966, the Gardners began teaching American Sign Language (Ameslan), the standardized language of the deaf, to an infant chimpanzee named Washoe. Washoe's progress with ASL was rapid; by 1971, she had a vocabulary of 160 signs, which she used in conversation. She also made up new word combinations for things she had never seen before: when shown watermelon for the first time, she signed it "water fruit."

The Gardners' work was highly controversial; it turned out that many scientists had an investment in the idea that apes were incapable of language. (As one researcher said, "My God, think of all those eminent names attached to all those scholarly papers for all those decades—and everyone agreeing that only man had language. What a mess.")

Washoe's skills provoked a variety of other experiments in teaching language. A chimpanzee named Lucy was taught to communicate through a computer; another, Sarah, was taught to use plastic markers on a board. Other apes were studied as well. An orangutan named Alfred began instruction in 1971; a lowland gorilla named Koko in 1972; and in 1973 Peter Elliot began with a mountain gorilla, Amy.

At his first visit to the hospital to meet Amy, he found a pathetic little creature, heavily sedated, with restraining straps on her frail black arms and legs. He stroked her head and said gently, "Hello, Amy, I'm Peter."

Amy promptly bit his hand, drawing blood.

From this inauspicious beginning emerged a singularly successful research program. In 1973, the basic teaching technique, called molding, was well understood. The animal was shown an object and the researcher simultaneously molded the animal's hand into the correct sign, until the association was firmly made. Subsequent testing confirmed that the animal understood the meaning of the sign.

But if the basic methodology was accepted, the application was highly competitive. Researchers competed over the rate of sign acquisition, or vocabulary. (Among human beings, vocabulary was considered the best measure of intelligence.) The rate of sign acquisition could be taken as a measure of either the scientist's skill or the animal's intelligence.

It was by now clearly recognized that different apes had different personalities. As one researcher commented, "Pongid studies are perhaps the only field in which academic gossip centers on the students and not the teachers." In the increasingly competitive and disputatious world of primate research, it was said that Lucy was a drunk, that Koko was an ill-mannered brat, that Lana's head was turned by her celebrity ("she only works when there is an interviewer present"), and that Nim was so stupid he should have been named Dim.

At first glance, it may seem odd that Peter Elliot should have come under attack, for this handsome, rather shy man—the son of a Marin County librarian—had avoided controversy during his years of work with Amy. Elliot's publications were modest and temperate; his progress with Amy was well documented; he showed no interest in publicity, and was not among those researchers who took their apes on the Carson or the Griffin show.

But Elliot's diffident manner concealed not only a quick intelligence, but a fierce ambition as well. If he avoided controversy, it was only because he didn't have time for it—he had been working nights and weekends for years, and driving his staff and Amy just as hard. He was very good at the business of science, getting grants; at all the animal behaviorist conferences, where others showed up in jeans and plaid lumberjack shirts, Elliot arrived in a three-piece suit. Elliot intended to be the foremost ape researcher, and he intended Amy to be the foremost ape.

Elliot's success in obtaining grants was such that in 1975, Project Amy had an annual budget of $160,000 and a staff of eight, including a child psychologist and a computer programmer. A staff member of the Bergren Institute later said that Elliot's appeal lay in the fact that he was "a good investment; for example, Project Amy got fifty percent more computer time for our money because he went on line with his time-sharing terminal at night and on weekends, when the time was cheaper. He was very cost-effective. And dedicated, of course: Elliot obviously cared about nothing in life except his work with Amy. That made him a boring conversationalist but a very good bet, from our standpoint. It's hard to decide who's truly brilliant; it's easier to see who's driven, which in the long run may be more important. We anticipated great things from Elliot."

Peter Elliot's difficulties began on the morning of February 2, 1979. Amy lived in a mobile home on the Berkeley campus; she spent nights there alone, and usually provided an effusive greeting the next day. However, on that morning the Project Amy staff found her in an uncharacteristic sullen mood; she was irritable and bleary-eyed, behaving as if she had been wronged in some fashion.

Elliot felt that something had upset her during the night. When asked, she kept making signs for "sleep box," a new word pairing he did not understand. That in itself was not unusual; Amy made up new word pairings all the time, and they were often hard to decipher. Just a few days before, she had bewildered them by talking about "crocodile milk." Eventually they realized that Amy's milk had gone sour, and that since she disliked crocodiles (which she had only seen in picture books), she somehow decided that sour milk was "crocodile milk."

Now she was talking about "sleep box." At first they thought she might be referring to her nestlike bed. It turned out she was using "box" in her usual sense, to refer to the television set.

Everything in her trailer, including the television, was controlled on a twenty-four-hour cycle by the computer. They ran a check to see if the television had been turned on during the night, disturbing her sleep. Since Amy liked to watch television, it was conceivable that she had managed to turn it on herself. But Amy looked scornful as they examined the actual television in the trailer. She clearly meant something else.

Finally they determined that by "sleep box" she meant "sleep pictures." When asked about these sleep pictures, Amy signed that they were "bad pictures" and "old pictures," and that they "make Amy cry."

She was dreaming.

The fact that Amy was the first primate to report dreams caused tremendous excitement among Elliot's staff. But the excitement was short-lived. Although Amy continued to dream on succeeding nights, she refused to discuss her dreams; in fact, she seemed to blame the researchers for this new and confusing intrusion into her mental life. Worse, her waking behavior deteriorated alarmingly.

Her word acquisition rate fell from 2.7 words a week to 0.8 words a week, her spontaneous word formation rate from 1.9 to 0.3. Monitored attention span was halved. Mood swings increased; erratic and unmotivated behavior became commonplace; temper tantrums occurred daily. Amy was four and a half feet tall, and weighed 130 pounds. She was

an immensely strong animal. The staff began to wonder if
they could control her.

Her refusal to talk about her dreams frustrated them. They
tried a variety of investigative approaches; they showed her
pictures from books and magazines; they ran the ceiling-
mounted video monitors around the clock, in case she signed
something significant while alone (like young children, Amy
often "talked to herself"); they even administered a battery
of neurological tests, including an EEG.

Finally they hit on finger painting.

This was immediately successful. Amy was enthusiastic
about finger painting, and after they mixed cayenne pepper
with the pigments, she stopped licking her fingers. She drew
images swiftly and repetitively, and she seemed to become
somewhat more relaxed, more her old self.

David Bergman, the child psychologist, noted that "what
Amy actually draws is a cluster of apparently related images:
inverted crescent shapes, or semicircles, which are always
associated with an area of vertical green streaks. Amy says
the green streaks represent 'forest,' and she calls the semicircles 'bad houses' or 'old houses.' In addition she often
draws black circles, which she calls 'holes.' "

Bergman cautioned against the obvious conclusion that
she was drawing old buildings in the jungle. "Watching her
make drawings one after another, again and again, convinces
me of the obsessive and private nature of the imagery. Amy
is troubled by these pictures, and she is trying to get them
out, to banish them to paper."

In fact, the nature of the imagery remained mysterious to
the Project Amy staff. By late April, 1979, they had concluded that her dreams could be explained in four ways. In
order of seriousness, they were:

1. *The dreams are an attempt to rationalize events in her
daily life.* This was the usual explanation of (human) dreams,
but the staff doubted that it applied in Amy's case.

2. *The dreams are a transitional adolescent manifestation.*
At seven years of age, Amy was a gorilla teenager, and for
nearly a year she had shown many typical teenage traits,

including rages and sulks, fussiness about her appearance, a new interest in the opposite sex.

3. *The dreams are a species-specific phenomenon.* It was possible that all gorillas had disturbing dreams, and that in the wild the resultant stresses were handled in some fashion by the behavior of the group. Although gorillas had been studied in the wild for the past twenty years, there was no evidence for this.

4. *The dreams are the first sign of incipient dementia.* This was the most feared possibility. To train an ape effectively, one had to begin with an infant; as the years progressed, researchers waited to see if their animal would grow up to be bright or stupid, recalcitrant or pliable, healthy or sickly. The health of apes was a constant worry; many programs collapsed after years of effort and expense when the apes died of physical or mental illness. Timothy, an Atlanta chimp, became psychotic in 1976 and committed suicide by coprophagia, choking to death on his own feces. Maurice, a Chicago orang, became intensely neurotic, developing phobias that halted work in 1977. For better or worse, the very intelligence that made apes worthwhile subjects for study also made them as unstable as human beings.

But the Project Amy staff was unable to make further progress. In May, 1979, they made what turned out to be a momentous decision: they decided to publish Amy's drawings, and submitted her images to the *Journal of Behavioral Sciences*.

2. Breakthrough

"DREAM BEHAVIOR IN A MOUNTAIN GORILLA" WAS never published. The paper was routinely forwarded to three scientists on the editorial board for review, and one copy somehow (it is still unclear just how) fell into the hands of the Primate Preservation Agency, a New York group formed in 1975 to prevent the "unwarranted and illegitimate exploitation of intelligent primates in unnecessary laboratory research."*

On June 3, the PPA began picketing the Zoology Department at Berkeley, and calling for the "release" of Amy. Most of the demonstrators were women, and several young children were present; videotapes of an eight-year-old boy holding a placard with Amy's photograph and shouting "Free Amy! Free Amy!" appeared on local television news.

In a tactical error, the Project Amy staff elected to ignore the protests except for a brief press release stating that the PPA was "misinformed." The release went out under the Berkeley Information Office letterhead.

On June 5, the PPA released comments on Professor Elliot's work from other primatologists around the country. (Many later denied the comments or claimed they were misquoted.) Dr. Wayne Turman, of the University of Oklahoma at Norman, was quoted as saying that Elliot's work was "fanciful and unethical." Dr. Felicity Hammond, of the Yerkes Primate Research Center in Atlanta, said that "neither Elliot nor his research is of the first rank." Dr. Richard Aronson at the University of Chicago called the research "clearly fascist in nature."

None of these scientists had read Elliot's paper before commenting; but the damage, particularly from Aronson, was incalculable. On June 8, Eleanor Vries, the spokesperson for the PPA, referred to the "criminal research of Dr. Elliot and his Nazi staff"; she claimed Elliot's research caused Amy to have nightmares, and that Amy was being subjected to torture, drugs, and electroshock treatments.

Belatedly, on June 10, the Project Amy staff prepared a lengthy press release, explaining their position in detail and

*The following account of Elliot's persecution draws heavily on J. A. Peebles, "Infringement of Academic Freedom by Press Innuendo and Hearsay: The Experience of Dr. Peter Elliot," in the *Journal of Academic Law and Psychiatry* 52, no. 12 (1979): 19–38.

referring to the unpublished paper. But the University Information Office was now "too busy" to issue the release.

On June 11, the Berkeley faculty scheduled a meeting to consider "issues of ethical conduct" within the university. Eleanor Vries announced that the PPA had hired the noted San Francisco attorney Melvin Belli "to free Amy from subjugation." Belli's office was not available for comment.

On the same day, the Project Amy staff had a sudden, unexpected breakthrough in their understanding of Amy's dreams.

Through all the publicity and commotion, the group had continued to work daily with Amy, and her continued distress—and flaring temper tantrums—was a constant reminder that they had not solved the initial problem. They persisted in their search for clues, although when the break finally came, it happened almost by accident.

Sarah Johnson, a research assistant, was checking prehistoric archaeological sites in the Congo, on the unlikely chance that Amy might have seen such a site ("old buildings in the jungle") in her infancy, before she was brought to the Minneapolis zoo. Johnson quickly discovered the pertinent facts about the Congo: the region had not been explored by Western observers until a hundred years ago; in recent times, hostile tribes and civil war had made scientific inquiry hazardous; and finally, the moist jungle environment did not lend itself to artifact preservation.

This meant remarkably little was known about Congolese prehistory, and Johnson completed her research in a few hours. But she was reluctant to return so quickly from her assignment, so she stayed on, looking at other books in the anthropology library—ethnographies, histories, early accounts. The earliest visitors to the interior of the Congo were Arab slave traders and Portuguese merchants, and several had written accounts of their travels. Because Johnson could read neither Arabic nor Portuguese, she just looked at the plates.

And then she saw a picture that, she said, "sent a chill up my spine."

It was a Portuguese engraving originally dated 1642 and

reprinted in an 1842 volume. The ink was yellowing on frayed
brittle paper, but clearly visible was a ruined city in the jungle, overgrown with creeper vines and giant ferns. The doors
and windows were constructed with semicircular arches, exactly as Amy had drawn them.

"It was," Elliot said later, "the kind of opportunity that
comes to a researcher once in his lifetime—if he's lucky. Of
course we knew nothing about the picture; the caption was
written in flowing script and included a word that looked like
'Zinj,' and the date 1642. We immediately hired translators
skilled in archaic Arabic and seventeenth-century Portuguese, but that wasn't the point. The point was we had a
chance to verify a major theoretical question. Amy's pictures
seemed to be a clear case of specific genetic memory."

Genetic memory was first proposed by Marais in 1911,
and it has been vigorously debated ever since. In its simplest
form, the theory proposed that the mechanism of genetic
inheritance, which governed the transmission of all physical
traits, was not limited to physical traits alone. Behavior was
clearly genetically determined in lower animals, which were
born with complex behavior that did not have to be learned.
But higher animals had more flexible behavior, dependent
on learning and memory. The question was whether higher
animals, particularly apes and men, had any part of their
psychic apparatus fixed from birth by their genes.

Now, Elliot felt, with Amy they had evidence for such a
memory. Amy had been taken from Africa when she was
only seven months old. Unless she had seen this ruined city
in her infancy, her dreams represented a specific genetic
memory which could be verified by a trip to Africa. By the
evening of June 11, the Project Amy staff was agreed. If they
could arrange it—and pay for it—they would take Amy back
to Africa.

On June 12, the team waited for the translators to complete
work on the source material. Checked translations were expected to be ready within two days. But a trip to Africa for
Amy and two staff members would cost at least thirty thousand dollars, a substantial fraction of their total annual op-

erating budget. And transporting a gorilla halfway around
the world involved a bewildering tangle of customs regulations and bureaucratic red tape.

Clearly, they needed expert help, but they were not sure
where to turn. And then, on June 13, a Dr. Karen Ross from
one of their granting institutions, the Earth Resources Wildlife Fund, called from Houston to say that she was leading
an expedition into the Congo in two days' time. And although she showed no interest in taking Peter Elliot or Amy
with her, she conveyed—at least over the telephone—a confident familiarity with the way expeditions were assembled
and managed in faroff places around the world.

When she asked if she could come to San Francisco to
meet with Dr. Elliot, Dr. Elliot replied that he would be
delighted to meet with her, at her convenience.

3. Legal Issues

PETER ELLIOT REMEMBERED JUNE 14, 1979, AS A
day of sudden reverses. He began at 8 A.M. in the San Francisco law firm of Sutherland, Morton & O'Connell, because
of the threatened custody suit from the PPA—a suit which
became all the more important now that he was planning to
take Amy out of the country.

He met with John Morton in the firm's wood-paneled library overlooking Grant Street. Morton took notes on a yellow legal pad. "I think you're all right," Morton began,
"but let me get a few facts. Amy is a gorilla?"

"Yes, a female mountain gorilla."

"Age?"

"She's seven now."

"So she's still a child?"

Elliot explained that gorillas matured in six to eight years, so that Amy was late adolescent, the equivalent of a sixteen-year-old human female.

Morton scratched notes on a pad. "Could we say she's still a minor?"

"Do we want to say that?"

"I think so."

"Yes, she's still a minor," Elliot said.

"Where did she come from? I mean originally."

"A woman tourist named Swenson found her in Africa, in a village called Bagimindi. Amy's mother had been killed by the natives for food. Mrs. Swenson bought her as an infant."

"So she was not bred in captivity," Morton said, writing on his pad.

"No. Mrs. Swenson brought her back to the States and donated her to the Minneapolis zoo."

"She relinquished her interest in Amy?"

"I assume so," Elliot said. "We've been trying to reach Mrs. Swenson to ask about Amy's early life, but she's out of the country. Apparently she travels constantly; she's in Borneo. Anyway, when Amy was sent to San Francisco, I called the Minneapolis zoo to ask if I could keep her for study. The zoo said yes, for three years."

"Did you pay any money?"

"No."

"Was there a written contract?"

"No, I just called the zoo director."

Morton nodded. "Oral agreement . . ." he said, writing. "And when the three years were up?"

"That was the spring of 1976. I asked the zoo for an extension of six years, and they gave it to me."

"Again orally?"

"Yes. I called on the phone."

"No correspondence?"

"No. They didn't seem very interested when I called. To tell you the truth, I think they had forgotten about Amy. The zoo has four gorillas, anyway."

Morton frowned. "Isn't a gorilla a pretty expensive animal? I mean, if you wanted to buy one for a pet or for the circus.''

"Gorillas are on the endangered list; you can't buy them as pets. But yes, they'd be pretty expensive.''

"How expensive?''

"Well, there's no established market value, but it would be twenty or thirty thousand dollars.''

"And all during these years, you have been teaching her language?''

"Yes,'' Peter said. "American Sign Language. She has a vocabulary of six hundred and twenty words now.''

"Is that a lot?''

"More than any known primate.''

Morton nodded, making notes. "You work with her every day in ongoing research?''

"Yes.''

"Good,'' Morton said. "That's been very important in the animal custody cases so far.''

For more than a hundred years, there had been organized movements in Western countries to stop animal experimentation. They were led by the anti-vivisectionists, the RSPCA, the ASPCA. Originally these organizations were a kind of lunatic fringe of animal lovers, intent on stopping all animal research.

Over the years, scientists had evolved a standard defense acceptable to the courts. Researchers claimed that their experiments had the goal of bettering the health and welfare of mankind, a higher priority than animal welfare. They pointed out that no one objected to animals being used as beasts of burden or for agricultural work—a life of drudgery to which animals had been subjected for thousands of years. Using animals in scientific experiments simply extended the idea that animals were the servants of human enterprises.

In addition, animals were literally brutes. They had no self-awareness, no recognition of their existence in nature. This meant, in the words of philosopher George H. Mead, that ''animals have no rights. We are at liberty to cut off their lives; there is no wrong committed when an animal's life is taken away. He has not lost anything. . . .''

Many people were troubled by these views, but attempts to establish guidelines quickly ran into logical problems. The most obvious concerned the perceptions of animals further down the phylogenetic scale. Few researchers operated on dogs, cats, and other mammals without anesthesia, but what about annelid worms, crayfish, leeches, and squid? Ignoring these creatures was a form of "taxonomic discrimination." Yet if these animals deserved consideration, shouldn't it also be illegal to throw a live lobster into a pot of boiling water?

The question of what constituted cruelty to animals was confused by the animal societies themselves. In some countries, they fought the extermination of rats; and in 1968 there was the bizarre Australian pharmaceutical case.* In the face of these ironies, the courts hesitated to interfere with animal experimentation. As a practical matter, researchers were free to do as they wished. The volume of animal research was extraordinary: during the 1970s, sixty-four million animals were killed in experiments in the United States each year.

But attitudes had slowly changed. Language studies with dolphins and apes made it clear that these animals were not only intelligent but self-aware; they recognized themselves in mirrors and photographs. In 1974, scientists themselves formed the International Primate Protection League to monitor research involving monkeys and apes. In March, 1978, the Indian government banned the export of rhesus monkeys to research laboratories around the world. And there were court cases which concluded that in some instances animals did, indeed, have rights.

The old view was analogous to slavery: the animal was the property of its owner, who could do whatever he wished. But now ownership became secondary. In February, 1977,

---

*A new pharmaceutical factory was built in Western Australia. In this factory all the pills came out on a conveyor belt; a person had to watch the belt, and press buttons to sort the pills into separate bins by size and color. A Skinnerian animal behaviorist pointed out that it would be simple to teach pigeons to watch the pills and peck colored keys to do the sorting process. Incredulous factory managers agreed to a test; the pigeons indeed performed reliably, and were duly placed on the assembly line. Then the RSPCA stepped in and put a stop to it on the grounds that it represented cruelty to animals; the job was turned over to a human operator, for whom it did not, apparently, represent cruelty.

there was a case involving a dolphin named Mary, released by a lab technician into the open ocean. The University of Hawaii prosecuted the technician, charging loss of a valuable research animal. Two trials resulted in hung juries; the case was dropped.

In November, 1978, there was a custody case involving a chimpanzee named Arthur, who was fluent in sign language. His owner, Johns Hopkins University, decided to sell him and close the program. His trainer, William Levine, went to court and obtained custody on the grounds that Arthur knew language and thus was no longer a chimpanzee.

"One of the pertinent facts," Morton said, "was that when Arthur was confronted by other chimpanzees, he referred to them as 'black things.' And when Arthur was twice asked to sort photographs of people and photographs of chimps, he sorted them correctly except that both times he put his own picture in the stack with the people. He obviously did not consider himself a chimpanzee, and the court ruled that he should remain with his trainer, since any separation would cause him severe psychic distress."

"Amy cries when I leave her," Elliot said.

"When you conduct experiments, do you obtain her permission?"

"Always." Elliot smiled. Morton obviously had no sense of day-to-day life with Amy. It was essential to obtain her permission for any course of action, even a ride in a car. She was a powerful animal, and she could be willful and stubborn.

"Do you keep a record of her acquiescence?"

"Videotapes."

"Does she understand the experiments you propose?"

He shrugged. "She says she does."

"You follow a system of rewards and punishments?"

"All animal behaviorists do."

Morton frowned. "What forms do her punishments take?"

"Well, when she's a bad girl I make her stand in the corner facing the wall. Or else I send her to bed early without her peanut-butter-and-jelly snack."

"What about torture and shock treatments?"

"Ridiculous."

"You never physically punish the animal?"

"She's a pretty damn big animal. Usually I worry that she'll get mad and punish *me*."

Morton smiled and stood. "You're going to be all right," he said. "Any court will rule that Amy is your ward and that you must decide any ultimate disposition in her case." He hesitated. "I know this sounds strange, but could you put Amy on the stand?"

"I guess so," Elliot said. "Do you think it will come to that?"

"Not in this case," Morton said, "but sooner or later it will. You watch: within ten years, there will be a custody case involving a language-using primate, and the ape will be in the witness-box."

Elliot shook his hand, and said as he was leaving, "By the way, would I have any problem taking her out of the country?"

"If there *is* a custody case, you could have trouble taking her across state lines," Morton said. "Are you planning to take her out of the country?"

"Yes."

"Then my advice is to do it fast, and don't tell anyone," Morton said.

Elliot entered his office on the third floor of the Zoology Department building shortly after nine. His secretary, Carolyn, said: "A Dr. Ross called from that Wildlife Fund in Houston; she's on her way to San Francisco. A Mr. Morikawa called three times, says it's important. The Project Amy staff meeting is set for ten o'clock. And Windy is in your office."

"Really?"

James Weldon was a senior professor in the Department, a weak, blustery man. "Windy" Weldon was usually portrayed in departmental cartoons as holding a wet finger in the air: he was a master at knowing which way the wind was blowing. For the past several days, he had avoided Peter Elliot and his staff.

Elliot went into his office.

"Well, Peter my boy," Weldon said, reaching out to give his version of a hearty handshake. "You're in early."

Elliot was instantly wary. "I thought I'd beat the crowds," he said. The picketers did not show up until ten o'clock, sometimes later, depending on when they had arranged to meet the TV news crews. That was how it worked these days: protest by appointment.

"They're not coming anymore." Weldon smiled.

He handed Elliot the late city edition of the *Chronicle*, a front-page story circled in black pen. Eleanor Vries had resigned her position as regional director of the PPA, pleading overwork and personal pressures; a statement from the PPA in New York indicated that they had seriously misconstrued the nature and content of Elliot's research.

"Meaning what?" Elliot asked.

"Belli's office reviewed your paper and Vries's public statements about torture, and decided that the PPA was exposed to a major libel suit," Weldon said. "The New York office is terrified. They'll be making overtures to you later today. Personally, I hope you'll be understanding."

Elliot dropped into his chair. "What about the faculty meeting next week?"

"Oh, that's essential," Weldon said. "There's no question that the faculty will want to discuss unethical conduct—on the part of the media, and issue a strong statement in your support. I'm drawing up a statement now, to come from my office."

The irony of this was not lost on Elliot. "You sure you want to go out on a limb?" he asked.

"I'm behind you one thousand percent, I hope you know that," Weldon said. Weldon was restless, pacing around the office, staring at the walls, which were covered with Amy's finger paintings. Windy had something further on his mind. "She's still making these same pictures?" he asked, finally.

"Yes," Elliot said.

"And you still have no idea what they mean?"

Elliot paused; at best it was premature to tell Weldon what they thought the pictures meant. "No idea," he said.

"Are you sure?" Weldon asked, frowning. "I think somebody knows what they mean."

"Why is that?"

"Something very strange has happened," Weldon said. "Someone has offered to buy Amy."

"To *buy* her? What are you talking about, to buy her?"

"A lawyer in Los Angeles called my office yesterday and offered to buy her for a hundred and fifty thousand dollars."

"It must be some rich do-gooder," Elliot said, "trying to save Amy from torture."

"I don't think so," Weldon said. "For one thing, the offer came from Japan. Someone named Morikawa—he's in electronics in Tokyo. I found that out when the lawyer called back this morning, to increase his offer to two hundred and fifty thousand dollars."

"Two hundred and fifty thousand dollars?" Elliot said. "For Amy?" Of course it was out of the question. He would never sell her. But why would anyone offer so much money?

Weldon had an answer. "This kind of money, a quarter of a million dollars, can only be coming from private enterprise. Industry. Clearly, Morikawa has read about your work and found a use for speaking primates in an industrial context." Windy stared at the ceiling, a sure sign he was about to wax eloquent. "I think a new field might be opening up here, the training of primates for industrial applications in the real world."

Peter Elliot swore. He was not teaching Amy language in order to put a hard hat on her head and a lunch pail in her hand, and he said so.

"You're not thinking it through," Weldon said. "What if we are on the verge of a new field of applied behavior for the great apes? Think what it means. Not only funding to the Department, and an opportunity for applied research. Most important, there would be a reason to keep these animals alive. You know that the great apes are becoming extinct. The chimps in Africa are greatly reduced in number. The orangs of Borneo are losing their natural habitat to the timber cutters and will be extinct in ten years. The gorilla is down to three thousand in the central African forests. These animals will all disappear in our lifetime—*unless there is a reason to keep them alive*, as a species. You may provide that reason, Peter my boy. Think about it."

Elliot did think about it, and he discussed it at the Project Amy staff meeting at ten o'clock. They considered possible industrial applications for apes, and possible advantages to employers, such as the lack of unions and fringe benefits. In the late twentieth century, these were major considerations. (In 1978, for each new automobile that rolled off the Detroit assembly lines, the cost of worker health benefits exceeded the cost of all the steel used to build the car.)

But they concluded that a vision of "industrialized apes" was wildly fanciful. An ape like Amy was not a cheap and stupid version of a human worker. Quite the opposite: Amy was a highly intelligent and complex creature out of her element in the modern industrial world. She demanded a great deal of supervision; she was whimsical and unreliable; and her health was always at risk. It simply didn't make sense to use her in industry. If Morikawa had visions of apes wielding soldering irons on a microelectronic assembly line, building TVs and hi-fi sets, he was sorely misinformed.

The only note of caution came from Bergman, the child psychologist. "A quarter of a million is a lot of money," he said, "and Mr. Morikawa is probably no fool. He must have learned about Amy through her drawings, which imply she is neurotic and difficult. If he's interested in her, I'd bet it's *because of her drawings*. But I can't imagine why those drawings should be worth a quarter of a million dollars."

Neither could anyone else, and the discussion turned to the drawings themselves, and the newly translated texts. Sarah Johnson, in charge of research, started out with the flat comment "I have bad news about the Congo."*

For most of recorded history, she explained, nothing was

*Johnson's principal reference was the definitive work by A. J. Parkinson, *The Congo Delta in Myth and History* (London: Peters, 1904).

known about the Congo. The ancient Egyptians on the upper Nile knew only that their river originated far to the south, in a region they called the Land of Trees. This was a mysterious place with forests so dense they were as dark as night in the middle of the day. Strange creatures inhabited this perpetual gloom, including little men with tails, and animals half black and half white.

For nearly four thousand years afterward, nothing more substantial was learned about the interior of Africa. The Arabs came to East Africa in the seventh century A.D., in search of gold, ivory, spices, and slaves. But the Arabs were merchant seamen and did not venture inland. They called the interior Zinj—the Land of the Blacks—a region of fable and fantasy. There were stories of vast forests and tiny men with tails; stories of mountains that spewed fire and turned the sky black; stories of native villages overwhelmed by monkeys, which would have congress with the women; stories of great giants with hairy bodies and flat noses; stories of creatures half leopard, half man; stories of native markets where the fattened carcasses of men were butchered and sold as a delicacy.

Such stories were sufficiently forbidding to keep the Arabs on the coast, despite other stories equally alluring: mountains of shimmering gold, riverbeds gleaming with diamonds, animals that spoke the language of men, great jungle civilizations of unimaginable splendor. In particular, one story was repeated again and again in early accounts: the story of the Lost City of Zinj.

According to legend, a city known to the Hebrews of Solomonic times had been a source of inconceivable wealth in diamonds. The caravan route to the city had been jealously guarded, passed from father to son, as a sacred trust for generation after generation. But the diamond mines were exhausted and the city itself now lay in crumbling ruins, somewhere in the dark heart of Africa. The arduous caravan routes were long since swallowed up by jungle, and the last trader who remembered the way had carried his secret with him to the grave many hundreds of years before.

This mysterious and alluring place the Arabs called the

Lost City of Zinj.* Yet despite its enduring fame, Johnson could find few detailed descriptions of the city. In 1187 Ibn Baratu, an Arab in Mombasa, recorded that "the natives of the region tell . . . of a lost city far inland, called Zinj. There the inhabitants, who are black, once lived in wealth and luxury, and even the slaves decorated themselves with jewels and especially blue diamonds, for a great store of diamonds is there."

In 1292, a Persian named Mohammed Zaid stated that "a large diamond [the size] of a man's clenched fist . . . was exhibited on the streets of Zanzibar, and all said it had come from the interior, where the ruins of a city called Zinj may be found, and it is here that such diamonds may be found in profusion, scattered upon the ground and also in rivers. . . ."

In 1334, another Arab, Ibn Mohammed, stated that "our number made arrangements to seek out the city of Zinj, but quitted our quest upon learning that the city was long since abandoned, and much ruined. It is said that the aspect of the city is wondrous strange, for doors and windows are built in the curve of a half-moon, and the residences are now overtaken by a violent race of hairy men who speak in whispers no known language. . . ."

Then the Portuguese, those indefatigable explorers, arrived. By 1544, they were venturing inland from the west coast up the mighty Congo River, but they soon encountered all the obstacles that would prevent exploration of central Africa for hundreds of years to come. The Congo was not navigable beyond the first set of rapids, two hundred miles inland (at what was once Léopoldville, and is now Kinshasa). The natives were hostile and cannibalistic. And the hot steaming jungle was the source of disease—malaria, sleeping sickness, bilharzia, blackwater fever—which decimated foreign intruders.

The Portuguese never managed to penetrate the central

*The fabled city of Zinj formed the basis for H. Rider Haggard's popular novel *King Solomon's Mines*, first published in 1885. Haggard, a gifted linguist, had served on the staff of the Governor of Natal in 1875, and he presumably heard of Zinj from the neighboring Zulus at that time.

Congo. Neither did the English, under Captain Brenner, in 1644; his entire party was lost. The Congo would remain for two hundred years as a blank spot on the civilized maps of the world.

But the early explorers repeated the legends of the interior, including the story of Zinj. A Portuguese artist, Juan Diego de Valdez, drew a widely acclaimed picture of the Lost City of Zinj in 1642. "But," Sarah Johnson said, "he also drew pictures of men with tails, and monkeys having carnal knowledge of native women."

Somebody groaned.

"Apparently Valdez was crippled," she continued. "He lived all his life in the town of Setúbal, drinking with sailors and drawing pictures based on his conversations."

Africa was not thoroughly explored until the mid-nineteenth century, by Burton and Speke, Baker and Livingstone, and especially Stanley. No trace of the Lost City of Zinj was found by any of them. Nor had any trace of the apocryphal city been found in the hundred years since.

The gloom that descended over the Project Amy staff meeting was profound. "I told you it was bad news," Sarah Johnson said.

"You mean," Peter Elliot said, "that this picture is based on a description, and we don't know whether the city actually exists or not."

"I'm afraid so," Sarah Johnson said. "There is no proof that the city in the picture exists at all. It's just a story."

4. Resolution

PETER ELLIOT'S UNQUESTIONED RELIANCE ON twentieth-century hard data—facts, figures, graphs—left him unprepared for the possibility that the 1642 engraving, in all its detail, was merely the fanciful speculation of an uninhibited artist. The news came as a shock.

Their plans to take Amy to the Congo suddenly appeared childishly naïve; the resemblance of her sketchy, schematic drawings to the 1642 Valdez engraving was obviously coincidental. How could they ever have imagined that a Lost City of Zinj was anything but the stuff of ancient fable? In the seventeenth-century world of widening horizons and new wonders, the idea of such a city would have seemed perfectly reasonable, even compelling. But in the computerized twentieth century, the Lost City of Zinj was as unlikely as Camelot or Xanadu. They had been fools ever to take it seriously. "The lost city doesn't exist," he said.

"Oh, it exists, all right," she said. "There's no doubt about *that*."

Elliot glanced up quickly, and then he saw that Sarah Johnson had not answered him. A tall gangly girl in her early twenties stood at the back of the room. She might have been considered beautiful except for her cold, aloof demeanor. This girl was dressed in a severe, businesslike suit, and she carried a briefcase, which she now set on the table, popping the latches.

"I'm Dr. Ross," she announced, "from the Wildlife Fund, and I'd like your opinion of these pictures."

She passed around a series of photographs, which were viewed by the staff with an assortment of whistles and sighs. At the head of the table, Elliot waited impatiently until the photographs came down to him.

They were grainy black-and-white images with horizontal scanning line streaks, photographed off a video screen. But the image was unmistakable: a ruined city in the jungle, with curious inverted crescent-shaped doors and windows.

5. Amy

"BY SATELLITE?" ELLIOT REPEATED, HEARING THE tension in his voice.

"That's right, the pictures were transmitted by satellite from Africa two days ago."

"Then you know the location of this ruin?"

"Of course."

"And your expedition leaves in a matter of hours?"

"Six hours and twenty-three minutes, to be exact," Ross said, glancing at her digital watch.

Elliot adjourned the meeting, and talked privately with Ross for more than an hour. Elliot later claimed that Ross had "deceived" him about the purpose of the expedition and the hazards they would face. But Elliot was eager to go, and probably not inclined to be too fussy about the reasons behind Ross's coming expedition, or the dangers involved. As a skilled grantsman, he had long ago grown comfortable with situations where other peoples' money and his own motivations did not exactly coincide. This was the cynical side of academic life: how much pure research had been funded because it might cure cancer? A researcher promised anything to get his money.

Apparently it never occurred to Elliot that Ross might be using him as coldly as he was using her. From the start Ross was never entirely truthful; she had been instructed by Travis to explain the ERTS Congo mission "with a little data dropout." Data dropout was second nature to her; everyone at ERTS had learned to say no more than was necessary. Elliot treated her as if she were an ordinary funding agency, and that was a serious mistake.

In the final analysis, Ross and Elliot misjudged each other, for each presented a deceptive appearance, and in the same way. Elliot appeared so shy and retiring that one Berkeley faculty member had commented, "It's no wonder he's devoted his life to apes; he can't work up the nerve to talk to people." But Elliot had been a tough middle linebacker in college, and his diffident academic demeanor concealed a head-crunching ambitious drive.

Similarly, Karen Ross, despite her youthful cheerleader beauty and soft, seductive Texas accent, possessed great intelligence and a deep inner toughness. (She had matured early, and a high-school teacher had once appraised her as "the very flower of virile Texas womanhood.") Ross felt responsible for the previous ERTS expedition, and she was determined to rectify past errors. It was at least possible that Elliot and Amy could help her when she got onsite; that was reason enough to take them with her. Beyond that, Ross was concerned about the consortium, which was obviously seeking Elliot, since Morikawa was calling. If she took Elliot and Amy with her, she removed a possible advantage to the consortium—again, reason enough to take them with her. Finally, she needed a cover in case her expedition was stopped at one of the borders—and a primatologist and an ape provided a perfect cover.

But in the end Karen Ross wanted only the Congo diamonds—and she was prepared to say anything, do anything, sacrifice anything to get them.

In photographs taken at San Francisco airport, Elliot and Ross appeared as two smiling, youthful academics, embarking on a lark of an expedition to Africa. But in fact, their motivations were different, and grimly held. Elliot was reluctant to tell her how theoretical and academic his goals were—and Ross was reluctant to admit how pragmatic were hers.

In any case, by midday on June 14, Karen Ross found herself riding with Peter Elliot in his battered Fiat sedan along Hallowell Road, going past the University athletic field. She had some misgivings: they were going to meet Amy.

Elliot unlocked the door with its red sign DO NOT DISTURB

ANIMAL EXPERIMENTATION IN PROGRESS. Behind the door, Amy was grunting and scratching impatiently. Elliot paused.

"When you meet her," he said, "remember that she is a gorilla and not a human being. Gorillas have their own etiquette. Don't speak loudly or make any sudden movements until she gets used to you. If you smile, don't show your teeth, because bared teeth are a threat. And keep your eyes downcast, because direct stares from strangers are considered hostile. Don't stand too close to me or touch me, because she's very jealous. If you talk to her, don't lie. Even though she uses sign language, she understands most human speech, and we usually just talk to her. She can tell when you're lying and she doesn't like it."

"She doesn't like it?"

"She dismisses you, won't talk to you, and gets bitchy."

"Anything else?"

"No, it should be okay." He smiled reassuringly. "We have this traditional greeting, even though she's getting a little big for it." He opened the door, braced himself, and said, "Good morning, Amy."

A huge black shape came leaping out through the open door into his arms. Elliot staggered back under the impact. Ross was astonished by the size of the animal. She had been imagining something smaller and cuter. Amy was as large as an adult human female.

Amy kissed Elliot on the cheek with her large lips, her black head seeming enormous alongside his. Her breath steamed his glasses. Ross smelled a sweetish odor, and watched as he gently unwrapped her long arms from around his shoulders. "Amy happy this morning?" he asked.

Amy's fingers moved quickly near her cheek, as if she were brushing away flies.

"Yes, I was late today," Elliot said.

She moved her fingers again, and Ross realized that Amy was signing. The speed was surprising; she had expected something much slower and more deliberate. She noticed that Amy's eyes never left Elliot's face. She was extraordinarily attentive, focusing on him with total animal watchfulness. She seemed to absorb everything, his posture, his expression, his tone of voice, as well as his words.

"I had to work," Elliot said. She sighed again quickly, like human gestures of dismissal. "Yes, that's right, people work." He led Amy back into the trailer, and motioned for Karen Ross to follow. Inside the trailer, he said, "Amy, this is Dr. Ross. Say hello to Dr. Ross."

Amy looked at Karen Ross suspiciously.

"Hello, Amy," Karen Ross said, smiling at the floor. She felt a little foolish behaving this way, but Amy was large enough to frighten her.

Amy stared at Karen Ross for a moment, then walked away, across the trailer to her easel. She had been finger-painting, and now resumed this activity, ignoring them.

"What's that mean?" Ross said. She distinctly felt she was being snubbed.

"We'll see," Elliot said.

After a few moments, Amy ambled back, walking on her knuckles. She went directly to Karen Ross, sniffed her crotch, and examined her minutely. She seemed particularly interested in Ross's leather purse, which had a shiny brass clasp. Ross said later that "it was just like any cocktail party in Houston. I was being checked out by another woman. I had the feeling that any minute she was going to ask me where I bought my clothes."

That was not the outcome, however. Amy reached up and deliberately streaked globs of green finger paint on Ross's skirt.

"I don't think this is going too well," Karen Ross said.

Elliot had watched the progress of this first meeting with more apprehension than he was willing to admit. Introducing new humans to Amy was often difficult, particularly if they were women.

Over the years, Elliot had come to recognize many distinctly "feminine" traits in Amy. She could be coy, she responded to flattery, she was preoccupied with her appearance, loved makeup, and was very fussy about the color of the sweaters she wore in the winter. She preferred men to women, and she was openly jealous of Elliot's girl friends. He rarely brought them around to meet her, but sometimes in the morning she would sniff him for perfume, and she always commented if he had not changed his clothing overnight.

This situation might have been amusing if not for the fact that Amy made occasional unprovoked attacks on strange women. And an attack by Amy was never amusing.

Amy returned to the easel and signed, *No like woman no like Amy no like go away away.*

"Come on, Amy, be a good gorilla," Peter said.

"What did she say?" Ross asked, going to the sink to wash the finger paint from her dress. Peter noticed that she did not squeal and shriek as many visitors did when they received an unfriendly greeting from Amy.

"She said she likes your dress," he said.

Amy shot him a look, as she always did whenever Elliot mistranslated her. *Amy not lie. Peter not lie.*

"Be nice, Amy," he said. "Karen is a nice human person."

Amy grunted, and returned to her work, painting rapidly.

"What happens now?" Karen Ross said.

"Give her time." He smiled reassuringly. "She needs time to adjust."

He did not bother to explain that it was much worse with chimpanzees. Chimps threw feces at strangers, and even at workers they knew well; they sometimes attacked to establish dominance. Chimpanzees had a strong need to determine who was in charge. Fortunately, gorillas were much less formal in their dominance hierarchies, and less violent.

At that moment, Amy ripped the paper from the easel and shredded it noisily, flinging the pieces around the room.

"Is this part of the adjustment?" Karen Ross asked. She seemed more amused than frightened.

"Amy, cut it out," Peter said, allowing his tone to convey irritation. "Amy . . ."

Amy sat in the middle of the floor, surrounded by the paper. She tore it angrily and signed, *This woman. This woman.* It was classic displacement behavior. Whenever gorillas did not feel comfortable with direct aggression, they did something symbolic. In symbolic terms, she was now tearing Karen Ross apart.

And she was getting worked up, beginning what the Project Amy staff called "sequencing." Just as human beings first became red-faced, and then tensed their bodies, and then shouted and threw things before they finally resorted to direct physical aggression, so gorillas passed through a stereotyped behavioral sequence on the way to physical aggression. Tearing up paper, or grass, would be followed by lateral crablike movements and grunts. Then she would slap the ground, making as much noise as possible.

And then Amy would charge, if he didn't interrupt the sequence.

"Amy," he said sternly. "Karen button woman."

Amy stopped shredding. In her world, "button" was the acknowledged term for a person of high status.

Amy was extremely sensitive to individual moods and behavior, and she had no difficulty observing the staff and deciding who was superior to whom. But among strangers, Amy as a gorilla was utterly impervious to formal human status cues; the principal indicators—clothing, bearing, and speech—had no meaning to her.

As a young animal, she had inexplicably attacked policemen. After several biting episodes and threatened lawsuits, they finally learned that Amy found police uniforms with their shiny buttons clownlike and ridiculous; she assumed that anyone so foolishly dressed must be of inferior status and safe to attack. After they had taught her the concept of "button," she treated anyone in uniform with deference.

Amy now stared at "button" Ross with new respect. Surrounded by the torn paper, she seemed suddenly embarrassed, as if she had made a social error. Without being told, she went and stood in the corner, facing the wall.

"What's that about?" Ross said.

"She knows she's been bad."

"You make her stand in the corner, like a child? She didn't mean any harm." Before Elliot could warn against it, she went over to Amy. Amy stared steadfastly at the corner.

Ross unshouldered her purse and set it on the floor within Amy's reach. Nothing happened for a moment. Then Amy took the purse, looked at Karen, then looked at Peter.

Peter said, "She'll wreck whatever's inside."

"That's all right."

Amy immediately opened the brass clasp, and dumped the contents on the floor. She began sifting through, signing, *Lipstick lipstick, Amy like Amy want lipstick want.*

"She wants lipstick."

Ross bent over and found it for her. Amy removed the cap and smeared a red circle on Karen's face. She then smiled and grunted happily, and crossed the room to her mirror, which was mounted on the floor. She applied lipstick.

"I think we're doing better," Karen Ross said.

Across the room, Amy squatted by the mirror, happily making a mess of her face. She grinned at her smart image, then applied lipstick to her teeth. It seemed a good time to ask her the question. "Amy want take trip?" Peter said.

Amy loved trips, and regarded them as special treats. After an especially good day, Elliot often took her for a ride to a nearby drive-in, where she would have an orange drink, sucking it through the straw and enjoying the commotion she caused among the other people there. Lipstick and an offer of a trip was almost too much pleasure for one morning. She signed, *Car trip?*

"No, not in the car. A long trip. Many days."

Leave house?

"Yes, leave house. Many days."

This made her suspicious. The only times she had left the house for many days had been during hospitalizations for pneumonia and urinary-tract infections; they had not been pleasant trips. She signed, *Where go trip?*

"To the jungle, Amy."

There was a long pause. At first he thought she had not understood, but she knew the word for jungle, and she should be able to put it all together. Amy signed thoughtfully to herself, repetitively as she always did when she was mulling things over: *Jungle trip trip jungle go trip jungle go.* She set aside her lipstick. She stared at the bits of paper on the floor,

and then she began to pick them up and put them in the
wastebasket.

"What does that mean?" Karen Ross asked.

"That means Amy wants to take a trip," Peter Elliot said.

6. Departure

THE HINGED NOSE OF THE BOEING 747 CARGO JET
lay open like a jaw, exposing the cavernous, brightly lit interior. The plane had been flown up from Houston to San
Francisco that afternoon; it was now nine o'clock at night,
and puzzled workers were loading on the large aluminum
travel cage, boxes of vitamin pills, a portable potty, and cartons of toys. One workman pulled out a Mickey Mouse
drinking cup and stared at it, shaking his head.

Outside on the concrete, Elliot stood with Amy, who covered her ears against the whine of the jet engines. She signed
to Peter, *Birds noisy.*

"We fly bird, Amy," he said.

Amy had never flown before, and had never seen an airplane at close hand. *We go car,* she decided, looking at the
plane.

"We can't go by car. We fly."

Fly where fly? Amy signed.

"Fly jungle."

This seemed to perplex her, but he did not want to explain
further. Like all gorillas, Amy had an aversion to water,
refusing to cross even small streams. He knew she would be
distressed to hear that they would be flying over large bodies
of water. Changing the subject, he suggested they board the
plane and look around. As they climbed the sloping ramp up
the nose, Amy signed, *Where button woman?*

He had not seen Ross for the last five hours, and was surprised to discover that she was already on board, talking on a telephone mounted on a wall of the cargo hold, one hand cupped over her free ear to block the noise. Elliot overheard her say, "Well, Irving seems to think it's enough. . . . Yes, we have four nine-oh-seven units and we are prepared to match and absorb. Two micro HUDs, that's all. . . . Yes, why not?" She finished the call, turned to Elliot and Amy.

"Everything okay?" he asked.

"Fine. I'll show you around." She led him deeper into the cargo hold, with Amy at his side. Elliot glanced back and saw the chauffeur coming up the ramp with a series of numbered metal boxes marked INTEC, INC. followed by serial numbers.

"This," Karen Ross said, "is the main cargo hold." It was filled with four-wheel-drive trucks, Land Cruisers, amphibious vehicles, inflatable boats, and racks of clothing, equipment, food—all tagged with computer codes, all loaded in modules. Ross explained that ERTS could outfit expeditions to any geographical and climatic condition in a matter of hours. She kept emphasizing the speed possible with computer assembly.

"Why the rush?" Elliot asked.

"It's business," Karen Ross said. "Four years ago, there were no companies like ERTS. Now there are nine around the world, and what they all sell is competitive advantage, meaning speed. Back in the sixties, a company—say, an oil company—might spend months or years investigating a possible site. But that's no longer competitive; business decisions are made in weeks or days. The pace of everything has speeded up. We're already looking to the nineteen-eighties, where we'll provide answers in *hours*. Right now the average ERTS contract runs a little under three weeks, or five hundred hours. But by 1990 there will be 'close of business' data—an executive can call us in the morning for information anywhere in the world, and have a complete report transmitted by computer to his desk before close of business that evening, say ten to twelve hours."

As they continued the tour, Elliot noticed that although

the trucks and vehicles caught the eye first, much of the aircraft storage space was given over to aluminum modules marked "C3I."

"That's right," Ross said. "Command-Control Communications and Intelligence. They're micronic components, the most expensive budget item we carry. When we started outfitting expeditions, twelve percent of the cost went to electronics. Now it's up to thirty-one percent, and climbing every year. It's field communications, remote sensing, defense, and so on."

She led them to the rear of the plane, where there was a modular living area, nicely furnished, with a large computer console, and bunks for sleeping.

Amy signed, *Nice house.*

"Yes, it is nice."

They were introduced to Jensen, a young bearded geologist, and to Irving, who announced that he was the "triple E." The two men were running some kind of probability study on the computer but they paused to shake hands with Amy, who regarded them gravely, and then turned her attention to the screen. Amy was captivated by the colorful screen images and bright LEDs, and kept trying to punch the keys herself. She signed, *Amy play box.*

"Not now, Amy," Elliot said, and swatted her hands away.

Jensen asked, "Is she always this way?"

"I'm afraid so," Elliot said. "She likes computers. She's worked around them ever since she was very young, and she thinks of them as her private property." And then he added, "What's a triple E?"

"Expedition electronic expert," Irving said cheerfully. He was a short man with an impish quick smile. "Doing the best I can. We picked up some stuff from Intec, that's about all. God knows what the Japanese and the Germans will throw at us."

"Oh, damn, there she goes," Jensen said, laughing as Amy pushed the keyboard.

Elliot said, "Amy, no!"

"It's just a game. Probably not interesting to apes," Jensen said. And he added, "She can't hurt anything."

Amy signed, *Amy good gorilla,* and pushed the keys on the computer again. She appeared relaxed, and Elliot was grateful for the distraction the computer provided. He was always amused by the sight of Amy's heavy dark form before a computer console. She would touch her lower lip thoughtfully before pushing the keys, in what seemed a parody of human behavior.

Ross, practical as always, brought them back to mundane matters. "Will Amy sleep on one of the bunks?"

Elliot shook his head. "No. Gorillas expect to make a fresh bed each night. Give her some blankets, and she'll twist them into a nest on the floor and sleep there."

Ross nodded. "What about her vitamins and medications? Will she swallow pills?"

"Ordinarily you have to bribe her, or hide the pills in a piece of banana. She tends to gulp banana, without chewing it."

"Without chewing." Ross nodded as if that were important. "We have a standard issue," she said. "I'll see that she gets them."

"She takes the same vitamins that people do, except that she'll need lots of ascorbic acid."

"We issue three thousand units a day. That's enough? Good. And she'll tolerate anti-malarials? We have to start them right away."

"Generally speaking," Elliot said, "she has the same reaction to medication as people."

Ross nodded. "Will the cabin pressurization bother her? It's set at five thousand feet."

Elliot shook his head. "She's a mountain gorilla, and they live at five thousand to nine thousand feet, so she's actually altitude-adapted. But she's acclimated to a moist climate and she dehydrates quickly; we'll have to keep forcing fluids on her."

"Can she use the head?"

"The seat's probably too high for her," Elliot said, "but I brought her potty."

"She'll use her potty?"

"Sure."

"I have a new collar for her; will she wear it?"

"If you give it to her as a gift."

As they reviewed other details of Amy's requirements, Elliot realized that something had happened during the last few hours, almost without his knowing it: Amy's unpredictable, dream-driven neurotic behavior had fallen away. It was as if the earlier behavior was irrelevant; now that she was going on a trip, she was no longer moody and introspective, her interests were outgoing; she was once again a youthful female gorilla. He found himself wondering whether her dreams, her depression—finger paintings, everything—were a result of her confined laboratory environment for so many years. At first the laboratory had been agreeable, like a crib for young children. But perhaps in later years it pinched. Perhaps, he thought, Amy just needed a little excitement.

Excitement was in the air: as he talked with Ross, Elliot felt something remarkable was about to happen. This expedition with Amy was the first example of an event primate researchers had predicted for years—the Pearl thesis.

Frederick Pearl was a theoretical animal behaviorist. At a meeting of the American Ethnological Society in New York in 1972, he had said, "Now that primates have learned sign language, it is only a matter of time until someone takes an animal into the field to assist the study of wild animals of the same species. We can imagine language-skilled primates acting as interpreters or perhaps even as ambassadors for mankind, in contact with wild creatures."

Pearl's thesis attracted considerable attention, and funding from the U.S. Air Force, which had supported linguistic research since the 1960s. According to one story, the Air Force had a secret project called CONTOUR, involving possible contact with alien life forms. The official military position was that UFOs were of natural origin—but the military was covering its bets. Should alien contact occur, linguistic fundamentals were obviously critically important. And taking primates into the field was seen as an example of contact with "alien intelligence"; hence the Air Force funding.

Pearl predicted that fieldwork would be undertaken before 1976, but in fact no one had yet done it. The reason was that on closer examination, no one could figure out quite what the advantages were—most language-using primates were as baffled by wild primates as human beings were. Some, like the chimpanzee Arthur, denied any association with their own kind, referring to them as "black things." (Amy, who had been taken to the zoo to view other gorillas, recognized them but was haughty, calling them "stupid gorillas" once she found that when she signed to them, they did not reply.)

Such observations led another researcher, John Bates, to say in 1977 that "we are producing an educated animal élite which demonstrates the same snobbish aloofness that a Ph.D. shows toward a truck driver. . . . It is highly unlikely that the generation of language-using primates will be skillful ambassadors in the field. They are simply too disdainful."

But the truth was that no one really knew what would happen when a primate was taken into the field. Because no one had done it: Amy would be the first.

At eleven o'clock, the ERTS cargo plane taxied down the runway at San Francisco International, lifted ponderously into the air, and headed east through the darkness toward Africa.

DAY 3: TANGIER

June 15, 1979

1. Ground Truth

PETER ELLIOT HAD KNOWN AMY SINCE INFANCY. He prided himself on his ability to predict her responses, although he had only known her in a laboratory setting. Now, as she was faced with new situations, her behavior surprised him.

Elliot had anticipated Amy would be terrified of the takeoff, and had prepared a syringe with Thoralen tranquilizer. But sedation proved unnecessary. Amy watched Jensen and Levine buckle their seat belts, and she immediately buckled herself in, too; she seemed to regard the procedure as an amusing, if simpleminded, game. And although her eyes widened when she heard the full roar of the engines, the human beings around her did not seem disturbed, and Amy imitated their bored indifference, raising her eyebrows and sighing at the tedium of it all.

Once airborne, however, Amy looked out the window and immediately panicked. She released her seat belt and scurried back and forth across the passenger compartment, moving from window to window, knocking people aside in whimpering terror while she signed, *Where ground ground where ground?* Outside, the ground was black and indistinct. *Where ground?* Elliot shot her with Thoralen and then began grooming her, sitting her down and plucking at her hair.

In the wild, primates devoted several hours each day to grooming one another, removing ticks and lice. Grooming behavior was important in ordering the group's social dominance structure—there was a pattern by which animals groomed each other, and with what frequency. And, like back rubs for people, grooming seemed to have a soothing,

69

calming effect. Within minutes, Amy had relaxed enough to notice that the others were drinking, and she promptly demanded a "green drop drink"—her term for a martini with an olive—and a cigarette. She was allowed this on special occasions such as departmental parties, and Elliot now gave her a drink and a cigarette.

But the excitement proved too much for her: an hour later, she was quietly looking out the window and signing *Nice picture* to herself when she vomited. She apologized abjectly, *Amy sorry Amy mess Amy Amy sorry.*

"It's all right, Amy," Elliot assured her, stroking the back of her head. Soon afterward, signing *Amy sleep now,* she twisted the blankets into a nest on the floor and went to sleep, snoring loudly through her broad nostrils. Lying next to her, Elliot thought, how do other gorillas get to sleep with this racket?

Elliot had his own reaction to the journey. When he had first met Karen Ross, he assumed she was an academic like himself. But this enormous airplane filled with computerized equipment, the acronymic complexity of the entire operation suggested that Earth Resources Technology had powerful resources behind it, perhaps even a military association.

Karen Ross laughed. "We're much too organized to be military." She then told him the background of the ERTS interest in Virunga. Like the Project Amy staff, Karen Ross had also stumbled upon the legend of the Lost City of Zinj. But she had drawn very different conclusions from the story.

During the last three hundred years, there had been several attempts to reach the lost city. In 1692, John Marley, an English adventurer, led an expedition of two hundred into the Congo; it was never heard from again. In 1744, a Dutch expedition went in; in 1804, another British party led by a Scottish aristocrat, Sir James Taggert, approached Virunga from the north, getting as far as the Rawana bend of the Ubangi River. He sent an advance party farther south, but it never returned.

In 1872, Stanley passed near the Virunga region but did not enter it; in 1899, a German expedition went in, losing more than half its party. A privately financed Italian expedition disappeared entirely in 1911. There had been no more recent searches for the Lost City of Zinj.

"So no one has ever found it," Elliot said.

Ross shook her head. "I think several expeditions found the city," she said. "But nobody ever got back out again."

Such an outcome was not necessarily mysterious. The early days of African exploration were incredibly hazardous. Even carefully managed expeditions lost half of their party or more. Those who did not succumb to malaria, sleeping sickness, and blackwater fever faced rivers teeming with crocodiles and hippos, jungles with leopards and suspicious, cannibalistic natives. And, for all its luxuriant growth, the rain forest provided little edible food; a number of expeditions had starved to death.

"I began," Ross said to Elliot, "with the idea that the city existed, after all. Assuming it existed, where would I find it?"

The Lost City of Zinj was associated with diamond mines, and diamonds were found with volcanoes. This led Ross to look along the Great Rift Valley—an enormous geological fault thirty miles wide, which sliced vertically up the eastern third of the continent for a distance of fifteen hundred miles. The Rift Valley was so huge that its existence was not recognized until the 1890s, when a geologist named Gregory noticed that the cliff walls thirty miles apart were composed of the same rocks. In modern terms the Great Rift was actually an abortive attempt to form an ocean, for the eastern third of the continent had begun splitting off from the rest of the African land mass two hundred million years ago; for some reason, it had stopped before the break was complete.

On a map the Great Rift depression was marked by two features: a series of thin vertical lakes—Malawi, Tanganyika, Kivu, Mobutu—and a series of volcanoes, including the only active volcanoes in Africa at Virunga. Three volcanoes in the Virunga chain were active: Mukenko, Mubuti, and Kanagarawi. They rose 11,000–15,000 feet above the Rift Valley to the east, and the Congo Basin to the west. Thus Virunga seemed a good place to look for diamonds. Her next step was to investigate the ground truth.

"What's ground truth?" Peter asked.

"At ERTS, we deal mostly in remote sensing," she explained. "Satellite photographs, aerial run-bys, radar side scans. We carry millions of remote images, but there's no substitute for ground truth, the experience of a team actually on the site, finding out what's there. I started with the preliminary expedition we sent in looking for gold. They found diamonds as well." She punched buttons on the console, and the screen images changed, glowing with dozens of flashing pinpoints of light.

"This shows the placer deposit locations in streambeds near Virunga. You see the deposits form concentric semicircles leading back to the volcanoes. The obvious conclusion is that diamonds were eroded from the slopes of the Virunga volcanoes, and washed down the streams to their present locations."

"So you sent in a party to look for the source?"

"Yes." She pointed to the screen. "But don't be deceived by what you see here. This satellite image covers fifty thousand square kilometers of jungle. Most of it has never been seen by white men. It's hard terrain, with visibility limited to a few meters in any direction. An expedition could search that area for years, passing within two hundred meters of the city and failing to see it. So I needed to narrow the search sector. I decided to see if I could find the city."

"Find the city? From satellite pictures?"

"Yes," she said. "And I found it."

The rain forests of the world had traditionally frustrated remote-sensing technology. The great jungle trees spread an impenetrable canopy of vegetation, concealing whatever lay beneath. In aerial or satellite pictures, the Congo rain forest appeared as a vast, undulating carpet of featureless and monotonous green. Even large features, rivers fifty or a hundred feet wide, were hidden beneath this leafy canopy, invisible from the air.

So it seemed unlikely she would find any evidence for a

lost city in aerial photographs. But Ross had a different idea: she would utilize the very vegetation that obscured her vision of the ground.

The study of vegetation was common in temperate regions, where the foliage underwent seasonal changes. But the equatorial rain forest was unchanging: winter or summer, the foliage remained the same. Ross turned her attention to another aspect, the differences in vegetation albedo.

Albedo was technically defined as the ratio of electromagnetic energy reflected by a surface to the amount of energy incident upon it. In terms of the visible spectrum, it was a measure of how "shiny" a surface was. A river had a high albedo, since water reflected most of the sunlight striking it. Vegetation absorbed light, and therefore had a low albedo. Starting in 1977, ERTS developed computer programs which measured albedo precisely, making very fine distinctions.

Ross asked herself the question: If there was a lost city, what signature might appear in the vegetation? There was an obvious answer: late secondary jungle.

The untouched or virgin rain forest was called primary jungle. Primary jungle was what most people thought of when they thought of rain forests: huge hardwood trees, mahogany and teak and ebony, and underneath a lower layer of ferns and palms, clinging to the ground. Primary jungle was dark and forbidding, but actually easy to move through. However, if the primary jungle was cleared by man and later abandoned, an entirely different secondary growth took over. The dominant plants were softwoods and fast-growing trees, bamboo and thorny tearing vines, which formed a dense and impenetrable barrier.

But Ross was not concerned about any aspect of the jungle except its albedo. Because the secondary plants were different, secondary jungle had a different albedo from primary jungle. And it could be graded by age: unlike the hardwood trees of primary jungle, which lived hundreds of years, the softwoods of secondary jungle lived only twenty years or so. Thus as time went on, the secondary jungle was replaced by another form of secondary jungle, and later by still another form.

By checking regions where late secondary jungle was generally found—such as the banks of large rivers, where innumerable human settlements had been cleared and abandoned—Ross confirmed that the ERTS computers could, indeed, measure the necessary small differences in reflectivity.

She then instructed the ERTS scanners to search for albedo differences of .03 or less, with a unit signature size of a hundred meters or less, across the fifty thousand square kilometers of rain forest on the western slopes of the Virunga volcanoes. This job would occupy a team of fifty human aerial photographic analysts for thirty-one years. The computer scanned 129,000 satellite and aerial photographs in under nine hours.

And found her city.

In May, 1979, Ross had a computer image showing a very old secondary jungle pattern laid out in a geometric, gridlike form. The pattern was located 2 degrees north of the equator, longitude 3 degrees, on the western slopes of the active volcano Mukenko. The computer estimated the age of the secondary jungle at five hundred to eight hundred years.

"So you sent an expedition in?" Elliot said.

Ross nodded. "Three weeks ago, led by a South African named Kruger. The expedition confirmed the placer diamond deposits, went on to search for the origin, and found the ruins of the city."

"And then what happened?" Elliot asked.

He ran the videotape a second time.

Onscreen he saw black-and-white images of the camp, destroyed, smoldering. Several dead bodies with crushed skulls were visible. As they watched, a shadow moved over the dead bodies, and the camera zoomed back to show the outline of the lumbering shadow. Elliot agreed that it looked like the shadow of a gorilla, but he insisted, "Gorillas couldn't do this. Gorillas are peaceful, vegetarian animals."

They watched as the tape ran to the end. And then they reviewed her final computer-reconstituted image, which clearly showed the head of a male gorilla.

"That's ground truth," Ross said.

Elliot was not so sure. He reran the last three seconds of videotape a final time, staring at the gorilla head. The image was fleeting, leaving a ghostly trail, but something was wrong with it. He couldn't quite identify what. Certainly this was atypical gorilla behavior, but there was something else. . . . He pushed the freeze-frame button and stared at the frozen image. The face and the fur were both gray: unquestionably gray.

"Can we increase contrast?" he asked Ross. "This image is washed out."

"I don't know," Ross said, touching the controls. "I think this is a pretty good image." She was unable to darken it.

"It's very gray," he said. "Gorillas are much darker."

"Well, this contrast range is correct for video."

Elliot was sure this creature was too light to be a mountain gorilla. Either they were seeing a new race of animal, *or a new species*. A new species of great ape, gray in color, aggressive in behavior, discovered in the eastern Congo. . . . He had come on this expedition to verify Amy's dreams—a fascinating psychological insight—but now the stakes were suddenly much higher.

Ross said, "You don't think this is a gorilla?"

"There are ways to test it," he said. He stared at the screen, frowning, as the plane flew onward in the night.

2. B-8 Problems

"YOU WANT ME TO *WHAT*?" TOM SEAMANS SAID, cradling the phone in his shoulder and rolling over to look at his bedside clock. It was 3 A.M.

"Go to the zoo," Elliot repeated. His voice sounded garbled, as if coming from under water.

"Peter, where are you calling from?"

"We're somewhere over the Atlantic now," Elliot said. "On our way to Africa."

"Is everything all right?"

"Everything is fine," Elliot said. "But I want you to go to the zoo first thing in the morning."

"And do what?"

"Videotape the gorillas. Try to get them in movement. That's very important for the discriminant function, that they be moving."

"I'd better write this down," Seamans said. Seamans handled the computer programming for the Project Amy staff, and he was accustomed to unusual requests, but not in the middle of the night. "What discriminant function?"

"While you're at it, run any films we have in the library of gorillas—any gorillas, wild or in zoos or whatever. The more specimens the better, so long as they're moving. And for a baseline, you'd better use chimps. Anything we have on chimps. Transfer it to tape and put it through the function."

"What function?" Seamans yawned.

"The function you're going to write," Elliot said. "I want a multiple variable discriminant function based on total imagery—"

"You mean a pattern-recognition function?" Seamans had written pattern-recognition functions for Amy's language use, enabling them to monitor her signing around the clock. Seamans was proud of that program; in its own way, it was highly inventive.

"However you structure it," Elliot said. "I just want a function that'll discriminate gorillas from other primates like chimps. A species-differentiating function."

"Are you kidding?" Seamans said. "That's a B-8 problem." In the developing field of pattern-recognition computer programs, so-called B-8 problems were the most difficult; whole teams of researchers had devoted years to trying to teach computers the difference between "B" and

"8"—precisely because the difference was so obvious. But what was obvious to the human eye was not obvious to the computer scanner. The scanner had to be told, and the specific instructions turned out to be far more difficult than anyone anticipated, particularly for handwritten characters.

Now Elliot wanted a program that would distinguish between similar visual images of gorillas and chimps. Seamans could not help asking, "Why? It's pretty obvious. A gorilla is a gorilla, and a chimp is a chimp."

"Just do it," Elliot said.

"Can I use size?" On the basis of size alone, gorillas and chimps could be accurately distinguished. But visual functions could not determine size unless the distance from the recording instrument to the subject image was known, as well as the focal length of the recording lens.

"No, you can't use size," Elliot said. "Element morphology only."

Seamans sighed. "Thanks a lot. What resolution?"

"I need ninety-five-percent confidence limits on species assignment, to be based on less than three seconds of black-and-white scan imagery."

Seamans frowned. Obviously, Elliot had three seconds of videotape imagery of some animal and he was not sure whether it was a gorilla or not. Elliot had seen enough gorillas over the years to know the difference: gorillas and chimps were utterly different animals in size, appearance, movement, and behavior. They were as different as intelligent oceanic mammals—say, porpoises and whales. In making such discriminations, the human eye was far superior to any computer program that could be devised. Yet Elliot apparently did not trust his eye. What was he thinking of?

"I'll try," Seamans said, "but it's going to take a while. You don't write that kind of program overnight."

"I need it overnight, Tom," Elliot said. "I'll call you back in twenty-four hours."

3. Inside the Coffin

IN ONE CORNER OF THE 747 LIVING MODULE WAS A sound-baffled fiberglass booth, with a hinged hood and a small CRT screen; it was called "the coffin" because of the claustrophobic feeling that came from working inside it. As the airplane crossed the mid-Atlantic, Ross stepped inside the coffin. She had a last look at Elliot and Amy—both asleep, both snoring loudly—and Jensen and Irving playing "submarine chase" on the computer console, as she lowered the hood.

Ross was tired, but she did not expect to get much sleep for the next two weeks, which was as long as she thought the expedition would last. Within fourteen days—336 hours—Ross's team would either have beaten the Euro-Japanese consortium or she would have failed and the Zaire Virunga mineral exploration rights would be lost forever.

The race was already under way, and Karen Ross did not intend to lose it.

She punched Houston coordinates, including her own sender designation, and waited while the scrambler interlocked. From now on, there would be a signal delay of five seconds at both ends, because both she and Houston would be sending in coded burst transmissions to elude passive listeners.

The screen glowed: TRAVIS.

She typed back: ROSS. She picked up the telephone receiver.

"It's a bitch," Travis said, although it was not Travis's voice, but a computer-generated flat audio signal, without expression.

78

"Tell me," Ross said.

"The consortium's rolling," Travis's surrogate voice said.

"Details," Ross said, and waited for the five-second delay. She could imagine Travis in the CCR in Houston, hearing her own computer-generated voice. That flat voice required a change in speech patterns; what was ordinarily conveyed by phrasing and emphasis had to be made explicit.

"They know you're on your way," Travis's voice whined. "They are pushing their own schedule. The Germans are behind it—your friend Richter. I'm arranging a feeding in a matter of minutes. That's the good news."

"And the bad news?"

"The Congo has gone to hell in the last ten hours," Travis said. "We have a nasty GPU."

"Print," she said.

On the screen, she saw printed GEOPOLITICAL UP-DATE, followed by a dense paragraph. It read:

```
ZAIRE EMBASSY WASHINGTON STATES EASTERN BOR-
DERS VIA RWANDA CLOSED / NO EXPLANATION / PRE-
SUMPTION IDI AMIN TROOPS FLEEING TANZANIAN
INVASION UGANDA INTO EASTERN ZAIRE / CONSE-
QUENT DISRUPTION / BUT FACTS DIFFER / LOCAL
TRIBES {KIGANI} ON RAMPAGE / REPORTED ATROCI-
TIES AND CANNIBALISM ETC / FOREST-DWELLING
PYGMIES UNRELIABLE / KILLING ALL VISITORS
CONGO RAIN FOREST / ZAIRE GOVERNMENT DIS-
PATCHED GENERAL MUGURU (AKA BUTCHER OF STAN-
LEYVILLE) / PUT DOWN KIGANI REBELLION 'AT ALL
COSTS' / SITUATION HIGHLY UNSTABLE / ONLY LE-
GAL ENTRY INTO ZAIRE NOW WEST THROUGH KINSHASA
/ YOU ARE ON YOUR OWN / ACQUISITION WHITE HUNTER
MUNRO NOW PARAMOUNT IMPORTANCE WHATEVER COST
/ KEEP HIM FROM CONSORTIUM WILL PAY ANYTHING /
YOUR SITUATION EXTREME DANGER / MUST HAVE MUNRO
TO SURVIVE /
```

She stared at the screen. It was the worst possible news. She said, "Have you got a time course?"

EURO-JAPANESE CONSORTIUM NOW COMPRISES MORI-
KAWA (JAPAN) / GERLICH (GERMANY) / VOORSTER
(AMSTERDAM) / UNFORTUNATELY HAVE RESOLVED
DIFFERENCES NOW IN COMPLETE ACCORD / MONITOR-
ING US CANNOT ANTICIPATE SECURE TRANSMISSIONS
ANYTIME HENCEFORTH / ANTICIPATE ELECTRONIC
COUNTERMEASURES AND WARFARE TACTICS IN PUR-
SUIT OF TWO-B GOAL / THEY WILL ENTER CONGO (RE-
LIABLE SOURCE) WITHIN 48 HOURS NOW SEEKING
MUNRO /

"When will they reach Tangier?" she asked.

"In six hours. You?"

"Seven hours. And Munro?"

"We don't know about Munro," Travis said. "Can you
booby him?"

"Absolutely," Ross said. "I'll arrange the booby now.
If Munro doesn't see things our way, I promise you it'll
be seventy-two hours before he's allowed out of the country."

"What've you got?" Travis asked.

"Czech submachine guns. Found on the premises, with
his prints on them, carefully applied. That should do it."

"That should do it," Travis agreed. "What about your
passengers?" He was referring to Elliot and Amy.

"They're fine," Ross said. "They know nothing."

"Keep it that way," Travis said, and hung up.

4. Feeding Time

"IT'S FEEDING TIME," TRAVIS CALLED CHEER-fully. "Who's at the trough?"

"We've got five tap dancers on Beta dataline," Rogers said. Rogers was the electronic surveillance expert, the bug catcher.

"Anybody we know?"

"Know them all," Rogers said, slightly annoyed. "Beta line is our main cross-trunk line in-house, so whoever wants to tap in to our system will naturally plug in there. You get more bits and pieces that way. Of course we aren't using Beta anymore except for routine úncoded garbage—taxes and payroll, that stuff."

"We have to arrange a feed," Travis said. A feed meant putting false data out over a tapped line, to be picked up. It was a delicate operation. "You have the consortium on the line?"

"Sure. What do you want to feed them?"

"Coordinates for the lost city," Travis said.

Rogers nodded, mopping his brow. He was a portly man who sweated profusely. "How good do you want it?"

"Damned good," Travis said. "You won't fool the Japanese with static."

"You don't want to give them the actual co-ords?"

"God, no. But I want them reasonably close. Say, within two hundred kilometers."

"Can do," Rogers said.

"Coded?" Travis said.

"Of course."

"You have a code they can break in twelve to fifteen hours?"

81

Rogers nodded. "We've got a dilly. Looks like hell, but then when you work it, it pops out. Got an internal weakness in concealed lettering frequency. At the other end, looks like we made a mistake, but it's very breakable."

"It can't be too easy," Travis warned.

"Oh, no, they'll earn their yen. They'll never suspect a feed. We ran it past the army and they came back all smiles, teaching us a lesson. Never knew it was a setup."

"Okay," Travis said, "put the data out, and let's feed them. I want something that'll give them a sense of confidence for the next forty-eight hours or more—until they figure out that we've screwed them."

"Delighted," Rogers said, and he moved off to Beta terminal.

Travis sighed. The feeding would soon begin, and he hoped it would protect his team in the field—long enough for them to get to the diamonds first.

5. Dangerous Signatures

THE SOFT MURMUR OF VOICES WOKE HIM.

"How unequivocal is that signature?"

"Pretty damn unequivocal. Here's the pissup, nine days ago, and it's not even epicentered."

"That's cloud cover?"

"No, that's not cloud cover, it's too black. That's ejecta from the signature."

"Hell."

Elliot opened his eyes to see dawn breaking as a thin red line against blue-black through the windows of the passenger compartment. His watch read 5:11—five in the morning, San Francisco time. He had slept only two hours since calling

Seamans. He yawned and glanced down at Amy, curled up in her nest of blankets on the floor. Amy snored loudly. The other bunks were unoccupied.

He heard soft voices again, and looked toward the computer console. Jensen and Irving were staring at a screen and talking quietly. "Dangerous signature. We got a computer projection on that?"

"Coming. It'll take a while. I asked for a five-year run-back, as well as the other pissups."

Elliot climbed out of his cot and looked at the screen. "What's pissups?" he said.

"PSOPs are prior significant orbital passes by the satellite," Jensen explained. "They're called pissups because we usually ask for them when we're already pissing upwind. We've been looking at this volcanic signature here," Jensen said, pointing to the screen. "It's not too promising."

"What volcanic signature?" Elliot asked.

They showed him the billowing plumes of smoke—dark green in artificial computer-generated colors—which belched from the mouth of Mukenko, one of the active volcanoes of the Virunga range. "Mukenko erupts on the average of once every three years," Irving said. "The last eruption was March, 1977, but it looks like it's gearing up for another full eruption in the next week or so. We're waiting now for the probability assessment."

"Does Ross know about this?"

They shrugged. "She knows, but she doesn't seem worried. She got an urgent GPU—geopolitical update—from Houston about two hours ago, and she went directly into the cargo bay. Haven't seen her since."

Elliot went into the dimly lit cargo bay of the jet. The cargo bay was not insulated and it was chilly: the trucks had a thin frost on metal and glass, and his breath hissed from his mouth. He found Karen Ross working at a table under low pools of light. Her back was turned to him, but when he approached, she dropped what she was doing and turned to face him.

"I thought you were asleep," she said.

"I got restless. What's going on?"

"Just checking supplies. This is our advanced technology unit," she said, lifting up a small backpack. "We've developed a miniaturized package for field parties; twenty pounds of equipment contains everything a man needs for two weeks: food, water, clothing, everything."

"Even water?" Elliot asked.

Water was heavy: seven-tenths of human body weight was water, and most of the weight of food was water; that was why dehydrated food was so light. But water was far more critical to human life than food. Men could survive for weeks without food, but they would die in a matter of hours without water. And water was heavy.

Ross smiled. "The average man consumes four to six liters a day, which is eight to thirteen pounds of weight. On a two-week expedition to a desert region, we'd have to provide two hundred pounds of water for each man. But we have a NASA water-recycling unit which purifies all excretions, including urine. It weighs six ounces. That's how we do it."

Seeing his expression, she said, "It's not bad at all. Our purified water is cleaner than what you get from the tap."

"I'll take your word for it." Elliot picked up a pair of strange-looking sunglasses. They were very dark and thick, and there was a peculiar lens mounted over the forehead bridge.

"Holographic night goggles," Ross said. "Employing thin-film diffraction optics." She then pointed out a vibration-free camera lens with optical systems that compensated for movement, strobe infrared lights, and miniature survey lasers no larger than a pencil eraser. There was also a series of small tripods with rapid-geared motors mounted on the top, and brackets to hold something, but she did not explain these devices beyond saying they were "defensive units."

Elliot drifted toward the far table, where he found six submachine guns set out under the lights. He picked one up; it was heavy, and gleaming with grease. Clips of ammunition lay stacked nearby. Elliot did not notice the lettering on the stock; the machine guns were Russian AK-47s manufactured under license in Czechoslovakia.

He glanced at Ross.

"Just precautions," Ross said. "We carry them on every expedition. It doesn't mean anything."

Elliot shook his head. "Tell me about your GPU from Houston," he said.

"I'm not worried about it," she said.

"I am," Elliot said.

As Ross explained it, the GPU was just a technical report. The Zaire government had closed its eastern borders during the previous twenty-four hours; no tourist or commercial traffic could enter the country from Rwanda or Uganda; everyone now had to enter the country from the west, through Kinshasa.

No official reason was given for closing the eastern border, although sources in Washington speculated that Idi Amin's troops, fleeing across the Zaire border from the Tanzanian invasion of Uganda, might be causing "local difficulties." In central Africa, local difficulties usually meant cannibalism and other atrocities.

"Do you believe that?" Elliot asked. "Cannibalism and atrocities?"

"No," Ross said. "It's all a lie. It's the Dutch and the Germans and the Japanese—probably your friend Morikawa. The Euro-Japanese electronics consortium knows that ERTS is close to discovering important diamond reserves in Virunga. They want to slow us down as much as they can. They've got the fix in somewhere, probably in Kinshasa, and closed the eastern borders. It's nothing more than that."

"If there's no danger, why the machine guns?"

"Just precautions," she said again. "We'll never use machine guns on this trip, believe me. Now why don't you get some sleep? We'll be landing in Tangier soon."

"Tangier?"

"Captain Munro is there."

6. Munro

THE NAME OF "CAPTAIN" CHARLES MUNRO WAS not to be found on the list of the expedition leaders employed by any of the usual field parties. There were several reasons for this, foremost among them his distinctly unsavory reputation.

Munro had been raised in the wild Northern Frontier Province of Kenya, the illegitimate son of a Scottish farmer and his handsome Indian housekeeper. Munro's father had the bad luck to be killed by Mau Mau guerillas in 1956.* Soon afterward, Munro's mother died of tuberculosis, and Munro made his way to Nairobi where in the late 1950s he worked as a white hunter, leading parties of tourists into the bush. It was during this time that Munro awarded himself the title of "Captain," although he had never served in the military.

Apparently, Captain Munro found humoring tourists uncongenial; by 1960, he was reported running guns from Uganda into the newly independent Congo. After Moise Tshombe went into exile in 1963, Munro's activities became politically embarrassing, and ultimately forced him to disappear from East Africa in late 1963.

He appeared again in 1964, as one of General Mobutu's white mercenaries in the Congo, under the leadership of Colonel "Mad Mike" Hoare. Hoare assessed Munro as a "hard, lethal customer who knew the jungle and was highly effective, when we could get him away from the ladies." Follow-

---

*Although more than nineteen thousand people were killed in the Mau Mau uprisings, only thirty-seven whites were killed during seven years of terrorism. Each dead white was properly regarded more as a victim of circumstance than of emerging black politics.

x

ing the capture of Stanleyville in Operation Dragon Rouge, Munro's name was associated with the mercenary atrocities at a village called Avakabi. Munro again disappeared for several years.

In 1968, he re-emerged in Tangier, where he lived splendidly and was something of a local character. The source of Munro's obviously substantial income was unclear, but he was said to have supplied Communist Sudanese rebels with East German light arms in 1971, to have assisted the royalist Ethiopians in their rebellion in 1974–1975, and to have assisted the French paratroopers who dropped into Zaire's Shaba province in 1978.

His mixed activities made Munro a special case in Africa in the 1970s; although he was *persona non grata* in a half-dozen African states, he traveled freely throughout the continent, using various passports. It was a transparent ruse: every border official recognized him on sight, but these officials were equally afraid to let him enter the country or to deny him entry.

Foreign mining and exploration companies, sensitive to local feeling, were reluctant to hire Munro as an expedition leader for their parties. It was also true that Munro was by far the most expensive of the bush guides. Nevertheless, he had a reputation for getting tough, difficult jobs done. Under an assumed name, he had taken two German tin-mining parties into the Cameroons in 1974; and he had led one previous ERTS expedition into Angola during the height of the armed conflict in 1977. He quit another ERTS field group headed for Zambia the following year after Houston refused to meet his price: Houston had canceled the expedition.

In short, Munro was acknowledged as the best man for dangerous travel. That was why the ERTS jet stopped in Tangier.

At the Tangier airport, the ERTS cargo jet and its contents were bonded, but all ongoing personnel except Amy passed through customs, carrying their personal belongings. Jensen and Irving were pulled aside for searches; trace quantities of heroin were discovered in their hand baggage.

This bizarre event occurred through a series of remarkable coincidences. In 1977, United States customs agents began to employ neutron backscatter devices, as well as chemical vapor detectors, or sniffers. Both were hand-held electronic devices manufactured under contract by Morikawa Electronics in Tokyo. In 1978, questions arose about the accuracy of these devices; Morikawa suggested that they be tested at other ports of entry around the world, including Singapore, Bangkok, Delhi, Munich, and Tangier.

Thus Morikawa Electronics knew the capabilities of the detectors at Tangier airport, and they also knew that a variety of substances, including ground poppy seeds and shredded turnip, would produce a false-positive registration on airport sensors. And the "false-positive net" required forty-eight hours to untangle. (It was later shown that both men had somehow acquired traces of turnip on their briefcases.)

Both Irving and Jensen vigorously denied any knowledge of illicit material, and appealed to the local U.S. consular office. But the case could not be resolved for several days; Ross telephoned Travis in Houston, who determined it was a "Dutch herring." There was nothing to be done except to carry on, and continue with the expedition as best they could.

"They think this will stop us," Travis said, "but it won't."

"Who's going to do the geology?" Ross asked.

"You are," Travis said.

"And the electronics?"

"You're the certified genius," Travis said. "Just make sure you have Munro. He's the key to everything."

The song of the muezzin floated over the pastel jumble of houses in the Tangier Casbah at twilight, calling the faithful to evening prayer. In the old days, the muezzin himself appeared in the minarets of the mosque, but now a recording played over loudspeakers: a mechanized call to the Muslim ritual of obeisance.

Karen Ross sat on the terrace of Captain Munro's house overlooking the Casbah and waited for her audience with the man himself. Beside her, Peter Elliot sat in a chair and snored noisily, exhausted from the long flight.

They had been waiting nearly three hours, and she was worried. Munro's house was of Moorish design, and open to the outdoors. From the interior she could hear voices, faintly carried by the breeze, speaking some Oriental language.

One of the graceful Moroccan servant girls that Munro seemed to have in infinite supply came onto the terrace carrying a telephone. She bowed formally. Ross saw that the girl had violet eyes; she was exquisitely beautiful, and could not have been more than sixteen. In careful English the girl said, "This is your telephone to Houston. The bidding will now begin."

Karen nudged Peter, who awoke groggily. "The bidding will now begin," she said.

Peter Elliot was surprised from the moment of his first entrance into Munro's house. He had anticipated a tough military setting and was amazed to see delicate carved Moroccan arches and soft gurgling fountains with sunlight sparkling on them.

Then he saw the Japanese and Germans in the next room, staring at him and at Ross. The glances were distinctly unfriendly, but Ross stood and said, "Excuse me a moment," and she went forward and embraced a young blond German man warmly. They kissed, chattered happily, and in general appeared to be intimate friends.

Elliot did not like this development, but he was reassured to see that the Japanese—identically dressed in black suits—were equally displeased. Noticing this, Elliot smiled benignly, to convey a sense of approval for the reunion.

But when Ross returned, he demanded, "Who was that?"

"That's Richter," she said. "The most brilliant topologist in Western Europe; his field is n-space extrapolation. His work's extremely elegant." She smiled. "Almost as elegant as mine."

"But he works for the consortium?"

"Naturally. He's German."

"And you're talking with him?"

"I was delighted for the opportunity," she said. "Karl has a fatal limitation. He can only deal with pre-existing data. He takes what he is given, and does cartwheels with it in *n*-space. But he cannot imagine anything new at all. I had a professor at M.I.T. who was the same way. Tied to facts, a hostage to reality." She shook her head.

"Did he ask about Amy?"

"Of course."

"And what did you tell him?"

"I told him she was sick and probably dying."

"And he believed that?"

"We'll see. There's Munro."

Captain Munro appeared in the next room, wearing khakis, smoking a cigar. He was a tall, rugged-looking man with a mustache, and soft dark watchful eyes that missed nothing. He talked with the Japanese and Germans, who were evidently unhappy with what he was saying. Moments later, Munro entered their room, smiling broadly.

"So you're going to the Congo, Dr. Ross."

"We are, Captain Munro," she said.

Munro smiled. "It seems as though everyone is going."

There followed a rapid exchange which Elliot found incomprehensible. Karen Ross said, "Fifty thousand U.S. in Swiss francs against point oh two of first-year adjusted extraction returns."

Munro shook his head. "A hundred in Swiss francs and point oh six of first-year return on the primary deposits, crude-grade accounting, no discounting.

"A hundred in U.S. dollars against point oh one of the first-year return on all deposits, with full discounting from point of origin."

"Point of origin? In the middle of the bloody Congo? I would want three years from point of origin: what if you're shut down?"

"You want a piece, you gamble. Mobutu's clever."

"Mobutu's barely in control, and I am still alive because I am no gambler," Munro said. "A hundred against point oh four of first year on primary with front-load discount only. Or I'll take point oh two of yours."

"If you're no gambler, I'll give you a straight buy-out for two hundred."

Munro shook his head. "You've paid more than that for your MER in Kinshasa."

"Prices for everything are inflated in Kinshasa, including mineral exploration rights. And the current exploration limit, the computer CEL, is running well under a thousand."

"If you say so." He smiled, and headed back into the other room, where the Japanese and Germans were waiting for his return.

Ross said quickly, "That's not for them to know."

"Oh, I'm sure they know it anyway," Munro said, and walked into the other room.

"Bastard," she whispered to his back. She talked in low tones on the telephone. "He'll never accept that. . . . No, no, he won't go for it . . . they want him bad. . . ."

Elliot said, "You're bidding very high for his services."

"He's the best," Ross said, and continued whispering into the telephone. In the next room, Munro was shaking his head sadly, turning down an offer. Elliot noticed that Richter was very red in the face.

Munro came back to Karen Ross. "What was your projected CEL?"

"Under a thousand."

"So you say. Yet you know there's an ore intercept."

"I don't know there's an ore intercept."

"Then you're foolish to spend all this money to go to the Congo," Munro said. "Aren't you?"

Karen Ross made no reply. She stared at the ornate ceiling of the room.

"Virunga's not exactly a garden spot these days," Munro continued. "The Kigani are on the rampage, and they're cannibals. Pygmies aren't friendly anymore either. Likely to find an arrow in your back for your troubles. Volcanoes always threatening to blow. Tsetse flies. Bad water. Corrupt officials. Not a place to go without a very good reason, hmm? Perhaps you should put off your trip until things settle down."

Those were precisely Peter Elliot's sentiments, and he said so.

"Wise man," Munro said, with a broad smile that annoyed Karen Ross.

"Evidently," Karen Ross said, "we will never come to terms."

"That seems clear." Munro nodded.

Elliot understood that negotiations were broken off. He got up to shake Munro's hand and leave—but before he could do that, Munro walked into the next room and conferred with the Japanese and Germans.

"Things are looking up," Ross said.

"Why?" Elliot said. "Because he thinks he's beaten you down?"

"No. Because he thinks we know more than they do about the site location and are more likely to hit an ore body and pay off."

In the next room, the Japanese and Germans abruptly stood, and walked to the front door. At the door, Munro shook hands with the Germans, and bowed elaborately to the Japanese.

"I guess you're right," Elliot said to Ross. "He's sending them away."

But Ross was frowning, her face grim. "They can't do this," she said. "They can't just quit this way."

Elliot was confused again. "I thought you wanted them to quit."

"Damn," Ross said. "We've been screwed." She whispered into the telephone, talking to Houston.

Elliot didn't understand it at all. And his confusion was not resolved when Munro locked the door behind the last of the departing men, then came back to Elliot and Ross to say that supper was served.

They ate Moroccan-style, sitting on the floor and eating with their fingers. The first course was a pigeon pie, and it was followed by some sort of stew.

"So you sent the Japanese off?" Ross said. "Told them no?"

"Oh, no," Munro said. "That would be impolite. I told them I would think about it. And I will."

"Then why did they leave?"

Munro shrugged. "Not my doing, I assure you. I think they heard something on the telephone which changed their whole plan."

Karen Ross glanced at her watch, making a note of the time. "Very good stew," she said. She was doing her best to be agreeable.

"Glad you like it. It's *tajin*. Camel meat."

Karen Ross coughed. Peter Elliot noticed that his own appetite had diminished. Munro turned to him. "So you have the gorilla, Professor Elliot?"

"How did you know that?"

"The Japanese told me. The Japanese are fascinated by your gorilla. Can't figure the point of it, drives them mad. A young man with a gorilla, and a young woman who is searching for—"

"Industrial-grade diamonds," Karen Ross said.

"Ah, industrial-grade diamonds." He turned to Elliot. "I enjoy a frank conversation. Diamonds, fascinating." His manner suggested that he had been told nothing of importance.

Ross said, "You've got to take us in, Munro."

"World's full of industrial-grade diamonds," Munro said. "You can find them in Africa, India, Russia, Brazil, Canada, even in America—Arkansas, New York, Kentucky— everywhere you look. But you're going to the Congo."

The obvious question hung in the air.

"We are looking for Type IIb boron-coated blue diamonds," Karen Ross said, "which have semiconducting properties important to microelectronics applications."

Munro stroked his mustache. "Blue diamonds," he said, nodding. "It makes sense."

Ross said that of course it made sense.

"You can't dope them?" Munro asked.

"No. It's been tried. There was a commercial boron-doping process, but it was too unreliable. The Americans had one and so did the Japanese. Everyone gave it up as hopeless."

"So you've got to find a natural source."

"That's right. I want to get there as soon as possible," Ross said, staring at him, her voice flat.

"I'm sure you do," Munro said. "Nothing but business for our Dr. Ross, eh?" He crossed the room and, leaning against one of the arches, looked out on the dark Tangier night. "I'm not surprised at all," he said. "As a matter of—"

At the first blast of machine-gun fire, Munro dived for cover, the glassware on the table splattered, one of the girls screamed, and Elliot and Ross threw themselves to the marble floor as the bullets whined around them, chipping the plaster overhead, raining plaster dust down upon them. The blast lasted thirty seconds or so, and it was followed by complete silence.

When it was over, they got up hesitantly, staring at one another.

"The consortium plays for keeps." Munro grinned. "Just my sort of people."

Ross brushed plaster dust off her clothes. She turned to Munro. "Five point two against the first two hundred, no deductions, in Swiss francs, adjusted."

"Five point seven, and you have me."

"Five point seven. Done."

Munro shook hands with them, then announced that he would need a few minutes to pack his things before leaving for Nairobi.

"Just like that?" Ross asked. She seemed suddenly concerned, glancing again at her watch.

"What's your problem?" Munro asked.

"Czech AK-47s," she said. "In your warehouse."

Munro showed no surprise. "Better get them out," he said. "The consortium undoubtedly has something similar in the works, and we've got a lot to do in the next few hours." As he spoke, they heard the police Klaxons approaching from a distance. Munro said, "We'll take the back stair."

An hour later, they were airborne, heading toward Nairobi.

DAY 4: NAIROBI

June 16, 1979

1. Timeline

IT WAS FARTHER ACROSS AFRICA FROM TANGIER TO Nairobi than it was across the Atlantic Ocean from New York to London—3,600 miles, an eight-hour flight. Ross spent the time at the computer console, working out what she called "hyperspace probability lines."

The screen showed a computer-generated map of Africa, with streaking multicolored lines across it. "These are all timelines," Ross said. "We can weight them for duration and delay factors." Beneath the screen was a total-elapsed-time clock, which kept shifting numbers.

"What's that mean?" Elliot asked.

"The computer's picking the fastest route. You see it's just identified a timeline that will get us on-site in six days eighteen hours and fifty-one minutes. Now it's trying to beat that time."

Elliot had to smile. The idea of a computer predicting *to the minute* when they would reach their Congo location seemed ludicrous to him. But Ross was totally serious.

As they watched, the computer clock shifted to 5 days 22 hours 24 minutes.

"Better," Ross said, nodding. "But still not very good." She pressed another key and the lines shifted, stretching like rubber bands over the African continent. "This is the consortium route," she said, "based on our assumptions about the expedition. They're going in big—thirty or more people, a full-scale undertaking. And they don't know the exact location of the city; at least, we don't think they know. But they have a substantial start on us, at least twelve hours, since their aircraft is already forming up in Nairobi."

97

The clock registered total elapsed time: 5 days 09 hours 19 minutes. Then she pressed a button marked DATE and it shifted to 06 21 79 0814. "According to this, the consortium will reach the Congo site a little after eight o'clock in the morning on June 21."

The computer clicked quietly; the lines continued to stretch and pull, and the clock read a new date: 06 21 79 1224.

"Well," she said, "that's where we are now. Given maximum favorable movements for us and them, the consortium will beat us to the site by slightly more than four hours, five days from now."

Munro walked past, eating a sandwich. "Better lock another path," he said. "Or go radical."

"I hesitate to go radical with the ape."

Munro shrugged. "Have to do something, with a timeline like that."

Elliot listened to them with a vague sense of unreality: they were discussing a difference of hours, five days in the future. "But surely," Elliot said, "over the next few days, with all the arrangements at Nairobi, and then getting into the jungle—you can't put too much faith in those figures."

"This isn't like the old days of African exploration," Ross said, "where parties disappeared into the wilds for months. At most, the computer is off by minutes—say, roughly half an hour in the total five-day projection." She shook her head. "No. We have a problem here, and we've got to do something about it. The stakes are too great."

"You mean the diamonds."

She nodded, and pointed to the bottom of the screen, where the words BLUE CONTRACT appeared. He asked her what the Blue Contract was.

"One hell of a lot of money," Ross said. And she added, "I think." For in truth she did not really know.

Each new contract at ERTS was given a code name. Only Travis and the computer knew the name of the company buying the contract; everyone else at ERTS, from computer programmers to field personnel, knew the projects only by their color-code names: Red Contract, Yellow Contract, White Contract. This was a business protection for the firms involved. But the ERTS mathematicians could not resist a lively guessing game about contract sources, which was the staple of daily conversation in the company canteen.

The Blue Contract had come to ERTS in December, 1978. It called for ERTS to locate a natural source of industrial-grade diamonds in a friendly or neutralist country. The diamonds were to be Type IIb, "nitrogen-poor" crystals. No dimensions were specified, so crystal size did not matter; nor were recoverable quantities specified: the contractor would take what he could get. And, most unusual, there was no UECL.

Nearly all contracts arrived with a unit extraction cost limit. It was not enough to find a mineral source; the minerals had to be extractable at a specified unit cost. This unit cost in turn reflected the richness of the ore body, its remoteness, the availability of local labor, political conditions, the possible need to build airfields, roads, hospitals, mines, or refineries.

For a contract to come in without a UECL meant only one thing: somebody wanted blue diamonds so badly he didn't care what they cost.

Within forty-eight hours, the ERTS canteen had explained the Blue Contract. It turned out that Type IIb diamonds were blue from trace quantities of the element boron, which rendered them worthless as gemstones but altered their electronic properties, making them semiconductors with a resistivity on the order of 100 ohms centimeters. They also had light-transmissive properties.

Someone then found a brief article in *Electronic News* for November 17, 1978: "McPhee Doping Dropped." It explained that the Waltham, Massachusetts, firm of Silec, Inc., had abandoned the experimental McPhee technique to dope diamonds artificially with a monolayer boron coating. The McPhee process had been abandoned as too expensive and too unreliable to produce "desirable semiconducting properties." The article concluded that "other firms have underestimated problems in boron monolayer doping; Morikawa (Tokyo) abandoned the Nagaura process in September of this year.'' Working backward, the ERTS canteen fitted additional pieces of the puzzle into place.

Back in 1971, Intec, the Santa Clara microelectronics firm, had first predicted that diamond semiconductors would be important to a future generation of "superconducting" computers in the 1980s.

The first generation of electronic computers, ENIAC and UNIVAC, built in the wartime secrecy of the 1940s, employed vacuum tubes. Vacuum tubes had an average life span of twenty hours, but with thousands of glowing hot tubes in a single machine, some computers shut down every seven to twelve minutes. Vacuum-tube technology imposed a limit on the size and power of planned second-generation computers.

But the second generation never used vacuum tubes. In 1947, the invention of the transistor—a thumbnail-sized sandwich of solid material which performed all the functions of a vacuum tube—ushered in an era of "solid state" electronic devices which drew little power, generated little heat, and were smaller and more reliable than the tubes they replaced. Silicon technology provided the basis for three generations of increasingly compact, reliable, and cheap computers over the next twenty years.

But by the 1970s, computer designers began to confront the inherent limitations of silicon technology. Although circuits had been shrunk to microscopic dimensions, computation speed was still dependent on circuit length. To miniaturize circuits still more, where distances were already on the order of millionths of an inch, brought back an old problem: heat. Smaller circuits would literally melt from the heat produced. What was needed was some method to eliminate heat and reduce resistance at the same time.

It had been known since the 1950s that many metals when cooled to extremely low temperatures became "superconducting," permitting the unimpeded flow of electrons through them. In 1977, IBM announced it was designing an ultra-high-speed computer the size of a grapefruit, chilled with liquid nitrogen. The superconducting computer required a radically new technology, and a new range of low-temperature construction materials.

Doped diamonds would be used extensively throughout.

Several days later, the ERTS canteen came up with an alternative explanation. According to the new theory, the 1970s had been a decade of unprecedented growth in computers. Although the first computer manufacturers in the 1940s had predicted that four computers would do the computing work of the entire world for the foreseeable future, experts anticipated that by 1990 there would actually be *one billion* computers—most of them linked by communications networks to other computers. Such networks didn't exist, and might even be theoretically impossible. (A 1975 study by the Hanover Institute concluded there was insufficient metal in the earth's crust to construct the necessary computer transmission lines.)

According to Harvey Rumbaugh, the 1980s would be characterized by a critical shortage of computer data transmission systems: "Just as the fossil fuel shortage took the industrialized world by surprise in the 1970s, so will the data transmission shortage take the world by surprise in the next ten years. People were denied *movement* in the 1970s; but they will be denied *information* in the 1980s, and it remains to be seen which shortage will prove more frustrating."

Laser light represented the only hope for handling these massive data requirements, since laser channels carried twenty thousand times the information of an ordinary metal coaxial trunk line. Laser transmission demanded whole new technologies—including thin-spun fiber optics, and doped semiconducting diamonds, which Rumbaugh predicted would be "more valuable than oil" in the coming years.

Even further, Rumbaugh anticipated that within ten years *electricity itself would become obsolete.* Future computers would utilize only light circuits, and interface with light-transmission data systems. The reason was speed. "Light," Rumbaugh said, "moves at the speed of light. Electricity doesn't. We are living in the final years of microelectronic technology."

Certainly microelectronics did not look like a moribund technology. In 1979, microelectronics was a major industry throughout the industrialized world, accounting for eighty billion dollars annually in the United States alone; six of the top twenty corporations in the Fortune 500 were deeply involved in microelectronics. These companies had a history of extraordinary competition and advance, over a period of less than thirty years.

In 1958, a manufacturer could fit 10 electronic components onto a single silicon chip. By 1970, it was possible to fit 100 units onto a chip of the same size—a tenfold increase in slightly more than a decade.

But by 1972, it was possible to fit 1,000 units on a chip, and by 1974, 10,000 units. It was expected that by 1980, there would be one million units on a single chip the size of a thumbnail, but, using electronic photoprojection, this goal was actually realized in 1978. By the spring of 1979, the new goal was ten million units—or, even better, one billion units—on a single silicon chip by 1980. But nobody expected to wait past June or July of 1979 for this development.

Such advances within an industry are unprecedented. Comparison to older manufacturing technologies makes this clear. Detroit was content to make trivial product design changes at three-year intervals, but the electronics industry routinely expected *order of magnitude* advances in the same time. (To keep pace, Detroit would have had to increase automobile gas mileage from 8 miles per gallon in 1970 to 80,000,000 miles per gallon in 1979. Instead, Detroit went from 8 to 16 miles per gallon during that time, further evidence of the coming demise of the automotive industry as the center of the American economy.)

In such a competitive market, everyone worried about foreign powers, particularly Japan, which since 1973 had maintained a Japanese Cultural Exchange in San Jose—which some considered a cover organization for well-financed industrial espionage.

The Blue Contract could only be understood in the light of an industry making major advances every few months. Travis had said that the Blue Contract was "the biggest thing we'll see in the next ten years. Whoever finds those diamonds has a jump on the technology for at least five years. *Five years*. Do you know what that means?''

Ross knew what it meant. In an industry where competitive edges were measured in months, companies had made fortunes by beating competitors by a matter of weeks with some new techniques or device; Syntel in California had been the first to make a 256K memory chip while everyone else was still making 16K chips and dreaming of 64K chips. Syntel kept their advantage for only sixteen weeks, but realized a profit of more than a hundred and thirty million dollars.

''And we're talking about *five years*,'' Travis said. ''That's an advantage measured in billions of dollars, maybe tens of billions of dollars. If we can get to those diamonds.''

These were the reasons for the extraordinary pressure Ross felt as she continued to work with the computer. At the age of twenty-four, she was team leader in a high-technology race involving a half-dozen nations around the globe, all secretly pitting their business and industrial resources against one another.

The stakes made any conventional race seem ludicrous. Travis told her before she left, ''Don't be afraid when the pressure makes you crazy. You have *billions of dollars* riding on your shoulders. Just do the best you can.''

Doing the best she could, she managed to reduce the expedition timeline by another three hours and thirty-seven minutes—but they were still slightly behind the consortium projection. Not too far to make up the time, especially with Munro's cold-blooded shortcuts, but nevertheless behind—which could mean total disaster in a winner-take-all race.

And then she received bad news.

The screen printed PIGGYBACK SLURP / ALL BETS OFF.

''Hell,'' Ross said. She felt suddenly tired. Because if there really had been a piggyback slurp, their chances of winning the race were vanishing—before any of them had even set foot in the rain forests of central Africa.

2. Piggyback Slurp

TRAVIS FELT LIKE A FOOL.

He stared at the hard copy from Goddard Space Flight Center, Greenbelt, Maryland.

ERTS WHY ARE YOU SENDING US ALL THIS MUKENKO
DATA WE DON'T REALLY CARE THANKS ANYWAY.

That had arrived an hour ago from GSFC/Maryland, but it was already too late by more than five hours.

"Damn!" Travis said, staring at the telex.

The first indication to Travis that anything was wrong was when the Japanese and Germans broke off negotiations with Munro in Tangier. One minute they had been willing to pay anything; the next minute they could hardly wait to leave. The break-off had come abruptly, discontinuously; it implied the sudden introduction of new data into the consortium computer files.

New data from where?

There could be only one explanation—and now it was confirmed in the GSFC telex from Greenbelt.

ERTS WHY ARE YOU SENDING ALL THIS MUKENKO DATA

There was a simple answer to that: ERTS *wasn't* sending any data. At least, not willingly. ERTS and GSFC had an arrangement to exchange data updates—Travis had made that deal in 1978 to obtain cheaper satellite imagery from orbiting

104

Landsats. Satellite imagery was his company's single greatest expense. In return for a look at derived ERTS data, GSFC agreed to supply satellite CCTs at 30 percent below gross rate.

It seemed like a good deal at the time, and the coded locks were specified in the agreement.

But now the potential drawbacks loomed large before Travis; his worst fears were confirmed. Once you put a line over two thousand miles from Houston to Greenbelt, you begged for a piggyback data slurp. Somewhere between Texas and Maryland someone had inserted a terminal linkup—probably in the carrier telephone lines—and had begun to slurp out data on a piggyback terminal. This was the form of industrial espionage they most feared.

A piggyback-slurp terminal tapped in between two legitimate terminals, monitoring the back and forth transmissions. After a time, the piggyback operator knew enough to begin making transmissions on line, slurping out data from both ends, pretending to be GSFC to Houston, and Houston to GSFC. The piggyback terminal could continue to function until one or both legitimate terminals realized that they were being slurped.

Now the question was: how much data had been slurped out in the last seventy-two hours?

He had called for twenty-four-hour scanner checks, and the readings were disheartening. It looked as though the ERTS computer had yielded up not only original database elements, but also data-transformation histories—the sequence of operations performed on the data by ERTS over the last four weeks.

If that was true, it meant that the Euro-Japanese consortium piggyback knew what transformations ERTS had carried out on the ·Mukenko data—and therefore they knew where the lost city was located, with pinpoint accuracy. They now knew the location of the city as precisely as Ross did.

Timelines had to be adjusted, unfavorably to the ERTS team. And the updated computer projections were unequivocal—Ross or no Ross, the likelihood of the ERTS team reaching the site ahead of the Japanese and Germans was now almost nil.

From Travis's viewpoint, the entire ERTS expedition was now a futile exercise, and a waste of time. There was no hope of success. The only unfactorable element was the gorilla Amy, and Travis's instincts told him that a gorilla named Amy would not prove decisive in the discovery of mineral deposits in the northeastern Congo.

It was hopeless.

Should he recall the ERTS team? He stared at the console by his desk. "Call cost-time," he said.

The computer blinked COST-TIME AVAILABLE.

"Congo Field Survey," he said.

The screen printed out numbers for the Congo Field Survey: expenditures by the hour, accumulated costs, committed future costs, cutoff points, future branch-point deletions. . . . The project was now just outside Nairobi, and was running at an accumulated cost of slightly over $189,000.

Cancellation would cost $227,455.

"Factor BF," he said.

The screen changed. B F . He now saw a series of probabilities. "Factor BF" was *bona fortuna*, good luck—the imponderable in all expeditions, especially remote, dangerous expeditions.

THINKING A MOMENT, the computer flashed.

Travis waited. He knew that the computer would require several seconds to perform the computations to assign weights to random factors that might influence the expedition, still five or more days from the target site.

His beeper buzzed. Rogers, the tap dancer, said, "We've traced the piggyback slurp. It's in Norman, Oklahoma, nominally at the North Central Insurance Corporation of America. NCIC is fifty-one percent owned by a Hawaiian holding company, Halekuli, Inc., which is in turn owned by mainland Japanese interests. What do you want?"

"I want a very bad fire," Travis said.

"Got you," Rogers said. He hung up the phone.

The screen flashed ASSESSED FACTOR BF and a probability: .449. He was surprised: that figure meant that ERTS had an almost even chance of attaining the target site before the consortium. Travis didn't question the mathematics; .449 was good enough.

The ERTS expedition would continue to the Congo, at least for the time being. And in the meantime he would do whatever he could to slow down the consortium. Off the top of his head, Travis could think of one or two ideas to accomplish that.

3. Additional Data

THE JET WAS MOVING SOUTH OVER LAKE RUDOLPH in northern Kenya when Tom Seamans called Elliot.

Seamans had finished his computer analysis to discriminate gorillas from other apes, principally chimpanzees. He had then obtained from Houston a videotape of three seconds of a garbled video transmission which seemed to show a gorilla smashing a dish antenna and staring into a camera.

"Well?" Elliot said, looking at the computer screen. The data flashed up:

```
DISCRIMINANT FUNCTION GORILLA / CHIMP
FUNCTIONAL GROUPINGS DISTRIBUTED AS:
GORILLA: .9934
CHIMP: .1132
TEST VIDEOTAPE (HOUSTON): .3349
```

"Hell," Elliot said. At those figures, the study was equivocal, useless.

"Sorry about that," Seamans said over the phone. "But

part of the trouble comes from the test material itself. We had to factor in the computer derivation of that image. The image has been cleaned up, and that means it's been regularized; the critical stuff has been lost. I'd like to work with the original digitized matrix. Can you get me that?''

Karen Ross was nodding yes. ''Sure,'' Elliot said.

''I'll go another round with it,'' Seamans said. ''But if you want my gut opinion, it is never going to turn out. The fact is that gorillas show a considerable individual variation in facial structure, just as people do. If we increase our sample base, we're going to get more variation, and a larger population interval. I think you're stuck. You can never prove it's not a gorilla—but for my money, it's not.''

''Meaning what?'' Elliot asked.

''It's something new,'' Seamans said. ''I'm telling you, if this was really a gorilla, it would have showed up .89 or .94, somewhere in there, on this function. But the image comes out at .39. That's just not good enough. It's not a gorilla, Peter.''

''Then what is it?''

''It's a transitional form. I ran a function to measure where the variation was. You know what was the major differential? Skin color. Even in black-and-white, it's not dark enough to be a gorilla, Peter. This is a whole new animal, I promise you.''

Elliot looked at Ross. ''What does this do to your timeline?''

''For the moment, nothing,'' she said. ''Other elements are more critical, and this is unfactorable.''

The pilot clicked on the intercom. ''We are beginning our descent into Nairobi,'' he said.

4. Nairobi

FIVE MILES OUTSIDE NAIROBI, ONE CAN FIND WILD game of the East African savannah. And within the memory of many Nairobi residents the game could be found closer still—gazelles, buffalo, and giraffe wandering around backyards, and the occasional leopard slipping into one's bedroom. In those days, the city still retained the character of a wild colonial station; in its heyday, Nairobi was a fast-living place indeed: "Are you married or do you live in Kenya?" went the standard question. The men were hard-drinking and rough, the women beautiful and loose, and the pattern of life no more predictable than the fox hunts that ranged over the rugged countryside each weekend.

But modern Nairobi is almost unrecognizable from the time of those freewheeling colonial days. The few remaining Victorian buildings lie stranded in a modern city of half a million, with traffic jams, stoplights, skyscrapers, supermarkets, same-day dry cleaners, French restaurants, and air pollution.

The ERTS cargo plane landed at Nairobi International Airport at dawn on the morning of June 16, and Munro contacted porters and assistants for the expedition. They intended to leave Nairobi within two hours—until Travis called from Houston to inform them that Peterson, one of the geologists on the first Congo expedition, had somehow made it back to Nairobi.

Ross was excited by the news. "Where is he now?" she asked.

"At the morgue," Travis said.

* * *

109

Elliot winced as he came close: the body on the stainless steel table was a blond man his own age. The man's arms had been crushed; the skin was swollen, a ghastly purple color. He glanced at Ross. She seemed perfectly cool, not blinking or turning away. The pathologist stepped on a foot petal, activating a microphone overhead. "Would you state your name, please."

"Karen Ellen Ross."

"Your nationality and passport number?"

"American, F 1413649."

"Can you identify the man before you, Miss Ross?"

"Yes," she said. "He is James Robert Peterson."

"What is your relation to the deceased James Robert Peterson?"

"I worked with him," she said dully. She seemed to be examining a geological specimen, scrutinizing it unemotionally. Her face showed no reaction.

The pathologist faced the microphone. "Identity confirmed as James Robert Peterson, male Caucasian, twenty-nine years old, nationality American." He turned back to Ross. "When was the last time you saw Mr. Peterson?"

"In May of this year. He was leaving for the Congo."

"You have not seen him in the last month?"

"No," she said. "What happened?"

The pathologist touched the puffy purple injuries on his arms. His fingertips sank in, leaving indentations like teeth in the flesh. "Damned strange story," the pathologist said.

The previous day, June 15, Peterson had been flown to Nairobi airport aboard a small charter cargo plane, in end-stage terminal shock. He died several hours later without regaining consciousness. "Extraordinary he made it at all. Apparently the aircraft made an unscheduled stop for a mechanical problem at Garona field, a dirt track in Zaire. And then this fellow comes stumbling out of the woods, collapsing at their feet." The pathologist pointed out that the bones had been shattered in both arms. The injuries, he explained, were not new; they had occurred at least four days earlier, perhaps more. "He must have been in incredible pain."

Elliot said, "What could cause that injury?"

The pathologist had never seen anything like it. "Superficially, it resembles mechanical trauma, a crush injury from an automobile or truck. We see a good deal of those here; but mechanical crush injuries are never bilateral, as they are in this case."

"So it wasn't a mechanical injury?" Karen Ross asked.

"Don't know what it was. It's unique in my experience," the pathologist said briskly. "We also found traces of blood under his nails, and a few strands of gray hair. We're running a test now."

Across the room, another pathologist looked up from his microscope. "The hair is definitely not human. Cross section doesn't match. Some kind of animal hair, close to human."

"The cross section?" Ross said.

"Best index we have of hair origin," the pathologist said. "For instance, human pubic hair is more elliptical in cross section than other body hair, or facial hair. It's quite characteristic—admissible in court. But especially in this laboratory, we come across a great deal of animal hair, and we're expert in that as well."

A large stainless-steel analyzer began pinging. "Blood's coming through," the pathologist said.

On a video screen they saw twin patterns of pastel-colored streaks. "This is the electrophoresis pattern," the pathologist explained. "To check serum proteins. That's ordinary human blood on the left. On the right we have the blood sample from under the nails. You can see it's definitely not human blood."

"Not human blood?" Ross said, glancing at Elliot.

"It's *close* to human blood," the pathologist said, staring at the pattern. "But it's not human. Could be a domestic or farm animal—a pig, perhaps. Or else a primate. Monkeys and apes are very close serologically to human beings. We'll have a computer analysis in a minute."

On the screen, the computer printed ALPHA AND BETA SERUM GLOBULINS MATCH: GORILLA BLOOD.

The pathologist said, "There's your answer to what he had under his nails. Gorilla blood."

5. Examination

"SHE WON'T HURT YOU," ELLIOT TOLD THE frightened orderly. They were in the passenger compartment of the 747 cargo jet. "See, she's smiling at you."

Amy was indeed giving her most winning smile, being careful not to expose her teeth. But the orderly from the private clinic in Nairobi was not familiar with these fine points of gorilla etiquette. His hands shook as he held the syringe.

Nairobi was the last opportunity for Amy to receive a thorough checkup. Her large, powerful body belied a constitutional fragility, as her heavy-browed, glowering face belied a meek, rather tender nature. In San Francisco, the Project Amy staff subjected her to a thorough medical regimen—urine samples every other day, stool samples checked weekly for occult blood, complete blood studies monthly, and a trip to the dentist every three months for removal of the black tartar that accumulated from her vegetarian diet.

Amy took it all in stride, but the terrified orderly did not know that. He approached her holding the syringe in front of him like a weapon. "You sure he won't bite?"

Amy, trying to be helpful, signed, *Amy promise no bite.* She was signing slowly, deliberately, as she always did when confronted by someone who did not know her language.

"She promises not to bite you," Elliot said.

"So you say," the orderly said. Elliot did not bother to explain that he hadn't said it; she had.

After the blood samples were drawn, the orderly relaxed a little. Packing up, he said, "Certainly is an ugly brute."

"You've hurt her feelings," Elliot said.

And, indeed, Amy was signing vigorously, *What ugly?*

"Nothing, Amy," Elliot said. "He's just never seen a gorilla before."

The orderly said, "I beg your pardon?"

"You've hurt her feelings. You'd better apologize."

The orderly snapped his medical case shut. He stared at Elliot and then at Amy. "Apologize to *him*?"

"Her," Elliot said. "Yes. How would you like to be told you're ugly?"

Elliot felt strongly about this. Over the years, he had come to feel acutely the prejudices that human beings showed toward apes, considering chimpanzees to be cute children, orangs to be wise old men, and gorillas to be hulking, dangerous brutes. They were wrong in every case.

Each of these animals was unique, and did not fit the human stereotypes at all. Chimps, for example, were much more callous than gorillas ever were. Because chimps were extroverts, an angry chimp was far more dangerous than an angry gorilla; at the zoo, Elliot would watch in amazement as human mothers pushed their children closer to look at the chimps, but recoiled protectively at the sight of the gorillas. These mothers obviously did not know that wild chimpanzees caught and ate human infants—something gorillas never did.

Elliot had witnessed repeatedly the human prejudice against gorillas, and had come to recognize its effect on Amy. Amy could not help the fact that she was huge and black and heavy-browed and squash-faced. Behind the face people considered so repulsive was an intelligent and sensitive consciousness, sympathetic to the people around her. It pained her when people ran away, or screamed in fear, or made cruel remarks.

The orderly frowned. "You mean that he understands English?"

"Yes, *she* does." The gender change was something else

Elliot didn't like. People who were afraid of Amy always assumed she was male.

The orderly shook his head. "I don't believe it."

"Amy, show the man to the door."

Amy lumbered over to the door and opened it for the orderly, whose eyes widened as he left. Amy closed the door behind him.

Silly human man, Amy signed.

"Never mind," Elliot said. "Come, Peter tickle Amy." And for the next fifteen minutes, he tickled her as she rolled on the floor and grunted in deep satisfaction. Elliot never noticed the door open behind him, never noticed the shadow falling across the floor, until it was too late and he turned his head to look up and saw the dark cylinder swing down, and his head erupted with blinding white pain and everything went black.

6. Kidnapped

HE AWOKE TO A PIERCING ELECTRONIC SHRIEK.

"Don't move, sir," a voice said.

Elliot opened his eyes and stared into a bright light shining down on him. He was still lying on his back in the aircraft; someone was bent over him.

"Look to the right . . . now to the left. . . . Can you flex your fingers?"

He followed the instructions. The light was taken away and he saw a black man in a white suit crouched beside him. The man touched Elliot's head; his fingers came away red with blood. "Nothing to be alarmed about," the man said; "it's quite superficial." He looked off. "How long would you estimate he was unconscious?"

"Couple of minutes, no more," Munro said.

The high-pitched squeal came again. He saw Ross moving around the passenger section, wearing a shoulder pack, and holding a wand in front of her. There was another squeal. "Damn," she said, and plucked something from the molding around the window. "That's five. They really did a job."

Munro looked down at Elliot. "How do you feel?" he asked.

"He should be put under observation for twenty-four hours," the black man said. "Just as a precaution."

"Twenty-four hours!" Ross said, moving around the compartment.

Elliot said, "Where is she?"

"They took her," Munro said. "They opened the rear door, inflated the pneumatic slide, and were gone before anyone realized what happened. We found this next to you."

Munro gave him a small glass vial with Japanese markings. The sides of the vial were scratched and scored; at one end was a rubber plunger, at the other end a broken needle.

Elliot sat up.

"Easy there," the doctor said.

"I feel fine," Elliot said, although his head was throbbing. He turned the vial over in his hand. "There was frost on it when you found it?"

Munro nodded. "Very cold."

"CO_2," Elliot said. It was a dart from a gas gun. He shook his head. "They broke the needle off in her." He could imagine Amy's screams of outrage. She was unaccustomed to anything but the tenderest treatment. Perhaps that was one of the shortcomings of his work with her; he had not prepared her well enough for the real world. He sniffed the vial, smelled a pungent odor. "Lobaxin. Fast-acting soporific, onset within fifteen seconds. It's what they'd use." Elliot was angry. Lobaxin was not often used on animals because it caused liver damage. And they had broken the needle—

He got to his feet and leaned on Munro, who put his arm around him. The doctor protested.

"I'm fine," Elliot said.

Across the room, there was another squeal, this one loud

and prolonged. Ross was moving her wand over the medicine cabinet, past the bottles of pills and supplies. The sound seemed to embarrass her; quickly she moved away, shutting the cabinet.

She crossed the passenger compartment, and a squeal was heard again. Ross removed a small black device from the underside of one seat. "Look at this. They must have brought an extra person just to plant the bugs. It'll take hours to sterilize the plane. We can't wait."

She went immediately to the computer console and began typing.

Elliot said, "Where are they now? The consortium?"

"The main party left from Kubala airport outside Nairobi six hours ago," Munro said.

"Then they didn't take Amy with them."

"Of course they didn't take her," Ross said, sounding annoyed. "They've got no use for her."

"Have they killed her?" Elliot asked.

"Maybe," Munro said quietly.

"Oh, *Jesus* . . ."

"But I doubt it," Munro continued. "They don't want any publicity, and Amy's famous—as famous in some circles as an ambassador or a head of state. She's a talking gorilla, and there aren't many of those. She's been on television news, she's had her picture in the newspapers. . . . They'd kill you before they killed her."

"Just so they don't kill her," Elliot said.

"They won't," Ross said, with finality. "The consortium isn't interested in Amy. They don't even know why we brought her. They're just trying to blow our timeline—but they won't succeed."

Something in her tone suggested that she planned to leave Amy behind. The idea appalled Elliot. "We've got to get her back," he said. "Amy is my responsibility, I can't possibly abandon her here—"

"Seventy-two minutes," Ross said, pointing to the screen. "We have exactly one hour and twelve minutes before we blow the timeline." She turned to Munro. "And we have to switch over to the second contingency."

"Fine," Munro said. "I'll get the men working on it."

"In a new plane," Ross said. "We can't take this one, it's contaminated." She was punching in call letters to the computer console, her fingers clicking on the keys. "We'll take it straight to point M," Ross said. "Okay?"

"Absolutely," Munro said.

Elliot said, "I won't leave Amy. If you're going to leave her behind, you'll have to leave me as well—" Elliot stopped.

Printed on the screen was the message FORGET GORILLA PROCEED TO NEXT CHECKPOINT URGENT APE NOT SIG-NIFICANT TIMELINE OUTCOME COMPUTER VERIFI-CATION REPEAT PROCEED WITHOUT AMY.

"You can't leave her behind," Elliot said. "I'll stay behind, too."

"Let me tell you something," Ross said. "I never believed that Amy was important to this expedition—or you either. From the very beginning she was just a diversion. When I came to San Francisco, I was followed. You and Amy provided a diversion. You threw the consortium into a spin. It was worth it. Now it's not worth it. We'll leave you both behind if we have to. I couldn't care less."

7. Bugs

"WELL, GODDAMN IT," ELLIOT BEGAN, "DO YOU mean to tell me that . . ."

"That's right," Ross said coldly. "You're expendable." But even as she spoke, she grabbed his arm firmly and led him out of the airplane while she held her finger to her lips.

Elliot realized that she intended to pacify him in private, Amy was his responsibility, and to hell with all the diamonds and international intrigue. Outside on the concrete runway he repeated stubbornly, "I'm not leaving without Amy."

"Neither am I." Ross walked quickly across the runway toward a police helicopter.

Elliot hurried to catch up. "What?"

"Don't you understand *anything*?" Ross said. "That airplane's *not clean*. It's full of bugs, and the consortium's listening in. I made that speech for their benefit."

"But who was following you in San Francisco?"

"Nobody. They're going to spend hours trying to figure out who was."

"Amy and I weren't just a diversion?"

"Not at all," she said. "Look: we don't know what happened to the last ERTS Congo team, but no matter what you or Travis or anyone else says, *I* think gorillas were involved. And I think that Amy will help us when we get there."

"As an ambassador?"

"We need information," Ross said. "And she knows more about gorillas than we do."

"But can you find her in an hour and ten minutes?"

"Hell, no," Ross said, checking her watch. "This won't take more than twenty minutes."

"Lower! Lower!"

Ross was shouting into her radio headset as she sat alongside the police helicopter pilot. The helicopter was circling the tower of Government House, turning and moving north, toward the Hilton.

"This is not acceptable, madam," the pilot said politely. "We fly below airspace limitations."

"You're too damn high!" Ross said. She was looking at a box on her knees, with four compass-point digital readouts. She flicked switches quickly, while the radio crackled with angry complaints from Nairobi tower.

"East now, due east," she instructed, and the helicopter tilted and moved east, toward the poor outskirts of the city.

In the back, Elliot felt his stomach twist with each banking turn on the helicopter. His head pounded and he felt awful, but he had insisted on coming. He was the only person knowledgeable enough to minister to Amy if she was in medical trouble.

Now, sitting alongside the pilot, Ross said, "Get a reading," and she pointed to the northeast. The helicopter thumped over crude shacks, junked automobile lots, dirt roads. "Slower now, slower . . ."

The readouts glowed, the numbers shifting. Elliot saw them all go to zero, simultaneously.

"Down!" Ross shouted, and the helicopter descended in the center of a vast garbage dump.

The pilot remained with the helicopter; his final words were disquieting. "Where there's garbage, there's rats," he said.

"Rats don't bother me," Ross said, climbing out with her box in her hand.

"Where there's rats, there's cobras," the pilot said.

"Oh," Ross said.

She crossed the dump with Elliot. There was a stiff breeze; papers and debris ruffled at their feet. Elliot's head ached, and the odors arising from the dump nauseated him.

"Not far now," Ross said, watching the box. She was excited, glancing at her watch.

"Here?"

She bent over and picked through the trash, her hand making circles, digging deeper in frustration, elbow-deep in the trash.

Finally she came up with a necklace—a necklace she had given Amy when they first boarded the airplane in San Francisco. She turned it over, examining the plastic name tag on it, which Elliot noticed was unusually thick. There were fresh scratches on the back.

"Hell," Ross said. "Sixteen minutes shot." And she hurried back to the waiting helicopter.

Elliot fell into step beside her. "But how can you find her if they got rid of her necklace bug?"

"Nobody," Ross said, "plants only one bug. This was just a decoy, they were supposed to find it." She pointed to the scratches on the back. "But they're clever, they reset the frequencies."

"Maybe they got rid of the second bug, too," Elliot said.

"They didn't," Ross said. The helicopter lifted off, a thuddering whirr of blades, and the paper and trash of the dump swirled in circles beneath them. She pressed her mouthpiece to her lips and said to the pilot, "Take me to the largest scrapmetal source in Nairobi."

Within nine minutes, they had picked up another very weak signal, located within an automobile junkyard. The helicopter landed in the street outside, drawing dozens of shouting children. Ross went with Elliot into the junkyard, moving past the rusting hulks of cars and trucks.

"You're sure she's here?" Elliot said.

"No question. They have to surround her with metal, it's the only thing they can do."

"Why?"

"Shielding." She picked her way around the broken cars, pausing frequently to refer to her electronic box.

Then Elliot heard a grunt.

It came from inside an ancient rust-red Mercedes bus. Elliot climbed through the shattered doors, the rubber gaskets crumbling in his hands, into the interior. He found Amy on her back, tied with adhesive tape. She was groggy, but complained loudly when he tore the tape off her hair.

He located the broken needle in her right chest and plucked it out with forceps, Amy shrieked, then hugged him. He heard the far-off whine of a police siren.

"It's all right, Amy, it's all right," he said. He set her down and examined her more carefully. She seemed to be okay.

And then he said, "Where's the second bug?"

Ross grinned. "She swallowed it."

Now that Amy was safe, Elliot felt a wave of anger. "You made her swallow it? An electronic bug? Don't you realize that she is a very delicate animal and her health is extremely precarious—"

"Don't get worked up," Ross said. "Remember the vitamins I gave you? You swallowed one, too." She glanced at her watch. "Thirty-two minutes," she said. "Not bad at all. We have forty minutes before we have to leave Nairobi."

8. Present Point

MUNRO SAT IN THE 747, PUNCHING KEYS ON THE computer. He watched as the lines crisscrossed over the maps, ticking out datalines, timelines, information lock coordinates.

The computer ran through possible expedition routines quickly, testing a new one every ten seconds. After each data fit, outcomes were printed—cost, logistical difficulties, supply problems, total elapsed times from Houston, from Present Point (Nairobi), where they were now.

Looking for a solution.

It wasn't like the old days, Munro thought. Even five years ago, expeditions were still run on guesswork and luck. But now every expedition employed real-time computer planning; Munro had long since been forced to learn BASIC and TW/GESHUND and other major interactive languages. Nobody did it by the seat of the pants anymore. The business had changed.

Munro had decided to join the ERTS expedition precisely because of those changes. Certainly he hadn't joined because of Karen Ross, who was stubborn and inexperienced. But ERTS had the most elaborate working database, and the most sophisticated planning programs. In the long run, he expected those programs to make the crucial difference. And he liked a smaller team; once the consortium was in the field, their working party of thirty was going to prove unwieldy.

But he had to find a faster timeline to get them in. Munro

pressed the buttons, watching the data flash up. He set trajectories, intersections, junctions. Then, with a practiced eye, he began to eliminate alternatives. He closed out pathways, shut down airfields, eliminated truck routes, avoided river crossings.

The computer kept coming back with reduced times, but from Present Point (Nairobi) the total elapsed times were always too long. The best projection beat the consortium by thirty-seven minutes—which was nothing to rely on. He frowned, and smoked a cigar. Perhaps if he crossed the Liko River at Mugana . . .

He punched the buttons.

It didn't help. Crossing the Liko was *slower*. He tried trekking through the Goroba Valley, even though it was probably too hazardous to execute.

PROPOSED ROUTING EXCESSIVELY HAZARDOUS

"Great minds think alike," Munro said, smoking his cigar. But it started him wondering: were there other, unorthodox approaches they had overlooked? And then he had an idea.

The others wouldn't like it, but it might work. . . .

Munro called the logistics equipment list. Yes, they were equipped for it. He punched in the routing, smiling as he saw the line streak straight across Africa, within a few miles of their destination. He called for outcomes.

PROPOSED ROUTING UNACCEPTABLE.

He pressed the override button, got the data outcomes anyway. It was just as he thought—they could beat the consortium by a full forty hours. Nearly two full days!

The computer went back to the previous statement:

PROPOSED ROUTING UNACCEPTABLE / ALTITUDE FACTORS / HAZARDS TO PERSONNEL EXCESSIVE / PROBABILITY SUCCESS UNDER LIMITS /

Munro didn't think that was true. He thought they could pull it off, especially if the weather was good. The altitude wouldn't be a problem, and the ground although rough would be reasonably yielding.

In fact, the more Munro thought about it, the more certain he was that it would work.

9. Departure

THE LITTLE FOKKER S-144 PROP PLANE WAS PULLED up alongside the giant 747 cargo jet, like an infant nursing at its mother's breast. Two cargo ramps were in constant motion as men transferred equipment from the larger plane to the smaller one. Returning to the airfield, Ross explained to Elliot that they would be taking the smaller plane, since the 747 had to be debugged, and since it was "too large" for their needs now.

"But the jet must be faster," Elliot said.

"Not necessarily," Ross said, but she did not explain further.

In any case, things were now happening very fast, and Elliot had other concerns. He helped Amy aboard the Fokker, and checked her thoroughly. She seemed to be bruised all over her body—at least she complained that everything hurt when he touched her—but she had no broken bones, and she was in good spirits.

Several black men were loading equipment into the airplane, laughing and slapping each other on the back, having a fine time. Amy was intrigued with the men, demanding to know *What joke?* But they ignored her, concentrating on the work at hand. And she was still groggy from her medication. Soon she fell asleep.

Ross supervised the loading, and Elliot moved toward the rear of the plane, where she was talking with a jolly black man, whom she introduced as Kahega.

"Ah," Kahega said, shaking Elliot's hand. "Dr. Elliot. Dr. Ross and Dr. Elliot, two doctors, very excellent."

Elliot was not sure why it was excellent.

Kahega laughed infectiously. "Very good *cover*," he announced. "Not like the old days with Captain Munro. Now two doctors—a medical mission, yes? Very excellent. Where are the 'medical supplies'?" He cocked an eyebrow.

"We have no medical supplies." Ross sighed.

"Oh, very excellent, Doctor, I like your manner," Kahega said. "You are American, yes? We take what, M-16s? Very good rifle, M-16. I prefer it myself."

"Kahega thinks we are running guns," Ross said. "He just can't believe we aren't."

Kahega was laughing. "You are with Captain Munro!" he said, as if this explained everything. And then he went off to see about the other workmen.

"You sure we aren't running guns?" Elliot asked when they were alone.

"We're after something more valuable than guns," Ross said. She was repacking the equipment, working quickly. Elliot asked if he could help, but she shook her head. "I've got to do this myself. We have to get it down to forty pounds per person."

"Forty pounds? For everything?"

"That's what the computer projection allows. Munro's brought in Kahega and seven other Kikuya assistants. With the three of us, that makes eleven people all together, plus Amy—she gets her full forty pounds. But it means a total of four hundred eighty pounds." Ross continued to weigh packs and parcels of food.

The news gave Elliot serious, misgivings. The expedition was taking yet another turn, into still greater danger. His immediate desire to back out was checked by his memory of the video screen, and the gray gorillalike creature that he suspected was a new, unknown animal. That was a discovery worth risk. He stared out the window at the porters. "They're Kikuyu?"

"Yes," she said. "They're good porters, even if they never shut up. Kikuyu tribesmen love to talk. They're all brothers, by the way, so be careful what you say. I just hope Munro didn't have to tell them too much."

"The Kikuyu?"

"No, the NCNA."

"The NCNA," Elliot repeated.

"The Chinese. The Chinese are very interested in computers and electronic technology," Ross said. "Munro must be telling them something in exchange for the advice they're giving him." She gestured to the window, and Elliot looked out. Sure enough, Munro stood under the shadow of the 747 wing, talking with four Chinese men.

"Here," Ross said, "stow these in that corner." She pointed to three large Styrofoam cartons marked AMERICAN SPORT DIVERS, LAKE ELSINORE, CALIF.

"We doing underwater work?" Elliot asked, puzzled.

But Ross wasn't paying attention. "I just wish I knew what he was telling them," she said. But as it turned out, Ross needn't have worried, for Munro paid the Chinese in something more valuable to them than electronics information.

The Fokker lifted off from the Nairobi runway at 14:24 hours, three minutes ahead of their new timeline schedule.

During the sixteen hours following Amy's recovery, the ERTS expedition traveled 560 miles across the borders of four countries—Kenya, Tanzania, Rwanda, and Zaire—as they went from Nairobi to the Barawana Forest, at the edge of the Congo rain forest. The logistics of this complex move would have been impossible without the assistance of an outside ally. Munro said that he "had friends in low places," and in this case he had turned to the Chinese Secret Service, in Tanzania.

The Chinese had been active in Africa since the early 1960s, when their spy networks attempted to influence the course of the Congolese civil war because China wanted access to the Congo's rich supplies of uranium. Field operatives were run out of the Bank of China or, more commonly, the New China News Agency. Munro had dealt with a number of NCNA "war correspondents" when he was running arms from 1963 to 1968, and he had never lost his contacts.

The Chinese financial commitment to Africa was considerable. In the late 1960s, more than half of China's two billion dollars in foreign aid went to African nations. An equal sum was spent secretly; in 1973, Mao Tse-tung complained publicly about the money he had wasted trying to overthrow the Zaire government of President Mobutu.

The Chinese mission in Africa was meant to counter the Russian influence, but since World War II the Chinese bore no great love for the Japanese, and Munro's desire to beat the Euro-Japanese consortium fell on sympathetic ears. To celebrate the alliance, Munro had brought three grease-stained cardboard cartons from Hong Kong.

The two chief Chinese operatives in Africa, Li T'ao and Liu Shu-wen, were both from Hunan province. They found their African posting tedious because of the bland African food, and gratefully accepted Munro's gift of a case of tree ears fungus, a case of hot bean sauce, and a case of chili paste with garlic. The fact that these spices came from neutral Hong Kong, and were not the inferior condiments produced in Taiwan, was a subtle point; in any case, the gift struck exactly the proper note for an informal exchange.

NCNA operatives assisted Munro with paperwork, some difficult-to-obtain equipment, and information. The Chinese possessed excellent maps, and remarkably detailed information about conditions along the northeast Zaire border—since they were assisting the Tanzanian troops invading Uganda. The Chinese had told him that the jungle rivers were flooding, and had advised him to procure a balloon for crossings. But Munro did not bother to take their advice; indeed, he seemed to have some plan to reach his destination without crossing any rivers at all. Although how, the Chinese could not imagine.

At 10 P.M. on June 16, the Fokker stopped to refuel at Rawamagena airport, outside Kigali in Rwanda. The local traffic control officer boarded the plane with a clipboard and forms, asking their next destination. Munro said that it was Rawamagena airport, meaning that the aircraft would make a loop, then return.

Elliot frowned. "But we're going to land somewhere in the—"

"Sh-h-h," Ross said, shaking her head. "Leave it alone."

Certainly the traffic officer seemed content with this flight plan; once the pilot signed the clipboard, he departed. Ross explained that flight controllers in Rwanda were accustomed to aircraft that did not file full plans. "He just wants to know when the plane will be back at his field. The rest is none of his business."

Rawamagena airport was sleepy; they had to wait two hours for petrol to be brought, yet the normally impatient Ross waited quietly. And Munro dozed, equally indifferent to the delay.

"What about the timeline?" Elliot asked.

"No problem," she said. "We can't leave for three hours anyway. We need the light over Mukenko."

"That's where the airfield is?" Elliot asked.

"If you call it an airfield," Munro said, and he pulled his safari hat down over his eyes and went back to sleep.

This worried Elliot until Ross explained to him that most outlying African airfields were just dirt strips cut into the bush. The pilots couldn't land at night, or in the foggy morning, because there were often animals on the field, or encamped nomads, or another plane that had put down and was unable to take off again. "We need the light," she explained. "That's why we're waiting. Don't worry: it's all factored in."

Elliot accepted her explanation, and went back to check on Amy. Ross sighed. "Don't you think we'd better tell him?" she asked.

"Why?" Munro said, not lifting his hat.

"Maybe there's a problem with Amy."

"I'll take care of Amy," Munro said.

"It's going to upset Elliot when he finds out," Ross said.

"Of course it's going to upset him," Munro said. "But

there's no point upsetting him until we have to. After all, what's this jump worth to us?''

"Forty hours, at least. It's dangerous, but it'll give us a whole new timeline. We could still beat them.''

"Well, there's your answer,'' Munro said. "Now keep your mouth shut, and get some rest.''

DAY 5: MORUTI

June 17, 1979

1. Zaire

FIVE HOURS OUT OF RAWAMAGENA, THE LAND-
scape changed. Once past Goma, near the Zaire border, they
found themselves flying over the easternmost fingers of the
Congo rain forest. Elliot stared out the window, fascinated.

Here and there in the pale morning light, a few fragile
wisps of fog clung like cotton to the canopy of trees. And
occasionally they passed the dark snaking curve of a muddy
river, or the straight deep red gash of a road. But for the most
part they looked down upon an unbroken expanse of dense
forest, extending away into the distance as far as the eye
could see.

The view was boring, and simultaneously frightening—it
was frightening to be confronted by what Stanley had called
"the indifferent immensity of the natural world." As one sat
in the air-conditioned comfort of an airplane seat, it was
impossible not to recognize that this vast, monotonous forest
was a giant creation of nature, utterly dwarfing in scale the
greatest cities or other creations of mankind. Each individual
green puff of a tree had a trunk forty feet in diameter, soaring
two hundred feet into the air; a space the size of a Gothic
cathedral was concealed beneath its billowing foliage. And
Elliot knew that the forest extended to the west for nearly
two thousand miles, until it finally stopped at the Atlantic
Ocean, on the west coast of Zaire.

Elliot had been anticipating Amy's reaction to this first
view of the jungle, her natural environment. She looked out
the window with a fixed stare. She signed *Here jungle* with
the same emotional neutrality that she named color cards, or
objects spread out on her trailer floor in San Francisco. She

131

was identifying the jungle, giving a name to what she saw, but he sensed no deeper recognition.

Elliot said to her, "Amy like jungle?"

Jungle here, she signed. *Jungle is.*

He persisted, probing for the emotional context that he was sure must be there. Amy like jungle?

Jungle here. Jungle is. Jungle place here Amy see jungle here.

He tried another approach. "Amy live jungle here?"

No. Expressionless.

"Where Amy live?"

Amy live Amy house. Referring to her trailer in San Francisco.

Elliot watched her loosen her seat belt, cup her chin on her hand as she stared lazily out the window. She signed, *Amy want cigarette.*

She had noticed Munro smoking.

"Later, Amy," Elliot said.

At seven in the morning, they flew over the shimmering metal roofs of the tin and tantalum mining complex at Masisi. Munro, Kahega, and the other porters went to the back of the plane, where they worked on the equipment, chattering excitedly in Swahili.

Amy, seeing them go, signed, *They worried.*

"Worried about what, Amy?"

They worried men worry they worried problems. After a while, Elliot moved to the rear of the plane to find Munro's men half buried under great heaps of straw, stuffing equipment into oblong torpedo-shaped muslin containers, then packing straw around the supplies. Elliot pointed to the muslin torpedoes. "What are these?"

"They're called Crosslin containers," Munro said. "Very reliable."

"I've never seen equipment packed this way," Elliot said, watching the men work. "They seem to be protecting our supplies very carefully."

"That's the idea," Munro said. And he moved up the aircraft to the cockpit, to confer with the pilot.

Amy signed, *Nosehair man lie Peter.* "Nosehair man" was her term for Munro, but Elliot ignored her. He turned to Kahega. "How far to the airfield?"

Kahega glanced up. "Airfield?"

"At Mukenko."

Kahega paused, thinking it over. "Two hours," he said. And then he giggled. He said something in Swahili and all his brothers laughed, too.

"What's funny?" Elliot said.

"Oh, Doctor," Kahega said, slapping him on the back. "You are humorous by your nature."

The airplane banked, making a slow wide circle in the air. Kahega and his brothers peered out the windows, and Elliot joined them. He saw only unbroken jungle—and then a column of green jeeps, moving down a muddy track far below. It looked like a military formation. He heard the word "Muguru" repeated several times.

"What's the matter?" Elliot said. "Is this Muguru?"

Kahega shook his head vigorously. "No hell. This damn pilot, I warn Captain Munro, this damn pilot lost."

"Lost?" Elliot repeated. Even the word was chilling.

Kahega laughed. "Captain Munro set him right, give him dickens."

The airplane now flew east, away from the jungle toward a wooded highland area, rolling hills and stands of deciduous trees. Kahega's brothers chattered excitedly, and laughed and slapped one another; they seemed to be having a fine time.

Then Ross came back, moving quickly down the aisle, her face tense. She unpacked cardboard boxes, withdrawing several basketball-sized spheres of tightly wrapped metal foil.

The foil reminded him of Christmas-tree tinsel. "What's that for?" Elliot asked.

And then he heard the first explosion, and the Fokker shuddered in the air.

Running to the window, he saw a straight thin white vapor trail terminating in a black smoke cloud off to their right. The Fokker was banking, tilting toward the jungle. As he watched, a second trail streaked up toward them from the green forest below.

It was a missile, he realized. A guided missile.

"Ross!" Munro shouted.

"Ready!" Ross shouted back.

There was a bursting red explosion, and his view through the windows was obscured by dense smoke. The airplane shook with the blast, but continued the turn. Elliot couldn't believe it: *someone was shooting missiles at them.*

"Radar!" Munro shouted. "Not optical! Radar!"

Ross gathered up the silver basketballs in her arms and moved back down the aisle. Kahega was opening the rear door, the wind whipping through the compartment.

"What the hell's happening?" Elliot said.

"Don't worry," Ross said over her shoulder. "We'll make up the time." There was a loud whoosh, followed by a third explosion. With the airplane still banked steeply, Ross tore the wrappings from the basketballs and threw them out into the open sky.

Engines roaring, the Fokker swung eight miles to the south and climbed to twelve thousand feet, then circled the forest in a holding pattern. With each revolution, Elliot could see the foil strips hanging in the air like a glinting metallic cloud. Two more rockets exploded within the cloud. Even from a distance, the noise and the shock waves disturbed Amy; she was rocking back and forth in her seat, grunting softly.

"That's chaff," Ross explained, sitting in front of her portable computer console, pushing keys. "It confuses radar weapons systems. Those radar-guided SAMs read us as somewhere in the cloud."

Elliot heard her words slowly, as if in a dream. It made no sense to him. "But who's shooting at us?"

"Probably the FZA," Munro said. "Forces Zairoises Armoises—the Zaire army."

"The Zaire army? Why?"

"It's a mistake," Ross said, still punching buttons, not looking up.

"A mistake? They're shooting surface-to-air missiles at us

and *it's a mistake?* Don't you think you'd better call them
and tell them it's a mistake?''

"Can't," Ross said.

"Why not?"

"Because," Munro said, "we didn't want to file a flight
plan in Rawamagena. That means we are technically in vi-
olation of Zaire airspace.''

"Jesus Christ," Elliot said.

Ross said nothing. She continued to work at the computer
console, trying to get the static to resolve on the screen,
pressing one key after another.

"When I agreed to join this expedition," Elliot said, beginning to shout, "I didn't expect to get into a shooting war."

"Neither did I," Ross said. "It looks as if we both got
more than we bargained for."

Before Elliot could reply, Munro put an arm around his
shoulder and took him aside. "It's going to be all right," he
told Elliot. "They're outdated sixties SAMs and most of them
are blowing up because the solid propellant's cracked with
age. We're in no danger. Just look after Amy, she needs your
help now. Let me work with Ross."

Ross was under intense pressure. With the airplane circling eight miles from the chaff cloud, she had to make a
decision quickly. But she had just been dealt a devastating—
and wholly unexpected—setback.

The Euro-Japanese consortium had been ahead of them
from the very start, by approximately eighteen hours and
twenty minutes. On the ground in Nairobi, Munro had
worked out a plan with Ross which would erase that difference and put the ERTS expedition on-site *forty hours* ahead
of the consortium team. This plan—which for obvious reasons she had not told Elliot—called for them to parachute
onto the barren southern slopes of Mount Mukenko.

From Mukenko, Munro estimated it was thirty-six hours
to the ruined city; Ross expected to jump at two o'clock that
afternoon. Depending on cloud cover over Mukenko and the
specific drop zone, they might reach the city as early as noon
on June 19.

The plan was extremely hazardous. They would be jumping untrained personnel into a wilderness area, more than three days' walk from the nearest large town. If anyone suffered a serious injury, the chances of survival were slight. There was also a question about the equipment: at altitudes of 8,000-10,000 feet on the volcanic slopes, air resistance was reduced, and the Crosslin packets might not provide enough protection.

Initially Ross had rejected Munro's plan as too risky, but he convinced her it was feasible. He pointed out that the parafoils were equipped with automated altimeter-release devices; that the upper volcanic scree was as yielding as a sandy beach; that the Crosslin containers could be over-packed; and that he could carry Amy down himself.

Ross had double-checked outcome probabilities from the Houston computer, and the results were unequivocal. The probability of a successful jump was .7980, meaning there was one chance in five that someone would be badly hurt. However, *given a successful jump*, the probability of expedition success was .9934, making it virtually certain they would beat the consortium to the site.

No alternate plan scored so high. She had looked at the data and said, "I guess we jump."

"I think we do," Munro had said.

The jump solved many problems, for the geopolitical updates were increasingly unfavorable. The Kigani were now in full rebellion; the pygmies were unstable; the Zaire army had sent armored units into the eastern border area to put down the Kigani—and African field armies were notoriously trigger-happy. By jumping onto Mukenko, they expected to bypass all these hazards.

But that was before the Zaire army SAMs began exploding all around them. They were still eighty miles south of the intended drop zone, circling over Kigani territory, wasting time and fuel. It looked as if their daring plan, so carefully worked out and confirmed by computer, was suddenly irrelevant.

And to add to her difficulties, she could not confer with Houston; the computer refused to link up by satellite. She spent fifteen minutes working with the portable unit, boosting power and switching scrambler codes, until she finally realized that her transmission was being electronically jammed.

For the first time in her memory, Karen Ross wanted to cry.

"Easy now," Munro said quietly, lifting her hand away from the keyboard. "One thing at a time, no point in getting upset." Ross had been pressing the keys over and over again, unaware of what she was doing.

Munro was conscious of the deteriorating situation with both Elliot and Ross. He had seen it happen on expeditions before, particularly when scientists and technical people were involved. Scientists worked all day in laboratories where conditions could be rigorously regulated and monitored. Sooner or later, scientists came to believe that the outside world was just as controllable as their laboratories. Even though they knew better, the shock of discovering that the natural world followed its own rules and was indifferent to them represented a harsh psychic blow. Munro could read the signs.

"But this," Ross said, "is obviously a non-military aircraft, how can they do it?"

Munro stared at her. In the Congolese civil war, civilian aircraft had been routinely shot down by all sides. "These things happen," he said.

"And the jamming? Those bastards haven't got the capability to jam us. We're being jammed between our transmitter and our satellite transponder. To do that requires another satellite somewhere, and—" She broke off, frowning.

"You didn't expect the consortium to sit by idly," Munro said. "The question is, can you fix it? Have you got countermeasures?"

"Sure, I've got countermeasures," Ross said. "I can encode a burst bounce, I can transmit optically on an IR carrier, I can link a ground-base cable—but there's nothing I can put together in the next few minutes, and we need information now. Our plan is shot."

"One thing at a time," Munro repeated quietly. He saw the tension in her features, and he knew she was not thinking clearly. He also knew he could not do her thinking for her; he had to get her calm again.

In Munro's judgment, the ERTS expedition was already finished—they could not possibly beat the consortium to the Congo site. But he had no intention of quitting; he had led expeditions long enough to know that anything could happen, so he said, "We can still make up the lost time."

"Make it up? How?"

Munro said the first thing that came to mind: "We'll take the Ragora north. Very fast river, no problem."

"The Ragora's too dangerous."

"We'll have to see," Munro said, although he knew that she was right. The Ragora was much too dangerous, particularly in June. Yet he kept his voice calm, soothing, reassuring. "Shall I tell the others?" he asked finally.

"Yes," Ross said. In the distance, they heard another rocket explosion. "Let's get out of here."

Munro moved swiftly to the rear of the Fokker and said to Kahega, "Prepare the men."

"Yes, boss," Kahega said. A bottle of whiskey was passed around, and each of the men took a long swallow.

Elliot said, "What the hell is this?"

"The men are getting prepared," Munro said.

"Prepared for what?" Elliot asked.

At that moment, Ross came back, looking grim. "From here on, we'll continue on foot," she said.

Elliot looked out the window. "Where's the airfield?"

"There is no airfield," Ross said.

"What do you mean?"

"I mean there is no airfield."

"Is the plane going to put down in the fields?" Elliot asked.

"No," Ross said. "The plane is not going to put down at all."

"Then how do we get down?" Elliot asked, but even as he asked the question, his stomach sank, because he knew the answer.

* * *

"Amy will be fine," Munro said cheerfully, cinching Elliot's straps tightly around his chest. "I gave her a shot of your Thoralen tranquilizer, and she'll be quite calm. No problem at all, I'll keep a good grip on her."

"Keep a good grip on her?" Elliot asked.

"She's too small to fit a harness," Munro said. "I'll have to carry her down." Amy snored loudly, and drooled on Munro's shoulder. He set Amy on the floor; she lay limply on her back, still snoring.

"Now, then," Munro said. "Your parafoil opens automatically. You'll find you have lines in both hands, left and right. Pull left to go left, right to go right, and—"

"What happens to her?" Elliot asked, pointing to Amy.

"I'll take her. Pay attention now. If anything goes wrong, your reserve chute is here, on your chest." He tapped a cloth bundle with a small black digital box, which read 4757. "That's your rate-of-fall altimeter. Automatically pops your reserve chute if you hit thirty-six hundred feet and are still falling faster than two feet per second. Nothing to worry about; whole thing's automatic."

Elliot was chilled, drenched in sweat. "What about landing?"

"Nothing to it," Munro grinned. "You'll land automatically too. Stay loose and relax, take the shock in the legs. Equivalent of jumping off a ten-foot ledge. You've done it a thousand times."

Behind him Elliot saw the open door, bright sunlight glaring into the plane. The wind whipped and howled. Kahega's men jumped in quick succession, one after another. He glanced at Ross, who was ashen, her lower lip trembling as she gripped the doorway.

"Karen, you're not going to go along with—"

She jumped, disappearing into the sunlight. Munro said, "You're next."

"I've never jumped before," Elliot said.

"That's the best way. You won't be frightened."

"But I *am* frightened."

"I can help you with that," Munro said, and he pushed Elliot out of the plane.

Munro watched him fall away, his grin instantly gone. Munro had adopted his hearty demeanor only for Elliot's benefit. "If a man has to do something dangerous," he said later, "it helps to be angry. It's for his own protection, really. Better he should hate someone than fall apart. I wanted Elliot to hate me all the way down."

Munro understood the risks. The minute they left the aircraft, they also left civilization, and all the unquestioned assumptions of civilization. They were jumping not only through the air, but through time, backward into a more primitive and dangerous way of life—the eternal realities of the Congo, which had existed for centuries before them. "Those were the facts of life," Munro said, "but I didn't see any reason to worry the others before they jumped. My job was to get those people into the Congo, not scare them to death. There was plenty of time for that."

Elliot fell, scared to death.

His stomach jumped into his throat, and he tasted bile; the wind screamed around his ears and tugged at his hair; and the air was so cold—he was instantly chilled and shivering. Below him the Barawana Forest lay spread across rolling hills. He felt no appreciation for the beauty before him, and in fact he closed his eyes, for he was plummeting at hideous speed toward the ground. But with his eyes shut he was more aware of the screaming wind.

Too much time had passed. Obviously the parafoil (whatever the hell that was) was not going to open. His life now depended on the parachute attached to his chest. He clutched it, a small tight bundle near his churning stomach. Then he pulled his hands away: he didn't want to interfere with its opening. He dimly remembered that people had died that way, when they interfered with the opening of their parachute.

The screaming wind continued; his body rushed sickeningly downward. *Nothing was happening.* He felt the fierce wind tugging at his feet, whipping his trousers, flapping his shirt against his arms. *Nothing was happening.* It had been at least three minutes since he'd jumped from the plane. He dared not open his eyes, for fear of seeing the trees rushing up close as his body crashed downward toward them in his final seconds of conscious life. . . .

He was going to throw up.

Bile dribbled from his mouth, but since he was falling head downward, the liquid ran up his chin to his neck and then inside his shirt. It was freezing cold. His shivering was becoming uncontrollable.

He snapped upright with a bone-twisting jolt.

For an instant he thought he had hit the ground, and then he realized that he was still descending through the air, but more slowly. He opened his eyes and stared at pale blue sky.

He looked down, and was shocked to see that he was still thousands of feet from the earth. Obviously he had only been falling a few seconds from the airplane above him—

Looking up, he could not see the plane. Directly overhead was a giant rectangular shape, with brilliant red, white, and blue stripes: the parafoil. Finding it easier to look up than down, he studied the parafoil intently. The leading edge was curved and puffy; the rear edge thin, fluttering in the breeze. The parafoil looked very much like an airplane wing, with cords running down to his body.

He took a deep breath and looked down. He was still very high over the landscape. There was some comfort in the slowness with which he was descending. It was really rather peaceful.

And then he noticed he wasn't moving down; he was moving sideways. He could see the other parafoils below, Kahega and his men and Ross; he tried to count them, and thought there were six, but he had difficulty concentrating. He appeared to be moving laterally away from them.

He tugged on the lines in his left hand, and he felt his body twist as the parafoil moved, taking him to the left.

Not bad, he thought.

He pulled harder on the left cords, ignoring the fact that this seemed to make him move faster. He tried to stay near the rectangles descending beneath him. He heard the scream of the wind in his ears. He looked up, hoping to see Munro, but all he could see was the stripes of his own parafoil.

He looked back down, and was astonished to find that the ground was a great deal closer. In fact, it seemed to be rushing up to him at brutal speed. He wondered where he had got the idea that he was drifting gently downward. There was nothing gentle about his descent at all. He saw the first of the parafoils crumple gently as Kahega touched ground, then the second, and the third.

It wouldn't be long before he landed. He was approaching the level of the trees, but his lateral movement was very fast. He realized that his left hand was rigidly pulling on the cords. He released his grip, and his lateral movement ceased. He drifted forward.

Two more parafoils crumpled on impact. He looked back to see Kahega and his men, already down, gathering up the cloth. They were all right; that was encouraging.

He was sliding right into a dense clump of trees. He pulled his cords and twisted to the right, his whole body tilting. He was moving very fast now. The trees could not be avoided. He was going to smash into them. The branches seemed to reach up like fingers, grasping for him.

He closed his eyes, and felt the branches scratching at his face and body as he crashed down, knowing that any second he was going to hit, that he was going to hit the ground and roll—

He never hit.

Everything became silent. He felt himself bobbing up and down. He opened his eyes and saw that he was swinging four feet above the ground. His parafoil had caught in the trees.

He fumbled with his harness buckles, and fell out onto the earth. As he picked himself up, Kahega and Ross came running over to ask if he was all right.

"I'm fine," Elliot said, and indeed he felt extraordinarily fine, more alive than he could ever remember feeling. The next instant he fell over on rubber legs and promptly threw up.

Kahega laughed. "Welcome to the Congo," he said.

Elliot wiped his chin and said, "Where is Amy?"

A moment later Munro landed, with a bleeding ear where Amy had bitten him in terror. But Amy was not the worse for the experience, and came running on her knuckles over to Elliot, making sure that he was all right, and then signing, *Amy fly no like*.

"Look out!"

The first of the torpedo-shaped Crosslin packets smashed down, exploding like a bomb when it hit the ground, spraying equipment and straw in all directions.

"There's the second one!"

Elliot dived for safety. The second bomb hit just a few yards away; he was pelted with foil containers of food and rice. Overhead, he heard the drone of the circling Fokker airplane. He got to his feet in time to see the final two Crosslin containers crash down, and Kahega's men running for safety, with Ross shouting, "Careful, those have the lasers!"

It was like being in the middle of a blitz, but as swiftly as it had begun it was over. The Fokker above them flew off, and the sky was silent; the men began repacking the equipment and burying the parafoils, while Munro barked instructions in Swahili.

Twenty minutes later, they were moving single-file through the forest, starting a two-hundred-mile trek that would lead them into the unexplored eastern reaches of the Congo, to a fabulous reward.

If they could reach it in time.

2. Kigani

ONCE PAST THE INITIAL SHOCK OF HIS JUMP, ELLIOT enjoyed the walk through the Barawana Forest. Monkeys chattered in the trees, and birds called in the cool air; the Kikuyu porters were strung out behind them, smoking cigarettes and joking with one another in an exotic tongue. Elliot found all his emotions agreeable—the sense of freedom from a crass civilization; the sense of adventure, of unexpected events that might occur at any future moment; and finally the sense of romance, of a quest for the poignant past while omnipresent danger kept sensation at a peak of intense feeling. It was in this heightened mood that he listened to the forest animals around him, viewed the play of sunlight and shadow, felt the springy ground beneath his boots, and looked over at Karen Ross, whom he found beautiful and graceful in an utterly unexpected way.

Karen Ross did not look back at him.

As she walked, she twisted knobs on one of her black electronic boxes, trying to establish a signal. A second electronic box hung from a shoulder strap, and since she did not turn to look at him, he had time to notice that there was already a dark stain of sweat at her shoulder, and another running down the back of her shirt. Her dark blonde hair was damp, clinging unattractively to the back of her head. And he noticed that her trousers were wrinkled, streaked with dirt from the fall. She still did not look back.

"Enjoy the forest," Munro advised him. "This is the last time you'll feel cool and dry for quite a while."

Elliot agreed that the forest was pleasant.

"Yes, very pleasant." Munro nodded, with an odd expression on his face.

The Barawana Forest was not virginal. From time to time, they passed cleared fields and other signs of human habitation, although they never saw farmers. When Elliot mentioned that fact, Munro just shook his head. As they moved deeper into the forest Munro turned self-absorbed, unwilling to talk. Yet he showed an interest in the fauna, frequently pausing to listen intently to bird cries before signaling the expedition to continue on.

During these pauses, Elliot would look back down the line of porters with loads balanced on their heads, and feel acutely his kinship with Livingstone and Stanley and the other explorers who had ventured through Africa a century before. And in this, his romantic associations were accurate. Central African life was little changed since Stanley explored the Congo in the 1870s, and neither was the basic nature of expeditions to that region. Serious exploration was still carried out on foot; porters were still necessary; expenses were still daunting—and so were the dangers.

By midday, Elliot's boots had begun to hurt his feet, and he found that he was exceedingly tired. Apparently the porters were tired too, because they had fallen silent, no longer smoking cigarettes and shouting jokes to one another up and down the line. The expedition proceeded in silence until Elliot asked Munro if they were going to stop for lunch.

"No," Munro said.

"Good," Karen Ross said, glancing at her watch.

Shortly after one o'clock, they heard the thumping of helicopters. The reaction of Munro and the porters was immediate—they dived under a stand of large trees and waited, looking upwards. Moments later, two large green helicopters passed overhead; Elliot clearly read white stenciling: "FZA."

Munro squinted at the departing craft. They were American-made Hueys; he had not been able to see the armament. "It's the army," he said. "They're looking for Kigani."

An hour later, they arrived at a clearing where manioc was being grown. A crude wooden farmhouse stood in the center, with pale smoke issuing from a chimney and laundry on a wash line flapping in the gentle breeze. But they saw no inhabitants.

The expedition had circled around previous farm clearings, but this time Munro raised his hand to call for a halt. The porters dropped their loads and sat in the grass, not speaking.

The atmosphere was tense, although Elliot could not understand why. Munro squatted with Kahega at the edge of the clearing, watching the farmhouse and the surrounding fields. After twenty minutes, when there was still no sign of movement, Ross, who was crouched near Munro, became impatient. "I don't see why we are—"

Munro clapped his hand over her mouth. He pointed to the clearing, and mouthed one word: Kigani.

Ross's eyes went wide. Munro took his hand away.

They all stared at the farmhouse. Still there was no sign of life. Ross made a circular movement with her arm, suggesting that they circle around the clearing and move on. Munro shook his head, and pointed to the ground, indicating that she should sit. Munro looked questioningly at Elliot, and pointed to Amy, who foraged in the tall grass off to one side. He seemed to be concerned that Amy would make noise. Elliot signed to Amy to be quiet, but it was not necessary. Amy had sensed the general tension, and glanced warily from time to time toward the farmhouse.

Nothing happened for several more minutes; they listened to the buzz of the cicadas in the hot midday sun, and they waited. They watched the laundry flutter in the breeze.

Then the thin wisp of blue smoke from the chimney stopped.

Munro and Kahega exchanged glances. Kahega slipped back to where the porters sat, opened one load, and brought out a machine gun. He covered the safety with his hand, muffling the click as he released it. It was incredibly quiet in the clearing. Kahega resumed his place next to Munro and handed him the gun. Munro checked the safety, then set the gun on the ground. They waited several minutes more. Elliot looked at Ross but she was not looking at him.

There was a soft creak as the farmhouse door opened. Munro picked up the machine gun.

No one came out. They all stared at the open door, waiting. And then finally the Kigani stepped into the sunlight.

Elliot counted twelve tall muscular men armed with bows and arrows, and carrying long *pangas* in their hands. Their legs and chests were streaked with white, and their faces were solid white, which gave their heads a menacing, skull-like appearance. As the Kigani moved off through the tall manioc, only their white heads were visible, looking around tensely.

Even after they were gone, Munro remained watching the silent clearing for another ten minutes. Finally he stood and sighed. When he spoke, his voice seemed incredibly loud. "Those were Kigani," Munro said.

"What were they doing?" Ross said.

"Eating," Munro said. "They killed the family in that house, and then ate them. Most farmers have left, because the Kigani are on the rampage."

He signaled Kahega to get the men moving again, and they set off, skirting around the clearing. Elliot kept looking at the farmhouse, wondering what he would see if he went inside. Munro's statement had been so casual; *They killed the family . . . and then ate them.*

"I suppose," Ross said, looking over her shoulder, "that we should consider ourselves lucky. We're probably among the last people in the world to see these things."

Munro shook his head. "I doubt it," he said. "Old habits die hard."

During the Congolese civil war in the 1960s, reports of widespread cannibalism and other atrocities shocked the Western world. But in fact cannibalism had always been openly practiced in central Africa.

In 1897, Sidney Hinde wrote that "nearly all the tribes in the Congo Basin either are, or have been, cannibals; and among some of them the practice is on the increase." Hinde was impressed by the undisguised nature of Congolese cannibalism: "The captains of steamers have often assured me that whenever they try to buy goats from the natives, slaves are demanded in exchange; the natives often come aboard with tusks of ivory with the intention of buying a slave, complaining that *meat is now scarce in their neighborhood.*"

In the Congo, cannibalism was not associated with ritual or religion or war; it was a simple dietary preference. The Reverend Holman Bentley, who spent twenty years in the region, quoted a native as saying, "You white men consider pork to be the tastiest of meat, but pork is not to be compared with human flesh." Bentley felt that the natives "could not understand the objections raised to the practice. 'You eat fowls and goats, and we eat men; why not? What is the difference?' "

This frank attitude astonished observers, and led to bizarre customs. In 1910, Herbert Ward wrote of markets where slaves were sold "piecemeal whilst still alive. Incredible as it may appear, captives are led from place to place in order that individuals may have the opportunity of indicating, by external marks on the body, the portion they desire to acquire. The distinguishing marks are generally made by means of coloured clay or strips of grass tied in a peculiar fashion. The astounding stoicism of the victims, who thus witness the bargaining for their limbs piecemeal, is only equalled by the callousness with which they walk forward to meet their fate."

Such reports cannot be dismissed as late-Victorian hysteria, for all observers found the cannibals likable and sympathetic. Ward wrote that "the cannibals are not schemers and they are not mean. In direct opposition to all natural conjectures, they are among the best types of men." Bentley described them as "merry, manly fellows, very friendly in conversation and quite demonstrative in their affection."

Under Belgian colonial administration, cannibalism became much rarer—by the 1950s, there were even a few graveyards to be found—but no one seriously thought it had been eradicated. In 1956, H. C. Engert wrote, "Cannibalism is far from being dead in Africa. . . . I myself once lived in a cannibal village for a time, and found some [human] bones. The natives . . . were pleasant enough people. It was just an old custom which dies hard."

Munro considered the 1979 Kigani uprising a political insurrection. The tribesmen were rebelling against the demand by the Zaire government that the Kigani change from hunting to farming, as if that were a simple matter. The Kigani were a poor and backward people; their knowledge of hygiene was rudimentary, their diet lacked proteins and vitamins, and they were prey to malaria, hookworm, bilharzia, and African sleeping sickness. One child in four died at birth, and few Kigani adults lived past the age of twenty-five. The hardships of their life required explanation, supplied by Angawa, or sorcerers. The Kigani believed that most deaths were super-natural: either the victim was under a sorcerer's spell, had broken some taboo, or was killed by vengeful spirits from the dead. Hunting also had a supernatural aspect: game was strongly influenced by the spirit world. In fact, the Kigani considered the supernatural world far more real than the day-to-day world, which they felt to be a "waking dream," and they attempted to control the supernatural through magical spells and potions, provided by the Angawa. They also car-ried out ritual body alterations, such as painting the face and hands white, to render an individual more powerful in battle. The Kigani believed that magic also resided in the bodies of their adversaries, and so to overcome spells cast by other Angawa they ate the bodies of their enemies. The magical power invested in the enemy thus became their own, frus-trating enemy sorcerers.

These beliefs were very old, and the Kigani had long since settled on a pattern of response to threat, which was to eat other human beings. In 1890, they went on the rampage in the north, following the first visits by foreigners bearing fire-arms, which had frightened off the game. During the civil war in 1961, starving, they attacked and ate other tribes.

"And why are they eating people now?" Elliot asked Munro.

"They want their right to hunt," Munro said. "Despite the Kinshasa bureaucrats."

In the early afternoon, the expedition mounted a hill from which they could overlook the valleys behind them to the south. In the distance they saw great billowing clouds of smoke and licking flames; there were the muffled explosions of air-to-ground rockets, and the helicopters wheeling like mechanical vultures over a kill.

"Those are Kigani villages," Munro said, looking back, shaking his head. "They haven't a prayer, especially since the men in those helicopters and the troops on the ground are all from the Abawe tribe, the traditional enemy of the Kigani."

The twentieth-century world did not accommodate man-eating beliefs; indeed, the government in Kinshasa, two thousand miles away, had already decided to "expunge the embarrassment" of cannibals within its borders. In June, the Zaire government dispatched five thousand armed troops, six rocket-armed American UH-2 helicopters, and ten armored personnel carriers to put down the Kigani rebellion. The military leader in charge, General Ngo Muguru, had no illusions about his directive. Muguru knew that Kinshasa wanted him to eliminate the Kigani as a tribe. And he intended to do exactly that.

During the rest of the day, they heard distant explosions of mortar and rockets. It was impossible not to contrast the modernity of this equipment with the bows and arrows of the Kigani they had seen. Ross said it was sad, but Munro replied that it was inevitable.

"The purpose of life," Munro said, "is to stay alive. Watch any animal in nature—all it tries to do is stay alive. It doesn't care about beliefs or philosophy. Whenever any animal's behavior puts it out of touch with the realities of its existence, it becomes extinct. The Kigani haven't seen that times have changed and their beliefs don't work. And they're going to be extinct."

"Maybe there is a higher truth than merely staying alive," Ross said.

"There isn't," Munro said.

They saw several other parties of Kigani, usually from a distance of many miles. At the end of the day, after they had crossed the swaying wooden bridge over the Moruti Gorge, Munro announced that they were now beyond the Kigani territory and, at least for the time being, safe.

3. Moruti Camp

IN A HIGH CLEARING ABOVE MORUTI, THE "PLACE of soft winds," Munro shouted Swahili instructions and Kahega's porters began to unpack their loads. Karen Ross looked at her watch. "Are we stopping?"

"Yes," Munro said.

"But it's only five o'clock. There's still two hours of light left."

"We stop here," Munro said. Moruti was located at 1,500 feet; another two hours' walking would put them down in the rain forest below. "It's much cooler and more pleasant here."

Ross said that she did not care about pleasantness.

"You will," Munro said.

To make the best time, Munro intended to keep out of the rain forest wherever possible. Progress in the jungle was slow and uncomfortable; they would have more than enough experience with mud and leeches and fevers.

Kahega called to him in Swahili; Munro turned to Ross and said, "Kahega wants to know how to pitch the tents."

Kahega was holding a crumpled silver ball of fabric in his outstretched hand; the other porters were just as confused, rummaging through their loads, looking for familiar tent poles or stakes, finding none.

The ERTS camp had been designed under contract by a NASA team in 1977, based on the recognition that wilderness expedition equipment was fundamentally unchanged since the eighteenth century. "Designs for modern exploration are long overdue," ERTS said, and asked for state-of-the-art improvements in lightness, comfort, and efficiency of

151

expedition gear. NASA had redesigned everything, from clothing and boots to tents and cooking gear, food and menus, first-aid kits, and communications systems for ERTS wilderness parties.

The redesigned tents were typical of the NASA approach. NASA had determined that tent weight consisted chiefly of the structural supports. In addition, single-ply tents were poorly insulated. If tents could be properly insulated, clothing and sleeping-bag weight could be reduced, as could the daily caloric requirements of expedition members. Since air was an excellent insulator, the obvious solution was an unsupported, pneumatic tent: NASA designed one that weighed six ounces.

Using a little hissing foot pump, Ross inflated the first tent. It was made from double-layer silvered Mylar, and looked like a gleaming ribbed Quonset hut. The porters clapped their hands with delight; Munro shook his head, amused; Kahega produced a small silver unit, the size of a shoebox. "And this, Doctor? What is this?"

"We won't need that tonight. That's an air conditioner," Ross said.

"Never go anywhere without one," Munro said, still amused.

Ross glared at him. "Studies show," she said, "that the single greatest factor limiting work efficiency is ambient temperature, with sleep deprivation as the second factor."

"Really."

Munro laughed and looked to Elliot, but Elliot was studiously examining the view of the rain forest in the evening sun. Amy came up and tugged at his sleeve.

Woman and nosehair man fight, she signed.

Amy had liked Munro from the beginning, and the feeling was mutual. Instead of patting her on the head and treating her like a child, as most people did, Munro instinctively treated her like a female. Then, too, he had been around enough gorillas to have a feeling for their behavior. Although he didn't know ASL, when Amy raised her arms, he understood that she wanted to be tickled, and would oblige her for a few moments, while she rolled grunting with pleasure on the ground.

But Amy was always distressed by conflict, and she was frowning now. "They're just talking," Elliot assured her.

She signed, *Amy want eat.*

"In a minute." Turning back, he saw Ross setting up the transmitting equipment; this would be a daily ritual during the rest of the expedition, and one which never failed to fascinate Amy. Altogether, the equipment to send a transmission ten thousand miles by satellite weighed six pounds, and the electronic countermeasures, or ECM devices, weighed an additional three pounds.

First, Ross popped open the collapsed umbrella of the silver dish antenna, five feet in diameter. (Amy particularly liked this; as each day progressed, she would ask Ross when she would "open metal flower.") Then Ross attached the transmitter box, plugging in the krylon-cadmium fuel cells. Next she linked the anti-jamming modules, and finally she hooked up the miniaturized computer terminal with its tiny keyboard and three-inch video screen.

This miniature equipment was highly sophisticated. Ross's computer had a 189K memory and all circuitry was redundant; housings were hermetically sealed and shockproof; even the keyboard was impedance-operated, so there were no moving parts to get gummed up, or admit water or dust.

And it was incredibly rugged. Ross remembered their "field tests." In the ERTS parking lot, technicians would throw new equipment against the wall, kick it across the concrete, and leave it in a bucket of muddy water overnight. Anything found working the next day was certified as field-worthy.

Now, in the sunset at Moruti, she punched in code coordinates to lock the transmission to Houston, checked signal strength, and waited the six minutes until the transponders matched up. But the little screen continued to show only gray static, with intermittent pulses of color. That meant someone was jamming them with a "symphony."

In ERTS slang, the simplest level of electronic jamming was called "tuba." Like a kid next door practicing his tuba, this jamming was merely annoying; it occurred within limited frequencies, and was often random or accidental, but transmissions could generally pass through it. At the next level was "string quartet," where multiple frequencies were jammed in an orderly fashion; next was "big band," where the electronic music covered a wider frequency range; and finally "symphony," where virtually the full transmission range was blocked.

Ross was now getting hit by a "symphony." To break through demanded coordination with Houston—which she was unable to arrange—but ERTS had several prearranged routines. She tried them one after another and finally broke the jamming with a technique called interstitial coding. (Interstitial coding utilized the fact that even dense music had periods of silence, or interstices, lasting microseconds. It was possible to monitor the jamming signals, identify regularities in the interstices, and then transmit in bursts during the silences.)

Ross was gratified to see the little screen glow in a multicolored image—a map of their position in the Congo. She punched in the field position lock, and a light blinked on the screen. Words appeared in "shortline," the compressed language devised for small-screen imagery. FILD TME-POSITN CHEK; PLS CONFRM LOCL TME 18:04 H 6/17/79. She confirmed that it was indeed just after 6 P.M. at their location. Immediately, overlaid lines produced a scrambled pattern as their Field Time-Position was measured against the computer simulation run in Houston before their departure.

Ross was prepared for bad news. According to her mental calculations, they had fallen some seventy-odd hours behind their projected timeline, and some twenty-odd hours behind the consortium.

Their original plan had called for them to jump onto the slopes of Mukenko at 2 P.M. on June 17, arriving at Zinj approximately thirty-six hours later, around midday of June 19. This would have put them onsite nearly two days before the consortium.

However, the SAM attack forced them to jump eighty

miles south of their intended drop zone. The jungle terrain before them was varied, and they could expect to pick up time rafting on rivers, but it would still take a minimum of three days to go eighty miles.

That meant that they could no longer expect to beat the consortium to the site. Instead of arriving forty-eight hours ahead, they would be lucky if they arrived only twenty-four hours too late.

To her surprise, the screen blinked: FILD TME-POSITN CHEK:-09:04 H WEL DUN. They were only nine hours off their simulation timeline.

"What does that mean?" Munro asked, looking at the screen.

There was only one possible conclusion. "Something has slowed the consortium," Ross said.

On the screen they read EURO / NIPON CONSRTIM LEGL TRUBL GOMA AIRPRT ZAIR THEIR AIRCRFT FOUND RA-DIOACTIVE TUF LUK FOR THEM.

"Travis has been working back in Houston," Ross said. She could imagine what it must have cost ERTS to put in the fix at the rural airport in Goma. "But it means we can still do it, if we can make up the nine hours."

"We can do it," Munro said.

In the light of the setting equatorial sun, Moruti camp gleamed like a cluster of dazzling jewels—a silver dish antenna, and five silver-domed tents, all reflecting the fiery sun. Peter Elliot sat on the hilltop with Amy and stared at the rain forest spread out below them. As night fell, the first hazy strands of mist appeared; and as the darkness deepened and water vapor condensed in the cooling air, the forest became shrouded in dense, darkening fog.

DAY 6: LIKO

June 18, 1979

1. Rain Forest

THE NEXT MORNING THEY ENTERED THE HUMID perpetual gloom of the Congo rain forest.

Munro noted the return of old feelings of oppression and claustrophobia, tinged with a strange, overpowering lassitude. As a Congo mercenary in the 1960s, he had avoided the jungle wherever possible. Most military engagements had occurred in open spaces—in the Belgian colonial towns, along riverbanks, beside the red dirt roads. Nobody wanted to fight in the jungle; the mercenaries hated it, and the superstitious Simbas feared it. When the mercenaries advanced, the rebels often fled into the bush, but they never went very far, and Munro's troops never pursued them. They just waited for them to come out again.

Even in the 1960s the jungle remained *terra incognita*, an unknown land with the power to hold the technology of mechanized warfare beyond its periphery. And with good reason, Munro thought. Men just did not belong there. He was not pleased to be back.

Elliot, never having been in a rain forest, was fascinated. The jungle was different from the way he had imagined it to be. He was totally unprepared for the scale—the gigantic trees soaring over his head, the trunks as broad as a house, the thick snaking moss-covered roots. To move in the vast space beneath these trees was like being in a very dark cathedral: the sun was completely blocked, and he could not get an exposure reading on his camera.

He had also expected the jungle to be much denser than it was. Their party moved through it freely; in a surprising way it seemed barren and silent—there were occasional birdcalls

159

and cries from monkeys, but otherwise a profound stillness settled over them. And it was oddly monotonous: although he saw every shade of green in the foliage and the clinging creeper vines, there were few flowers or blooms. Even the occasional orchids seemed pale and muted.

He had expected rotting decay at every turn, but that was not true either. The ground underfoot was often firm, and the air had a neutral smell. But it was incredibly hot, and it seemed as though everything was wet—the leaves, the ground, the trunks of the trees, the oppressively still air itself, trapped under the overhanging trees.

Elliot would have agreed with Stanley's description from a century before: "Overhead the wide-spreading branches absolutely shut out the daylight. . . . We marched in a feeble twilight. . . . The dew dropped and pattered on us incessantly. . . . Our clothes were heavily saturated with it. . . . Perspiration exuded from every pore, for the atmosphere was stifling. . . . What a forbidding aspect had the Dark Unknown which confronted us!"

Because Elliot had looked forward to his first experience of the equatorial African rain forest, he was surprised at how quickly he felt oppressed—and how soon he entertained thoughts of leaving again. Yet the tropical rain forests had spawned most new life forms, including man. The jungle was not one uniform environment but many different microenvironments, arranged vertically like a layer cake. Each microenvironment supported a bewildering profusion of plant and animal life, but there were typically few members of each species. The tropical jungle supported four times as many species of animal life as a comparable temperate forest. As he walked through the forest, Elliot found himself thinking of it as an enormous hot, dark womb, a place where new species were nourished in unchanging conditions until they were ready to migrate out to the harsher and more variable temperate zones. That was the way it had been for millions of years.

Amy's behavior immediately changed as she entered the vast humid darkness of her original home. In retrospect, Elliot believed he could have predicted her reaction, had he thought it through clearly.

Amy no longer kept up with the group.

She insisted on foraging along the trail, pausing to sit and chew tender shoots and grasses. She could not be budged or hurried, and ignored Elliot's requests that she stay with them. She ate lazily, a pleasant, rather vacant expression on her face. In shafts of sunlight, she would lie on her back, and belch, and sigh contentedly.

"What the hell is this all about?" Ross asked, annoyed. They were not making good time.

"She's become a gorilla again," Elliot said. "Gorillas are vegetarians, and they spend nearly all day eating; they're large animals, and they need a lot of food." Amy had immediately reverted to these traits.

"Well, can't you make her keep up with us?"

"I'm trying. She won't pay attention to me." And he knew why—Amy was finally back in a world where Peter Elliot was irrelevant, where she herself could find food and security and shelter, and everything else that she wanted.

"School's out," Munro said, summarizing the situation. But he had a solution. "Leave her," he said crisply, and he led the party onward. He took Elliot firmly by the elbow. "Don't look back," he said. "Just walk on. Ignore her."

They continued for several minutes in silence.

Elliot said, "She may not follow us."

"Come, come, Professor," Munro said. "I thought you knew about gorillas."

"I do," Elliot said.

"Then you know there are none in this part of the rain forest."

Elliot nodded; he had seen no nests or spoor. "But she has everything she needs here."

"Not everything," Munro said. "Not without other gorillas around."

Like all higher primates, gorillas were social animals. They lived in a group, and they were not comfortable—or safe—in isolation. In fact, most primatologists assumed that there was a need for social contact as strongly perceived as hunger, thirst, or fatigue.

"We're her troop," Munro said. "She won't let us get far."

Several minutes later, Amy came crashing through the underbrush fifty yards ahead. She watched the group, and glared at Peter.

"Now come here, Amy," Munro said, "and I'll tickle you." Amy bounded up and lay on her back in front of him. Munro tickled her.

"You see, Professor? Nothing to it."

Amy never strayed far from the group again.

If Elliot had an uncomfortable sense of the rain forest as the natural domain of his own animal, Karen Ross viewed it in terms of earth resources—in which it was poor. She was not fooled by the luxuriant, oversized vegetation, which she knew represented an extraordinarily efficient ecosystem built in virtually barren soil.*

The developing nations of the world did not understand this fact; once cleared, the jungle soil yielded disappointing crops. Yet the rain forests were being cleared at the incredible rate of fifty acres a minute, day and night. The rain forests of the world had circled the equator in a green belt for at least sixty million years—but man would have cleared them within twenty years.

This widespread destruction had caused some alarm Ross did not share. She doubted that the world climate would change or the atmospheric oxygen be reduced. Ross was not an alarmist, and not impressed by the calculations of those who were. The only reason she felt uneasy was that the forest was so little understood. A clearing rate of fifty acres a minute meant that plant and animal species were becoming extinct at the incredible rate of *one species per hour*. Life forms that had evolved for millions of years were being wiped out

---

* The rain forest ecosystem is an energy utilization complex far more efficient than any energy conversion system developed by man. See C. F. Higgins et al., *Energy Resources and Ecosystem Utilization* (Englewood Cliffs, N.J.: Prentice Hall, 1977), pp. 232–255.

every few minutes, and no one could predict the consequences of this stupendous rate of destruction. The extinction of species was proceeding much faster than anybody recognized, and the publicized lists of "endangered" species told only a fraction of the story; the disaster extended all the way down the animal phyla to insects, worms, and mosses.

The reality was that entire ecosystems were being destroyed by man without a care or a backward glance. And these ecosystems were for the most part mysterious, poorly understood. Karen Ross felt herself plunged into a world entirely different from the exploitable world of mineral resources; this was an environment in which plant life reigned supreme. It was no wonder, she thought, that the Egyptians called this the Land of Trees. The rain forest provided a hothouse environment for plant life, an environment in which gigantic plants were much superior to—and much favored over—mammals, including the insignificant human mammals who were now picking their way through its perpetual darkness.

The Kikuyu porters had an immediate reaction to the forest: they began to laugh and joke and make as much noise as possible. Ross said to Kahega, "They certainly are jolly."

"Oh, no," Kahega said. "They are warning."

"Warning?"

Kahega explained that the men made noise to warn off the buffalo and leopards. And the *tembo*, he added, pointing to the trail.

"Is this a *tembo* trail?" she asked.

Kahega nodded.

"The *tembo* live nearby?"

Kahega laughed. "I hope no," Kahega said. "*Tembo*. Elephant."

"So this is a game trail. Will we see elephants?"

"Maybe yes, maybe no," Kahega said. "I hope no. They are very big, elephants."

There was no arguing with his logic. Ross said, "They

tell me these are your brothers," nodding down the line of
porters.

"Yes, they are my brothers."

"Ah."

"But you mean that my brothers, we have the same
mother?"

"Yes, you have the same mother."

"No," Kahega said.

Ross was confused. "You are not real brothers?"

"Yes, we are real brothers. But we do not have the same
mother."

"Then why are you brothers?"

"Because we live in the same village."

"With your father and mother?"

Kahega looked shocked. *"No,"* he said emphatically.
"Not the same village."

"A different village, then?"

"Yes, of course—we are Kikuyu."

Ross was perplexed. Kahega laughed.

Kahega offered to carry the electronic equipment that Ross
had slung over her shoulder, but she declined. Ross was
obliged to try and link up with Houston at intervals throughout the day, and at noon she found a clear window, probably
because the consortium jamming operator took a break for
lunch. She managed to link through and register another Field
Time–Position.

The console read: F I L D T M E – P O S I T N C H E K – 1 0 : 0 3 H

They had lost nearly an hour since the previous check the
night before. "We've got to go faster," she told Munro.

"Perhaps you'd prefer to jog," Munro said. "Very good
exercise." And then, because he decided he was being too
hard on her, he added, "A lot can happen between here and
Virunga."

They heard the distant growl of thunder and minutes later
were drenched in a torrential rain, the drops so dense and
heavy that they actually hurt. The rain fell solidly for the next
hour, then stopped as abruptly as it had begun. They were

all soaked and miserable, and when Munro called a halt for food, Ross did not protest.

Amy promptly went off into the forest to forage; the porters cooked curried meat gravy on rice; Munro, Ross, and Elliot burned leeches off their legs with cigarettes. The leeches were swollen with blood. "I didn't even notice them," Ross said.

"Rain makes 'em worse," Munro said. Then he looked up sharply, glancing at the jungle.

"Something wrong?"

"No, nothing," Munro said, and he went into an explanation of why leeches had to be burned off; if they were pulled off, a part of the head remained lodged in the flesh and caused an infection.

Kahega brought them food, and Munro said in a low voice, "Are the men all right?"

"Yes," Kahega said. "The men are all right. They will not be afraid."

"Afraid of what?" Elliot said.

"Keep eating. Just be natural," Munro said.

Elliot looked nervously around the little clearing.

"Eat!" Munro whispered. "Don't insult them. You're not supposed to know they're here."

The group ate in silence for several minutes. And then the nearby brush rustled and a pygmy stepped out.

2. The Dancers of God

HE WAS A LIGHT-SKINNED MAN ABOUT FOUR AND A half feet tall, barrel-chested, wearing only a loincloth, with a bow and arrow over his shoulder. He looked around the expedition, apparently trying to determine who was the leader.

Munro stood, and said something quickly in a language that was not Swahili. The pygmy replied. Munro gave him one of the cigarettes they had been using to burn off the leeches. The pygmy did not want it lit; instead he dropped it into a small leather pouch attached to his quiver. A brief conversation followed. The pygmy pointed off into the jungle several times.

"He says a white man is dead in their village," Munro said. He picked up his pack, which contained the first-aid kit. "I'll have to hurry."

Ross said, "We can't afford the time."

Munro frowned at her.

"Well, the man's dead anyway."

"He's not *completely* dead," Munro said. "He's not dead-for-ever."

The pygmy nodded vigorously. Munro explained that pygmies graded illness in several stages. First a person was hot, then he was with fever, then ill, then dead, then completely dead—and finally dead-for-ever.

From the bush, three more pygmies appeared. Munro nodded. "Knew he wasn't alone," he said. "These chaps never are alone. Hate to travel alone. The others were watching us; if we'd made a wrong move, we'd get an arrow for our trouble. See those brown tips? Poison."

Yet the pygmies appeared relaxed now—at least until Amy came crashing back through the underbrush. Then there were shouts and swiftly drawn bows; Amy was terrified and ran to Peter, jumping up on him and clutching his chest—and making him thoroughly muddy.

The pygmies engaged in a lively discussion among themselves, trying to decide what Amy's arrival meant. Several questions were asked of Munro. Finally, Elliot set Amy back down on the ground and said to Munro, "What did you tell them?"

"They wanted to know if the gorilla was yours, and I said yes. They wanted to know if the gorilla was female, and I said yes. They wanted to know if you had relations with the gorilla; I said no. They said that was good, that you should not become too attached to the gorilla, because that would cause you pain.''

"Why pain?"

"They said when the gorilla grows up, she will either run away into the forest and break your heart or kill you.''

Ross still opposed making a detour to the pygmy village, which was several miles away on the banks of the Liko River. "We're behind on our timeline," she said, "and slipping further behind every minute.''

For the first and last time during the expedition, Munro lost his temper. "Listen, Doctor," he said, "this isn't downtown Houston, this is the middle of the goddamn Congo and it's no place to be injured. We have medicines. That man may need it. You don't leave him behind. You just don't.''

"If we go to that village," Ross said, "we blow the rest of the day. It puts us nine or ten hours further back. Right now we can still make it. With another delay, we won't have a chance.''

One of the pygmies began talking quickly to Munro. He nodded, glancing several times at Ross. Then he turned to the others.

"He says that the sick white man has some writing on his shirt pocket. He's going to draw the writing for us.''

Ross glanced at her watch and sighed.

The pygmy picked up a stick and drew large characters in the muddy earth at their feet. He drew carefully, frowning in concentration as he reproduced the alien symbols: E R T S.

"Oh, God," Ross said softly.

The pygmies did not walk through the forest: they ran at a brisk trot, slipping through the forest vines and branches, dodging rain puddles and gnarled tree roots with deceptive ease. Occasionally they glanced over their shoulders and giggled at the difficulties of the three white people who followed.

For Elliot, it was a difficult pace—a succession of roots to stumble over, tree limbs to strike his head on, thorny vines to tear at his flesh. He was gasping for breath, trying to keep up with the little men who padded effortlessly ahead of him. Ross was doing no better than he, and even Munro, although surprisingly agile, showed signs of fatigue.

Finally they came to a small stream and a sunlit clearing. The pygmies paused on the rocks, squatting and turning their faces up to the sun. The white people collapsed, panting and gasping. The pygmies seemed to find this hilarious, their laughter good-natured.

The pygmies were the earliest human inhabitants of the Congo rain forest. Their small size, distinctive manner, and deft agility had made them famous centuries before. More than four thousand years ago, an Egyptian commander named Herkouf entered the great forest west of the Mountains of the Moon; there he found a race of tiny men who sang and danced to their god. Herkouf's amazing report had the ring of fact, and Herodotus and later Aristotle insisted that these stories of the tiny men were true, and not fabulous. The Dancers of God inevitably acquired mythical trappings as the centuries passed.

As late as the seventeenth century, Europeans remained unsure whether tiny men with tails who had the power to fly through the trees, make themselves invisible, and kill elephants actually existed. That skeletons of chimpanzees were sometimes mistaken for pygmy skeletons added to the confusion. Colin Turnbull notes that many elements of the fable are actually true: the pounded-bark loincloths hang down and look like tails; the pygmies can blend into the forest and become virtually invisible; and they have always hunted and killed elephants.

The pygmies were laughing now as they got to their feet and padded off again. Sighing, the white people struggled up and lumbered after them. They ran for another half hour, never pausing or hesitating, and then Elliot smelled smoke and they came into a clearing beside a stream where the village was located.

He saw ten low rounded huts no more than four feet high, arranged in a semicircle. The villagers were all outside in the afternoon light, the women cleaning mushrooms and ber-

ries picked during the day, or cooking grubs and turtles on
crackling fires; children tottered around, bothering the men
who sat before their houses and smoked tobacco while the
women worked.

At Munro's signal, they waited at the edge of the camp
until they were noticed, and then they were led in. Their
arrival provoked great interest; the children giggled and
pointed; the men wanted tobacco from Munro and Elliot;
the women touched Ross's blonde hair, and argued about it.
A little girl crawled between Ross's legs, peering up her
trousers. Munro explained that the women were uncertain
whether Ross painted her hair, and the girl had taken it upon
herself to settle the question of artifice.

"Tell them it's natural," Ross said, blushing.

Munro spoke briefly to the women. "I told them it was
the color of your father's hair," he told Ross. "But I'm not
sure they believe it." He gave Elliot cigarettes to pass out,
one to each man; they were received with broad smiles and
odd girlish giggles.

Preliminaries concluded, they were taken to a newly constructed house at the far end of the village where the dead
white man was said to be. They found a filthy, bearded man
of thirty, sitting cross-legged in the small doorway, staring
outward. After a moment Elliot realized the man was cata-
tonic—he was not moving at all.

"Oh, my God," Ross said. "It's Bob Driscoll."

"You know him?" Munro said.

"He was a geologist on the first Congo expedition." She
leaned close to him, waved her hand in front of his face.
"Bobby, it's me, Karen. Bobby, what happened to you?"

Driscoll did not respond, did not even blink. He continued
to stare forward.

One of the pygmies offered an explanation to Munro. "He
came into their camp four days ago," Munro said. "He was
wild and they had to restrain him. They thought he had blackwater fever, so they made a house for him and gave him some
medicines, and he was not wild anymore. Now he lets them
feed him, but he never speaks. They think perhaps he was

captured by General Muguru's men and tortured, or else he is *agudu*—a mute.''

Ross moved back in horror.

"I don't see what we can do for him," Munro said. "Not in his condition. Physically he's okay but . . ." He shook his head.

"I'll give Houston the location," Ross said, "and they'll send help from Kinshasa."

During all this, Driscoll never moved. Elliot leaned forward to look at his eyes, and as he approached, Driscoll wrinkled his nose. His body tensed. He broke into a high-pitched wail—"Ah-ah-ah-ah"—like a man about to scream.

Appalled, Elliot backed off, and Driscoll relaxed, falling silent again. "What the hell was that all about?"

One of the pygmies whispered to Munro. "He says," Munro said, "that you smell like gorilla."

3. Ragora

TWO HOURS LATER, THEY WERE REUNITED WITH Kahega and the others, led by a pygmy guide across the rain forest south of Gabutu. They were all sullen, uncommunicative—and suffering from dysentery.

The pygmies had insisted they stay for an early dinner, and Munro felt they had no choice but to accept. The meal was mostly a slender wild potato called *kitsombe*, which looked like a shriveled asparagus; forest onions, called *otsa*; and *modoke*, wild manioc leaves, along with several kinds of mushrooms. There were also small quantities of sour, tough turtle meat and occasional grasshoppers, caterpillars, worms, frogs, and snails.

This diet actually contained twice as much protein by

weight as beefsteak, but it did not sit well on unaccustomed stomachs. Nor was the news around the campfire likely to improve their spirits.

According to the pygmies, General Muguru's men had established a supply camp up at the Makran escarpment, which was where Munro was headed. It seemed wise to avoid the troops. Munro explained there was no Swahili word for chivalry or sportsmanship, and the same was true of the Congolese variant, Lingala. "In this part of the world, it's kill or be killed. We'd best stay away."

Their only alternate route took them west, to the Ragora River. Munro frowned at his map, and Ross frowned at her computer console.

"What's wrong with the Ragora River?" Elliot asked.

"Maybe nothing," Munro said. "Depends on how hard it's rained lately."

Ross glanced at her watch. "We're now twelve hours behind," she said. "The only thing we can do is continue straight through the night on the river."

"I'd do that anyway," Munro said.

Ross had never heard of an expedition guide leading a party through a wilderness area at night. "You would? Why?"

"Because," Munro said, "the obstacles on the lower river will be much easier at night."

"What obstacles?"

"We'll discuss them when we come to them," Munro said.

A mile before they reached the Ragora, they heard the distant roar of powerful water. Amy was immediately anxious, signing *What water?* again and again. Elliot tried to reassure her, but he was not inclined to do much; Amy was going to have to put up with the river, despite her fears.

But when they got to the Ragora they found that the sound came from tumbling cataracts somewhere upstream; directly before them, the river was fifty feet wide and a placid muddy brown.

"Doesn't look too bad," Elliot said.

"No," Munro said, "it doesn't."

But Munro understood about the Congo. The fourth largest river in the world (after the Nile, the Amazon, and the Yangtze) was unique in many ways. It twisted like a giant snake across the face of Africa, twice crossing the equator—the first time going north, toward Kisangani, and later going south, at Mbandaka. This fact was so remarkable that even a hundred years ago geographers did not believe it was true. Because the Congo flowed both north and south of the equator, there was always a rainy season somewhere along its path; the river was not subject to the seasonal fluctuations that characterized rivers such as the Nile. The Congo poured a steady 1,500,000 cubic feet of water every second into the Atlantic Ocean, a flow greater than any river except the Amazon.

But this tortuous course also made the Congo the least navigable of the great rivers. Serious disruptions began with the rapids of Stanley Pool, three hundred miles from the Atlantic. Two thousand miles inland, at Kisangani, where the river was still a mile wide, the Wagenia Cataract blocked all navigation. And as one moved farther upriver along the fan of tributaries, the impediments became even more pronounced, for above Kisangani the tributaries were descending rapidly into the low jungle from their sources—the highland savannahs to the south, and the 16,000-foot snowcapped Ruwenzori Mountains to the east.

The tributaries cut a series of gorges, the most striking of which was the Portes d'Enfer—the Gates of Hell—at Kongolo. Here the placid Lualaba River funneled through a gorge half a mile deep and a hundred yards wide.

The Ragora was a minor tributary of the Lualaba, which it joined near Kisangani. The tribes along the river referred to it as *baratawani*, "the deceitful road," for the Ragora was notoriously changeable. Its principal feature was the Ragora Gorge, a limestone cut two hundred feet deep and in places only ten feet wide. Depending on recent rainfall, the Ragora Gorge was either a pleasant scenic spectacle or a boiling whitewater nightmare.

At Abutu, they were still fifteen miles upriver from the

gorge, and conditions on the river told them nothing about conditions within the gorge. Munro knew all that, but he did not feel it necessary to explain it to Elliot, particularly since at the moment Elliot was fully occupied with Amy.

Amy had watched with growing uneasiness as Kahega's men inflated the two Zodiac rafts. She tugged Elliot's sleeve and demanded to know *What balloons?*

"They're boats, Amy," he said, although he sensed she had already figured that out, and was being euphemistic. "Boat" was a word she had learned with difficulty; since she disliked water, she had no interest in anything intended to ride upon it.

Why boat? she asked.

"We ride boat now," Elliot said.

Indeed, Kahega's men were pushing the boats to the edge of the water, and loading the equipment on, lashing it to the rubber stanchions at the gunwales.

Who ride? she asked.

"We all ride," Elliot said.

Amy watched a moment longer. Unfortunately, everyone was nervous, Munro barking orders, the men working hastily. As she had often shown, Amy was sensitive to the moods of those around her. Elliot always remembered how she had insisted that something was wrong with Sarah Johnson for days before Sarah finally told the Project Amy staff that she had split up with her husband. Now Elliot was certain that Amy sensed their apprehension. *Cross water in boat?* she asked.

"No, Amy," he said. "Not cross. Ride boat."

No, Amy signed, stiffening her back, tightening her shoulders.

"Amy," he said, "we can't leave you here."

She had a solution for that. *Other people go. Peter stay Amy.*

"I'm sorry, Amy," he said. "I have to go. You have to go."

No, she signed. *Amy no go.*

"Yes, Amy." He went to his pack and got his syringe and a bottle of Thoralen.

With her body stiff and angry, she tapped the underside of her chin with a clenched fist.

"Watch your language, Amy," he warned her.

Ross came over with orange life vests for him and Amy. "Something wrong?"

"She's swearing," Elliot said. "Better leave us alone." Ross took one look at Amy's tense, rigid body, and left hurriedly.

Amy signed Peter's name, then tapped the underside of her chin again. This was the Ameslan sign politely translated in scholarly reports as "dirty," although it was most often employed by apes when they needed to go to the potty. Primate investigators were under no illusions about what the animals really meant. Amy was saying, *Peter shitty.*

Nearly all language-skilled primates swore, and they employed a variety of words for swearing. Sometimes the pejorative seemed to be chosen at random, "nut" or "bird" or "wash." But at least eight primates in different laboratories had independently settled on the clenched-fist sign to signify extreme displeasure. The only reason this remarkable coincidence hadn't been written up was that no investigator was willing to try and explain it. It seemed to prove that apes, like people, found bodily excretions suitable terms to express denigration and anger.

Peter shitty, she signed again.

"Amy . . ." He doubled the Thoralen dose he was drawing into the syringe.

Peter shitty boat shitty people shitty.

"Amy, cut it out." He stiffened his own body and hunched over, imitating a gorilla's angry posture; that often made her back off, but this time it had no effect.

Peter no like Amy. Now she was sulking, turned away from him, signing to nobody.

"Don't be ridiculous," Elliot said, approaching her with the syringe held ready. "Peter like Amy."

She backed away and would not let him come close to her. In the end he was forced to load the CO_2 gun and shoot a dart into her chest. He had only done this three or four times in all their years together. She plucked out the dart with a sad expression. *Peter no like Amy.*

"Sorry," Peter Elliot said, and ran forward to catch her as her eyes rolled back and she collapsed into his arms.

Amy lay on her back in the second boat at Elliot's feet, breathing shallowly. Ahead, Elliot saw Munro standing in the first boat, leading the way as the Zodiacs slid silently downstream.

Munro had divided the expedition into two rafts of six each; Munro went in the first, and Elliot, Ross, and Amy went in the second, under Kahega's command. As Munro put it, the second boat would "learn from our misfortunes."

But for the first two hours on the Ragora, there were no misfortunes. It was an extraordinarily peaceful experience to sit in the front of the boat and watch the jungle on both sides of the river glide past them in timeless, hypnotic silence. It was idyllic, and very hot; Ross began to trail her hand over the side in the muddy water, until Kahega put a stop to it.

"Where there is water, there is always *mamba*," he said.

Kahega pointed to the muddy banks, where crocodiles basked in the sunshine, indifferent to their approach. Occasionally one of the huge reptiles yawned, lifting jagged jaws into the air, but for the most part they seemed sluggish, hardly noticing the boats.

Elliot was secretly disappointed. He had grown up on the jungle movies where the crocodiles slithered menacingly into the water at the first approach of boats. "Aren't they going to bother us?" he asked.

"Too hot," Kahega said. "*Mamba* sleepy except at cool times, eat morning and night, not now. In daytime, Kikuyu say *mamba* have joined army, one-two-three-four." And he laughed.

It took some explaining before it was clear that Kahega's tribesmen had noticed that during the day the crocodiles did pushups, periodically lifting their heavy bodies off the ground on their stubby legs in a movement that reminded Kahega of army calisthenics.

"What is Munro so worried about?" Elliot asked. "The crocodiles?"

"No," Kahega said.

"The Ragora Gorge?"

"No," Kahega said.

"Then what?"

"*After* the gorge," Kahega said.

Now the Ragora twisted, and they came around a bend, and they heard the growing roar of the water. Elliot felt the boat gathering speed, the water rippling along the rubber gunwales. Kahega shouted, "Hold fast, Doctors!"

And they were into the gorge.

Afterward, Elliot had only fragmented, kaleidoscopic impressions: the churning muddy water that boiled white in the sunlight; the erratic wrenching of his own boat, and the way Munro's boat up ahead seemed to reel and upend, yet miraculously remain upright.

They were moving so fast it was hard to focus on the passing blur of craggy red canyon walls, bare rock except for sparse green clinging scrub; the hot humid air and the shockingly cold muddy water that smashed over them, drenching them time and again; the pure white surge of water boiling around the black protruding rocks, like the bald heads of drowned men.

Everything was happening too fast.

Ahead, Munro's boat was often lost from sight for minutes at a time, concealed by giant standing waves of leaping, roaring muddy water. The roar echoed off the rock walls, reverberating, becoming a constant feature of their world; in the depths of the gorge, where the afternoon sun did not reach the narrow strip of dark water, the boats moved through a rushing, churning inferno, careening off rocky walls, spinning end around end, while the boatmen shouted and cursed and fended off the rock walls with paddles.

Amy lay on her back, lashed to the side of the boat, and Elliot was in constant fear that she would drown from the muddy waves that crashed over the gunwales. Not that Ross was doing much better; she kept repeating "Oh my God oh

my God oh my God" over and over, in a low monotone, as
the water smashed down on them in successive waves, soaking them to the skin.

Other indignities were forced upon them by nature. Even
in the boiling, pounding heart of the gorge, black clouds of
mosquitoes hung in the air, stinging them again and again.
Somehow it did not seem possible that there could be mosquitoes in the midst of the roaring chaos of the Ragora Gorge,
but they were there. The boats moved with gut-wrenching
fury through the standing waves, and in the growing darkness
the passengers baled out the boats and slapped at the mosquitoes with equal intensity.

And then suddenly the river broadened, the muddy water
slowed, and the walls of the canyon moved apart. The river
became peaceful again. Elliot slumped back in the boat, exhausted, feeling the fading sun on his face and the water
moving beneath the inflated rubber of the boat.

"We made it," he said.

"So far," Kahega said. "But we Kikuyu say no one es-
capes from life alive. No relaxing now, Doctors!"

"Somehow," Ross said wearily, "I believe him."

They drifted gently downstream for another hour, and the
rock walls receded farther away on each side, until finally
they were in flat African rain forest once more. It was as if
the Ragora Gorge had never existed; the river was wide and
sluggish gold in the descending sun.

Elliot stripped off his soaking shirt and changed it for a
pullover, for the evening air was chilly. Amy snored at his
feet, covered with a towel so she would not get too cold.
Ross checked her transmitting equipment, making sure it
was all right. When she was finished, the sun had set and it
was rapidly growing dark. Kahega broke out a shotgun and
inserted yellow stubby shells.

"What's that for?" Elliot said.

"*Kiboko,*" Kahega said. "I do not know the word in English." He shouted, *"Mzee! Nini maana kiboko?"*

In the lead boat, Munro glanced back. "Hippopotamus,"
he said.

"Hippo," Kahega said.

"Are they dangerous?" Elliot asked.

"At night, we hope no," Kahega said. "But me, I think yes."

The twentieth century had been a period of intensive wild-life study, which overturned many long-standing conceptions about animals. It was now recognized that the gentle, soft-eyed deer actually lived in a ruthless, nasty society, while the supposedly vicious wolf was devoted to family and off-spring in exemplary fashion. And the African lion—the proud king of beasts—was relegated to the status of slinking scav-enger, while the loathed hyena assumed new dignity. (For decades, observers had come upon a dawn kill to find lions feeding on the carcass, while the scavenging hyenas circled at the periphery, awaiting their chance. Only after scientists began night tracking the animals did a new interpretation emerge: hyenas actually made the kill, only to be driven off by opportunistic and lazy lions; hence the traditional dawn scene. This coincided with the discovery that lions were in many ways erratic and mean, while the hyenas had a finely developed social structure—yet another instance of long-standing human prejudice toward the natural world of animals.)

But the hippopotamus remained a poorly understood an-imal. Herodotus's "river horse" was the largest African mammal after the elephant, but its habit of lying in the water with just eyes and nostrils protruding made it difficult to study. Hippos were organized around a male. A mature male had a harem of several females and their offspring, a group of eight to fourteen animals altogether.

Despite their obese, rather humorous appearance, hippos were capable of unusual violence. The bull hippopotamus was a formidable creature, fourteen feet long and weighing nearly ten thousand pounds. Charging, he moved with ex-traordinary speed for such a large animal, and his four stubby blunted tusks were actually razor sharp on the sides. A hippo attacked by slashing, moving his cavernous mouth from side to side, rather than biting. And, unlike most animals, a fight between bulls often resulted in the death of one animal from deep slashing wounds. There was nothing symbolic about a hippopotamus fight.

The animal was dangerous to man, as well. In river areas where herds were found, half of native deaths were attributed to hippos; elephants and predatory cats accounted for the remainder. The hippopotamus was vegetarian, and at night the animals came onto the land, where they ate enormous quantities of grass to sustain their great bulk. A hippo separated from the water was especially dangerous; anyone finding himself between a landed hippo and the river he was rushing to return to did not generally survive the experience.

But the hippo was essential to Africa's river ecology. His fecal matter, produced in prodigious quantities, fertilized the river grasses, which in turn allowed river fish and other creatures to live. Without the hippopotamus African rivers would be sterile, and where they had been driven away, the rivers died.

This much was known, and one thing more. The hippopotamus was fiercely territorial. Without exception, the male defended his river against any intruder. And as had been recorded on many occasions, intruders included other hippos, crocodiles, and passing boats. And the people in them.

DAY 7: MUKENKO

June 19, 1979

1. Kiboko

MUNRO'S INTENTION IN CONTINUING THROUGH the night was two-fold. First, he hoped to make up precious time, for all the computer projections assumed that they would stop each night. But it took no effort to ride the river in the moonlight; most of the party could sleep, and they would advance themselves another fifty or sixty miles by dawn.

But more important, he hoped to avoid the Ragora hippos, which could easily destroy their flimsy rubber boats. During the day, the hippos were found in pools beside the river-banks, and the bulls would certainly attack any passing boat. At night, when the animals went ashore to forage, the expedition could slip down the river and avoid a confrontation entirely.

It was a clever plan, but it ran into trouble for an unexpected reason—their progress on the Ragora was too rapid. It was only nine o'clock at night when they reached the first hippo areas, too early for the animals to be eating. The hippos would attack the boats—but they would attack in the dark.

The river twisted and turned in a series of curves. At each curve there was a still pool, which Kahega pointed out as the kind of quiet water that hippos liked to inhabit. And he pointed to the grass on the banks, cut short as if the banks had been mown.

"Soon now," Kahega said.

They heard a low grunting, *"Haw-huh-huh-huh."* It sounded like an old man trying to clear his throat of phlegm.

183

Munro tensed in the lead boat. They drifted around another curve, carried smoothly in the flow of current. The two boats were now about ten yards apart. Munro held his loaded shotgun ready.

The sound came again, this time in a chorus: *"Haw-huh-huh-huh."*

Kahega plunged his paddle into the water. It struck bottom quickly. He pulled it out; only three feet of it was wet. "Not deep," he said, shaking his head.

"Is that bad?" Ross said.

"Yes, I think it is bad."

They came around the next bend, and Elliot saw a half-dozen partially submerged black rocks near the shore, gleaming in the moonlight. Then one of the "rocks" crashed upward and he saw an enormous creature lift entirely out of the shallow water so that he could see the four stubby legs, and the hippo churned forward toward Munro's boat.

Munro fired a low magnesium flare as the animal charged; in the harsh white light Elliot saw a gigantic mouth, four huge glistening blunted teeth, the head lifted upward as the animal roared. And then the hippo was engulfed in a cloud of pale yellow gas. The gas drifted back, and stung their eyes.

"He's using tear gas," Ross said.

Munro's boat had already moved on. With a roar of pain the male hippo had plunged down into the water and disappeared from sight. In the second boat, they blinked back tears and watched for him as they approached the pool. Overhead, the magnesium flare sizzled and descended, lengthening sharp shadows, glaring off the water.

"Perhaps he's given up," Elliot said. They could not see the hippo anywhere. They drifted in silence.

And suddenly the front of the boat bucked up, and the hippo roared and Ross screamed. Kahega toppled backward, discharging his gun into the air. The boat slapped down with a wrenching crash and a spray of water over the sides, and Elliot scrambled to his feet to check Amy and found himself staring into a huge pink cavernous mouth and hot breath.

The mouth came down with a lateral slash on the side of the rubber boat, and the air began to hiss and sizzle in the water.

The mouth opened again, and the hippo grunted, but by then Kahega had got to his feet and fired a stinging cloud of gas. The hippo backed off and splashed down, rocking the boat and propelling them onward, down the river. The whole right side of the boat was collapsing swiftly as the air leaked out of the huge cuts in the rubber. Elliot tried to pull them shut with his hands; the hissing continued unabated. They would sink within a minute.

Behind them, the bull hippo charged, racing down the shallow river like a powerboat, churning water in a wake from both sides of his body, bellowing in anger.

"Hold on, hold on!" Kahega shouted, and fired again. The hippo disappeared behind a cloud of gas, and the boat drifted around another curve. When the gas cleared the animal was gone. The magnesium flare sputtered into the water and they were plunged into darkness again. Elliot grabbed Amy as the boat sank, and they found themselves standing knee-deep in the muddy water.

They managed to beach the Zodiac on the dark riverbank. In the lead boat, Munro paddled over, surveyed the damage, and announced that they would inflate another boat and go on. He called for a rest, and they all lay in the moonlight on the river's edge swatting mosquitoes away.

Their reverie was interrupted by the screaming whine of ground-to-air rockets, blossoming explosions in the sky overhead. With each explosion, the riverbank glowed bright red, casting long shadows, then fading black once more.

"Muguru's men firing from the ground," Munro said, reaching for his field glasses.

"What're they shooting at?" Elliot said, staring up into the sky.

"Beats me," Munro said.

Amy touched Munro's arm, and signed, *Bird come.* But they heard no sound of an aircraft, only the bursting of rockets in the sky.

Munro said, "You think she hears something?"

"Her hearing is very acute."

And then they heard the drone of a distant aircraft, approaching from the south. As it came into view, they saw it twist, maneuvering among the brilliant yellow-red explosions that burst in the moonlight and glinted off the metal body of the aircraft.

"Those poor bastards are trying to make time," Munro said, scanning the plane through field glasses. "That's a C-130 transport with Japanese markings on the tail. Supply plane for the consortium base camp—if it makes it through."

As they watched, the transport twisted left and right, running a zigzag course through the bursting fireballs of exploding missiles.

"Breaking a snake's back," Munro said. "The crew must be terrified; they didn't buy into this."

Elliot felt a sudden sympathy for the crew; he imagined them staring out the windows as the fireballs exploded with brilliant light, illuminating the interior of the plane. Were they chattering in Japanese? Wishing they had never come?

A moment later, the aircraft droned onward to the north, out of sight, a final missile with a red-hot tail chasing after it, but it was gone over the jungle trees, and he listened to the distant explosion of the missile.

"Probably got through," Munro said, standing. "We'd better move on." And he shouted in Swahili for Kahega to put the men on the river once more.

2. Mukenko

ELLIOT SHIVERED, ZIPPED HIS PARKA TIGHTER, AND waited for the hailstorm to stop. They were huddled beneath a stand of evergreen trees above 8,000 feet on the alpine slopes of Mount Mukenko. It was ten o'clock in the morning, and the air temperature was 38 degrees. Five hours before, they had left the river behind and begun their pre-dawn climb in 100-degree steaming jungle.

Alongside him, Amy watched the golfball-sized white pellets bounce on the grass and slap the branches of the tree over their heads. She had never seen hail before.

She signed, *What name?*

"Hail," he told her.

Peter make stop.

"I wish I could, Amy."

She watched the hail for a moment, then signed, *Amy want go home.*

She had begun talking about going home the night before. Although the Thoralen had worn off, she remained depressed and withdrawn. Elliot had offered her some food to cheer her up. She signed that she wanted milk. When he told her they had none (which she knew perfectly well), she signed that she wanted a banana. Kahega had produced a bunch of small, slightly sour jungle bananas. Amy had eaten them without objection on previous days, but she now threw them into the water contemptuously, signing she wanted "real bananas."

When Elliot told her that they had no real bananas, she signed, *Amy want go home.*

"We can't go home now, Amy."

Amy good gorilla Peter take Amy home.

She had only known him as the person in charge, the final arbiter of her daily life in the experimental setting of Project Amy. He could think of no way to make clear to her that he was no longer in charge, and that he was not punishing her by keeping her here.

In fact, they were all discouraged. Each of the expedition members had looked forward to escaping the oppressive heat of the rain forest, but now that they were climbing Mukenko, their enthusiasm had quickly faded. "Christ," Ross said. "From hippos to hail."

As if on cue, the hail stopped. "All right," Munro said, "let's get moving."

* * *

Mukenko had never been climbed until 1933. In 1908, a German party under von Ranke ran into storms and had to descend; a Belgian team in 1913 reached 10,000 feet but could not find a route to the summit; and another German team was forced to quit in 1919 when two team members fell and died, about 12,000 feet. Nevertheless Mukenko was classified as a fairly easy (non-technical) climb by most mountaineers, who generally devoted a day to the ascent; after 1943, a new route up the southeast was found which was frustratingly slow but not dangerous, and it was this route that most climbers followed.

Above 9,000 feet, the pine forest disappeared and they crossed weak grassy fields cloaked in chilly mist; the air was thinner, and they called frequently for a rest. Munro had no patience with the complaints of his charges. "What did you expect?" he demanded. "It's a mountain. Mountains are high." He was especially merciless with Ross, who seemed the most easily fatigued. "What about your timetable?" he would ask her. "We're not even to the difficult part. It's not even interesting until eleven thousand feet. You quit now and we'll never make it to the summit before nightfall, and that means we lose a full day."

"I don't care," Ross said finally, dropping to the ground, gasping for breath.

"Just like a woman," Munro said scornfully, and smiled when Ross glared at him. Munro humiliated them, chided them, encouraged them—and somehow kept them moving.

Above 10,000 feet, the grass disappeared and there was only mossy ground cover; they came upon the solitary peculiar fat-leafed lobelia trees, emerging suddenly from the cold gray mist. There was no real cover between 10,000 feet and the summit, which was why Munro pushed them; he did not want to get caught in a storm on the barren upper slopes.

The sun broke out at 11,000 feet, and they stopped to position the second of the directional lasers for the ERTS laser-fix system. Ross had already set the first laser several miles to the south that morning, and it had taken thirty minutes.

The second laser was more critical, since it had to be matched to the first. Despite the electronic jamming, the transmitting equipment had to be connected with Houston, in order that the little laser—it was the size of a pencil eraser, mounted on a tiny steel tripod—could be accurately aimed. The two lasers on the volcano were positioned so that their beams crossed many miles away, above the jungle. And if Ross's calculations were correct, that intersection point was directly over the city of Zinj.

Elliot wondered if they were inadvertently assisting the consortium, but Ross said no. "Only at night," she said, "when they aren't moving. During the day, they won't be able to lock on our beacons—that's the beauty of the system."

Soon they smelled sulfurous volcanic fumes drifting down from the summit, now 1,500 feet above them. Up here there was no vegetation at all, only bare hard rock and scattered patches of snow tinged yellow from the sulfur. The sky was clear dark blue, and they had spectacular views of the south Virunga range—the great cone of Nyiragongo, rising steeply from the deep green of the Congo forests, and, beyond that, Mukenko, shrouded in fog.

The last thousand feet were the most difficult, particularly for Amy, who had to pick her way barefoot among the sharp lava rocks. Above 12,000 feet, the ground was loose volcanic scree. They reached the summit at five in the afternoon, and gazed over the eight-mile-wide lava lake and smoking crater of the volcano. Elliot was disappointed in the landscape of black rock and gray steam clouds. "Wait until night," Munro said.

That night the lava glowed in a network of hot red through the broken dark crust; hissing red steam slowly lost its color as it rose into the sky. On the crater rim, their little tents reflected the red glow of the lava. To the west scattered clouds were silver in the moonlight, and beneath them the Congo jungle stretched away for miles. They could see the straight green laser beams, intersecting over the black forest. With any luck they would reach that intersection tomorrow.

Ross connected her transmitting equipment to make the nightly report to Houston. After the regular six-minute delay, the signal linked directly through to Houston, without interstitial encoding or other evasive techniques.

"Hell," Munro said.

"But what does it mean?" Elliot asked.

"It means," Munro said gloomily, "the consortium has stopped jamming us."

"Isn't that good?"

"No," Ross said. "It's bad. They must already be on the site, and they've found the diamonds." She shook her head, and adjusted the video screen:

```
HUSTN CONFRMS CONSRTUM ONSITE ZINJ PROBA-
BILTY 1.000. TAK NO FURTHR RSKS. SITUTN HOPE-
LSS.
```

"I can't believe it," Ross said. "It's all over."

Elliot sighed. "My feet hurt," he said.

"I'm tired," Munro said.

"The hell with it," Ross said.

Utterly exhausted, they all went to bed.

DAY 8: KANYAMAGUFA

June 20, 1979

1. Descent

EVERYONE SLEPT LATE ON THE MORNING OF JUNE 20. They had a leisurely breakfast, taking the time to cook a hot meal. They relaxed in the sun, and played with Amy, who was delighted by this unexpected attention. It was past ten o'clock before they started down Mukenko to the jungle.

Because the western slopes of Mukenko are sheer and impassible, they descended inside the smoking volcanic crater to a depth of half a mile. Munro led the way, carrying a porter's load on his head; Asari, the strongest porter, had to carry Amy, because the rocks were much too hot for her bare feet.

Amy was terrified, and regarded the human persons trekking single-file down the steep inner cone to be mad. Elliot was not sure she was wrong: the heat was intense; as they approached the lava lake, the acrid fumes made eyes water and nostrils burn; they heard the lava pop and crackle beneath the heavy black crust.

Then they reached the formation called Naragema—the Devil's Eye. It was a natural arch 150 feet high, and so smooth it appeared polished on the inside. Through this arch a fresh breeze blew, and they saw the green jungle below. They paused to rest in the arch, and Ross examined the smooth inner surface. It was part of a lava tube formed in some earlier eruption; the main body of the tube had been blown away, leaving just the slender arch.

"They call it the Devil's Eye," Munro said, "because from below, during an eruption, it glows like a red eye."

From the Devil's Eye they descended rapidly through an alpine zone, and from there across the unworldly jagged ter-

193

rain of a recent lava flow. Here they encountered black craters of scorched earth, some as deep as five or six feet. Munro's first thought was that the Zaire army had used this field for mortar practice. But on closer examination, they saw a scorched pattern etched into the rock, extending like tentacles outward from the craters. Munro had never seen anything like it; Ross immediately set up her antenna, hooked in the computer, and got in touch with Houston. She seemed very excited.

The party rested while she reviewed the data on the little screen, Munro said, "What are you asking them?"

"The date of the last Mukenko eruption, and the local weather. It was in March—Do you know somebody named Seamans?"

"Yes," Elliot said. "Tom Seamans is the computer programmer for Project Amy. Why?"

"There's a message for you," she said, pointing to the screen.

Elliot came around to look: SEMNS MESG FOR ELYT STNDBY.

"What's the message?" Elliot asked.

"Push the transmit button," she said.

He pushed the button and the message flashed: REVUWD ORGNL TAPE HUSTN NU M.

"I don't understand," Elliot said. Ross explained that the "M" meant that there was more message, and he had to press the transmit button again. He pushed the button several times before he got the message, which in its entirety read:

REVUWD ORGNL TAPE HUSTN NU FINDNG RE AURL SIGNL INFO–COMPUTR ANLYSS COMPLTE THNK ITS LNGWGE.

Elliot found he could read the compressed shortline language by speaking it aloud: "Reviewed original tape Houston, new finding regarding aural signal information, computer analysis complete think it's language." He frowned. "Language?"

Ross said, "Didn't you ask him to review Houston's original tape material from the Congo?"

"Yes, but that was for visual identification of the animal

on the screen. I never said anything to him about aural information." Elliot shook his head. "I wish I could talk to him."

"You can," Ross said. "If you don't mind waking him up." She pushed the interlock button, and fifteen minutes later Elliot typed, Hello Tom How Are You? The screen printed HLO TOM HOWRU.

"We don't usually waste satellite time with that kind of thing," Ross said.

The screen printed SLEPY WHRERU.

He typed, Virunga. VIRNGA.

"Travis is going to scream when he sees this transcript," Ross said. "Do you realize what the transmission costs are?" But Ross needn't have worried; the conversation soon became technical:

RECVD MESG AURL INFO PLS XPLN.

AXIDENTL DISKVRY VRY XCITNG-DISCRIMNT FUNXN
COMPTR ANLSS 99 CONFDNCE LIMTS TAPD AURL INFO
{BRETHNG SOUNS} DEMNSTRTS CHRCTRISTX SPECH.

SPSFY CHRCTRISTX.

REPETNG   ELMNTS-ARBTRARY   PATRN-STRXRAL
RLATNSHPS-PROBLY THRFOR SPOKN LNGWGE.

KN U TRNSLTE?

NOT SOFR.

WHT RESN?

COMPUTR HAS INSFSNT INFO IN AURL MESG-WNT MOR
DATA-ST WORKNG-MAYB MOR TOMORO-FINGRS X.

RLY THNK GORILA LNGWGE?

YES IF GORILA.

"I'll be damned," Elliot said. He ended the satellite transmission, but the final message from Seamans remained on the screen, glowing bright green:

YES IF GORILA.

2. The Hairy Men

WITHIN TWO HOURS OF RECEIVING THIS UNEX-
pected news, the expedition had its first contact with gorillas.

They were by now back in the darkness of the equatorial
rain forest. They proceeded directly toward the site, following the overhead laser beams. They could not see these beams
directly, but Ross had brought a weird optical track guide, a
cadmium photocell filtered to record the specific laser wave-
length emission. Periodically during the day, she inflated a
small helium balloon, attached the track guide with a wire,
and released it. Lifted by the helium, the guide rose into the
sky above the trees. There it rotated, sighted one of the laser
lines, and transmitted coordinates down the wire to the computer. They followed the track of diminishing laser intensity
from a single beam, and waited for the "blip reading," the
doubled intensity value that would signal the intersection of
two beams above them.

This was a slow job and their patience was wearing thin
when, toward midday, they came upon the characteristic
three-lobed feces of gorilla, and they saw several nests made
of eucalyptus leaves on the ground and in the trees.

Fifteen minutes later, the air was shattered by a deafening
roar. "Gorilla," Munro announced. "That was a male telling somebody off."

Amy signed, *Gorillas say go away.*

"We have to continue, Amy," he said.

Gorilla no want human people come.

"Human people won't harm gorillas," Elliot assured her.
But Amy just looked blank at this, and shook her head, as if
Elliot had missed the point.

Days later he realized that he had indeed missed the point. Amy was not telling him that the gorillas were afraid of being harmed by people. She was saying that the gorillas were afraid that the people would be harmed, by gorillas.

They had progressed halfway across a small jungle clearing when the large silverback male reared above the foliage and bellowed at them.

Elliot was leading the group, because Munro had gone back to help one of the porters with his pack. He saw six animals at the edge of the clearing, dark black shapes against the green, watching the human intruders. Several of the females cocked their heads and compressed their lips in a kind of disapproval. The dominant male roared again.

He was a large male with silver hair down his back. His massive head stood more than six feet above the ground, and his barrel chest indicated that he weighed more than four hundred pounds. Seeing him, Elliot understood why the first explorers to the Congo had believed gorillas to be "hairy men," for this magnificent creature looked like a gigantic man, both in size and shape.

At Elliot's back Ross whispered, "What do we do?"

"Stay behind me," Elliot said, "and don't move."

The silverback male dropped to all fours briefly, and began a soft *ho-ho-ho* sound, which grew more intense as he leapt to his feet again, grabbing handfuls of grass as he did so. He threw the grass in the air, and then beat his chest with flat palms, making a hollow thumping sound.

"Oh, no," Ross said.

The chest-beating lasted five seconds, and then the male dropped to all fours again. He ran sideways across the grass, slapping the foliage and making as much noise as possible, to frighten the intruders off. Finally he began the *ho-ho-ho* sound once more.

The male stared at Elliot, expecting that this display would send him running. When it did not, the male leapt to his feet, pounded his chest, and roared with even greater fury.

And then he charged.

With a howling scream he came crashing forward at frightening speed, directly toward Elliot. Elliot heard Ross gasp behind him. He wanted to turn and run, his every bodily instinct screamed that he should run, but he forced himself to stand absolutely still—and to look down at the ground.

Staring at his feet while he listened to the gorilla crashing through the tall grass toward him, he had the sudden sensation that all his abstract book knowledge was wrong, that everything that scientists around the world thought about gorillas was wrong. He had a mental image of the huge head and the deep chest and the long arms swinging wide as the powerful animal rushed toward an easy kill, a stationary target foolish enough to believe all the academic misinformation sanctified by print. . . .

The gorilla (who must have been quite close) made a snorting noise, and Elliot could see his heavy shadow on the grass near his feet. But he did not look up until the shadow moved away.

When Elliot raised his head, he saw the male gorilla retreating backward, toward the far edge of the clearing. There the male turned, and scratched his head in a puzzled way, as if wondering why his terrifying display had not driven off the intruders. He slapped the ground a final time, and then he and the rest of the troop melted away into the tall grass. It was silent in the clearing until Ross collapsed into Elliot's arms.

"Well," Munro said as he came up, "it seems you know a thing or two about gorillas after all." Munro patted Ross's arm. "It's all right. They don't do anything unless you run away. Then they bite you on the ass. That's the mark for cowardice in these regions—because it means you ran away."

Ross was sobbing quietly, and Elliot discovered that his own knees were shaky; he went to sit down. It had all happened so fast that it was a few moments before he realized that these gorillas had behaved in exactly the textbook manner, which included not making any verbalizations even remotely like speech.

3. The Consortium

AN HOUR LATER THEY FOUND THE WRECKAGE OF the C-130 transport. The largest airplane in the world appeared in correct scale as it lay half buried in the jungle, the gigantic nose crushed against equally gigantic trees, the enormous tail section twisted toward the ground, the massive wings buckled casting shadows on the jungle floor.

Through the shattered cockpit windshield, they saw the body of the pilot, covered with black flies. The flies buzzed and thumped against the glass as they peered in. Moving aft, they tried to look into the fuselage windows, but even on crumpled landing gear the body of the plane stood too high above the jungle floor.

Kahega managed to climb an overturned tree, and from there moved onto one wing and looked into the interior. "No people," he said.

"Supplies?"

"Yes, many supplies. Boxes and containers."

Munro left the others, walking beneath the crushed tail section to examine the far side of the plane. The port wing, concealed from their view, was blackened and shattered, the engines gone. That explained why the plane crashed—the last FZA missile had found its target, blowing away most of the port wing. Yet the wreck remained oddly mysterious to Munro; something about its appearance was wrong. He looked along the length of the fuselage, from the crushed nose, down the line of windows, past the stump of wing, past the rear exit doors. . . .

"I'll be damned," Munro said softly.

He hurried back to the others, who were sitting on one of the tires, in the shadow of the starboard wing. The tire was so enormous that Ross could sit on it and swing her feet in the air without touching the ground.

"Well," Ross said, with barely concealed satisfaction. "They didn't get their damn supplies."

"No," Munro said. "And we saw this plane the night before last, which means it's been down at least thirty-six hours."

Munro waited for Ross to figure it out.

"Thirty-six hours?"

"That's right. Thirty-six hours."

"And they never came back to get their supplies. . . ."

"They didn't even *try* to get them," Munro said. "Look at the main cargo doors, fore and aft—no one has tried to open them. I wonder why they never came back?"

In a section of dense jungle, the ground underfoot crunched and crackled. Pushing aside the palm fronds, they saw a carpeting of shattered white bones.

"*Kanyamagufa*," Munro said. The place of bones. He glanced quickly at the porters to see what their reaction was, but they showed only puzzlement, no fear. They were East African Kikuyu and they had none of the superstitions of the tribes that bordered the rain forest.

Amy lifted her feet from the sharp bleached fragments. She signed, *Ground hurt.*

Elliot signed, What place this?

We come bad place.

What bad place?

Amy had no reply.

"These are bones!" Ross said, staring down at the ground.

"That's right," Munro said quickly, "but they're not human bones. Are they, Elliot?"

Elliot was also looking at the ground. He saw bleached skeletal remains from several species, although he could not immediately identify any of them.

"Elliot? Not human?"

"They don't look human," Elliot agreed, staring at the

ground. The first thing he noticed was that the majority of the bones came from distinctly small animals—birds, monkeys, and tiny forest rodents. Other small pieces were actually fragments from larger animals, but how large was hard to say. Perhaps large monkeys—but there weren't any large monkeys in the rain forest.

Chimpanzees? There were no chimps in this part of the Congo. Perhaps they might be gorillas: he saw one fragment from a cranium with heavy frontal sinuses, and he saw the beginning of the characteristic sagittal crest.

"Elliot?" Munro said, his voice tense, insistent. "Non-human?"

"Definitely non-human," Elliot said, staring. *What could shatter a gorilla skull?* It must have happened after death, he decided. A gorilla had died and after many years the bleached skeleton had been crushed in some fashion. Certainly it could not have happened during life.

"Not human," Munro said, looking at the ground. "Hell of a lot of bones, but nothing human." As he walked past Elliot, he gave him a look. *Keep your mouth shut.* "Kahega and his men know that you are expert in these matters," Munro said, looking at him steadily.

What had Munro seen? Certainly he had been around enough death to know a human skeleton when he saw one. Elliot's glance fell on a curved bone. It looked a bit like a turkey wishbone, only much larger and broader, and white with age. He picked it up. It was a fragment of the zygomatic arch from a human skull. A cheekbone, from beneath the eye.

He turned the fragment in his hands. He looked back at the jungle floor, and the creepers that spread reaching tentacles over the white carpet of bones. He saw many very fragile bones, some so thin they were translucent—bones that he assumed had come from small animals.

Now he was not sure.

A question from graduate school returned to him. What seven bones compose the orbit of the human eye? Elliot tried to remember. The zygoma, the nasal, the inferior orbital, the sphenoid—that was four—the ethmoid, five—something must come from beneath, from the mouth—the palatine, six—one more to go—he couldn't think of the last bone. Zygoma, nasal, inferior orbital, sphenoid, ethmoid, palatine . . . delicate bones, translucent bones, small bones.

Human bones.

"At least these aren't human bones," Ross said.

"No," Elliot agreed. He glanced at Amy.

Amy signed, *People die here.*

"What did she say?"

"She said people don't benefit from the air here."

"Let's push on," Munro said.

Munro led him a little distance ahead of the others. "Well done," he said. "Have to be careful about the Kikuyu. Don't want to panic them. What'd your monkey say?"

"She said people died there."

"That's more than the others know," Munro said, nodding grimly. "Although they suspect."

Behind them, the party walked single-file, nobody talking.

"What the hell happened back there?" Elliot said.

"Lots of bones," Munro said. "Leopard, colobus, forest rat, maybe a bush baby, human . . ."

"And gorilla," Elliot said.

"Yes," Munro said. "I saw that, too. Gorilla." He shook his head. "What can kill a gorilla, Professor?"

Elliot had no answer.

The consortium camp lay in ruins, the tents shredded and shattered, the dead bodies covered with dense black clouds of flies. In the humid air, the stench was overpowering, the buzzing of the flies an angry monotonous sound. Everybody except Munro hung back at the edge of the camp.

"No choice," he said. "We've got to know what happened to these—" He went inside the camp itself, stepping over the flattened fence.

As Munro moved inside, the perimeter defenses were set off, emitting a screaming high-frequency signal. Outside the fence, the others cupped their hands over their ears and Amy snorted her displeasure.

Bad noise.

Munro glanced back at them. "Doesn't bother me," he said. "That's what you get for staying outside." Munro went to one dead body, turning it over with his foot. Then he bent down, swatting away the cloud of buzzing flies, and carefully examined the head.

Ross glanced over at Elliot. He seemed to be in shock, the typical scientist, immobilized by disaster. At his side, Amy covered her ears and winced. But Ross was not immobilized; she took a deep breath and crossed the perimeter. "I have to know what defenses they installed."

"Fine," Elliot said. He felt detached, light-headed, as if he might faint; the sight and the smells made him dizzy. He saw Ross pick her way across the compound, then lift up a black box with an odd baffled cone. She traced a wire back toward the center of the camp. Soon afterward the high-frequency signal ceased; she had turned it off at the source.

Amy signed, *Better now.*

With one hand, Ross rummaged through the electronics equipment in the center of the units in the camp, while with the other she held her nose against the stench.

Kahega said, "I'll see if they have guns, Doctor," and he, too, moved into the camp. Hesitantly, the other porters followed him.

Alone, Elliot remained with Amy. She impassively surveyed the destruction, although she reached up and took his hand. He signed, Amy what happened this place?

Amy signed, *Things come.*

What things?

Bad things.

What things?

Bad things come things come bad.

What things?

Bad things.

Obviously he would get nowhere with this line of questioning. He told her to remain outside the camp, and went in himself, moving among the bodies and the buzzing flies.

Ross said, "Anybody find the leader?"

Across the camp, Munro said, "Menard."

"Out of Kinshasa?"

Munro nodded. "Yeah."

"Who's Menard?" Elliot asked.

"He's got a good reputation, knows the Congo." Ross picked her way through the debris. "But he wasn't good enough." A moment later she paused.

Elliot went over to her. She stared at a body lying face down on the ground.

"Don't turn it over," she said. "It's Richter."

Elliot did not understand how she could be sure. The body was covered with black flies. He bent over.

"Don't touch him!"

"Okay," Elliot said.

"Kahega," Munro shouted, raising a green plastic twenty-liter can. The can sloshed with liquid in his hand. "Let's get this done."

Kahega and his men moved swiftly, splashing kerosene over the tents and dead bodies. Elliot smelled the sharp odor.

Ross, crouched under a torn nylon supply tent, shouted, "Give me a minute!"

"Take all the time you want," Munro said. He turned to Elliot, who was watching Amy outside the camp.

Amy was signing to herself: *People bad. No believe people bad things come.*

"She seems very calm about it," Munro said.

"Not really," Elliot said. "I think she knows what took place here."

"I hope she'll tell us," Munro said. "Because all these men died in the same way. Their skulls were crushed."

The flames from the consortium camp licked upward into the air, and the black smoke bellowed as the expedition moved onward through the jungle. Ross was silent, lost in thought. Elliot said, "What did you find?"

"Nothing good," she said. "They had a perfectly adequate peripheral system, quite similar to our ADP—animal defense perimeter. Those cones I found are audio-sensing units, and when they pick up a signal, they emit an ultra-high-frequency signal that is very painful to auditory systems. Doesn't work for reptiles, but it's damn effective on mammalian systems. Send a wolf or a leopard running for the hills.''

"But it didn't work here," Elliot said.

"No," Ross said. "And it didn't bother Amy very much."

Elliot said, "What does it do to human auditory systems?''

"You felt it. It's annoying, but that's all." She glanced at Elliot. "But there aren't any human beings in this part of the Congo. Except us."

Munro asked, "Can we make a better perimeter defense?''

"Damn right we can," Ross said. "I'll give you the next generation perimeter—it'll stop anything except elephants and rhinos.'' But she didn't sound convinced.

Late in the afternoon, they came upon the remains of the first ERTS Congo camp. They nearly missed it, for during the intervening eight days the jungle vines and creepers had already begun to grow back over it, obliterating all traces. There was not much left—a few shreds of orange nylon, a dented aluminum cooking pan, the crushed tripod, and the broken video camera, its green circuit boards scattered across the ground. They found no bodies, and since the light was fading they pressed on.

Amy was distinctly agitated, She signed, *No go*.

Peter Elliot paid no attention.

Bad place old place no go.

"We go, Amy," he said.

Fifteen minutes later they came to a break in the overhanging trees. Looking up, they saw the dark cone of Mukenko rising above the forest, and the faint crossed green beams of the lasers glinting in the humid air. And directly beneath the beams were the moss-covered stone blocks, half concealed in jungle foliage, of the Lost City of Zinj.

Elliot turned to look at Amy.

Amy was gone.

4. WEIRD

He could not believe it.

At first he thought she was just punishing him, running off to make him sorry for shooting the dart at her on the river. He explained to Munro and Ross that she was capable of such things, and they spent the next half hour wandering through the jungle, calling her name. But there was no response, just the eternal silence of the rain forest. The half hour became an hour, then almost two hours.

Elliot was panic-stricken.

When she still did not emerge from the foliage, another possibility had to be considered. "Maybe she ran off with the last group of gorillas," Munro said.

"Impossible," Elliot said.

"She's seven, she's near maturity." Munro shrugged. "She *is* a gorilla."

"Impossible," Elliot insisted.

But he knew what Munro was saying. Inevitably, people who raised apes found at a certain point they could no longer keep them. With maturity the animals became too large, too powerful, too much their own species to be controllable. It was no longer possible to put them in diapers and pretend they were cute humanlike creatures. Their genes coded inevitable differences that ultimately became impossible to overlook.

"Gorilla troops aren't closed," Munro reminded him. "They accept strangers, particularly female strangers."

"She wouldn't do that," Elliot insisted. "She couldn't."

Amy had been raised from infancy among human beings. She was much more familiar with the Westernized world of

206

freeways and drive-ins than she was with the jungle. If Elliot drove his car past her favorite drive-in, she was quick to tap his shoulder and point out his error. What did she know of the jungle? It was as alien to her as it was to Elliot himself. And not only that—

"We'd better make camp," Ross said, glancing at her watch. "She'll come back—if she wants to. After all," she said, "we didn't leave her. She left us."

They had brought a bottle of Dom Pérignon champagne but nobody was in a mood to celebrate. Elliot was remorseful over the loss of Amy; the others were horrified by what they had seen of the earlier camp; with night rapidly falling, there was much to do to set up the ERTS system known as WEIRD (Wilderness Environmental Intruder Response Defenses).

The exotic WEIRD technology recognized the fact that perimeter defenses were traditional throughout the history of Congo exploration. More than a century before, Stanley observed that "no camp is to be considered complete until it is fenced around by bush or trees." In the years since there was little reason to alter the essential nature of that instruction. But defensive technology had changed, and the WEIRD system incorporated all the latest innovations.

Kahega and his men inflated the silvered Mylar tents, arranging them close together. Ross directed the placement of the tubular infrared night lights on telescoping tripods. These were positioned shining outward around the camp.

Next the perimeter fence was installed. This was a lightweight metalloid mesh, more like cloth than wire. Attached to stakes, it completely enclosed the campsite, and when hooked to the transformer carried 10,000 volts of electrical current. To reduce drain on the fuel cells, the current was pulsed at four cycles a second, creating a throbbing, intermittent hum.

Dinner on the night of June 20 was rice with rehydrated Creole shrimp sauce. The shrimps did not rehydrate well, remaining little cardboard-tasting chunks in the mix, but nobody complained about this failure of twentieth-century technology as they glanced around them at the deepening jungle darkness.

Munro positioned the sentries. They would stand four-hour watches; Munro announced that he, Kahega, and Elliot would take the first watch.

With night goggles in place, the sentries looked like mysterious grasshoppers peering out at the jungle. The night goggles intensified ambient light and overlaid this on the pre-existing imagery, rimming it in ghostly green. Elliot found the goggles heavy, and the electronic view through them difficult to adjust to. He pulled them off after several minutes, and was astonished to see that the jungle was inky black around him. He put them back on hastily.

The night passed quietly, without incident.

DAY 9: ZINJ

June 21, 1979

1. Tiger Tail

THEIR ENTRANCE INTO THE LOST CITY OF ZINJ ON the morning of June 21 was accomplished with none of the mystery and romance of nineteenth-century accounts of similar journeys. These twentieth-century explorers sweated and grunted under a burdensome load of technical equipment—optical range finders, data-lock compasses, RF directionals with attached transmitters, and microwave transponders—all deemed essential to the modern high-speed evaluation of a ruined archaeological site.

They were only interested in diamonds. Schliemann had been only interested in gold when he excavated Troy, and he had devoted three years to it. Ross expected to find her diamonds in three days.

According to the ERTS computer simulation the best way to do this was to draw up a ground plan of the city. With a plan in hand, it would be relatively simple to deduce mine locations from the arrangement of urban structures.

They expected a usable plan of the city within six hours. Using RF transponders, they had only to stand in each of the four corners of a building, pressing the radio beeper at each corner. Back in camp, two widely spaced receivers recorded their signals so that their computer could plot them in two dimensions. But the ruins were extensive, covering more than three square kilometers. A radio survey would separate them widely in dense foliage—and, considering what had happened to the previous expedition, this seemed unwise.

Their alternative was what ERTS called the non-systematic survey, or "the tiger-tail approach." (It was a joke at ERTS that one way to find a tiger was to keep walking until you stepped on its tail.) They moved through the ruined buildings, avoiding slithering snakes and giant spiders that scurried into dark recesses. The spiders were the size of a man's hand, and to Ross's astonishment made a loud clicking noise.

They noticed that the stonework was of excellent quality, although the limestonc in many places was pitted and crumbling. And everywhere they saw the half-moon curve of doors and windows, which seemed to be a cultural design motif.

But aside from that curved shape, they found almost nothing distinctive about the rooms they passed through. In general, the rooms were rectangular and roughly the same size; the walls were bare, lacking decoration. After so many intervening centuries they found no artifacts at all—although Elliot finally came upon a pair of disc-shaped stone paddles, which they presumed had been used to grind spices or grain.

The bland, characterless quality of the city grew more disturbing as they continued; it was also inconvenient, since they had no way to refer to one place or another; they began assigning arbitrary names to different buildings. When Karen Ross found a series of cubby holes carved into the wall of one room, she announced that this must be a post office, and from then on it was referred to as "the post office."

They came upon a row of small rooms with postholes for wooden bars. Munro thought these were cells of a jail, but the cells were extremely small. Ross said that perhaps the people were small, or perhaps the cells were intentionally small for punishment. Elliot thought perhaps they were cages for a zoo. But in that case, why were all the cages of the same size? And Munro pointed out there was no provision for viewing the animals; he repeated his conviction that it was a jail, and the rooms became known as "the jail."

Near to the jail they found an open court they called "the gymnasium." It was apparently an athletic field or training ground. There were four tall stone stakes with a crumbling stone ring at the top; evidently these had been used for some kind of game like tetherball. In a corner of the court stood a horizontal overhead bar, like a jungle gym, no more than five feet off the ground. The low bar led Elliot to conclude that this was a playground for children. Ross repeated her belief that the people were small. Munro wondered if the gymnasium was a training area for soldiers.

As they continued their search, they were all aware that their reactions simply mirrored their preoccupations. The city was so neutral, so uninformative, that it became a kind of Rorschach for them. What they needed was objective information about the people who had built the city, and their life.

It was there all along, although they were slow to realize it. In many rooms, one wall or another was overgrown with black-green mold. Munro noticed that this mold did not grow in relation to light from a window, or air currents, or any other factor they could identify. In some rooms, the mold grew thickly halfway down a wall, only to stop in a sharp horizontal line, as if cut by a knife.

"Damn strange," Munro said, peering at the mold, rubbing his finger against it. His finger came away with traces of blue paint.

That was how they discovered the elaborate bas-reliefs, once painted, that appeared throughout the city. However, the overgrowth of mold on the irregular carved surface and the pitting of the limestone made any interpretation of the images impossible.

At lunch, Munro mentioned that it was too bad they hadn't brought along a group of art historians to recover the bas-relief images. "With all their lights and machines, they could see what's there in no time," he said.

The most recent examination techniques for artwork, as devised by Degusto and others, employed infrared light and image intensification, and the Congo expedition had the necessary equipment to contrive such a method on the spot. At least it was worth a try. After lunch they returned to the ruins, lugging in the video camera, one of the infrared night lights, and the tiny computer display screen.

After an hour of fiddling they had worked out a system. By shining infrared light on the walls and recording the image with the video camera—and then feeding that image via satellite through the digitizing computer programs in Hous-

ton, and returning it back to their portable display unit—they
were able to reconstitute the pictures on the walls.

Seeing the bas-reliefs in this way reminded Peter Elliot of
the night goggles. If you looked directly at the walls, you
saw nothing but dark moss and lichen and pitted stone. But
if you looked at the little computer screen, you saw the original painted scenes, vibrant and lifelike. It was, he remembered, "very peculiar. There we were in the middle of the
jungle, but we could only examine our environment indi-
rectly, with the machines. We used goggles to see at night,
and video to see during the day. We were using machines to
see what we could not see otherwise, and we were totally
dependent on them."

He also found it odd that the information recorded by the
video camera had to travel more than twenty thousand miles
before returning to the display screen, only a few feet away.
It was, he said later, the "world's longest spinal cord," and
it produced an odd effect. Even at the speed of light, the
transmission required a tenth of a second, and since there
was a short processing time in the Houston computer, the
images did not appear on the screen instantaneously, but
arrived about half a second late. The delay was just barely
noticeable. The scenes they saw provided them with their
first insight into the city and its inhabitants.

The people of Zinj were relatively tall blacks, with round
heads and muscular bodies; in appearance they resembled
the Bantu-speaking people who had first entered the Congo
from the highland savannahs to the north, two thousand years
ago. They were depicted here as lively and energetic: despite
the climate, they favored elaborately decorated, colorful long
robes; their attitudes and gestures were expansive; in all ways
they contrasted sharply with the bland and crumbling structures, now all that remained of their civilization.

The first decoded frescoes showed marketplace scenes:
sellers squatted on the ground beside beautiful woven baskets
containing round objects, while buyers stood and bargained
with them. At first they thought the round objects were fruit,
but Ross decided they were stones.

"Those are uncut diamonds in a surrounding matrix," she said, staring at the screen. "They're selling diamonds."

The frescoes led them to consider what had happened to the inhabitants of the city of Zinj, for the city was clearly abandoned, not destroyed—there was no sign of war or invaders, no evidence of any cataclysm or natural disaster.

Ross, voicing her deepest fears, suspected the diamond mines had given out, turning this city into a ghost town like so many other mining settlements in history. Elliot thought that a plague or disease had overcome the inhabitants. Munro said he thought the gorillas were responsible.

"Don't laugh," he said. "This is a volcanic area. Eruptions, earthquakes, drought, fires on the savannah—the animals go berserk, and don't behave in the ordinary way at all."

"Nature on the rampage?" Elliot asked, shaking his head. "There are volcanic eruptions here every few years, and we know this city existed for centuries. It can't be that."

"Maybe there was a palace revolution, a coup."

"What would that matter to gorillas?" Elliot laughed.

"It happens," Munro said. "In Africa, the animals always get strange when there's a war on, you know." He then told them stories of baboons attacking farmhouses in South Africa and buses in Ethiopia.

Elliot was unimpressed. These ideas of nature mirroring the affairs of man were very old—at least as old as Aesop, and about as scientific. "The natural world is indifferent to man," he said.

"Oh, no question," Munro said, "but there isn't much natural world left."

Elliot was reluctant to agree with Munro, but in fact a well-known academic thesis argued just that. In 1955, the French anthropologist Maurice Cavalle published a controversial paper entitled "The Death of Nature." In it he said:

One million years ago the earth was characterized by a pervasive wilderness which we may call "nature." In the midst of this wild nature stood small enclaves of human habitation. Whether caves with artificial fire to keep men warm, or later cities with dwellings and artificial fields of cultivation, these enclaves were distinctly unnatural. In the succeeding millennia, the area of untouched nature surrounding artificial human enclaves progressively declined, although for centuries the trend remained invisible.

Even 300 years ago in France or England, the great cities of man were isolated by hectares of wilderness in which untamed beasts roamed, as they had for thousands of years before. And yet the expansion of man continued inexorably.

One hundred years ago, in the last days of the great European explorers, nature had so radically diminished that it was a novelty: it is for this reason that African explorations captured the imagination of nineteenth-century man. To enter a truly natural world was exotic, beyond the experience of most mankind, who lived from birth to death in entirely man-made circumstances.

In the twentieth century the balance has shifted so far that for all practical purposes one may say that nature has disappeared. Wild plants are preserved in hothouses, wild animals in zoos and game parks: artificial settings created by man as a souvenir of the once-prevalent natural world. But an animal in a zoo or a game park does not live its natural life, any more than a man in a city lives a natural life.

Today we are surrounded by man and his creations. Man is inescapable, everywhere on the globe, and nature is a fantasy, a dream of the past, long gone.

Ross called Elliot away from his dinner. "It's for you," she said, pointing to the computer next to the antenna. "That friend of yours again."

Munro grinned, "Even in the jungle, the phone never stops ringing."

Elliot went over to look at the screen: COMPUTR LNGWAGE ANALYSS NG REQUIR MOR INPUT KN PROVIDE?

WHT INPUT? Elliot typed back.
MOR AURL INPUT-TRNSMIT RECORDNGS.
Elliot typed back, Yes If Occurs. YES IF OCRS.
RCORD FREQNCY 22-50,000 CYCLS-CRITICL
Elliot typed back, Understood. UNDRSTOD.
There was a pause, then the screen printed: HOWS AMY?
Elliot hesitated. FINE.
STAF SNDS LOV came the reply, and the transmission was
momentarily interrupted.
HOLD TRSNMSN.
There was a long pause.
INCREDIBL NWZ, Seamans printed. HAV FOUND MRS
SWENSN.

2. Swensn NWZ

FOR A MOMENT ELLIOT DID NOT RECOGNIZE THE
name. Swensn? Who was Swensn? A transmission error?
And then he realized: *Mrs. Swenson!* Amy's discoverer, the
woman who had brought her from Africa and had donated
her to the Minneapolis zoo. The woman who had been in
Borneo all these weeks. IF WE HAD ONLY KNON AMY MOTHR
NOT KILD BY NATIVS.
Elliot waited impatiently for the next message from Sea-
mans.
Elliot stared at the message. He had always been told that
Amy's mother had been killed by natives in a village called
Bagimindi. The mother had been killed for food, and Amy
was orphaned. . . .
WHT MEANS?
MOTHR ALREDY DED NOT EATN.

The natives hadn't killed Amy's mother? She was already dead?

XPLN.

SWENSN HAS PICTR CAN TRANSMT?

Hastily, Elliot typed, his fingers fumbling at the keyboard.

TRANSMT.

There was a pause that seemed interminable, and then the video screen received the transmission, scanning it from top to bottom. Long before the picture filled the screen, Elliot realized what it showed.

A crude snapshot of a gorilla corpse with a crushed skull. The animal lay on its back in a packed-earth clearing, presumably in a native village.

In that moment Elliot felt as if the puzzle that preoccupied him, that had caused so much anguish for so many months, was explained. If only they had been able to reach her before . . .

The glowing electronic image faded to black.

Elliot was confronted by a rush of sudden questions. Crushed skulls occurred in the remote—and supposedly uninhabited—region of the Congo, *kanyamagufa*, the place of bones. But Bagimindi was a trading village on the Lubula River, more than a hundred miles away. How had Amy and her dead mother reached Bagimindi?

Ross said, "Got a problem?"

"I don't understand the sequence. I need to ask—"

"Before you do," she said, "review the transmission. It's all in memory." She pressed a button marked RE-PEAT.

The earlier transmitted conversation was repeated on the screen. As Elliot watched Seaman's answers, one line struck him: MOTHR ALREDY DED NOT EATN.

Why wasn't the mother eaten? Gorilla meat was an acceptable—indeed a prized—food in this part of the Congo basin. He typed in a question:

WHY MOTHR NOT EATN.

MOTHR / INFNT FWND BY NATIV ARMY PATRL DOWN

FRM SUDAN CARRIED CRPSE / INFNT 5 DAYS TO BAG-
MINDI VILLAG FOR SALE TOURISTS. SWENSN THERE.

Five days! Quickly, Elliot typed the important question:
WHER FWND?
The answer came back: UNKNWN AREA CONGO.
SPECFY.
NO DETALS. A short pause, then: THERS MOR PICTRS.

SND, he typed back.
The screen went blank, and then filled once more, from
top to bottom. Now he saw a closer view of the female gorilla's crushed skull. And alongside the huge skull, a small
black creature lying on the ground, hands and feet clenched,
mouth open in a frozen scream.
Amy.

Ross repeated the transmission several times, finishing on
the image of Amy as an infant—small, black, screaming.
"No wonder she's been having nightmares," Ross said.
"She probably saw her mother killed."
Elliot said, "Well, at least we can be sure it wasn't goril-
las. They don't kill each other."
"Right now," Ross said, "we can't be sure of anything at
all."

The night of June 21 was so quiet that by ten o'clock they
switched off the infrared night lights to save power. Almost
at once they became aware of movement in the foliage outside the compound. Munro and Kahega swung their guns
around. The rustling increased, and they heard an odd sighing sound, a sort of wheeze.
Elliot heard it too, and felt a chill: it was the same wheezing that had been recorded on the tapes from the first Congo
expedition. He turned on the tape recorder, and swung the
microphone around. They were all tense, alert, waiting.
But for the next hour nothing further happened. The foliage moved all around them, but they saw nothing. Then
shortly before midnight the electrified perimeter fence

erupted in sparks. Munro swung his gun around and fired; Ross hit the switch for the night lights and the camp was bathed in deep red.

"Did you see it?" Munro said. "Did you see what it was?"

They shook their heads. Nobody had seen anything. Elliot checked his tapes; he had only the harsh rattle of gunfire, and the sounds of sparks. No breathing.

The rest of the night passed uneventfully.

DAY 10: ZINJ

June 22, 1979

1. Return

THE MORNING OF JUNE 22 WAS FOGGY AND GRAY. Peter Elliot awoke at 6 A.M. to find the camp already up and active. Munro was stalking around the perimeter of the camp, his clothing soaked to the chest by the wet foliage. He greeted Elliot with a look of triumph, and pointed to the ground.

There, on the ground, were fresh footprints. They were deep and short, rather triangular-shaped, and there was a wide space between the big toe and the other four toes—as wide as the space between a human thumb and fingers.

"Definitely not human," Elliot said, bending to look closely.

Munro said nothing.

"Some kind of primate."

Munro said nothing.

"It can't be a gorilla," Elliot finished, straightening. His video communications from the night before had hardened his belief that gorillas were not involved. Gorillas did not kill other gorillas as Amy's mother had been killed. "It can't be a gorilla," he repeated.

"It's a gorilla, all right," Munro said. "Have a look at this." He pointed to another area of the soft earth. There were four indentations in a row. "Those are the knuckles, when they walk on their hands."

"But gorillas," Elliot said, "are shy animals that sleep at night and avoid contact with men."

"Tell the one that made this print."

"It's small for a gorilla," Elliot said. He examined the fence nearby, where the electrical short had occurred the night before. Bits of gray fur clung to the fence. "And go-rillas don't have gray fur."

"Males do," Munro said. "Silverbacks."

"Yes, but the silverback coloring is whiter than this. This fur is distinctly gray." He hesitated. "Maybe it's a *kakundakari*."

Munro looked disgusted.

The *kakundakari* was a disputed primate in the Congo. Like the yeti of the Himalayas and bigfoot of North America, he had been sighted but never captured. There were endless native stories of a six-foot-tall hairy ape that walked on his hind legs and otherwise behaved in a manlike fashion.

Many respected scientists believed the *kakundakari* existed; perhaps they remembered the authorities who had once denied the existence of the gorilla.

In 1774, Lord Monboddo wrote of the gorilla that "this wonderful and frightful production of nature walks upright like man; is from 7 to 9 feet high . . . and amazingly strong; covered with longish hair, jet black over the body, but longer on the head; the face more like the human than the Chimpenza, but the complexion black; and has no tail."

Forty years later, Bowditch described an African ape "generally five feet high, and four across the shoulders; its paw was said to be even more disproportionate than its breadth, and one blow of it to be fatal." But it was not until 1847 that Thomas Savage, an African missionary, and Jeffries Wyman, a Boston anatomist, published a paper describing "a second species in Africa . . . not recognized by naturalists," which they proposed to call *Troglodytes gorilla*. Their announcement caused enormous excitement in the scientific world, and a rush in London, Paris, and Boston to procure skeletons; by 1855, there was no longer any doubt—a second, very large ape existed in Africa.

Even in the twentieth century, new animal species were discovered in the rain forest: the blue pig in 1944, and the red-breasted grouse in 1961. It was perfectly possible that a rare, reclusive primate might exist in the jungle depths. But there was still no hard evidence for the *kakundakari*.

"This print is from a gorilla," Munro insisted. "Or rather

a group of gorillas. They're all around the perimeter fence. They've been scouting our camp.''

"Scouting our camp," Elliot repeated, shaking his head.

"That's right," Munro said. "Just look at the bloody prints."

Elliot felt his patience growing short. He said something about white-hunter campfire tales, to which Munro said something unflattering about people who knew everything from books.

At that point, the colobus monkeys in the trees overhead began to shriek and shake the branches.

They found Malawi's body just outside the compound. The porter had been going to the stream to get water when he had been killed; the collapsible buckets lay on the ground nearby. The bones of his skull had been crushed; the purple, swelling face was distorted, the mouth open.

The group was repelled by the manner of death; Ross turned away, nauseated; the porters huddled with Kahega, who tried to reassure them; Munro bent to examine the injury. "You notice these flattened areas of compression, as if the head was squeezed between something. . . ."

Munro then called for the stone paddles that Elliot had found in the city the day before. He glanced back at Kahega.

Kahega stood at his most erect and said, "We go home now, boss."

"That's not possible," Munro said.

"We go home. We must go home, one of our brothers is dead, we must make ceremony for his wife and his children, boss."

"Kahega . . ."

"Boss, we must go now."

"Kahega, we will talk." Munro straightened, put his arm over Kahega and led him some distance away, across the clearing. They talked in low voices for several minutes.

"It's awful," Ross said. She seemed genuinely affected with human feeling and instinctively Elliot turned to comfort her, but she continued, "The whole expedition is falling apart. It's awful. We have to hold it together somehow, or we'll *never* find the diamonds.''

''Is that all you care about?''

''Well, they *do* have insurance. . . .''

''For Christ's sake,'' Elliot said.

''You're just upset because you've lost your damned monkey,'' Ross said. ''Now get hold of yourself. They're watching us.''

The Kikuyu were indeed watching Ross and Elliot, trying to sense the drift of sentiment. But they all knew that the real negotiations were between Munro and Kahega, standing off to one side. Several minutes later Kahega returned, wiping his eyes. He spoke quickly to his remaining brothers, and they nodded. He turned back to Munro.

''We stay, boss.''

''Good,'' Munro said, immediately resuming his former imperious tone. ''Bring the paddles.''

When they were brought, Munro placed the paddles to either side of Malawi's head. They fitted the semicircular indentations on the head perfectly.

Munro then said something quickly to Kahega in Swahili, and Kahega said something to his brothers, and they nodded. Only then did Munro take the next horrible step. He raised his arms wide, and then swung the paddles back hard against the already crushed skull. The dull sound was sickening; droplets of blood spattered over his shirt, but he did not further damage the skull.

''A man hasn't the strength to do this,'' Munro said flatly. He looked up at Peter Elliot. ''Care to try?''

Elliot shook his head.

Munro stood. ''Judging by the way he fell, Malawi was standing when it happened.'' Munro faced Elliot, looking him in the eye. ''Large animal, the size of a man. Large, strong animal. A gorilla.''

Elliot had no reply.

There is no doubt that Peter Elliot felt a personal threat in these developments, although not a threat to his safety. ''I simply couldn't accept it,'' he said later. ''I knew my field, and I simply couldn't accept the idea of some unknown, radically violent behavior displayed by gorillas in the wild. And in any case, it didn't make sense. Gorillas making stone paddles that they used to crush human skulls? It was impossible."

After examining the body, Elliot went to the stream to wash the blood from his hands. Once alone, away from the others, he found himself staring into the clear running water and considering the possibility that he might be wrong. Certainly primate researchers had a long history of misjudging their subjects.

Elliot himself had helped eradicate one of the most famous misconceptions—the brutish stupidity of the gorilla. In their first descriptions, Savage and Wyman had written, "This animal exhibits a degree of intelligence inferior to that of the Chimpanzee; this might be expected from its wider departure from the organization of the human subject." Later observers saw the gorilla as "savage, morose, and brutal." But now there was abundant evidence from field and laboratory studies that the gorilla was in many ways brighter than the chimpanzee.

Then, too, there were the famous stories of chimpanzees kidnapping and eating human infants. For decades, primate researchers had dismissed such native tales as "wild and superstitious fantasy." But there was no longer any doubt that chimpanzees occasionally kidnapped—and ate—human infants; when Jane Goodall studied Gombe chimpanzees, she locked away her own infant to prevent his being taken and killed by the chimps.

Chimpanzees hunted a variety of animals, according to a complicated ritual. And field studies by Dian Fossey suggested that gorillas also hunted from time to time, killing small game and monkeys, whenever—

He heard a rustling in the bushes across the stream, and an enormous silverback male gorilla reared up in chest-high foliage. Peter was startled, although as soon as he got over his fright he realized that he was safe. Gorillas never crossed open water, even a small stream. Or was that a misconception, too?

The male stared at him across the water. There seemed to be no threat in his gaze, just a kind of watchful curiosity. Elliot smelled the musty odor of the gorilla, and he heard the breath hiss through his flattened nostrils. He was wondering what he should do when suddenly the gorilla crashed noisily away through the underbrush, and was gone.

This encounter perplexed him, and he stood, wiping the sweat from his face. Then he realized that there was still movement in the foliage across the stream. After a moment, another gorilla rose up, this one smaller: a female, he thought, though he couldn't be sure. The new gorilla gazed at him as implacably as the first. Then the hand moved.

Peter come give tickle.

"Amy!" he shouted, and a moment later he had splashed across the stream, and she had leapt into his arms, hugging him and delivering sloppy wet kisses and grunting happily.

Amy's unexpected return to camp nearly got her shot by the jumpy Kikuyu porters. Only by blocking her body with his own did Elliot prevent gunfire. Twenty minutes later, however, everyone had adjusted to her presence—and Amy promptly began making demands.

She was unhappy to learn that they had not acquired milk or cookies in her absence, but when Munro produced the bottle of warm Dom Pérignon, she agreed to accept champagne instead.

They all sat around her, drinking champagne from tin cups. Elliot was glad for the mitigating presence of the others, for now that Amy was sitting there, safely restored to him, calmly sipping her champagne and signing *Tickle drink Amy like*, he found himself overcome with anger toward her.

Munro grinned at Elliot as he gave him his champagne. "Calmly, Professor, calmly. She's just a child."

"The hell she is," Elliot said. He conducted the subsequent conversation entirely in sign language, not speaking.

Amy, he signed. Why Amy leave?

She buried her nose in her cup, singing *Tickle drink good drink.*

Amy, he signed. Amy tell Peter why leave.

Peter not like Amy.

Peter like Amy.

Peter hurt Amy Peter fly ouch pin Amy no like Peter no like Amy Amy sad sad.

In a detached corner of his mind, he thought he would have to remember that "ouch pin" had now been extended to the Thoralen dart. Her generalization pleased him, but he signed sternly, Peter like Amy. Amy know Peter like Amy. Amy tell Peter why—

Peter no tickle Amy Peter not nice Amy Peter not nice human person Peter like woman no like Amy Peter not like Amy Amy sad Amy sad.

This increasingly rapid signing was itself an indication that she was upset. Where Amy go?

Amy go gorillas good gorillas. Amy like.

Curiosity overcame his anger. Had she joined a troop of wild gorillas for several days? If so, it was an event of major importance, a crucial moment in modern primate history— a language-skilled primate had joined a wild troop and had come back again. He wanted to know more.

Gorillas nice to Amy?

With a smug look: *Yes.*

Amy tell Peter.

She stared off into the distance, not answering.

To catch her attention Elliot snapped his fingers. She turned to him slowly, her expression bored.

Amy tell Peter, Amy stay gorillas?

Yes.

In her indifference was the clear recognition that Elliot was desperate to learn what she knew. Amy was always very astute at recognizing when she had the upper hand—and she had it now.

Amy tell Peter, he signed as calmly as he could.

Good gorillas like Amy Amy good gorilla.

That told him nothing at all. She was composing phrases by rote: another way of ignoring him.

Amy.

She glanced at him.

Amy tell Peter. Amy come see gorillas?

Yes.

Gorillas do what?

Gorillas sniff Amy.

All gorillas?

Big gorillas white back gorillas sniff Amy baby sniff Amy all gorillas sniff gorillas like Amy.

So silverback males had sniffed her, then infants, then all the members of the troop. That much was clear—remarkably clear, he thought, making a mental note of her extended syntax. Afterward had she been accepted in the troop? He signed, What happen Amy then?

Gorillas give food.

What food?

No name Amy food give food.

Apparently they had shown her food. Or had they actually fed her? Such a thing had never been reported in the wild, but then no one had ever witnessed the introduction of a new animal into a troop. She was a female, and nearly of productive age. . . .

What gorillas give food?

All give food Amy take food Amy like.

Apparently it was not males, or males exclusively. But what had caused her acceptance? Granted that gorilla troops were not as closed to outsiders as monkey troops—what actually had happened?

Amy stay with gorillas?

Gorillas like Amy.

Yes. What Amy do?

Amy sleep Amy eat Amy live gorillas gorillas good gorillas Amy like.

So she had joined in the life of the troop, living the daily existence. Had she been totally accepted?

Amy like gorillas?

Gorillas dumb.

Why dumb?

Gorillas no talk.

No talk sign talk?

Gorillas no talk.

Evidently she had experienced frustration with the gorillas

because they did not know her sign language. (Language-using primates were commonly frustrated and annoyed when thrown among animals who did not understand the signs.)

Gorillas nice to Amy?

Gorillas like Amy Amy like gorillas like Amy like gorillas.

Why Amy come back?

Want milk cookies.

"Amy," he said, "you know we don't have any damn milk or cookies." His sudden verbalization startled the others. They looked questioningly at Amy.

For a long time she did not answer. *Amy like Peter. Amy sad want Peter.*

He felt like crying.

Peter good human person.

Blinking his eyes he signed, Peter tickle Amy. She jumped into his arms.

Later, he questioned her in more detail. But it was a painstakingly slow process, chiefly because of Amy's difficulty in handling concepts of time.

Amy distinguished past, present, and future—she remembered previous events, and anticipated future promises—but the Project Amy staff had never succeeded in teaching her exact differentiations. She did not, for example, distinguish yesterday from the day before. Whether this reflected a failing in teaching methods or an innate feature of Amy's conceptual world was an open question. (There was evidence for a conceptual difference. Amy was particularly perplexed by spatial metaphors for time, such as "that's behind us" or "that's coming up." Her trainers conceived of the past as behind them and the future ahead. But Amy's behavior seemed to indicate that she conceived of the past as in front of her—because she could see it—and the future behind her—because it was still invisible. Whenever she was impatient for the promised arrival of a friend, she repeatedly looked over her shoulder, even if she was facing the door.)

In any case, the time problem was a difficulty in talking to her now, and Elliot phrased his questions carefully. He asked, "Amy, what happened at night? With the gorillas?"

She gave him the look she always gave him when she
thought a question was obvious. *Amy sleep night.*

"And the other gorillas?"

Gorillas sleep night.

"All the gorillas?"

She disdained to answer.

"Amy," he said, "gorillas come to our camp at night."

Come this place?

"Yes, this place. Gorillas come at night."

She thought that over. *No.*

Munro said, "What did she say?"

Elliot said, "She said 'No.' Yes, Amy, they come."

She was silent a moment, and then she signed, *Things
come.*

Munro again asked what she had said.

"She said, 'Things come.' " Elliot translated the rest of
her responses for them.

Ross asked, "What things, Amy?"

Bad things.

Munro said, "Were they gorillas, Amy?"

*Not gorillas. Bad things. Many bad things come forest
come. Breath talk. Come night come.*

Munro said, "Where are they now, Amy?"

Amy looked around at the jungle. *Here. This bad old place
things come.*

Ross said, "What things, Amy? Are they animals?"

Elliot told them that Amy could not abstract the category
"animals." "She thinks people are animals," he explained.
"Are the bad things people, Amy? Are they human persons?"

No.

Munro said, "Monkeys?"

No. Bad things, not sleep night.

Munro said, "Is she reliable?"

What means?

"Yes," Elliot said. "Perfectly."

"She knows what gorillas are?"

Amy good gorilla, she signed.

"Yes, you are," Elliot said. "She's saying she's a good gorilla."

Munro frowned. "So she knows what gorillas are, but she says these things are not gorillas?"

"That's what she says."

2. Missing Elements

ELLIOT GOT ROSS TO SET UP THE VIDEO CAMERA AT the outskirts of the city, facing the campsite. With the videotape running he led Amy to the edge of the camp to look at the ruined buildings. Elliot wanted to confront Amy with the lost city, the reality behind her dreams—and he wanted a record of her responses to that moment. What happened was totally unexpected.

Amy had no reaction at all.

Her face remained impassive, her body relaxed. She did not sign. If anything she gave the impression of boredom, of suffering through another of Elliot's enthusiasms that she did not share. Elliot watched her carefully. She wasn't displacing; she wasn't repressing; she wasn't doing anything. She stared at the city with equanimity.

"Amy know this place?"

Yes.

"Amy tell Peter what place."

Bad place old place.

"Sleep pictures?"

This bad place.

"Why is it bad, Amy?"

Bad place old place.

"Yes, but why, Amy?"

Amy fear.

She showed no somatic indication of fear. Squatting on the ground alongside him she gazed forward, perfectly calm.

"Why Amy fear?"

Amy want eat.

"Why Amy fear?"

She would not answer, in the way that she did not deign to answer him whenever she was completely bored; he could not provoke her to discuss her dreams further. She was as closed on the subject as she had been in San Francisco. When he asked her to accompany them into the ruins, she calmly refused to do so. On the other hand, she did not seem distressed that Elliot was going into the city, and she cheerfully waved goodbye before going to demand more food from Kahega.

Only after the expedition was concluded and Elliot had returned to Berkeley did he find the explanation to this perplexing event—in Freud's *Interpretation of Dreams*, first published in 1887.

It may happen on rare occasions that a patient may be confronted by the reality behind his dreams. Whether a physical edifice, a person, or a situation that has the tenor of deep familiarity, the subjective response of the dreamer is uniformly the same. The emotive content held in the dream—whether frightening, pleasurable, or mysterious— is drained away upon sight of the reality. . . . We may be certain that the apparent boredom of the subject does not prove the dream-content is false. Boredom may be most strongly felt when the dream-content is *real*. The subject recognizes on some deep level his inability to alter the conditions that he feels, and so finds himself overcome by fatigue, boredom, and indifference, to conceal from him *his fundamental helplessness in the face of a genuine problem which must be rectified.*

Months later, Elliot would conclude that Amy's bland reaction only indicated the depth of her feeling, and that Freud's analysis was correct; it protected her from a situation that had to be changed, but that Amy felt powerless to alter,

especially considering whatever infantile memories remained from the traumatic death of her mother.

Yet at the time, Elliot felt disappointment with Amy's neutrality. Of all the possible reactions he had imagined when
he first set out for the Congo, boredom was the least expected, and he utterly failed to grasp its significance—that
the city of Zinj was so fraught with danger that Amy felt
obliged in her own mind to push it aside, and to ignore it.

Elliot, Munro, and Ross spent a hot, difficult morning
hacking their way through the dense bamboo and the clinging, tearing vines of secondary jungle growth to reach new
buildings in the heart of the city. By midday, their efforts
were rewarded as they entered structures unlike any they had
seen before. These buildings were impressively engineered,
enclosing vast cavernous spaces descending three and four
stories beneath the ground.

Ross was delighted by the underground constructions, for
it proved to her that the Zinj people had evolved the technology to dig into the earth, as was necessary for diamond
mines. Munro expressed a similar view: "These people,"
he said, "could do anything with earthworks."

Despite their enthusiasm, they found nothing of interest in
the depths of the city. They ascended to higher levels later
in the day, coming upon a building so filled with reliefs that
they termed it "the gallery." With the video camera hooked
to the satellite linkup, they examined the pictures in the gallery.

These showed aspects of ordinary city life. There were
domestic scenes of women cooking around fires, children
playing a ball game with sticks, scribes squatting on the
ground as they kept records on clay tablets. A whole wall of
hunting scenes, the men in brief loincloths, armed with
spears. And finally scenes of mining, men carrying baskets
of stones from tunnels in the earth.

In this rich panorama, they noticed certain missing elements. The people of Zinj had dogs, used for hunting, and
a variety of civet cat, kept as household pets—yet it had apparently never occurred to them to use animals as beasts of

burden. All manual labor was done by human slaves. And they apparently never discovered the wheel for there were no carts or rolling vehicles. Everything was carried by hand in baskets.

Munro looked at the pictures for a long time and finally said, "Something else is missing."

They were looking at a scene from the diamond mines, the dark pits in the ground from which men emerged carrying baskets heaped with gems.

"Of course!" Munro said, snapping his fingers. "No police!"

Elliot suppressed a smile: he considered it only too predictable that a character like Munro would wonder about police in this long-dead society.

But Munro insisted his observation was significant. "Look here," he said. "This city existed because of its diamond mines. It had no other reason for being, out here in the jungle. Zinj was a mining civilization—its wealth, its trade, its daily life, everything depended upon mining. It was a classic one-crop economy—and yet they didn't guard it, didn't regulate it, didn't control it?"

Elliot said, "There are other things we haven't seen— pictures of people eating, for example. Perhaps it was taboo to show the guards."

"Perhaps," Munro said, unconvinced. "But in every other mining complex in the world guards are ostentatiously prominent, as proof of control. Go to the South African diamond mines or the Bolivian emerald mines and the first thing you are made aware of is the security. But here," he said, pointing to the reliefs, *"there are no guards."*

Karen Ross suggested that perhaps they didn't need guards, perhaps the Zinjian society was orderly and peaceful. "After all, it was a long time ago," she said.

"Human nature doesn't change," Munro insisted.

When they left the gallery, they came to an open courtyard, overgrown with tangled vines. The courtyard had a formal quality, heightened by the pillars of a temple-like building to one side. Their attention was immediately drawn to the courtyard floor. Strewn across the ground were dozens of stone paddles, of the kind Elliot had previously found.

"I'll be damned," Elliot said. They picked their way through this field of paddles, and entered the building they came to call "the temple."

It consisted of a single large square room. The ceiling had been broken in several places, and hazy shafts of sunlight filtered down. Directly ahead, they saw an enormous mound of vines perhaps ten feet high, a pyramid of vegetation. Then they recognized it was a statue.

Elliot climbed up on the statue and began stripping away the clinging foliage. It was hard work; the creepers had dug tenaciously into the stone. He glanced back at Munro. "Better?"

"Come and look," Munro said, with an odd expression on his face.

Elliot climbed down, stepped back to look. Although the statue was pitted and discolored, he could clearly see an enormous standing gorilla, the face fierce, the arms stretched wide. In each hand, the gorilla held stone paddles like cymbals, ready to swing them together.

"My God," Peter Elliot said.

"Gorilla," Munro said with satisfaction.

Ross said, "It's all clear now. These people worshiped gorillas. It was their religion."

"But why would Amy say they weren't gorillas?"

"Ask her," Munro said, glancing at his watch. "I have to get us ready for tonight."

3. Attack

THEY DUG A MOAT OUTSIDE THE PERIMETER FENCE with collapsible metalloid shovels. The work continued long after sundown; they were obliged to turn on the red night lights while they filled the moat with water diverted from the nearby stream. Ross considered the moat a trivial obstacle— it was only a few inches deep and a foot wide. A man could step easily across it. In reply, Munro stood outside the moat and said, "Amy, come here, I'll tickle you."

With a delighted grunt, Amy came bounding toward him, but stopped abruptly on the other side of the water. "Come on, I'll tickle you," Munro said again, holding out his arms. "Come on, girl."

Still she would not cross. She signed irritably; Munro stepped over and lifted her across. "Gorillas hate water," he told Ross. "I've seen them refuse to cross a stream smaller than this." Amy was reaching up and scratching under his arms, then pointing to herself. The meaning was perfectly clear. "Women," Munro sighed, and bent over and tickled her vigorously. Amy rolled on the ground, grunting and snuffling and smiling broadly. When he stopped, she lay expectantly on the ground, waiting for more.

"That's all," Munro said.

She signed to him.

"Sorry, I don't understand. No," he laughed, "signing slower doesn't help." And then he understood what she wanted, and he carried her back across the moat again, into the camp. She kissed him wetly on the cheek.

"Better watch your monkey," Munro said to Elliot as he sat down to dinner. He continued in this light bantering fashion, aware of the need to loosen everybody up; they were all nervous, crouching around the fire. But when the dinner was finished, and Kahega was off setting out the ammunition and checking the guns, Munro took Elliot aside and said, "Chain her in your tent. If we start shooting tonight, I'd hate to have her running around in the dark. Some of the lads may not be too particular about telling one gorilla from another. Explain to her that it may get very noisy from the guns but she should not be frightened."

"Is it going to get very noisy?" Elliot said.

"I imagine," Munro said.

He took Amy into his tent and put on the sturdy chain leash she often wore in California. He tied one end to his cot, but it was a symbolic gesture; Amy could move it easily if she chose to. He made her promise to stay in the tent.

She promised. He stepped to the tent entrance, and she signed, *Amy like Peter*.

"Peter like Amy," he said, smiling. "Everything's going to be fine."

He emerged into another world.

The red night lights had been doused, but in the flickering glow of the campfire he saw the goggle-eyed sentries in position around the compound. With the low throbbing pulse of the electrified fence, this sight created an unearthly atmosphere. Peter Elliot suddenly sensed the precariousness of their position—a handful of frightened people deep in the Congo rain forest, more than two hundred miles from the nearest human habitation.

Waiting.

He tripped over a black cable on the ground. Then he saw a network of cables, snaking over the compound, running to the guns of each sentry. He noticed then that the guns had an unfamiliar shape—they were somehow too slender, too insubstantial—and that the black cables ran from the guns to squat, snub-nosed mechanisms mounted on short tripods at intervals around the camp.

He saw Ross near the fire, setting up the tape recorder.

"What the hell is all this?" he whispered, pointing to the cables.

"That's a LATRAP. For laser-tracking projectile," she whispered. "The LATRAP system consists of multiple LGSDs attached to sequential RFSDs."

She told him that the sentries held guns which were actually laser-guided sight devices, linked to rapid-firing sensor devices on tripods. "They lock onto the target," she said, "and do the actual shooting once the target is identified. It's a jungle warfare system. The RFSDs have marlan-baffle silencers so the enemy won't know where the firing is coming from. Just make sure you don't step in front of one, because they automatically lock onto body heat."

Ross gave him the tape recorder, and went off to check the fuel cells powering the perimeter fence. Elliot glanced at the sentries in the outer darkness; Munro waved cheerfully to him. Elliot realized that the sentries with their grasshopper goggles and their acronymic weapons could see him far better than he could see them. They looked like beings from another universe, dropped into the timeless jungle.

Waiting.

The hours passed. The jungle perimeter was silent except for the murmur of water in the moat. Occasionally the porters called to one another softly, making some joke in Swahili; but they never smoked because of the heat-sensing machinery. Eleven o'clock passed, and then midnight, and then one o'clock.

He heard Amy snoring in his tent, her noisy rasping audible above the throb of the electrified fence. He glanced over at Ross sleeping on the ground, her finger on the switch for the night lights. He looked at his watch and yawned; nothing was going to happen tonight; Munro was wrong.

Then he heard the breathing sound.

The sentries heard it too, swinging their guns in the darkness. Elliot pointed the recorder microphone toward the sound but it was hard to determine its exact location. The wheezing sighs seemed to come from all parts of the jungle at once, drifting with the night fog, soft and pervasive.

He watched the needles wiggle on the recording gauges.

And then the needles bounced into the red, as Elliot heard a dull thud, and the gurgle of water. Everyone heard it; the sentries clicked off their safeties.

Elliot crept with his tape recorder toward the perimeter fence and looked out at the moat. Foliage moved beyond the fence. The sighing grew louder. He heard the gurgle of water and saw a dead tree trunk lying across the moat.

That was what the slapping sound had been: a bridge being placed across the moat. In that instant Elliot realized they had vastly underestimated whatever they were up against. He signaled to Munro to come and look, but Munro was waving him away from the fence and pointing emphatically to the squat tripod on the ground near his feet. Before Elliot could move, the colobus monkeys began to shriek in the trees overhead—and the first of the gorillas silently charged.

He had a glimpse of an enormous animal, distinctly gray in color, racing up to him as he ducked down; a moment later, the gorillas hit the electrified fence with a shower of spitting sparks and the odor of burning flesh.

It was the start of an eerie, silent battle.

Emerald laser beams flashed through the air; the tripod-mounted machine guns made a soft *thew-thew-thew* as the bullets spit outward, the aiming mechanisms whining as the barrels spun and fired, spun and fired again. Every tenth bullet was a white phosphorous tracer; the air was criss-crossed green and white over Elliot's head.

The gorillas attacked from all directions; six of them simultaneously hit the fence and were repelled in a crackling burst of sparks. Still more charged, throwing themselves on the flimsy perimeter mesh, yet the sizzle of sparks and the shriek of the colobus monkeys was the loudest sound they heard. And then he saw gorillas in the trees overhanging the campsite. Munro and Kahega began firing upward, silent laser beams streaking into the foliage. He heard the sighing sound again. Elliot turned and saw more gorillas tearing at the fence, which had gone dead—there were no more sparks.

And he realized that this swift, sophisticated equipment was not holding the gorillas back—they needed the noise. Munro had the same thought, because he shouted in Swahili for the men to hold their fire, and called to Elliot, "Pull the silencers! The silencers!"

Elliot grabbed the black barrel on the first tripod mechanism and plucked it away, swearing—it was very hot. Immediately as he stepped away from the tripod, a stuttering sound filled the air, and two gorillas fell heavily from the trees, one still alive. The gorilla charged him as he pulled away the silencer from the second tripod. The stubby barrel swung around and blasted the gorilla at very close range; warm liquid spattered Elliot's face. He pulled the silencer from the third tripod and threw himself to the ground.

Deafening machine-gun fire and clouds of acrid cordite had an immediate effect on the gorillas; they backed off in disorder. There was a period of silence, although the sentries fired laser shots that set the tripod machines scanning rapidly across the jungle landscape, whirring back and forth, searching for a target.

Then the machines stopped hunting, and paused. The jungle around them was still.

The gorillas were gone.

DAY 11: ZINJ

June 23, 1979

1. Gorilla Elliotensis

THE GORILLA CORPSES LAY STRETCHED ON THE ground, the bodies already stiffening in the morning warmth. Elliot spent two hours examining the animals, both adult males in the prime of life.

The most striking feature was the uniform gray color. The two known races of gorilla, the mountain gorilla in Virunga, and the lowland gorilla near the coast, both had black hair. Infants were often brown with a white tuft of hair at the rump, but their hair darkened within the first five years. By the age of twelve, adult males had developed the silver patch along their back and rump, the sign of sexual maturity.

With age, gorillas turned gray in much the same way as people. Male gorillas first developed a spot of gray above each ear, and as the years passed more body hair turned gray. Old animals in their late twenties and thirties sometimes turned entirely gray except for their arms, which remained black.

But from their teeth Elliot estimated that these males were no more than ten years old. All their pigmentation seemed lighter, eye and skin color as well as hair. Gorilla skin was black, and eyes were dark brown. But here the pigmentation was distinctly gray, and the eyes were light yellow brown.

As much as anything it was the eyes that set him thinking.

Next Elliot measured the bodies. The crown-heel length was 139.2 and 141.7 centimeters. Male mountain gorillas had been recorded from 147 to 205 centimeters, with an average height of 175 centimeters—five feet eight inches. But these animals stood about four feet six inches tall. They were distinctly small for gorillas. He weighed them: 255 pounds

245

and 347 pounds. Most mountain gorillas weighed between 280 and 450 pounds.

Elliot recorded thirty additional skeletal measurements for later analysis by the computer back in San Francisco. Because now he was convinced that he was onto something. With a knife, he dissected the head of the first animal, cutting away the gray skin to reveal the underlying muscle and bone. His interest was the sagittal crest, the bony ridge running along the center of the skull from the forehead to the back of the neck. The sagittal crest was a distinctive feature of gorilla skull architecture not found in other apes or man; it was what gave gorillas a pointy-headed look.

Elliot determined that the sagittal crest was poorly developed in these males. In general, the cranial musculature resembled a chimpanzee's far more than a gorilla's. Elliot made additional measurements of the molar cusps, the jaw, the simian shelf, and the brain case.

By midday, his conclusion was clear: this was at least a new race of gorilla, equal to the mountain and lowland gorilla—and it was possibly a new species of animal entirely.

"Something happens to the man who discovers a new species of animal," wrote Lady Elizabeth Forstmann in 1879. "At once he forgets his family and friends, and all those who were near and dear to him; he forgets colleagues who supported his professional efforts; most cruelly he forgets parents and children; in short, he abandons all who knew him prior to his insensate lust for fame at the hands of the demon called Science."

Lady Forstmann understood, for her husband had just left her after discovering the Norwegian blue-crested grouse in 1878. "In vain," she observed, "does one ask what it matters that another bird or animal is added to the rich panoply of God's creations, which already number—by Linnaean reckoning—in the millions. There is no response to such a question, for the discoverer has joined the ranks of the immortals, at least as he imagines it, and he lies beyond the power of mere people to dissuade him from his course."

Certainly Peter Elliot would have denied that his own behavior resembled that of the dissolute Scottish nobleman. Nevertheless he found he was bored by the prospect of further exploration of Zinj; he had no interest in diamonds, or Amy's dreams; he wished only to return home with a skeleton of the new ape, which would astonish colleagues around the world. He suddenly remembered he did not own a tuxedo, and he found himself preoccupied with matters of nomenclature; he imagined in the future three species of African apes:

> *Pan troglodytes*, the chimpanzee.
> *Gorilla gorilla*, the gorilla.
> *Gorilla elliotensis*, a new species of gray gorilla.

Even if the species category and name were ultimately rejected, he would have accomplished far more than most scientists studying primates could ever hope to achieve.

Elliot was dazzled by his own prospects.

In retrospect, no one was thinking clearly that morning. When Elliot said he wanted to transmit the recorded breathing sounds to Houston, Ross replied it was a trivial detail that could wait. Elliot did not press her; they both later regretted their decision.

And when they heard booming explosions like distant artillery fire that morning, they paid no attention. Ross assumed it was General Muguru's men fighting the Kigani. Munro told her that the fighting was at least fifty miles away, too far for the sound to carry, but offered no alternative explanation for the noise.

And because Ross skipped the morning transmission to Houston, she was not informed of new geological changes that might have given new significance to the explosive detonations.

They were seduced by the technology employed the night before, secure in their sense of indomitable power. Only Munro remained immune. He had checked their ammunition supplies with discouraging results. "That laser system is splendid but it uses up bullets like there's no tomorrow," Munro said. "Last night consumed half of our total ammunition."

"What can we do?" Elliot asked.

"I was hoping you'd have an answer for that," Munro said. "You examined the bodies."

Elliot stated his belief that they were confronted with a new species of primate. He summarized the anatomical findings, which supported his beliefs.

"That's all well and good," Munro said. "But I'm interested in how they act, not how they look. You said it yourself—gorillas are usually diurnal animals, and these are nocturnal. Gorillas are usually shy and avoid men, while these are aggressive and attack men fearlessly. Why?"

Elliot had to admit that he didn't know.

"Considering our ammunition supplies, I think we'd better find out," Munro said.

2. The Temple

THE LOGICAL PLACE TO BEGIN WAS THE TEMPLE, with its enormous, menacing gorilla statue. They returned that afternoon, and found behind the statue a succession of small cubicle-like rooms. Ross thought that priests who worshiped the cult of the gorilla lived here.

She had an elaborate explanation: "The gorillas in the surrounding jungle terrorized the people of Zinj, who offered sacrifices to appease the gorillas. The priests were a separate class, secluded from society. Look here, at the entrance to the line of cubicles, there is this little room. A guard stayed here to keep people away from the priests. It was a whole system of belief.''

Elliot was not convinced, and neither was Munro. "Even religion is practical," Munro said. "It's supposed to benefit you."

"People worship what they fear," Ross said, "hoping to control it."

"But how could they control the gorillas?" Munro asked. "What could they do?"

When the answer finally came it was startling, for they had it all backward.

They moved past the cubicles to a series of long corridors, decorated with bas-reliefs. Using their infrared computer system, they were able to see the reliefs, which were scenes arranged in a careful order like a picture textbook.

The first scene showed a series of caged gorillas. A black man stood near the cages holding a stick in his hand.

The second picture showed an African standing with two gorillas, holding ropes around their necks.

A third showed an African instructing the gorillas in a courtyard. The gorillas were tethered to vertical poles, each with a ring at the top.

The final picture showed the gorillas attacking a line of straw dummies, which hung from an overhead stone support. They now knew the meaning of what they had found in the courtyard of the gymnasium, and the jail.

"My God," Elliot said. "They *trained* them."

Munro nodded. "Trained them as guards to watch over the mines. An animal élite, ruthless and incorruptible. Not a bad idea when you think about it."

Ross looked at the building around her again, realizing it wasn't a temple but a school. An objection occurred to her: these pictures were hundreds of years old, the trainers long gone. Yet the gorillas were still here. "Who teaches them now?"

"They do," Elliot said. "They teach each other."

"Is that possible?"

"Perfectly possible. Conspecific teaching occurs among primates."

This had been a longstanding question among researchers. But Washoe, the first primate in history to learn sign language, taught ASL to her offspring. Language-skilled primates freely taught other animals in captivity; for that matter, they would teach people, signing slowly and repeatedly until the stupid uneducated human person got the point.

So it was possible for a primate tradition of language and behavior to be carried on for generations. "You mean," Ross said, "that the people in this city have been gone for centuries, but the gorillas they trained are still here?"

"That's the way it looks," Elliot said.

"And they use stone tools?" she asked. "Stone paddles."

"Yes," Elliot said. The idea of tool use was not as far-fetched as it first seemed. Chimpanzees were capable of elaborate tool use, of which the most striking example was "termite fishing." Chimps would make a twig, carefully bending it to their specifications, and then spend hours over a termite mound, fishing with the stick to catch succulent grubs.

Human observers labeled this activity "primitive tool use" until they tried it themselves. It turned out that making a satisfactory twig and catching termites was not primitive at all; at least it proved to be beyond the ability of people who tried to duplicate it. Human fishermen quit, with a new respect for the chimpanzees, and a new observation—they now noticed that younger chimps spent days watching their elders make sticks and twirl them in the mound. Young chimps literally *learned* how to do it, and the learning process extended over a period of years.

This began to look suspiciously like culture; the apprenticeship of young Ben Franklin, printer, was not so different from the apprenticeship of young Chimpanzee, termite fisher. Both learned their skills over a period of years by observing their elders; both made mistakes on the way to ultimate success.

Yet manufactured stone tools implied a quantum jump beyond twigs and termites. The privileged position of stone tools as the special province of mankind might have remained sacrosanct were it not for a single iconoclastic researcher. In 1971, the British scientist R. V. S. Wright decided to teach an ape to make stone tools. His pupil was a five-year-old orangutan named Abang in the Bristol zoo. Wright presented Abang with a box containing food, bound with a rope; he showed Abang how to cut the rope with a flint chip to get the food. Abang got the point in an hour.

Wright then showed Abang how to make a stone chip by striking a pebble against a flint core. This was a more difficult lesson; over a period of weeks, Abang required a total of three hours to learn to grasp the flint core between his toes, strike a sharp chip, cut the rope, and get the food.

The point of the experiment was not that apes used stone tools, but that the ability to make stone tools was literally within their grasp. Wright's experiment was one more reason to think that human beings were not as unique as they had previously imagined themselves to be.

"But why would Amy say they weren't gorillas?"

"Because they're not," Elliot said. "These animals don't look like gorillas and they don't act like gorillas. They are physically and behaviorally different." He went on to voice his suspicion that not only had these animals been trained, they had been *bred*—perhaps interbred with chimpanzees or, more strangely still, with men.

They thought he was joking. But the facts were disturbing. In 1960, the first blood protein studies quantified the kinship between man and ape. Biochemically man's nearest relative was the chimpanzee, much closer than the gorilla. In 1964, chimpanzee kidneys were successfully transplanted into men; blood transfusions were also possible.

But the degree of similarity was not fully known until 1975, when biochemists compared the DNA of chimps and men. It was discovered that chimps differed from men by only 1 percent of their DNA strands. And almost no one wanted to acknowledge one consequence: with modern DNA hybridization techniques and embryonic implantation, ape-ape crosses were certain, and man-ape crosses were possible.

Of course, the fourteenth-century inhabitants of Zinj had no way to mate DNA strands. But Elliot pointed out that they had consistently underestimated the skills of the Zinj people, who at the very least had managed, five hundred years ago, to carry out sophisticated animal-training procedures only duplicated by Western scientists within the last ten years.

And as Elliot saw it, the animals the Zinjians had trained presented an awesome problem.

"We have to face the realities," he said. "When Amy was given a human IQ test, she scored ninety-two. For all practical purposes, Amy is as smart as a human being, and in many ways she is smarter—more perceptive and sensitive. She can manipulate us at least as skillfully as we can manipulate her.

"These gray gorillas possess that same intelligence, yet they have been single-mindedly bred to be the primate equivalent of Doberman pinschers—guard animals, attack animals, trained for cunning and viciousness. But they are much brighter and more resourceful than dogs. And they will continue their attacks until they succeed in killing us all, as they have killed everyone who has come here before."

3. Looking Through the Bars

IN 1975, THE MATHEMATICIAN S. L. BERENSKY reviewed the literature on primate language and reached a startling conclusion. "There is no doubt," he announced, "that primates are far superior in intelligence to man."

In Berensky's mind, "The salient question—which every human visitor to the zoo intuitively asks—is, who is behind the bars? Who is caged, and who is free? . . . On both sides of the bars primates can be observed making faces at each other. It is too facile to say that man is superior because he has made the zoo. We impose our special horror of barred captivity—a form of punishment among our species—and assume that other primates feel as we do."

Berensky likened primates to foreign ambassadors. "Apes have for centuries managed to get along with human beings, as ambassadors from their species. In recent years, they have even learned to communicate with human beings using sign language. But it is a one-sided diplomatic exchange; no human being has attempted to live in ape society, to master their language and customs, to eat their food, to live as they do. The apes have learned to talk to us, but we have never learned to talk to them. Who, then, should be judged the greater intellect?"

Berensky added a prediction. "The time will come," he said, "when circumstances may force some human beings to communicate with a primate society on its own terms. Only then human beings will become aware of their complacent egotism with regard to other animals."

The ERTS expedition, isolated deep in the Congo rain forest, now faced just such a problem. Confronted by a new species of gorilla-like animal, they somehow had to deal with it on its own terms.

During the evening, Elliot transmitted the taped breath sounds to Houston, and from there they were relayed to San Francisco. The transcript which followed the transmission was brief:

Seamans wrote: RECVD TRNSMISN. SHLD HELP.

IMPORTNT-NEED TRNSLATION SOON, Elliot typed back. WHN HAVE?

COMPUTR ANALYSS DIFICLT-PROBLMS XCEED MGNITUDE CSL / JSL TRNSLATN.

"What does that mean?" Ross said.

"He's saying that the translation problems exceed the problem of translating Chinese or Japanese sign language."

She hadn't known there was a Chinese or Japanese sign language, but Elliot explained that there were sign languages for all major languages, and each followed its own rules. For instance, BSL, British sign language, was totally different from ASL, American sign language, even though spoken and written English language was virtually identical in the two countries.

Different sign languages had different grammar and syntax, and even obeyed different sign traditions. Chinese sign language used the middle finger pointing outward for several signs, such as TWO WEEKS FROM NOW and BROTHER, although this configuration was insulting and unacceptable in American sign language.

"But this is a spoken language," Ross said.

"Yes," Elliot said, "but it's a complicated problem. We aren't likely to get it translated soon."

By nightfall, they had two additional pieces of information. Ross ran a computer simulation through Houston which came back with a probability course of three days and a standard deviation of two days to find the diamond mines. That meant they should be prepared for five more days at the site. Food was not a problem, but ammunition was: Munro proposed to use tear gas.

They expected the gray gorillas to try a different approach, and they did, attacking immediately after dark. The battle on the night of June 23 was punctuated by the coughing explosions of canisters and the sizzling hiss of the gas. The strategy was effective; the gorillas were driven away, and did not return again that night.

Munro was pleased. He announced that they had enough tear gas to hold off the gorillas for a week, perhaps more. For the moment, their problems appeared to be solved.

DAY 12: ZINJ

June 24, 1979

1. The Offensive

SHORTLY AFTER DAWN, THEY DISCOVERED THE bodies of Mulewe and Akari near their tent. Apparently the attack the night before had been a diversion, allowing one gorilla to enter the compound, kill the porters, and slip out again. Even more disturbing, they could find no clue to how the gorilla had got through the electrified fence and back out again.

A careful search revealed a section of fence torn near the bottom. A long stick lay on the ground nearby. The gorillas had used the stick to lift the bottom of the fence, enabling one to crawl through. And before leaving, the gorillas had carefully restored the fence to its original condition.

The intelligence implied by such behavior was hard to accept. "Time and again," Elliot said later, "we came up against our prejudices about animals. We kept expecting the gorillas to behave in stupid, stereotyped ways but they never did. We never treated them as flexible and responsive adversaries, though they had already reduced our numbers by one fourth."

Munro had difficulty accepting the calculated hostility of the gorillas. His experience had taught him that animals in nature were indifferent to man. Finally he concluded that "these animals had been trained by men, and I had to think of them as men. The question became what would I do if they were men?"

For Munro the answer was clear: take the offensive.

Amy agreed to lead them into the jungle where she said the gorillas lived. By ten o'clock that morning, they were moving up the hillsides north of the city armed with machine guns. It was not long before they found gorilla spoor—quantities of dung, and nests on the ground and in the trees. Munro was disturbed by what he saw; some trees held twenty or thirty nests, suggesting a large population of animals.

Ten minutes later, they came upon a group of ten gray gorillas feeding on succulent vines: four males and three females, a juvenile, and two scampering infants. The adults were lazy, basking in the sun, eating in desultory fashion. Several other animals slept on their backs, snoring loudly. They all seemed remarkably unguarded.

Munro gave a hand signal; the safeties clicked off the guns. He prepared to fire into the group when Amy tugged at his trouser leg. He looked off and "had the shock of my bloody life. Up the slope was another group, perhaps ten or twelve animals—and then I saw another group—and another—and another still. There must have been three hundred or more. The hillside was *crawling* with gray gorillas."

The largest gorilla group ever sighted in the wild had been thirty-one individuals, in Kabara in 1971, and even that sighting was disputed. Most researchers thought it was actually two groups seen briefly together, since the usual group size was ten to fifteen individuals. Elliot found three hundred animals "an awesome sight." But he was even more impressed by the behavior of the animals. As they browsed and fed in the sunlight, they behaved very much like ordinary gorillas in the wild, but there were important differences.

"From the first sighting, I never had any doubt that they had language. Their wheezing vocalizations were striking and clearly constituted a form of language. In addition they used sign language, although nothing like what we knew. Their hand gestures were delivered with outstretched arms in a graceful way, rather like Thai dancers. These hand movements seemed to complement or add to the sighing vocalizations. Obviously the gorillas had been taught, or had elaborated on their own, a language system far more sophisticated than the pure sign language of laboratory apes in the twentieth century."

Some abstract corner of Elliot's mind considered this discovery tremendously exciting, while at the same time he shared the fear of the others around him. Crouched behind the dense foliage they held their breath and watched the gorillas feed on the opposite hillside. Although the gorillas seemed peaceful, the humans watching them felt a tension approaching panic at being so close to such great numbers of them. Finally, at Munro's signal, they slipped back down the trail, and returned to the camp.

The porters were digging graves for Akari and Mulewe in camp. It was a grim reminder of their jeopardy as they discussed their alternatives. Munro said to Elliot, "They don't seem to be aggressive during the day."

"No," Elliot said. "Their behavior looks quite typical— if anything, it's more sluggish than that of ordinary gorillas in daytime. Probably most of the males are sleeping during the day."

"How many animals on the hillside are males?" Munro asked. They had already concluded that only male animals participated in the attacks; Munro was asking for odds.

Elliot said, "Most studies have found that adult males constitute fifteen percent of gorilla groupings. And most studies show that isolated observations underestimate troop size by twenty-five percent. There are more animals than you see at any given moment."

The arithmetic was disheartening. They had counted three hundred gorillas on the hillside, which meant there were probably four hundred, of which 15 percent were males. That meant that there were sixty attacking animals—and only nine in their defending group.

"Hard," Munro said, shaking his head.

Amy had one solution. She signed, *Go now.*

Ross asked what she said and Elliot told her, "She wants to leave. I think she's right."

"Don't be ridiculous," Ross said. "We haven't found the diamonds. We can't leave now."

Go now, Amy signed again.

They looked at Munro. Somehow the group had decided that Munro would make the decision of what to do next. "I want the diamonds as much as anyone," he said. "But they won't be much use to us if we're dead. We have no choice. We must leave if we can."

Ross swore, in florid Texan style.

Elliot said to Munro, "What do you mean, if we can?"

"I mean," Munro said, "that they may not let us leave."

2. Departure

FOLLOWING MUNRO'S INSTRUCTIONS, THEY CAR-ried only minimal supplies of food and ammunition. They left everything else—the tents, the perimeter defenses, the communications equipment, everything, in the sunlit clearing at midday.

Munro glanced back over his shoulder and hoped he was doing the right thing. In the 1960s, the Congo mercenaries had had an ironic rule: "Don't leave home." It had multiple meanings, including the obvious one that none of them should ever have come to the Congo in the first place. It also meant that once established in a fortified camp or colonial town you were unwise to step out into the surrounding jungle, whatever the provocation. Several of Munro's friends had bought it in the jungle because they had foolishly left home. The news would come to them: "Digger bought it last week outside Stanleyville." "Outside? Why'd he leave home?"

Munro was leading the expedition outside now, and home was the little silver camp with its perimeter defense behind them. Back in that camp, they were sitting ducks for the attacking gorillas. The mercenaries had had something to say about that, too: "Better a sitting duck than a dead duck."

As they marched through the rain forest, Munro was pain-fully aware of the single-file column strung out behind him, the least defensible formation. He watched the jungle foliage move in as their path narrowed. He did not remember this track being so narrow when they had come to the city. Now they were hemmed in by close ferns and spreading palms. The gorillas might be only a few feet away, concealed in the dense foliage, and they wouldn't know it until it was too late.

They walked on.

Munro thought if they could reach the eastern slopes of Mukenko, they would be all right. The gray gorillas were localized near the city, and would not follow them far. One or two hours walking, and they would be beyond danger.

He checked his watch: they had been gone ten minutes.

And then he heard the sighing sound. It seemed to come from all directions. He saw the foliage moving before him, shifting as if blown by a wind. Only there was no wind. He heard the sighing grow louder.

The column halted at the edge of a ravine, which followed a streambed past sloping jungle walls on both sides. It was the perfect spot for an ambush. Along the line he heard the safeties click on the machine guns. Kahega came up. "Captain, what do we do?"

Munro watched the foliage move, and heard the sighing. He could only guess at the numbers concealed in the bush. Twenty? Thirty? Too many, in any case.

Kahega pointed up the hillside to a track that ran above the ravine. "Go up there?"

For a long time, Munro did not answer. Finally, he said, "No, not up there."

"Then where, Captain?"

"Back," Munro said. "We go back."

When they turned away from the ravine, the sighing faded and the foliage ceased its movement. When he looked back over his shoulder for a last glimpse, the ravine appeared an ordinary passage in the jungle, without threat of any kind. But Munro knew the truth. They could not leave.

3. Return

ELLIOT'S IDEA CAME IN A FLASH OF INSIGHT. "IN the middle of the camp," he later related, "I was looking at Amy signing to Kahega. Amy was asking him for a drink, but Kahega didn't know Ameslan, and he kept shrugging helplessly. It occurred to me that the linguistic skill of the gray gorillas was both their great advantage and their Achilles' heel."

Elliot proposed to capture a single gray gorilla, learn its language, and use that language to establish communication with the other animals. Under normal circumstances it would take several months to learn a new ape language, but Elliot thought he could do it in a matter of hours.

Seamans was already at work on the gray-gorilla verbalizations; all he needed was further input. But Elliot had decided that the gray gorillas employed a combination of spoken sounds and sign language. And the sign language would be easy to work out.

Back at Berkeley, Seamans had developed a computer program called APE, for animal pattern explanation. APE was capable of observing Amy and assigning meanings to her signs. Since the APE program utilized declassified army software subroutines for code-breaking, it was capable of identifying new signs, and translating these as well. Although APE was intended to work with Amy in ASL, there was no reason why it would not work with an entirely new language.

If they could forge satellite links from the Congo to Houston to Berkeley, they could feed video data from a captive animal directly into the APE program. And APE promised a speed of translation far beyond the capacity·of any human observer. (The army software was designed to break enemy codes in minutes.)

Elliot and Ross were convinced it would work; Munro was not. He made some disparaging comments about interrogating prisoners of war. "What do you intend to do," he said, "torture the animal?"

"We will employ situational stress," Elliot said, "to elicit language usage." He was laying out test materials on the ground: a banana, a bowl of water, a piece of candy, a stick, a succulent vine, stone paddles. "We'll scare the hell out of her if we have to."

"Her?"

"Of course," Elliot said, loading the Thoralen dart gun. "Her."

4. Capture

HE WANTED A FEMALE WITHOUT AN INFANT. AN infant would create difficulties.

Pushing through waist-high undergrowth, he found himself on the edge of a sharp ridge and saw nine animals grouped below him: two males, five females, and two juveniles. They were foraging through the jungle twenty feet below. He watched the group long enough to be sure that all the females used language, and that there were no infants concealed in the foliage. Then he waited for his chance.

The gorillas fed casually among the ferns, plucking up tender shoots, which they chewed lazily. After several minutes, one female moved up from the group to forage nearer the top of the ridge where he was crouching. She was separated from the rest of the group by more than ten yards.

Elliot raised the dart pistol in both hands and squinted down the sight at the female. She was perfectly positioned. He watched, squeezed the trigger slowly—and lost his footing on the ridge. He fell crashing down the slope, right into the midst of the gorillas.

Elliot lay unconscious on his back, twenty feet below, but his chest was moving, and his arm twitched; Munro felt certain that he was all right. Munro was only concerned about the gorillas.

The gray gorillas had seen Elliot fall and now moved toward the body. Eight or nine animals clustered around him, staring impassively, signing.

Munro slipped the safety off his gun.

Elliot groaned, touched his head, and opened his eyes. Munro saw Elliot stiffen as he saw the gorillas, but he did not move. Three mature males crouched very close to him, and he understood the precariousness of his situation. Elliot lay motionless on the ground for nearly a minute. The gorillas whispered and signed, but they did not come any closer.

Finally Elliot sat up on one elbow, which caused a burst of signing but no direct threatening behavior.

On the hillside above, Amy tugged at Munro's sleeve, signing emphatically. Munro shook his head: he did not understand; he raised his machine gun again, and Amy bit his kneecap. The pain was excruciating. It was all Munro could do to keep from screaming.

Elliot, lying on the ground below, tried to control his breathing. The gorillas were very close—close enough for him to touch them, close enough to smell the sweet, musty odor of their bodies. They were agitated; the males had started grunting, a rhythmic *ho-ho-ho*.

He decided he had better get to his feet, slowly and methodically. He thought that if he could put some distance between himself and the animals, their sense of threat would be reduced. But as soon as he began to move the grunting grew louder, and one of the males began a sideways crablike movement, slapping the ground with his flat palms.

Immediately Elliot lay back down. The gorillas relaxed, and he decided he had done the correct thing. The animals were confused by this human being crashing down in their midst; they apparently did not expect contact with men in foraging areas.

He decided to wait them out, if necessary remaining on his back for several hours until they lost interest and moved off. He breathed slowly, regularly, aware that he was sweating. Probably he smelled of fear—but like men, gorillas had a poorly developed sense of smell. They did not react to the odor of fear. He waited. The gorillas were sighing and signing swiftly, trying to decide what to do. Then one male abruptly resumed his crabwise movements, slapping the ground and staring at Elliot. Elliot did not move. In his mind, he reviewed the stages of attack behavior: grunting, sideways movement, slapping, tearing up grass, beating chest—

Charging.

The male gorilla began tearing up grass. Elliot felt his heart pounding. The gorilla was a huge animal, easily three hundred pounds. He reared up on his hind legs and beat his chest with flat palms, making a hollow sound. Elliot wondered what Munro was doing above. And then he heard a crash, and he looked to see Amy tumbling down the hillside, breaking her fall by grabbing at branches and ferns. She landed at Elliot's feet.

The gorillas could not have been more surprised. The large male ceased beating his chest, dropped down from his upright posture, and glowered at Amy.

Amy grunted.

The large male moved menacingly toward Peter, but he never took his eyes off Amy. Amy watched him without response. It was a clear test of dominance. The male moved closer and closer, without hesitation.

Amy bellowed, a deafening sound; Elliot jumped in surprise. He had only heard her do it once or twice before in moments of extreme rage. It was unusual for females to roar, and the other gorillas were alarmed. Amy's forearms stiffened, her back went rigid, her face became tense. She stared aggressively at the male and roared again.

The male paused, tilted his head to one side. He seemed to be thinking it over. Finally he backed off, rejoining the semicircle of gray apes around Elliot's head.

Amy deliberately rested her hand on Elliot's leg, establishing possession. A juvenile male, four or five years old, impulsively scurried forward, baring his teeth. Amy slapped him across the face, and the juvenile whined and scrambled back to the safety of his group.

Amy glowered at the other gorillas. And then she began signing. *Go away leave Amy go away.*

The gorillas did not respond.

Peter good human person. But she seemed to be aware that the gorillas did not understand, for she then did something remarkable: she sighed, making the same wheezing sound that the gorillas made.

The gorillas were startled, and stared at one another.

But if Amy was speaking their language, it was without effect: they remained where they were. And the more she sighed, the more their reaction diminished, until finally they stared blandly at her.

She was not getting through to them.

Amy now came alongside Peter's head and began to groom him, plucking at his beard and scalp. The gray gorillas signed rapidly. Then the male began his rhythmic *ho-ho-ho* once more. When she saw this Amy turned to Peter and signed, *Amy hug Peter.* He was surprised: Amy never volunteered to hug Peter. Ordinarily she only wanted Peter to hug and tickle Amy.

Elliot sat up and she immediately pulled him to her chest, pressing his face into her hair. At once the male gorilla ceased grunting. The gray gorillas began to backpedal, as if they had committed some error. In that moment, Elliot understood: *she was treating him like her infant.*

This was classic primate behavior in aggressive situations. Primates carried strong inhibitions against harming infants, and this inhibition was invoked by adult animals in many contexts. Male baboons often ended their fight when one male grabbed an infant and clutched it to his chest; the sight of the small animal inhibited further attack. Chimpanzees showed more subtle variations of the same thing. If juvenile chimp play turned too brutal, a male would grab one juvenile and clutch it maternally, even though in this case both parent and child were symbolic. Yet the posture was sufficient to evoke the inhibition against further violence. In this case Amy was not only halting the male's attack but protecting Elliot as well, by treating him as an infant—if the gorillas would accept a bearded six-foot-tall infant.

They did.

They disappeared back into the foliage. Amy released Elliot from her fierce grip. She looked at him and signed, *Dumb things*.

"Thank you, Amy," he said and kissed her.

Peter tickle Amy Amy good gorilla.

"You bet," he said, and he tickled her for the next several minutes, while she rolled on the ground, grunting happily.

It was two o'clock in the afternoon when they returned to camp. Ross said, "Did you get a gorilla?"

"No," Elliot said.

"Well, it doesn't matter," Ross said, "because I can't raise Houston."

Elliot was stunned: "More electronic jamming?"

"Worse than that," Ross said. She had spent an hour trying to establish a satellite link with Houston, and had failed. Each time the link was broken within seconds. Finally, after confirming that there was no fault with her equipment, she had checked the date. "It's June 24," she said. "And we had communications trouble with the last Congo expedition on May 28. That's twenty-seven days ago."

When Elliot still didn't get it, Munro said, "She's telling you it's solar."

"That's right," Ross said. "This is an ionospheric disturbance of solar origin." Most disruptions of the earth's ionosphere—the thin layer of ionized molecules 50–250 miles up—were caused by phenomena such as sunspots on the surface of the sun. Since the sun rotated every twenty-seven days, these disturbances often recurred a month later.

"Okay," Elliot said, "it's solar. How long will it last?"

Ross shook her head. "Ordinarily, I would say a few hours, a day at most. But this seems to be a severe disturbance and it's come up very suddenly. Five hours ago we had perfect communications—and now we have none at all. Something unusual is going on. It could last a week."

"No communications for a week? No computer tie-ins, no nothing?"

"That's right," Ross said evenly. "From this moment on, we are entirely cut off from the outside world."

5. Isolation

THE LARGEST SOLAR FLARE OF 1979 WAS RECORDED on June 24, by the Kitt Peak Observatory near Tucson, Arizona, and duly passed on to the Space Environment Services Center in Boulder, Colorado. At first the SESC did not believe the incoming data: even by the gigantic standards of solar astronomy, this flare, designated 78/06/414aa, was a monster.

The cause of solar flares is unknown, but they are generally associated with sunspots. In this case the flare appeared as an extremely bright spot ten thousand miles in diameter, affecting not only alpha hydrogen and ionized calcium spectral lines but also the white light spectrum from the sun. Such a "continuous spectrum" flare was extremely rare.

Nor could the SESC believe the computed consequences. Solar flares release an enormous amount of energy; even a modest flare can double the amount of ultraviolet radiation emitted by the entire solar surface. But flare 78/06/414aa was almost *tripling* ultraviolet emissions. Within 8.3 minutes of its first appearances along the rotating rim—the time it takes light to reach the earth from the sun—this surge of ultraviolet radiation began to disrupt the ionosphere of the earth.

The consequence of the flare was that radio communications on a planet ninety-three million miles away were seriously disrupted. This was especially true for radio transmissions which utilized low signal strengths. Commercial radio stations generating kilowatts of power were hardly inconvenienced, but the Congo Field Survey, transmitting signals on the order of twenty thousand watts, was unable to establish satellite links. And since the solar flare also ejected X-rays and atomic particles which would not reach the earth for a full day, the radio disruption would last at least one day, and perhaps longer. At ERTS in Houston, technicians reported to Travis that the SESC predicted a time course of ionic disruption of four to eight days.

"That's how it looks. Ross'll probably figure it out," the technician said, "when she can't re-establish today."

"They need that computer hookup," Travis said. The ERTS staff had run five computer simulations and the outcome was always the same—short of airlifting in a small army, Ross's expedition was in serious trouble. Survival projections were running "point two four four and change"— only one chance in four that the Congo expedition would get out alive, assuming the help of the computer link which was now broken.

Travis wondered if Ross and the others realized how grave their situation was. "Any new Band Five on Mukenko?" Travis asked.

Band 5 on Landsat satellites recorded infrared data. On its last pass over the Congo, Landsat had acquired significant new information on Mukenko. The volcano had become much hotter in the nine days since the previous Landsat pass; the temperature increase was on the order of 8 degrees.

"Nothing new," the technician said. "And the computers don't project an eruption. Four degrees of orbital change are within sensor error on that system, and the additional four degrees have no predictive value."

"Well, that's something," Travis said. "But what are they

going to do about the apes now that they're cut off from the computer?"

That was the question the Congo Field Survey had been asking themselves for the better part of an hour. With communications disrupted the only computers available were the computers in their own heads. And those computers were not powerful enough.

Elliot found it strange to think that his own brain was inadequate. "We had all become accustomed to the availability of computing power," he said later. "In any decent laboratory you can get all the memory and all the computation speed you could want, day or night. We were so used to it we had come to take it for granted.

Of course they could have eventually worked out the ape language, but they were up against a time factor: they didn't have months to puzzle it out; they had hours. Cut off from the APE program their situation was ominous. Munro said that they could not survive another night of frontal attack, and they had every reason to expect an attack that night.

Amy's rescue of Elliot suggested their plan. Amy had shown some ability to communicate with the gorillas; perhaps she could translate for them as well. "It's worth a try," Elliot insisted.

Unfortunately, Amy herself denied that this was possible. In response to the question "Amy talk thing talk?" She signed, *No talk.*

"Not at all?" Elliot said, remembering the way she had signed. "Peter see Amy talk thing talk."

No talk. Make noise.

He concluded from this that she was able to mimic the gorilla verbalizations but had no knowledge of their meaning. It was now past two; they had only four or five hours until nightfall.

Munro said, "Give it up. She obviously can't help us." Munro preferred to break camp and fight their way out in daylight. He was convinced that they could not survive another night among the gorillas.

But something nagged at Elliot's mind.

After years of working with Amy, he knew she had the maddening literal-mindedness of a child. With Amy, especially when she was feeling uncooperative, it was necessary to be exact to elicit the appropriate response. Now he looked at Amy and said, "Amy talk thing talk?"

No talk.

"Amy understand thing talk?"

Amy did not answer. She was chewing on vines, preoccupied.

"Amy, listen to Peter."

She stared at him.

"Amy understand thing talk?"

Amy understand thing talk, she signed back. She did it so matter-of-factly that at first he wondered if she realized what he was asking her.

"Amy watch thing talk, Amy understand talk?"

Amy understand.

"Amy sure?"

Amy sure.

"I'll be goddamned," Elliot said.

Munro was shaking his head. "We've only got a few hours of daylight left," he said. "And even if you do learn their language, how are you going to talk to them?"

6. Amy Talk Thing Talk

AT 3 P.M., ELLIOT AND AMY WERE COMPLETELY concealed in the foliage along the hillside. The only sign of their presence was the slender cone of the microphone that protruded through the foliage. The microphone was connected to the videotape recorder at Elliot's feet, which he used to record the sounds of the gorillas on the hills beyond.

The only difficulty was trying to determine which gorilla the directional microphone had focused on—and which gorilla Amy had focused on, and whether they were the same gorilla. He could never be quite sure that Amy was translating the verbal utterances of the same animal that he was recording. There were eight gorillas in the nearest group and Amy kept getting distracted. One female had a six-month-old infant, and at one point, when the baby was bitten by a bee, Amy signed, *Baby mad*. But Elliot was recording a male.

Amy, he signed. Pay attention.

Amy pay attention. Amy good gorilla.

Yes, he signed. Amy good gorilla. Amy pay attention man thing.

Amy not like.

He swore silently, and erased half an hour of translations from Amy. She had obviously been paying attention to the wrong gorilla. When he started the tape again, he decided that this time he would record whatever Amy was watching. He signed, What thing Amy watch?

Amy watch baby.

That wouldn't work, because the baby didn't speak. He signed, Amy watch woman thing.

Amy like watch baby.

This dependency on Amy was like a bad dream. He was in the hands of an animal whose thinking and behavior he barely understood; he was cut off from the wider society of human beings and human machinery, thus increasing his dependency on the animal; and yet he had to trust her.

After another hour, with the sunlight fading, he took Amy back down the hillside to the camp.

Munro had planned as best he could.

First he dug a series of holes like elephant traps outside the camp; they were deep pits lined with sharp stakes, covered with leaves and branches.

He widened the moat in several places, and cleared away dead trees and underbrush that might be used as bridges.

He cut down the low tree branches overhanging the camp, so that if gorillas went into the trees, they would be kept at least thirty feet above the ground—too high to jump down.

He gave three of the remaining porters, Muzezi, Amburi, and Harawi, shotguns along with a supply of tear-gas canisters.

With Ross, he boosted power on the perimeter fence to almost 200 amps. This was the maximum the thin mesh could handle without melting; they had been obliged to reduce the pulses from four to two per second. But the additional current changed the fence from a deterrent to a lethal barrier. The first animals to hit that fence would be immediately killed, although the likelihood of shorts and a dead fence was considerably increased.

At sunset, Munro made his most difficult decision. He loaded the stubby tripod-mounted RFSDs with half their remaining ammunition. When that was gone, the machines would simply stop firing. From that point on, Munro was counting on Elliot and Amy and their translation.

And Elliot did not look very happy when he came back down the hill.

7. Final Defense

"HOW LONG UNTIL YOU'RE READY?" MUNRO asked him.

"Couple of hours, maybe more." Elliot asked Ross to help him, and Amy went to get food from Kahega. She seemed very proud of herself, and behaved like an important person in the group.

Ross said, "Did it work?"

"We'll know in a minute," Elliot said. His first plan was to run the only kind of internal check on Amy that he could, by verifying repetitions of sounds. If she had consistently translated sounds in the same way, they would have a reason for confidence.

But it was painstaking work. They had only the half-inch VTR and the small pocket tape recorder; there were no connecting cables. They called for silence from the others in the camp and proceeded to run the checks, taping, retaping, listening to the whispering sounds.

At once they found that their ears simply weren't capable of discriminating the sounds—everything sounded the same. Then Ross had an idea.

"These sounds taped," she said, "as electrical signals."

"Yes . . ."

"Well, the linkup transmitter has a 256K memory."

"But we can't link up to the Houston computer."

"I don't mean that," Ross said. She explained that the satellite linkup was made by having the 256K computer on-site match an internally generated signal—like a video test pattern—to a transmitted signal from Houston. That was how they locked on. The machine was built that way, but they could use the matching program for other purposes.

"You mean we can use it to compare these sounds?" Elliot said.

They could, but it was incredibly slow. They had to transfer the taped sounds to the computer memory, and rerecord it in the VTR, on another portion of the tape bandwidth. Then they had to input that signal into the computer memory, and run a second comparison tape on the VTR. Elliot found that he was standing by, watching Ross shuffle tape cartridges and mini floppy discs. Every half hour, Munro would wander over to ask how it was coming; Ross became increasingly snappish and irritable. "We're going as fast as we can," she said.

It was now eight o'clock.

But the first results were encouraging: Amy was indeed

consistent in her translations. By nine o'clock they had quantified matching on almost a dozen words:

FOOD	.9213	.112
EAT	.8844	.334
WATER	.9978	.004
DRINK	.7743	.334
{AFFIRMATION} YES	.6654	.441
{NEGATION} NO	.8883	.220
COME	.5459	.440
GO	.5378	.404
SOUND COMPLEX: ? AWAY	.5444	.343
SOUND COMPLEX: ? HERE	.6344	.344
SOUND COMPLEX: ? ANGER		
? BAD	.4232	.477

Ross stepped away from the computer. "All yours," she said to Elliot.

Munro paced across the compound. This was the worst time. Everyone waiting, on edge, nerves shot. He would have joked with Kahega and the other porters, but Ross and Elliot needed silence for their work. He glanced at Kahega.

Kahega pointed to the sky and rubbed his fingers together. Munro nodded.

He had felt it too, the heavy dampness in the air, the almost palpable feeling of electrical charge. Rain was coming. That was all they needed, he thought. During the afternoon, there had been more booming and distant explosions, which he had thought were far-off lightning storms. But the sound was not right; these were sharp, single reports, more like a sonic boom than anything else. Munro had heard them before, and he had an idea about what they meant.

He glanced up at the dark cone of Mukenko, and the faint glow of the Devil's Eye. He looked at the crossed green laser beams overhead. And he noticed one of the beams was moving where it struck foliage in the trees above.

At first he thought it was an illusion, that the leaf was moving and not the beam. But after a moment he was sure:

the beam itself was quivering, shifting up and down in the
night air.

Munro knew this was an ominous development, but it
would have to wait until later; at the moment, there were
more pressing concerns. He looked across the compound at
Elliot and Ross bent over their equipment, talking quietly
and in general behaving as if they had all the time in the
world.

Elliot actually was going as fast as he could. He had eleven
reliable vocabulary words recorded on tape. His problem
now was to compose an unequivocal message. This was not
as easy as it first appeared.

For one thing, the gorilla language was not a pure verbal
language. The gorillas used sign and sound combinations to
convey information. This raised a classic problem in language structure—how was the information actually conveyed? (L. S. Verinski once said that if alien visitors watched
Italians speaking they would conclude that Italian was basi-
cally a gestural sign language, with sounds added for emphasis only.) Elliot needed a simple message that did not
depend on accompanying hand signs.

But he had no idea of gorilla syntax, which could critically
alter meaning in most circumstances—the difference between "me beat" and "beat me." And even a short message
could be ambiguous in another language. In English, "Look
out!" generally meant the opposite of its literal meaning.

Faced with these uncertainties, Elliot considered broadcasting a single word. But none of the words on his list was
suitable. His second choice was to broadcast several short
messages, in case one was inadvertently ambiguous. He
eventually decided on three messages; GO AWAY, NO COME,
and BAD HERE; two of these combinations had the virtue of
being essentially independent of word order.

By nine o'clock, they had already isolated the specific
sound components. But they still had a complicated task
ahead. What Elliot needed was a loop, repeating the sounds
over and over. The closest they would come was the VCR,
which rewound automatically to play its message again. He

could hold the six sounds in the 256K memory and play them out, but the timing was critical. For the next hour, they frantically worked at the keyboard, trying to bring the word combinations close enough together to sound—to their ears—correct.

By then it was after ten.

Munro came over with his laser gun. "You think all this will work?"

Elliot shook his head. "There's no way to know." A dozen objections had come to mind. They had recorded a female voice, but would the gorillas respond to a female? Would they accept voice sounds without accompanying hand signals? Would the message be clear? Would the spacing of the sounds be acceptable? Would the gorillas pay attention at all?

There was no way to know. They would simply have to try.

Equally uncertain was the problem of broadcasting. Ross had made a speaker, removing the tiny speaker from the pocket tape recorder and gluing it to an umbrella on a collapsible tripod. This makeshift speaker produced surprisingly loud volume, but reproduction was muffled and unconvincing.

Shortly afterward, they heard the first sighing sounds.

Munro swung the laser gun through the darkness, the red activation light glowing on the electronic pod at the end of the barrel. Through his night goggles he surveyed the foliage. Once again, the sighing came from all directions; and although he heard the jungle foliage shifting, he saw no movement close to the camp. The monkeys overhead were silent. There was only the soft, ominous sighing. Listening now, Munro was convinced that the sounds represented a language of some form, and—

A single gorilla appeared and Kahega fired, his laser beam streaking arrow-straight through the night. The RFSD chattered and the foliage snapped with bullets. The gorilla ducked silently back into a stand of dense ferns.

Munro and the others quickly took positions along the perimeter, crouching tensely, the infrared night lights casting their shadows on the mesh fence and the jungle beyond.

The sighing continued for several minutes longer, and then slowly faded away, until all was silent again.

"What was that about?" Ross said.

Munro frowned. "They're waiting."

"For what?"

Munro shook his head. He circled the compound, looking at the other guards, trying to work it out. Many times he had anticipated the behavior of animals—a wounded leopard in the bush, a cornered buffalo—but this was different. He was forced to admit he didn't know what to expect. Had the single gorilla been a scout to look at their defenses? Or had an attack actually begun, only for some reason to be halted? Was it a maneuver designed to fray nerves? Munro had watched parties of hunting chimpanzees make brief threatening forays toward baboons, to raise the anxiety level of the entire troop before the actual assault, isolating some young animal for killing.

Then he heard the rumble of thunder. Kahega pointed to the sky, shaking his head. That was their answer.

"Damn," Munro said.

At 10:30 a torrential tropical rain poured down on them. Their fragile speaker was immediately soaked and drooping. The rain shorted the electrical cables and the perimeter fence went dead. The night lights flickered, and two bulbs exploded. The ground turned to mud; visibility was reduced to five yards. And worst of all, the rain splattering the foliage was so noisy they had to shout to each other. The tapes were unfinished; the loudspeaker probably would not work, and certainly would not carry over the rain. The rain would interfere with the lasers and prevent the dispersal of tear gas. Faces in camp were grim.

Five minutes later, the gorillas attacked.

The rain masked their approach; they seemed to burst out of nowhere, striking the fence from three directions simultaneously. From that first moment, Elliot realized the attack would be unlike the others. The gorillas had learned from the earlier assaults, and now were intent on finishing the job.

Primate attack animals, trained for cunning and vicious-

ness: even though that was Elliot's own assessment, he was astonished to see the proof in front of him. The gorillas charged in waves, like disciplined shock troops. Yet he found it more horrifying than an attack by human troops. To them we are just animals, he thought. An alien species, for which they have no feeling. We are just pests to be eliminated.

These gorillas did not care why human beings were there, or what reasons had brought them to the Congo. They were not killing for food, or defense, or protection of their young. They were killing because they were trained to kill.

The attack proceeded with stunning swiftness. Within seconds, the gorillas had breached the perimeter and trampled the mesh fence into the mud. Unchecked, they rushed into the compound, grunting and roaring. The driving rain matted their hair, giving them a sleek, menacing appearance in the red night lights. Elliot saw ten or fifteen animals inside the compound, trampling the tents and attacking the people. Azizi was killed immediately, his skull crushed between paddles.

Munro, Kahega, and Ross all fired laser bursts, but in the confusion and poor visibility their effectiveness was limited. The laser beams fragmented in the slashing rain; the tracer bullets hissed and sputtered. One of the RFSDs went haywire, the barrel swinging in wide arcs, bullets spitting out in all directions, while everyone dived into the mud. Several gorillas were killed by the RFSD bursts, clutching their chests in a bizarre mimicry of human death.

Elliot turned back to the recording equipment and Amy flung herself on him, panicked, grunting in fear. He pushed her away and switched on the tape replay.

By now the gorillas had overwhelmed everyone in the camp. Munro lay on his back, a gorilla on top of him. Ross was nowhere to be seen. Kahega had a gorilla clinging to his chest as he rolled in the mud. Elliot was hardly aware of the hideous scratching sounds now emanating from the loudspeaker, and the gorillas themselves paid no attention.

Another porter, Muzezi, screamed as he stepped in front of a firing RFSD; his frame shook with the impact of the bullets and he fell backward to the ground, his body smoking from the tracers. At least a dozen gorillas were dead or lying wounded in the mud, groaning. The haywire RFSD had run out of ammunition; the barrel swung back and forth, the empty chamber clicking. A gorilla kicked it over, and it lay writhing on its side in the mud like a living thing as the barrel continued to swing.

Elliot saw one gorilla crouched over, methodically tearing a tent apart, shredding the silver Mylar into strips. Across the camp, another arrival banged aluminum cook pans together, as if they were metal paddles. More gorillas poured into the compound, ignoring the rasping broadcast sounds. He saw a gorilla pass beneath the loudspeaker, very close, and pay no attention at all. Elliot had the sickening realization that their plan had failed.

They were finished; it was only a matter of time.

A gorilla charged him, bellowing in rage, swinging stone paddles wide. Terrified, Amy threw her hands over Elliot's eyes. "Amy!" he shouted, pulling her fingers away, expecting to feel at any moment the impact of the paddles and the instant of blinding pain.

He saw the gorilla bearing down on him. He tensed his body. Six feet away, the charging gorilla stopped so abruptly that he literally skidded in the mud and fell backward. He sat there surprised, cocking his head, listening.

Then Elliot realized that the rain had nearly stopped, that there was now only a light drizzle sifting down over the campsite. Looking across the compound, Elliot saw another gorilla stop to listen—then another—and another—and another. The compound took on the quality of a frozen tableau, as the gorillas stood silent in the mist.

They were listening to the broadcast sounds.

He held his breath, not daring to hope. The gorillas seemed uncertain, confused by the sounds they heard. Yet Elliot sensed that at any moment they could arrive at some group decision and resume their attack with the same intensity as before.

That did not happen. The gorillas stepped away from the people, listening. Munro scrambled to his feet, raising his gun from the mud. but he did not shoot; the gorilla standing

over him seemed to be in a trance, to have forgotten all about
the attack.

In the gentle rain, with the flickering night lights, the gorillas moved away, one by one. They seemed perplexed, off
balance. The rasping continued over the loudspeaker.

The gorillas left, moving back across the trampled perimeter fence, disappearing once more into the jungle. And then
the expedition members were alone, staring at each other,
shivering in the misty rain. The gorillas were gone.

Twenty minutes later, as they were trying to rebuild their
shattered campsite, the rain poured down again with unabated fury.

DAY 13: MUKENKO

June 25, 1979

1. Diamonds

IN THE MORNING A FINE LAYER OF BLACK ASH COV-
ered the campsite, and in the distance Mukenko was belching
great quantities of black smoke. Amy tugged at Elliot's
sleeve.

Leave now, she signed insistently.

"No, Amy," he said.

Nobody in the expedition was in a mood to leave, including Elliot. Upon arising, he found himself thinking of additional data he needed before leaving Zinj. Elliot was no
longer satisfied with a skeleton of one of these creatures; like
men, their uniqueness went beyond the details of physical
structure to their behavior. Elliot wanted videotapes of the
gray apes, and more recordings of verbalizations. And Ross
was more determined than ever to find the diamonds, with
Munro no less interested.

Leave now.

"Why leave now?" he asked her.

Earth bad. Leave now.

Elliot had no experience with volcanic activity, but what
he saw did not impress him. Mukenko was more active than
it had been in previous days, but the volcano had ejected
smoke and gas since their first arrival in Virunga.

He asked Munro, "Is there any danger?"

Munro shrugged. "Kahega thinks so, but he probably just
wants an excuse to go home."

Amy came running over to Munro raising her arms, slapping them down on the earth in front of him. Munro recognized this as her desire to play; he laughed and began to
tickle Amy. She signed to him.

"What's she saying?" Munro asked. "What are you saying, you little devil?"

Amy grunted with pleasure, and continued to sign.

"She says leave now," Elliot translated.

Munro stopped tickling her. "Does she?" he asked sharply. "What *exactly* does she say?"

Elliot was surprised at Munro's seriousness—although Amy accepted his interest in her communication as perfectly proper. She signed again, more slowly, for Munro's benefit, her eyes on his face.

"She says the earth is bad."

"Hmm," Munro said. "Interesting." He glanced at Amy and then at his watch.

Amy signed, *Nosehair man listen Amy go home now.*

"She says you listen to her and go home now," Elliot said.

Munro shrugged. "Tell her I understand."

Elliot translated. Amy looked unhappy, and did not sign again.

"Where is Ross?" Munro asked.

"Here," Ross said.

"Let's get moving," Munro said, and they headed for the lost city. Now they had another surprise—Amy signed she was coming with them, and she hurried to catch up with them.

This was their final day in the city, and all the participants in the Congo expedition described a similar reaction: the city, which had been so mysterious before, was somehow stripped of its mystery. On this morning, they saw the city for what it was: a cluster of crumbling old buildings in a hot stinking uncomfortable jungle.

They all found it tedious, except for Munro. Munro was worried.

Elliot was bored, talking about verbalizations and why he wanted tape recordings, and whether it was possible to preserve a brain from one of the apes to take back with them. It seemed there was some academic debate about where language came from; people used to think language was a development of animal cries, but now they knew that animal barks and cries were controlled by the limbic system of the brain, and that real language came from some other part of the brain called Broca's area. . . . Munro couldn't pay attention. He kept listening to the distant rumbling of Mukenko.

Munro had firsthand experience with volcanoes; he had been in the Congo in 1968, when Mbuti, another of the Virunga volcanoes, erupted. When he had heard the sharp explosions the day before, he had recognized them as brontides, the unexplained accompaniments of coming earthquakes. Munro had assumed that Mukenko would soon erupt, and when he had seen the flickering laser beam the night before, he had known there was new rumbling activity on the upper slopes of the volcano.

Munro knew that volcanoes were unpredictable—as witnessed by the fact that this ruined city at the base of an active volcano had been untouched after more than five hundred years. There were recent lava fields on the mountain slopes above, and others a few miles to the south, but the city itself was spared. This in itself was not so remarkable—the configuration of Mukenko was such that most eruptions occurred on the gentle south slopes. But it did not mean that they were now in any less danger. The unpredictability of volcanic eruptions meant that they could become life-threatening in a matter of minutes. The danger was not from lava, which rarely flowed faster than a man could walk; it would take hours for lava to flow down from Mukenko's summit. The real danger from volcanic eruptions was ash and gas.

Just as most people killed by fires actually died from smoke inhalation, most deaths from volcanoes were caused by asphyxiation from dust and carbon monoxide. Volcanic gases were heavier than air; the Lost City of Zinj, located in a valley, could be filled in minutes with a heavy, poisonous atmosphere, should Mukenko discharge a large quantity of gas.

The question was how rapidly Mukenko was building toward a major eruptive phase. That was why Munro was so interested in Amy's reactions: it was well known that primates could anticipate geological events such as earthquakes and eruptions. Munro was surprised that Elliot, babbling away about freezing gorilla brains, didn't know about that. And he was even more surprised that Ross, with her extensive geological knowledge, did not regard the morning ashfall as the start of a major volcanic eruption.

Ross knew a major eruption was building. That morning, she had routinely tried to establish contact with Houston; to her surprise, the transmission keys immediately locked through. After the scrambler notations registered, she began typing in field updates, but the screen went blank, and flashed:

HUSTN STATN OVRIDE CLR BANX.

This was an emergency signal; she had never seen it before on a field expedition. She cleared the memory banks and pushed the transmit button. There was a burst transmission delay, then the screen printed:

COMPUTR DESIGNATN MAJR ERUPTN SIGNATR MU-KENKO ADVIS LEAV SITE NOW EXPEDN JEPRDY DANGR REPET ALL LEAV SITE NOW.

Ross glanced across the campsite. Kahega was making breakfast; Amy squatted by the fire, eating a roasted banana (she had got Kahega to make special treats for her); Munro and Elliot were having coffee. Except for the black ashfall, it was a perfectly normal morning at the camp. She looked back at the screen.

MAJR ERUPTN SIGNATR MUKENKO ADVIS LEAV SITE NOW.

Ross glanced up at the smoking cone of Mukenko. The hell with it, she thought. She wanted the diamonds, and she had gone too far to quit now.

The screen blinked: PLS SIGNL REPLY.
Ross turned the transmitter off.

As the morning progressed they felt several sharp jolting
earth tremors, which released clouds of dust from the crumbling buildings. The rumblings of Mukenko became more
frequent. Ross paid no attention. "It just means this is elephant country," she said. That was an old geological adage:
"If you're looking for elephants, go to elephant country."
Elephant country meant a likely spot to find whatever minerals you were looking for. "And if you want diamonds,"
Ross said, shrugging, "you go to volcanoes."

The association of diamonds with volcanoes had been recognized for more than a century, but it was still poorly understood. Most theories postulated that diamonds, crystals
of pure carbon, were formed in the intense heat and pressure
of the upper mantle one thousand miles beneath the earth's
surface. The diamonds remained inaccessible at this depth
except in volcanic areas where rivers of molten magma carried them to the surface.

But this did not mean that you went to erupting volcanoes
to catch diamonds being spewed out. Most diamond mines
were at the site of extinct volcanoes, in fossilized cones called
kimberlite pipes, named for the geological formations in
Kimberley, South Africa. Virunga, near the geologically unstable Rift Valley, showed evidence of continuous volcanic
activity for more than fifty million years. They were now
looking for the same fossil volcanoes which the earlier inhabitants of Zinj had found.

Shortly before noon they found them, halfway up the hills
east of the city—a series of excavated tunnels running into
the mountain slopes of Mukenko.

Elliot felt disappointed. "I don't know what I was expecting," he said later, "but it was just a brown-colored
tunnel in the earth, with occasional bits of dull brown rock
sticking out. I couldn't understand why Ross got so excited."
Those bits of dull brown rock were diamonds; when cleaned,
they had the transparency of dirty glass.

"They thought I was crazy," Ross said, "because I began jumping up and down. But they didn't know what they were looking at."

In an ordinary kimberlite pipe, diamonds were distributed sparsely in the rock matrix. The average mine recovered only thirty-two karats—a fifth of an ounce—for every hundred tons of rock removed. When you looked down a diamond mineshaft, you saw no diamonds at all. But the Zinj mines were lumpy with protruding stones. Using his machete, Munro dug out six hundred karats. And Ross saw six or seven stones protruding from the wall, each as large as the one Munro had removed. "Just looking," she said later, "I could see easily four or five thousand karats. With no further digging, no separation, nothing. Just sitting there. It was a richer mine than the Premier in South Africa. It was *unbelievable.*"

Elliot asked the question that had already formed in Ross's own mind. "If this mine is so damn rich," he said, "why was it abandoned?"

"The gorillas got out of control," Munro said. "They staged a coup." He was laughing, plucking diamonds out of the rock.

Ross had considered that, as she had considered Elliot's earlier suggestion that the city had been wiped out by disease. She thought a less exotic explanation was likely. "I think," she said, "that as far as they were concerned, the diamond mines had dried up." Because as gemstones, these crystals were very poor indeed—blue, streaked with impurities.

The people of Zinj could not have imagined that five hundred years in the future these same worthless stones would be more scarce and desirable than any other mineral resources on the planet.

"What makes these blue diamonds so valuable?"

"They are going to change the world," Ross said, in a soft voice. "They are going to end the nuclear age."

2. War at the Speed of Light

IN JANUARY, 1979, TESTIFYING BEFORE THE SEN-
ate Armed Services Subcommittee, General Franklin F.
Martin of the Pentagon Advanced Research Project Agency
said, "In 1939, at the start of World War II, the most important country in the world to the American military effort
was the Belgian Congo." Martin explained that as a kind of
"accident of geography" the Congo, now Zaire, has for forty
years remained vital to American interests—and will assume
even more importance in the future. (Martin said bluntly that
"this country will go to war over Zaire before we go to war
over any Arab oil state.")

During World War II, in three highly secret shipments,
the Congo supplied the United States with uranium used to
build the atomic bombs exploded over Japan. By 1960 the
U.S. no longer needed uranium, but copper and cobalt were
strategically important. In the 1970s the emphasis shifted to
Zaire's reserves of tantalum, wolframite, germanium—
substances vital to semiconducting electronics. And in the
1980s, "so-called Type IIb blue diamonds will constitute
the most important military resource in the world"—and the
presumption was that Zaire had such diamonds. In General
Martin's view, blue diamonds were essential because "we
are entering a time when the brute destructive power of a
weapon will be less important than its speed and intelligence."

For thirty years, military thinkers had been awed by inter-
continental ballistic missiles. But Martin said that "ICBMs
are crude weapons. They do not begin to approach the theoretical limits imposed by physical laws. According to Ein-

291

steinian physics, nothing can happen faster than the speed of light, 186,000 miles a second. We are now developing high-energy pulsed lasers and particle beam weapons systems which operate *at the speed of light*. In the face of such weapons, ballistic missiles travelling a mere 17,000 miles an hour are slow-moving dinosaurs from a previous era, as inappropriate as cavalry in World War I, and as easily eliminated.''

Speed-of-light weapons were best suited to space, and would first appear in satellites. Martin noted that the Russians had made a "kill" of the American spy satellite VV/02 as early as 1973; in 1975, Hughes Aircraft developed a rapid aiming and firing system which locked onto multiple targets, firing eight high-energy pulses in less than one second. By 1978, the Hughes team had reduced response time to fifty nanoseconds—fifty billionths of a second—and increased beam accuracy to five hundred missile knockdowns in less than one minute. Such developments presaged the end of the ICBM as a weapon.

"Without the gigantic missiles, miniature, high-speed computers will be vastly more important in future conflicts than nuclear bombs, and their speed of computation will be the single most important factor determining the outcome of World War III. Computer speed now stands at the center of the armament race, as megaton power once held the center twenty years ago.

"We will shift from electronic circuit computers to light circuit computers simply because of speed—the Fabry-Perot Interferometer, the optical equivalent of a transistor, can respond in 1 picosecond (10^{-12} seconds), at least 1,000 times faster than the fastest Josephson junctions.'' The new generation of optical computers, Martin said, would be dependent on the availability of Type IIb boron-coated diamonds.

Elliot recognized at once the most serious consequence of the speed-of-light weapons—they were much too fast for human comprehension. Men were accustomed to mechanized warfare, but a future war would be a war of machines in a startlingly new sense: machines would actually govern the moment-to-moment course of a conflict which lasted only minutes from start to finish.

In 1956, in the waning years of the strategic bomber, military thinkers imagined an all-out nuclear exchange lasting 12 hours. By 1963, ICBMs had shrunk the time course to 3 hours. By 1974, military theorists were predicting a war that lasted just 30 minutes, yet this "half-hour war" was vastly more complex than any earlier war in human history.

In the 1950s, if the Americans and the Russians launched all the bombers and rockets at the same moment, there would still be no more than 10,000 weapons in the air, attacking and counterattacking. Total weapons interaction events would peak at 15,000 in the second hour. This represented the impressive figure of 4 weapons interactions every second around the world.

But given diversified tactical warfare, the number of weapons and "systems elements" increased astronomically. Modern estimates imagined 400 million computers in the field, with total weapons interactions at more than 15 billion in the first half hour of war. This meant there would be 8 million weapons interactions every second, in a bewildering ultrafast conflict of aircraft, missiles, tanks, and ground troops.

Such a war was only manageable by machines; human response times were simply too slow. World War III would not be a push-button war because as General Martin said, "It takes too long for a man to push the button—at least 1.8 seconds, which is an eternity in modern warfare."

This fact created what Martin called the "rock problem." Human responses were geologically slow, compared to a high-speed computer. "A modern computer performs 2,000,000 calculations in the time it takes a man to blink. Therefore, from the point of view of computers fighting the next war, human beings will be essentially fixed and unchanging elements, like rocks. Human wars have never lasted long enough to take into account the rate of geological change. In the future, computer wars will not last long enough to take into account the rate of human change."

Since human beings responded too slowly, it was necessary for them to relinquish decision-making control of the war to the faster intelligence of computers. "In the coming war, we must abandon any hope of regulating the course of the conflict. If we decide to 'run' the war at human speed, we will almost surely lose. Our only hope is to put our trust in machines. This makes human judgment, human values, human thinking utterly superfluous. World War III will be war by proxy: a pure war of machines, over which we dare exert no influence for fear of so slowing the decision-making mechanism as to cause our defeat." And the final, crucial transition—the transition from computers working at nanoseconds to computers working at picoseconds—was dependent on Type IIb diamonds.

Elliot was appalled by this prospect of turning control over to the creations of men.

Ross shrugged. "It's inevitable," she said. "In Olduvai Gorge in Tanzania, there are traces of a house two million years old. The hominid creature wasn't satisfied with caves and other natural shelters; he created his own accommodations. Men have always altered the natural world to suit their purposes."

"But you can't give up control," Elliot said.

"We've been doing it for centuries," Ross said. "What's a domesticated animal—or a pocket calculator—except an attempt to give up control? We don't want to plow fields or do square roots so we turn the job over to some other intelligence, which we've trained or bred or created."

"But you can't let your creations take over."

"We've been doing it for centuries," Ross repeated. "Look: even if we refused to develop faster computers, the Russians would. They'd be in Zaire right now looking for diamonds, if the Chinese weren't keeping them out. You can't stop technological advances. As soon as we know something is possible, we have to carry it out."

"No," Elliot said. "We can make our own decisions. I won't be a part of this."

"Then leave," she said. "The Congo's no place for academics, anyway."

She began unpacking her rucksack, taking out a series of white ceramic cones, and a number of small boxes with antennae. She attached a box to each ceramic cone, then entered the first tunnel, placed the cones flat against the walls, moving deeper into darkness.

Peter not happy Peter.

"No," Elliot said.

Why not happy?

"It's hard to explain, Amy," he said.

Peter tell Amy good gorilla.

"I know, Amy."

Karen Ross emerged from one tunnel, and disappeared into the second. Elliot saw the glow of her flashlight as she placed the cones, and then she was hidden from view.

Munro came out into the sunlight, his pockets bulging with diamonds. "Where's Ross?"

"In the tunnels."

"Doing what?"

"Some kind of explosive test, looks like." Elliot gestured to the three remaining ceramic cones on the ground near her pack.

Munro picked up one cone, and turned it over. "Do you know what these are?" he asked.

Elliot shook his head.

"They're RCs," Munro said, "and she's out of her mind to place them here. She could blow the whole place apart."

Resonant conventionals, or RCs, were timed explosives, a potent marriage of microelectronic and explosive technology. "We used RCs two years ago on bridges in Angola," Munro explained. "Properly sequenced, six ounces of explosive can bring down fifty tons of braced structural steel. You need one of those sensors"—he gestured to a control box lying near her pack—"which monitors shock waves from the early charges, and detonates the later charges in the timed sequence to set up resonating waves which literally shake the structure to pieces. Very impressive to see it happen." Munro glanced up at Mukenko, smoking above them.

At that moment, Ross emerged from the tunnel, all smiles. "We'll soon have our answers," she said.

"Answers?"

"About the extent of the kimberlite deposits. I've set twelve seismic charges, which is enough to give us definitive readings."

"You've set twelve *resonant* charges," Munro said.

"Well, they're all I brought. We've got to make do."

"They'll do," Munro said. "Perhaps too well. That volcano"—he pointed upwards—"is in an eruptive phase."

"I've placed a total of eight hundred grams of explosive," Ross said. "That's less than a pound and a half. It can't make the slightest difference."

"Let's not find out."

Elliot listened to their argument with mixed feelings. On the face of it, Munro's objections seemed absurd—a few trivial explosive charges, however timed, could not possibly trigger a volcanic eruption. It was ridiculous; Elliot wondered why Munro was so adamant about the dangers. It was almost as if Munro knew something that Elliot and Ross did not—and could not even imagine.

3. DOD/ARPD/VULCAN 7021

In 1978, MUNRO HAD LED A ZAMBIA EXPEDITION which included Robert Perry, a young geologist from the University of Hawaii. Perry had worked on PROJECT VULCAN, the most advanced program financed under the Department of Defense Advanced Research Project Division.

VULCAN was so controversial that during the 1975 House Armed Services Subcommittee hearings, project DOD/ARPD/VULCAN 7021 was carefully buried among "miscellaneous long-term fundings of national security significance." But the following year, Congressman David Inaga (D., Hawaii) challenged DOD/ARPD/VULCAN, demanding to know "its exact military purpose, and why it should be funded entirely within the state of Hawaii."

Pentagon spokesmen explained blandly that VULCAN was a "tsunami warning system" of value to the residents of the Hawaiian islands, as well as to military installations there. Pentagon experts reminded Inaga that in 1948 a tsunami had swept across the Pacific Ocean, first devastating Kauai, but moving so swiftly along the Hawaiian island chain that when it struck Oahu and Pearl Harbor twenty minutes later, no effective warning had been given.

"That tsunami was triggered by an underwater volcanic avalanche off the coast of Japan," they said. "But Hawaii has its own active volcanoes, and now that Honolulu is a city of half a million, and naval presence is valued at more than thirty-five billion dollars, the ability to predict tsunami activity secondary to eruptions by Hawaiian volcanoes assumes major long-term significance."

In truth, PROJECT VULCAN was not long-term at all; it was intended to be carried out at the next eruption of Mauna Loa, the largest active volcano in the world, located on the big island of Hawaii. The designated purpose of VULCAN was to control volcanic eruptions as they progressed; Mauna Loa was chosen because its eruptions were relatively mild and gentle.

Although it rose to an altitude of only 13,500 feet, Mauna Loa was the largest mountain in the world. Measured from its origin at the depths of the ocean floor, Mauna Loa had more than twice the cubic volume of Mount Everest; it was a unique and extraordinary geological formation. And Mauna Loa had long since become the most carefully studied volcano in history, having a permanent scientific observation station on its crater since 1928. It was also the most interfered-with volcano in history, since the lava that flowed down its slopes at three-year intervals had been diverted by everything from aerial bombers to local crews with shovels and sandbags.

VULCAN intended to alter the course of a Mauna Loa eruption by "venting" the giant volcano, releasing the enormous quantities of molten magma by a series of timed, non-nuclear explosions detonated along fault lines in the shield. In October, 1978, VULCAN was carried out in secret, using navy helicopter teams experienced in detonating high-explosive resonant conic charges. The VULCAN project lasted two days; on the third day, the civilian Mauna Loa Volcanic Laboratory publicly announced that "the October eruption of Mauna Loa has been milder than anticipated, and no further eruptive episodes are expected."

PROJECT VULCAN was secret but Munro had heard all about it one drunken night around the campfire near Bangazi. And he remembered it now as Ross was planning a resonant explosive sequence in the region of a volcano in its eruptive phase. The basic tenet of VULCAN was that enormous, pent-up geological forces—whether the forces of an earthquake, or a volcano, or a Pacific typhoon—could be devastatingly unleashed by a relatively small energy trigger.

Ross prepared to fire her conical explosives.

"I think," Munro said, "that you should try again to contact Houston."

"That's not possible," Ross said, supremely confident. "I'm required to decide on my own—and I've decided to assess the extent of diamond deposits in the hillsides now."

As the argument continued, Amy moved away. She picked up the detonating device lying alongside Ross's pack. It was a tiny handheld device with six glowing LEDs, more than enough to fascinate Amy. She raised her fingers to push the buttons.

Karen Ross looked over. "Oh God."

Munro turned. "Amy," he said softly. "Amy, no. No. Amy no good."

Amy good gorilla Amy good.

Amy held the detonating device in her hand. She was captivated by the winking LEDs. She glanced over at the humans.

"No, Amy," Munro said. He turned to Elliot. "Can't you stop her?"

"Oh, what the hell," Ross said. "Go ahead, Amy."

A series of rumbling explosions blasted gleaming diamond dust from the mine shafts, and then there was silence. "Well," Ross said finally, "I hope you're satisfied. It's perfectly clear that such a minimal explosive charge could not affect the volcano. In the future you can leave the scientific aspects to me, and—"

And then Mukenko rumbled, and the earth shook so hard that they were all knocked to the ground.

4. ERTS Houston

AT 1 A.M. HOUSTON TIME, R. B. TRAVIS FROWNED at the computer monitor in his office. He had just received the latest photosphere imagery from Kitt Peak Observatory, via GSFC telemetry. GSFC had kept him waiting all day for the data, which was only one of several reasons why Travis was in a bad humor.

The photospheric imagery was negative—the sphere of the sun appeared black on the screen, with a glowing white chain of sunspots. There were at least fifteen major sunspots across the sphere, one of which originated the massive solar flare that was making his life hell.

For two days now, Travis had been sleeping at ERTS. The entire operation had gone to hell. ERTS had a team in northern Pakistan, not far from the troubled Afghan border; another in central Malaysia, in an area of Communist insurrection; and the Congo team, which was facing rebelling natives and some unknown group of gorilla-like creatures.

Communications with all teams around the world had been cut off by the solar flare for more than twenty-four hours. Travis had been running computer simulations on all of them with six-hour updates. The results did not please him. The Pakistan team was probably all right, but would run six days over schedule and cost them an additional two hundred thousand dollars; the Malaysia team was in serious jeopardy; and the Congo team was classified CANNY—ERTS computer slang for "can not estimate." Travis had had two CANNY teams in the past—in the Amazon in 1976, and in Sri Lanka in 1978—and he had lost people from both groups.

Things were going badly. Yet this latest GSFC was much better than the previous report. They had—it seemed—managed a brief transmission contact with the Congo several hours earlier, although there was no verification response from Ross. He wondered whether the team had received the warning or not. He stared at the black sphere with frustration.

Richards, one of the main data programmers, stuck his head in the door. "I have something relevant to the CFS."

"Fire away," Travis said. Any news relevant to the Congo Field Survey was of interest.

"The South African seismological station at the University of Jo'burg reports tremors initiating at twelve oh four P.M. local time. Estimated epicenter coordinates are consistent with Mount Mukenko in the Virunga chain. The tremors are multiple, running Richter five to eight."

"Any confirmation?" Travis asked.

"Nairobi is the nearest station, and they're computing a Richter six to nine, or a Morelli Nine, with heavy downfall of ejecta from the cone. They are also predicting that the LAC, the local atmospheric conditions, are conducive to severe electrical discharges."

Travis glanced at his watch. "Twelve oh four local time is nearly an hour ago," he said. "Why wasn't I informed?"

Richards said, "It didn't come in from the African stations until now. I guess they figure it's no big deal, another volcano.''

Travis sighed. That was the trouble—volcanic activity was now recognized as a common phenomenon on the earth's surface. Since 1965, the first year that global records were kept, there had been twenty-two major eruptions each year, roughly one eruption every two weeks. Outlying stations were in no hurry to report such "ordinary" occurrences—to delay was proof of fashionable boredom.

"But they have problems," Richards said. "With the satellites disrupted by the sunspots, everybody has to transmit surface cable. And I guess as far as they're concerned, the northeast Congo is uninhabited.''

Travis said, "How bad is a Morelli Nine?''

Richards paused. "It's pretty bad, Mr. Travis.''

5. "Everything Was Moving"

IN THE CONGO, EARTH MOVEMENT WAS RICHTER scale 8, a Morelli scale IX. At this severity, the earth shakes so badly a man has difficulty standing. There are lateral shifts in the earth and rifts open up; trees and even steel-frame buildings topple.

For Elliot, Ross, and Munro, the five minutes following the onset of the eruption were a bizarre nightmare. Elliot recalled that "*everything* was moving. We were all literally knocked off our feet; we had to crawl on our hands and knees, like babies. Even after we got away from mine-shaft tunnels, the city swayed like a wobbling toy. It was quite a while—maybe half a minute—before the buildings began to collapse. Then everything came down at once: walls caving in, ceilings collapsing, big blocks of stone crashing down into the jungle. The trees were swaying too, and pretty soon they began falling over.''

The noise of this collapse was incredible, and added to that was the sound from Mukenko. The volcano wasn't rumbling anymore; they heard staccato explosions of lava blasting from the cone. These explosions produced shock waves; even when the earth was solid under their feet, they were knocked over without warning by blasts of hot air. "It was," Elliot recalled, "just like being in the middle of a war."

Amy was panic-stricken. Grunting in terror, she leapt into Elliot's arms—and promptly urinated on his clothes—as they began to run back toward the camp.

A sharp tremor brought Ross to the ground. She picked herself up, and stumbled onward, acutely aware of the humidity and the dense ash and dust ejected by the volcano. Within minutes, the sky above them was dark as night, and the first flashes of lightning cracked through the boiling clouds. It had rained the night before; the jungle surrounding them was wet, the air supersaturated with moisture. In short, they had all the requisites for a lightning storm. Ross felt herself torn between the perverse desire to watch this unique theoretical phenomenon and the desire to run for her life.

In a searing burst of blue-white light, the lightning storm struck. Bolts of electricity crackled all around them like rain; Ross later estimated there were two hundred bolts within the first minute—nearly three every second. The familiar shattering crack of lightning was not punctuation but a continuous sound, a roar like a waterfall. The booming thunder caused sharp ear pains, and the accompanying shock waves literally knocked them backward.

Everything happened so fast that they had little chance to absorb sensations. Their ordinary expectations were turned upside down. One of the porters, Amburi, had come back toward the city to find them. They saw him standing in a clearing, waving them ahead, when a lightning bolt crashed *up* through a nearby tree into the sky. Ross had known that the lightning flash came after the invisible downward flow of electrons and actually ran upward from the ground to the clouds above. But to see it! The explosive flash lifted Amburi off his feet and tossed him through the air toward them; he scrambled to his feet, shouting hysterically in Swahili.

All around them trees were cracking, splitting and hissing clouds of moisture as the lightning bolts shot upward through them. Ross later said, "The lightning was everywhere, the blinding flashes were continuous, with this terrible sizzling sound. That man [Amburi] was screaming and the next instant the lightning grounded through him. I was close enough to touch him but there was very little heat, just white light. He went rigid and there was this terrible smell as his whole body burst into flame, and he fell to the ground. Munro rolled on him to put out the fire but he was dead, and we ran on. There was no time to react; we kept falling down from the [earthquake] tremors. Soon we were all half-blinded from the lightning. I remember hearing somebody screaming but I didn't know who it was. I was sure we would all die."

Near camp, a gigantic tree crashed down before them, presenting an obstacle as broad and high as a three-story building. As they clambered through it, lightning sizzled through the damp branches, stripping off bark, glowing and scorching. Amy howled when a white bolt streaked across her hand as she gripped a wet branch. Immediately she dived to the ground, burying her head in the low foliage, refusing to move. Elliot had to drag her the remaining distance to the camp.

Munro was the first to reach camp. He found Kahega trying to pack the tents for their departure, but it was impossible with the tremors and the lightning crashing down through the dark ashen sky. One Mylar tent burst into flames. They smelled the harsh burning plastic. The dish antenna, resting on the ground, was struck and split apart, sending metal fragments flying.

"Leave!" Munro shouted. "Leave!"

"*Ndio mzee!*" Kahega shouted, grabbing his pack hastily. He glanced back toward the others, and in that moment Elliot stumbled out of the black gloom with Amy clinging to his chest. He had injured his ankle and was limping slightly. Amy quickly dropped to the ground.

"Leave!" Munro shouted.

As Elliot moved on, Ross emerged from the darkness of the ashen atmosphere, coughing, bent double. The left side of her body was scorched and blackened, and the skin of her left hand was burned. She had been struck by lightning, although she had no later memory of it. She pointed to her nose and throat, coughing. "Burns . . . hurts . . ."

"It's the gas," Munro shouted. He put his arm around her and half-lifted her from her feet, carrying her away. "We have to get uphill!"

An hour later, on higher ground, they had a final view of the city engulfed with smoke and ash. Farther up on the slopes of the volcano, they saw a line of trees burst into flames as an unseen dark wave of lava came sliding down the mountainside. They heard agonized bellows of pain from the gray gorillas on the hillside as hot lava rained down on them. As they watched, the foliage collapsed closer and closer to the city, until finally the city itself crumbled under a darkly descending cloud, and disappeared.

The Lost City of Zinj was buried forever.

Only then did Ross realize that her diamonds were buried forever as well.

6. Nightmare

THEY HAD NO FOOD, NO WATER, AND VERY LITTLE ammunition. They dragged themselves through the jungle, clothes burned and torn, faces haggard, exhausted. They did not speak to one another, but silently pressed on. Elliot said later they were "living through a nightmare."

The world through which they passed was grim and col-

orless. Sparkling white waterfalls and streams now ran black
with soot, splashing into scummy pools of gray foam. The
sky was dark gray, with occasional red flashes from the volcano. The very air became filmy gray; they coughed and
stumbled through a world of black soot and ash.

They were all covered with ash—their packs gritty on their
backs, their faces grimy when they wiped them, their hair
many shades darker. Their noses and eyes burned. There was
nothing to do about it; they could only keep going.

As Ross trudged through the dark air, she was aware of an
ironic ending to her personal quest. Ross had long since
acquired the expertise to tap into any ERTS data bank she
wanted, including the one that held her own evaluation. She
knew her assigned qualities by heart:
YOUTHFUL-ARROGANT (probably) / TENUOUS HUMAN
RAPPORT (she particularly resented that one) / DOMI-
NEERING (maybe) INTELLECTUALLY ARROGANT (only
natural) / INSENSITIVE (whatever that meant) / DRIVEN
TO SUCCEED AT ANY COST (was that so bad?)

And she knew her late-stage conclusions. All that flopover matrix garbage about parental figures and so on. And
the last line of her report: SUBJECT MUST BE MONITORED
IN LATE STAGE GOAL ORIENTED PROCEDURES.

But none of that was relevant. She had gone after the diamonds only to be beaten by the worst volcanic eruption in
Africa in a decade. Who could blame her for what had happened? It wasn't her fault. She would prove that on her next
expedition. . . .

Munro felt the frustration of a gambler who has placed
every bet correctly but still loses. He had been correct to
avoid the Euro-Japanese consortium; he had been correct to
go with ERTS; and yet he was coming out empty-handed.
Well, he reminded himself, feeling the diamonds in his pockets, not *quite* empty handed. . . .

Elliot was returning without photographs, videotapes,
sound recordings, or the skeleton of a gray gorilla. Even his
measurements had been lost. Without such proofs, he dared
not claim a new species—in fact, he would be unwise even

to discuss the possibility. A great opportunity had slipped away from him, and now, walking through the dark landscape, he had only a sense of the natural world gone mad: birds fell screeching from the sky, flopping at their feet, asphyxiated by the gases in the air above; bats skittered through the midday air; distant animals shrieked and howled. A leopard, fur burning on its hindquarters, ran past them at noon. Somewhere in the distance, elephants trumpeted with alarm.

They were trudging lost souls in a grim sooty world that seemed like a description of hell; perpetual fire and darkness, where tormented souls screamed in agony. And behind them Mukenko spat cinders and glowing rain. At one point, they were engulfed in a shower of red-hot embers that sizzled as they struck the damp canopy overhead, then turned the wet ground underfoot smoky, burning holes in their clothing, scorching their skin, setting hair smoldering as they danced in pain and finally sought shelter beneath tall trees, huddled together, awaiting the end of the fiery rain from the skies.

Munro planned from the first moments of the eruption to head directly for the wrecked C-130 transport, which would afford them shelter and supplies. He estimated they would reach the aircraft in two hours. In fact, six hours passed before the gigantic ash-covered hulk of the plane emerged from the murky afternoon darkness.

One reason it had taken them so long to move away from Mukenko was that they were obliged to avoid General Muguru and his troops. Whenever they came across jeep tracks, Munro led them farther west, into the depths of the jungle. "He's not a fellow you want to meet," Munro said. "And neither are his boys. And they'd think nothing of cutting your liver out and eating it raw."

Dark ash on wings and fuselage made the giant transport look as if it had crashed in black snow. Off one bent wing, a kind of waterfall of ash hissed over the metal down to the ground. Far in the distance, they heard the soft beating of Kigani drums, and thumping mortar from Muguru's troops. Otherwise it was ominously quiet.

Munro waited in the forest beyond the wreckage, watching the airplane. Ross took the opportunity to try to transmit on the computer, continuously brushing ash from the video screen, but she could not reach Houston.

Finally Munro signaled, and they all began to move forward. Amy, panicked, tugged at Munro's sleeve. *No go,* she signed. *People there.*

Munro frowned at her, glanced at Elliot. Elliot pointed to the airplane. Moments later, there was a crash, and two white-painted Kigani warriors emerged from the aircraft, onto the high wing. They were carrying cases of whiskey and arguing about how to get them down to the jungle floor below. After a moment, five more Kigani appeared beneath the wing, and the cases were passed to them. The two men above jumped down, and the group moved off.

Munro looked at Amy and smiled.

Amy good gorilla, she signed.

They waited another twenty minutes, and when no further Kigani appeared, Munro led the group to the airplane. They were just outside the cargo doors when a rain of white arrows began to whistle down on them.

"Inside!" Munro shouted, and hurried them all up the crumpled landing gear, onto the upper wing surface, and from there into the airplane. He slammed the emergency door; arrows clattered on the outer metal surface.

Inside the transport it was dark; the floor tilted at a crazy angle. Boxes of equipment had slid across the aisles, toppled over, and smashed. Broken glassware crunched underfoot. Elliot carried Amy to a seat, and then noticed that the Kigani had defecated on the seats.

Outside, they heard drums, and the steady rain of arrows on the metal and windows. Looking out through the dark ash, they glimpsed dozens of white-painted men, running through the trees, slipping under the wing.

"What are we going to do?" Ross asked.

"Shoot them," Munro said briskly, breaking open their supplies, removing machine-gun clips. "We aren't short of ammunition."

"But there must be a hundred men out there."

"Yes, but only one man is important. Kill the Kigani with red streaks painted beneath his eyes. That'll end the attack right away."

"Why?" Elliot asked.

"Because he's the *Angawa* sorcerer," Munro said, moving forward to the cockpit. "Kill him and we're off the hook."

Poison-tipped arrows clattered on the plastic windows and rang against the metal; the Kigani also threw feces, which thudded dully against the fuselage. The drums beat constantly.

Amy was terrified, and buckled herself into a seat, signing, *Amy leave now bird fly.*

Elliot found two Kigani concealed in the rear passenger compartment. To his own amazement he killed both without hesitation, firing the machine gun which bucked in his hands, blasting the Kigani back into the passenger seats, shattering windows, crumpling their bodies.

"Very good, Doctor." Kahega grinned, although by then Elliot was shaking uncontrollably. He slumped into a seat next to Amy.

People attack bird bird fly now bird fly Amy want go.

"Soon, Amy," he said, hoping it would prove true.

By now, the Kigani had abandoned their frontal assault; they were attacking from the rear, where there were no windows. Everyone could hear the sound of bare feet moving over the tail section and up onto the fuselage above their heads. Two warriors managed to climb through the open aft cargo door. Munro, who was in the cockpit, shouted, "If they get you, they eat you!"

Ross fired at the rear door, and blood spattered on her clothes as the intruding Kigani were knocked out backward.

Amy no like, she signed. *Amy want go home.* She clutched her seat belt.

"There's the son of a bitch," Munro shouted, and fired his machine gun. A young man of about twenty, his eyes smeared with red, fell onto his back, shuddering with machine-gun fire. "Got him," Munro said. "Got the *An-*

gawa." He sat back and allowed the warriors to remove the body."

It was then the Kigani attack ended, the warriors retreating into the silent bush. Munro bent over the slumped body of the pilot and stared out at the jungle.

"What happens now?" Elliot asked. "Have we won?"

Munro shook his head. "They'll wait for nightfall. Then they'll come back to kill us all."

Elliot said, "What will we do then?"

Munro had been thinking about that. He saw no possibility of their leaving the aircraft for at least twenty-four hours. They needed to defend themselves at night and they needed a wider clearing around the plane during the day. The obvious solution was to burn the waist-high bush in the immediate vicinity of the plane—if they could do that without exploding the residual fuel in the airplane tanks.

"Look for flamethrowers," he told Kahega, "or gas canisters." And he began to check for documents that would tell him tank locations on the C-130.

Ross approached him. "We're in trouble, aren't we."

"Yes," Munro said. He didn't mention the volcano.

"I suppose I made a mistake."

"Well, you can atone," Munro said, "by thinking of some way out."

"I'll see what I can do," she said seriously, and went aft. Fifteen minutes later, she screamed.

Munro spun back into the passenger compartment, his machine gun raised to fire. But he saw that Ross had collapsed into a seat, laughing hysterically. The others stared at her, not sure what to do. He grabbed her shoulders and shook her: "Get a grip on yourself," he said, but she just went on laughing.

Kahega stood next to a gas cylinder marked PROPANE. "She see this, and she ask how many more, I tell her six more, she begins to laugh."

Munro frowned. The cylinder was large, 20 cubic feet. "Kahega, what'd they carry that propane for?"

Kahega shrugged. "Too big for cooking. They need only five, ten cubic feet for cooking."

Munro said, "And there are six more like this?"

"Yes, boss. Six."

"That's a hell of a lot of gas," Munro said, and then he realized that Ross with her instinct for planning would have grasped at once the significance of all that propane, and Munro also knew what it meant, and he broke into a grin.

Annoyed, Elliot said, "Will someone please tell us what this means?"

"It means," Munro said through his laughter, "it means things are looking up."

Buoyed by 50,000 pounds of heated air from the propane gas ring, the gleaming plastic sphere of the consortium balloon lifted off from the jungle floor, and climbed swiftly into the darkening night air.

The Kigani came running from the forest, the warriors brandishing spears and arrows. Pale white arrows sliced up in the fading light, but they fell short, arcing back down to the ground again. The balloon rose steadily into the sky.

At an altitude of 2,000 feet, the sphere caught an easterly wind which carried it away from the dark expanse of the Congo forest, over the smoking red volcanic heart of Mount Mukenko, and across the sharp depression of the Rift Valley, vertical walls shimmering in the moonlight.

From there, the balloon slid across the Zaire border, moving southeast toward Kenya—and civilization.

Epilogue:
The Place of Fire

ON SEPTEMBER 18, 1979, THE LANDSAT 3 SATELlite, at a nominal altitude of 918 kilometers, recorded a 185-kilometer-wide scan on Band 6 (.7–.8 millimicrons in the infrared spectrum) over central Africa. Penetrating cloud cover over the rain forest, the acquired image clearly showed the eruption of Mount Mukenko still continuing after three months. A computer projection of ejecta estimated 6–8 cubic kilometers of debris dispersed into the atmosphere, and another 2--3 cubic kilometers of lava released down the western flanks of the mountain. The natives called it *Kanyalifeka*, "the place of fire."

On October 1, 1979, R. B. Travis formally canceled the Blue Contract, reporting that no natural source of Type IIb diamonds could be anticipated in the foreseeable future. The Japanese electronics firm of Morikawa revived interest in the Nagaura artificial boron-doping process. American firms had also begun work on doping; it was expected that the process would be perfected by 1984.

On October 23, Karen Ross resigned from ERTS to work for the U.S. Geological Survey EDC in Sioux Falls, South Dakota, where no military work was conducted, and no fieldwork was possible. She has since married John Bellingham, a scientist at EDC.

Peter Elliot took an indefinite leave of absence from the Berkeley Department of Zoology on October 30. A press release cited "Amy's increasing maturity and size . . . making further laboratory research difficult . . ." Project Amy was formally disbanded, although most of the staff accompanied Elliot and Amy to the Institut d'Etudes Ethnologiques

311

at Bukama, Zaire. Here Amy's interaction with wild gorillas continued to be studied in the field. In November, 1979, she was thought to be pregnant; by then she was spending most of her time with a local gorilla troop, so it was difficult to be sure. She disappeared in May 1980.*

The institute conducted a census of mountain gorillas from March to August 1980. The estimate was five thousand animals in all, approximately half the estimate of George Schaller, field biologist, twenty years before. These data confirm that the mountain gorilla is disappearing rapidly. Zoo reproduction rates have increased, and gorillas are unlikely to become technically extinct, but their habitats are shrinking under the press of mankind, and researchers suspect that the gorilla will vanish as a wild, free-roaming animal in the next few years.

Kahega returned to Nairobi in 1979, working in a Chinese restaurant which went bankrupt in 1980. He then joined the National Geographic Society expedition to Botswana to study hippos.

Aki Ubara, the eldest son of the porter Marawani and a radio astronomer at Cambridge, England, won the Herskovitz Prize in 1980 for research on X-ray emissions from the galactic source M322.

At a handsome profit, Charles Munro sold 31 karats of blue Type IIb diamonds on the Amsterdam *bourse* in late 1979; the diamonds were purchased by Intel, Inc., an American micronics company. Subsequently he was stabbed by a Russian agent in Antwerp in January 1980; the agent's body was later recovered in Brussels. Munro was arrested by an armed border patrol in Zambia in March 1980, but charges were dropped. He was reported in Somalia in May, but there is no confirmation. He still resides in Tangier.

A Landsat 3 image acquired on January 8, 1980, showed

*In May 1980, Amy disappeared for four months, but in September she returned with a male infant clinging to her chest. Elliot signed to her, and had the unexpected satisfaction of seeing the infant sign back to him *Amy like Peter like Peter*. The signing was crisp and correct and has been recorded on videotape. Amy would not approach closely with her infant; when the infant moved toward Elliot, Amy grabbed him to her chest, disappearing into the bush. She was later sighted among a troop of twelve gorillas on the slopes of Mt. Kyambara in northeastern Zaire.

that the eruption of Mount Mukenko had ceased. The faint signature of crossed laser beams, recorded on some earlier satellite passes, was no longer visible. The projected intersection point now marked a field of black quatermain lava with an average depth of eight hundred meters—nearly half a mile—over the Lost City of Zinj.

References

BALANDIER, GEORGES. *Daily Life in the Kingdom of the Kongo from the Sixteenth to the Eighteenth Century*. New York: Pantheon, 1968.

BANCHOFF, THOMAS F., and STRAUSS, CHARLES M. "Real-Time Computer Graphics Analysis of Figures in Four-Space." In *Hypergraphics*, edited by David W. Brisson, pp. 159–169. AAAS Selected Symposium 24. Boulder, Colo.: Westview Press, 1978.

BLEIBTREU, JOHN N. *The Parable of the Beast*. New York: Macmillan, 1967.

BROWN, HARRISON; BONNER, JAMES; and WEIR, JOHN. *The Next Hundred Years*. New York: Viking Press, 1963.

BURCHETT, WILFRED, and ROEBUCK, DEREK. *The Whores of War*. Harmondsworth, England: Penguin, 1977.

CAPLAN, ARTHUR L. "Ethics, Evolution and the Milk of Human Kindness." In *The Sociobiology Debate*, edited by Arthur L. Caplan, pp. 304–314. New York: Harper & Row, 1978.

CHURCHMAN, C. WEST. *The Systems Approach and Its Enemies*. New York: Basic Books, 1979.

CLARK, W. E. *The Antecedents of Man*. Edinburgh: University of Edinburgh Press, 1962.

COX, KEITH G. "Kimberlite Pipes." *Scientific American* 238, no. 4 (1978): 120–134.

DEACON, RICHARD. *The Chinese Secret Service*. New York: Taplinger, 1974.

DERJAGUIN, B. V., and FEDOSEEV, D. B. "The Synthesis of Diamonds at Low Pressure." *Scientific American* 233, no. 5 (1975): 102–110.

DESMOND, ADRIAN J. *The Ape's Reflexion*, New York: Dial, 1979.

DOUGLAS-HAMILTON, IAIN and ORIA. *Among the Elephants*. New York: Viking, 1975.

EVANS-PRITCHARD, E. E. "The Morphology and Function of Magic: A Comparative Study of Trobriand and Zande Ritual and Spells." In *Magic, Witchcraft and Curing*, edited by John Middleton, pp. 1–22. Garden City, N.Y.: Natural History Press, 1967.

————. *Witchcraft, Oracles and Magic Among the Azande*. Oxford: Clarendon Press, 1937.

FORBATH, PETER. *The River Congo*. New York: Harper & Row, 1977.

FOUTS, ROGER S. "Sign Language in Chimpanzees: Implications of the Visual Mode and the Comparative Approach." In *Sign Language and Language Acquisition in Man and Ape: New Dimensions in Comparative Pedolinguistics*, edited by Fred C. C. Peng, pp. 121–137. AAAS Selected Symposium 16. Boulder, Colo.: Westview Press, 1978.

FRANCIS, PETER. *Volcanoes*. Harmondsworth, England: Penguin, 1976.

GOLD, THOMAS, and SOTER, STEVEN. "Brontides: Natural Explosive Noises." *Science* 204, no. 4391 (1979): 371–375.

References

315

GOULD, R. G., and LUM, L. F., eds. *Communications Satellite Systems: An Overview of the Technology*. New York: Institute of Electrical and Electronics Engineers Press, 1976.

GRIBBIN, JOHN. "What Future for Futures?" *New Scientist* 84, no. 1187, pp. 21–23.

HALLET, JEAN-PIERRE. *Congo Kitabu*. New York: Random House, 1964.

HARRIS, MARVIN. *Cannibals and Kings: The Origins of Cultures*. New York: Random House, 1977.

HAWTHORNE, J. B. "Model of a Kimberlite Pipe." *Physics and Chemistry of the Earth* 9 (1975): 1–15.

HOARE, COLONEL MIKE. *Congo Mercenary*. London: Hale, 1967.

HOFF, CHRISTINA. "Immoral and Moral Uses of Animals." *New England Journal of Medicine* 302, no. 2, pp. 115–118.

HOGG, GARRY. *Cannibalism and Human Sacrifice*. New York: Citadel Press, 1966.

JENSEN, HOMER; GRAHAM, L. C.; PORCELLO, L. J. and LEITH, E. N. "Side-Looking Airborne Radar." *Scientific American* 237, no. 4 (1977): 84–96.

JONES, ROGER. *The Rescue of Emin Pasha*. New York: St. Martin's Press, 1972.

KAHN, HERMAN; BROWN, WILLIAM; and MARTEL, LEON. *The Next Two Hundred Years*. New York: Morrow, 1976.

LILLESAND, THOMAS M., and KIEFER, RALPH W. *Remote Sensing and Image Interpretation*. New York: Wiley, 1979.

LINDEN, EUGENE. *Apes, Men and Language*. New York: E. P. Dutton, 1975.

MARTIN, JAMES. *Telecommunications and the Computer*. Englewood Cliffs, N.J.: Prentice-Hall, 1969.

MARWICK, M. G. "The Sociology of Sorcery in a Central African Tribe." In *Magic, Witchcraft and Curing*, edited by John Middleton. Garden City. N.Y.: Natural History Press, 1967.

MIDGLEY, MARY. *Beast and Man: The Roots of Human Nature*. Ithaca, N.Y.: Cornell University Press, 1978.

MOORE, C. B., ed. *Chemical and Biochemical Applications of Lasers*. Vol. 3. New York: Academic Press, 1977.

MOOREHEAD, ALAN. *The White Nile*. New York: Harper & Brothers, 1960.

MOSS, CYNTHIA. *Portraits in the Wild: Animal Behavior in East Africa*. London: Hamilton, 1976.

NOYCE, ROBERT N. "Microelectronics." *Scientific American* 237, no. 3 (1977): 62–70.

NUGENT, JOHN PEER. *Call Africa 999*. New York: Coward-McCann, 1965.

ORLOV, YU L. *The Mineralogy of the Diamond*. New York: Wiley, 1977.

PATTERSON, FRANCINE. "Conversations with a Gorilla." *National Geographic* 154, no. 4 (1978): 438–467.

_____. "Linguistic Capabilities of a Lowland Gorilla." In *Sign Language and Language Acquisition in Man and Ape: New Dimensions in Comparative Pedolinguistics*, edited by Fred C. C. Peng, pp. 161–202. AAAS Selected Symposium 16. Boulder, Colo.: Westview Press, 1978.

PETERS, WILLIAM C. *Exploration and Mining Geology*. New York: Wiley, 1978.

PREMACK, ANN JAMES and DAVID. "Teaching Language to an Ape." *Scientific American* 227, no. 4 (1972): 92–100.

PREMACK, DAVID. "Language in a Chimpanzee?" *Science* 172, no. 3985 (1971): 808–822.

RICHARDS, PAUL W. "The Tropical Rain Forest." *Scientific American* 229, no. 6 (1973): 58–69.

ROTH, H. M. and others. *Zaire: A Country Study*. Area Handbook Series. Washington, D.C.: U.S. Government Printing Office, 1977.

RUMBAUGH, DUANE M., ed. *Language Learning by a Chimpanzee: The Lana Project.* New York: Academic Press, 1977.

SABINS, FLOYD F. *Remote Sensing Principles and Interpretation.* San Francisco: W. H. Freeman, 1978.

SANDVED, KJELL B., and EMSLEY, MICHAEL. *Rain Forests and Cloud Forests.* New York: Abrams, 1979.

SAPOLSKY, HARVEY M. *The Polaris System Development.* Cambridge, Mass.: Harvard, 1972.

SCHALLER, GEORGE B. *The Mountain Gorilla, Ecology and Behavior.* Chicago: University of Chicago Press, 1963.

_____. *The Year of the Gorilla.* Chicago: University of Chicago Press, 1964.

SPUHLER, J. N. "Somatic Paths to Culture." In *The Evolution of Man's Capacity for Culture,* edited by J. N. Spuhler, pp. 1–13. Detroit: Wayne State University Press, 1959.

STANLEY, HENRY M. *In Darkest Africa,* 2 vols. New York: 1890.

TERRACE, H. S. *Nim.* New York: Alfred A. Knopf, 1979.

_____. "How Nim Chimpsky Changed My Mind." *Psychology Today,* November, 1979, pp. 65–76.

TURNBULL, COLIN M. *The Forest People.* London: Jonathan Cape, 1961.

_____. *Man in Africa.* Garden City, N.Y.: Doubleday, 1976.

_____. *The Mountain People.* London: Jonathan Cape, 1973.

VAUGHAN, JAMES H. "Environment, Population, and Traditional Society." In *Africa,* edited by Phyllis M. Martin and Patrick O'Meara, pp. 9–23. Bloomington: Indiana University Press, 1977.

WILSON, EDWARD O. *On Human Nature.* Cambridge, Mass.: Harvard, 1978.

YERKES, ROBERT M. and ADA, W. *The Great Apes: A Study of Anthropoid Life.* New Haven: Yale University Press, 1929.

ZUCKERMAN, ED. "You Talkin' to Me?" *Rolling Stone,* June 16, 1977, pp. 45–48.

THE TERMINAL MAN

To Kurt Villadsen

Acknowledgment

Martin J. Nathan, M.D., and Demian Kuffler gave technical advice and assistance. Kay Kolman Tyler prepared the graphics. I am indebted to them all.

Contents

Author's Introduction

READERS WHO FIND THE SUBJECT MATTER OF this book shocking or frightening should not delude themselves by also thinking it is something quite new. The physical study of the brain, and the technology for modifying behavior through psychosurgery, has been developing for nearly a century. For decades, it was there for anyone to see, discuss, support, or oppose.

Nor has there been any lack of publicity. Research in neurobiology is spectacular enough to appear regularly in Sunday supplements. But the public has never really taken it seriously. There has been so much ominous talk and so much frivolous speculation for so many years that the public now regards "mind control" as a problem removed to the distant future: it might eventually happen, but not soon, and not in a way that would affect anyone now alive.

Scientists engaged in this research have sought public discussion. James V. McConnell of the University of Michigan told his students some years ago, "Look, we can do these things. We can control behavior. Now, who's going to decide what's to be done? If you don't get busy and tell me how I'm supposed to do it, I'll make up my own mind for you. And then it's too late.''

Many people today feel that they live in a world that is predetermined and running along a fixed pre-established course. Past decisions have left us with pollution, depersonalization, and urban blight; somebody else made the decisions for us, and we are stuck with the consequences.

That attitude represents a childish and dangerous denial of responsibility, and everyone should recognize it for what it is. In that spirit, the following chronology is presented:

HISTORY OF THERAPY OF PSYCHOSURGERY

1908   Horsley and Clarke (Great Britain) describe stereotaxic surgical techniques for use on animals.

1947   Spiegel and co-workers (U.S.A.) report the first stereotaxic surgery performed on a human being.

1950   Penfield and Flanagan (Canada) perform ablative surgery with favorable results in patients with seizure foci.

1958   Talairach and co-workers (France) begin chronic stereotaxic implantation of depth electrodes.

Author's Introduction

1963   Heath and co-workers (U.S.A.) allow patients to stimulate themselves, at will, via implanted electrodes.

1965   Narabayashi (Japan) reports on 98 patients with violent behavior treated by stereotaxic surgery.

1965   More than 24,000 stereotaxic procedures on human beings have been performed in various countries by this date.

1968   Delgado and co-workers (U.S.A.) attach "stimoceiver" (radio stimulator plus radio receiver) to freely ambulatory hospital patients.

1969   Chimpanzee at Alamogordo, N.M., is directly linked by radio to a computer which programs and delivers his brain stimulations.

1971   Patient Harold Benson is operated on in Los Angeles.

M.C.

Los Angeles
October 23, 1971

"I have come to the conclusion that my subjective account of my own motivation is largely mythical on almost all occasions. I don't know why I do things."

J. B. S. HALDANE

"The wilderness masters the colonist."

FREDERICK JACKSON TURNER

TUESDAY, MARCH 9, 1971:

Admission

1

THEY CAME DOWN TO THE EMERGENCY WARD at noon and sat on the bench just behind the swinging doors that led in from the ambulance parking slot. Ellis, the senior man, was tense, preoccupied, distant. The younger man, Morris, was eating a candy bar. He crumpled the wrapper into the pocket of his white jacket.

From where they sat, they could look at the sunlight outside, falling across the big sign that said EMERGENCY WARD and the smaller sign that said NO PARKING AMBULANCES ONLY. In the distance they heard sirens.

"Is that him?" Ellis asked.

Morris checked his watch. "I doubt it. It's too early."

They sat on the bench and listened to the sirens come closer. Ellis removed his glasses and wiped them with his tie. One of the emergency ward nurses, a girl Morris did not know by name, came over and said brightly, "Is this the welcoming committee?"

Ellis squinted at her. Morris said, "We'll be taking him straight through. Do you have his chart down here?"

The nurse said, "Yes, I think so, Doctor," and walked off looking irritated.

3

Ellis sighed. He replaced his glasses and frowned at the nurse. "I suppose the whole damned hospital knows."

"It's a pretty big secret to keep."

The sirens were very close now; through the windows they saw an ambulance back into the slot. Two orderlies opened the door and pulled out the stretcher. A frail elderly woman lay on the stretcher, gasping for breath, making wet gurgling sounds. Severe pulmonary edema, Morris thought as he watched her taken into one of the treatment rooms.

"I hope he's in good shape," Ellis said.

"Who?"

"Benson."

"Why shouldn't he be?"

"They might have roughed him up." Ellis stared morosely out the windows. He really is in a bad mood, Morris thought. He knew that meant Ellis was excited; he had scrubbed in on enough cases with Ellis to recognize the pattern. Irascibility under pressure while he waited—and then total, almost lazy calm when the operation began. "Where the hell is he?" Ellis said, looking at his watch again.

To change the subject, Morris said, "Are we all set for three-thirty?" At 3:30 that afternoon, Benson would be presented to the hospital staff at a special Neurosurgical Rounds.

"As far as I know," Ellis said. "Ross is making the presentation. I just hope Benson's in good shape."

Over the loudspeaker, a soft voice said, "Dr. Ellis, Dr. John Ellis, two-two-three-four. Dr. Ellis, two-two-three-four."

Ellis got up to answer the page. "Hell," he said.

Morris knew that two-two-three-four was the extension for the animal laboratories. The call probably meant something had gone wrong with the monkeys. Ellis had been doing three monkeys a week for the past month, just to keep himself and his staff ready.

He watched as Ellis crossed the room and answered from a wall phone. Ellis walked with a slight limp, the result of a childhood injury that had cut the common peroneal nerve in his right leg. Morris always wondered if the injury had had something to do with Ellis's later decision to become a neurosurgeon. Certainly Ellis had the attitude of a man determined to correct defects, to fix things up. That was what he always said to his patients: "We can fix you up." And he seemed to have more than his share of defects himself—the limp, the premature near-baldness, the weak eyes, and the heavy thick glasses. It produced a vulnerability about him that made his irascibility more tolerable.

Morris stared out the window at the sunlight and the parking lot. Afternoon visiting hours were beginning; relatives were driving into the parking lot, getting out of their cars, glancing up at the high buildings of the hospital. The apprehension was clear in their faces; the hospital was a place people feared.

Morris noticed how many of them had sun tans. It had been a warm, sunny spring in Los Angeles, yet he was still as pale as the white jacket and trousers he wore every day. He had to get outside more often, he told himself. He should start eating lunch outside. He played tennis, of course, but that was usually in the evenings.

Ellis came back, shaking his head. "It's Ethel. She tore out her sutures."

"How did it happen?" Ethel was a juvenile rhesus

monkey who had undergone brain surgery the day before. The operation had proceeded flawlessly. And Ethel
was unusually docile, as rhesus monkeys went.

"I don't know," Ellis said. "Apparently she worked
an arm loose from her restraints. Anyway, she's shrieking and the bone's exposed on one side."

"Did she tear out her wires?"

"I don't know. But I've got to go down and resew
her now. Can you handle this?"

"I think so."

"Are you all right with the police?" Ellis said. "I
don't think they'll give you any trouble."

"No, I don't think so."

"Just get Benson up to seven as fast as you can,"
Ellis said. "Then call Ross. I'll be up as soon as possible." He checked his watch. "It'll probably take forty
minutes to resew Ethel, if she behaves herself."

"Good luck with her," Morris said.

Ellis looked sour and walked away.

After he had gone, the emergency ward nurse came
back. "What's the matter with *him*?" she asked.

"Just edgy," Morris said.

"He sure is," the nurse said. She paused and looked
out the window, lingering.

Morris watched her with a kind of bemused detachment. He'd spent enough years in the hospital to recognize the subtle signs of status. He had begun as an
intern, with no status at all. Most of the nurses knew
more medicine than he did, and if they were tired they
didn't bother to conceal it. ("I don't think you want to
do that, Doctor.") As the years went by, he became a
surgical resident, and the nurses became more defer-
ential. When he was a senior resident, he was suffi-

ciently assured in his work that a few of the nurses called him by his first name. And finally, when he transferred to the Neuropsychiatric Research Unit as a junior staff member, the formality returned as a new mark of status.

But this was something else: a nurse hanging around, just being near him, because he had a special aura of importance. Because everyone in the hospital knew what was going to happen.

Staring out the window, the nurse said, "Here he comes."

Morris got up and looked out. A blue police van drove up toward the emergency ward, and turned around, backing into the ambulance slot. "All right," he said. "Notify the seventh floor, and tell them we're on our way."

"Yes, Doctor."

The nurse went off. Two ambulance orderlies opened the hospital doors. They knew nothing about Benson. One of them said to Morris, "You expecting this one?"

"Yes."

"EW case?"

"No, a direct admission."

The orderlies nodded, and watched as the police officer driving the van came around and unlocked the rear door. Two officers seated in the back emerged, blinking in the sunlight. Then Benson came out.

As always, Morris was struck by his appearance. Benson was a meek, pudgy, thirtyish man, with a bewildered air as he stood by the van, with his wrists handcuffed in front of him. When he saw Morris, he said, "Hello," and then looked away, embarrassed.

One of the cops said, "You in charge?"

"Yes. I'm Dr. Morris."

The cop gestured toward the interior of the hospital. "Lead the way, Doctor."

Morris said, "Would you mind taking off his handcuffs?"

Benson's eyes flicked up at Morris, then back down. "We don't have any orders about that." The cops exchanged glances. "I guess it's okay."

While they took the cuffs off, the driver brought Morris a form on a clipboard: "Transfer of Suspect to Institutional Care (Medical)." He signed it.

"And again here," the driver said.

As Morris signed again, he looked at Benson. Benson stood quietly, rubbing his wrists, staring straight ahead. The impersonality of the transaction, the forms and signatures, made Morris feel as if he were receiving a package from United Parcel.

"Okay," the driver said. "Thanks, Doc."

Morris led the other two policemen and Benson into the hospital. The orderlies shut the doors. A nurse came up with a wheelchair and Benson sat down in it. The cops looked confused.

"It's hospital policy," Morris said.

They all went to the elevators.

The elevator stopped at the lobby. A half-dozen relatives were waiting to go up to the higher floors, but they hesitated when they saw Morris, Benson in the wheelchair, and the two cops. "Please take the next car," Morris said smoothly. The doors closed. They continued up.

"Where is Dr. Ellis?" Benson asked. "I thought he was going to be here."

"He's in surgery. He'll be up shortly."

"And Dr. Ross?"

"You'll see her at the presentation."

"Oh, yes." Benson smiled. "The presentation."

The elevator arrived at the seventh floor, and they all got out.

Seven was the Special Surgical floor, where difficult and complex cases were treated. It was essentially a research floor. The most severe cardiac, kidney, and metabolic patients recuperated here. They went down to the nurses' station, a glasswalled area strategically located at the center of the X-shaped floor.

The nurse on duty at the station looked up. She was surprised to see the cops, but she said nothing. Morris said, "This is Mr. Benson. Have we got seven-ten ready?"

"All set for him," the nurse said, and gave Benson a cheery smile. Benson smiled bleakly back, and glanced from the nurse to the computer console in the corner of the nursing station.

"You have a time-sharing station up here?"

"Yes," Morris said.

"Where's the main computer?"

"In the basement."

"Of this building?"

"Yes. It draws a lot of power, and the power lines come to this building."

Benson nodded. Morris was not surprised at the questions. Benson was trying to distract himself from the thought of surgery, and he was, after all, a computer expert.

The nurse handed Morris the chart on Benson. It had the usual blue plastic cover with the seal of University

Hospital. But there was also a red tag, which meant neurosurgery, and a yellow tag, which meant intensive care, and a white tag, which Morris had almost never seen on a patient's chart. The white tag meant security precautions.

"Is that my record?" Benson asked as Morris wheeled him down the hall to 710. The cops followed along behind.

"Uh-huh."

"I always wondered what was in it."

"Lot of unreadable notes, mostly." Actually, Benson's chart was thick and very readable, with all the computer print-outs of different tests.

They came to 710. Before they entered the room, one of the cops went in and closed the door behind him. The second cop remained outside the door. "Just a precaution," he said.

Benson glanced up at Morris. "They're very careful about me," he said.

The first cop came out. "It's okay," he said.

Morris wheeled Benson into the room. It was a large room, on the south side of the hospital, so that it was sunny in the afternoon. Benson looked around and nodded approvingly. Morris said, "This is one of the best rooms in the hospital."

"Can I get up now?"

"Of course."

Benson got out of the wheelchair and sat on the bed. He bounced on the mattress. He pressed the buttons that made the bed move up and down, then bent over to look at the motorized mechanism beneath the bed. Morris went to the window and drew the blinds, reducing the direct light. "Simple," Benson said.

"What's that?"

"This bed mechanism. Remarkably simple. You should really have a feedback unit so that body movements by the person in the bed are automatically compensated for. . . ." His voice trailed off. He opened the closet doors, looked in, checked the bathroom, came back. Morris thought that he wasn't acting like an ordinary patient. Most patients were intimidated by the hospital, but Benson acted as if he were renting a hotel room.

"I'll take it," Benson said, and laughed. He sat down on the bed and looked at Morris, then at the cops. "Do they have to be here?"

"I think they can wait outside," Morris said.

The cops nodded and went out, closing the door behind them.

"I meant," Benson said, "do they have to be here at all?"

"Yes, they do."

"All the time?"

"Yes. Unless we can get charges against you dropped."

Benson frowned. "Was it . . . I mean, did I . . . Was it bad?"

"You gave him a black eye and you fractured one rib."

"But he's all right?"

"Yes. He's all right."

"I don't remember any of it," Benson said. "All my memory cores are erased."

"I know that."

"But I'm glad he's all right."

Morris nodded. "Did you bring anything with you? Pajamas, anything like that?"

Benson said, "No. But I can arrange for it."

"All right. I'll get you some hospital clothing in the meantime. Are you all right for now?"

"Yes. Sure." And he grinned. "I could do with a quick shot, maybe."

"That," Morris said, "is something you'll have to do without." He went out of the room.

The cops had brought a chair up to the door. One of them sat on it, the other stood alongside. Morris flipped open his notebook.

"You'll want to know the schedule," he said. "An admitting person will show up in the next half hour with financial waivers for Benson to sign. Then, at three-thirty he goes downstairs to the main amphitheater for Surgical Rounds. He comes back after about twenty minutes. His head will be shaved tonight. The operation is scheduled for six a.m. tomorrow morning. Do you have questions?"

"Can someone get us meals?" one of them asked.

"I'll have the nurse order extras. Will there be two of you, or just one?"

"Just one. We're working eight-hour shifts."

Morris said, "I'll tell the nurses. It'd help if you check in and out with them. They like to know who's on the floor."

The cops nodded. There was a moment of silence. Finally, one of them said, "What's wrong with him, anyway?"

"He has a special kind of brain damage. It gives him seizures."

"I saw the guy he beat up," one of the cops said. "Big strong guy, looked like a truck driver. You'd never think a little guy like that"—he jerked his arm toward Benson's room—"could do it."

"When he has seizures, he's violent."

They nodded. "What's this operation he's getting?"

"It's a kind of surgery we call a stage-three procedure," Morris said. He didn't bother to explain further. The policemen wouldn't understand. And, he thought, even if they understood, they wouldn't believe it.

2

NEUROSURGICAL GRAND ROUNDS, WHERE UN-usual cases were presented and discussed by all the surgeons of the hospital, were normally scheduled for Thursdays at nine. Special rounds were hardly ever called; it was too difficult for the staff to get together. But now the amphitheater was packed, tier after tier of white jackets and pale faces staring down at Ellis, who pushed his glasses up on his nose and said, "As many of you know, tomorrow morning the Neuropsychiatric Research Unit will perform a limbic pacing procedure—what we call a stage three—on a human patient."

There was no sound, no movement, from the audience. Janet Ross stood in the corner of the amphitheater near the doors and watched. She found it odd that there should be so little reaction. But then it was hardly a surprise. Everyone in the hospital knew that the Neuropsychiatric Service, or NPS, had been waiting for a good stage-three subject.

"I must ask you," Ellis said, "to restrain your questions when the patient is introduced. He is a sensitive man, and his disturbance is quite severe. We thought you should have the psychiatric background before we bring him in. The attending psychiatrist, Dr. Ross, will give you a summary." Ellis nodded to Ross. She came forward to the center of the room.

She stared up at the steeply banked rows of faces and felt a momentary hesitation. Janet Ross was good-looking in a lean, dark-blond way. She herself felt she was too bony and angular, and she often wished she were more softly feminine. But she knew her appearance was striking, and at thirty, after a decade of training in a predominantly masculine profession, she had learned to use it.

She clasped her hands behind her back, took a breath, and launched into the summary, delivering it in the rapid, stylized method that was standard for grand rounds.

"Harold Franklin Benson," she said, "is a thirty-four-year-old divorced computer scientist who was healthy until two years ago, when he was involved in an automobile accident on the Santa Monica Freeway. Following the accident, he was unconscious for an unknown period of time. He was taken to a local hospital for overnight observation and discharged the next day in good health. He was fine for six months, until he began to experience what he called 'blackouts.' "

The audience was silent, faces staring down at her, listening.

"These blackouts lasted several minutes, and occurred about once a month. They were often preceded by the sensation of peculiar, unpleasant odors. The blackouts frequently occurred after drinking alcohol. The patient consulted his local physician, who told him he was working too hard, and recommended he reduce his alcohol intake. Benson did this, but the blackouts continued.

"One year ago—a year after the accident—he realized that the blackouts were becoming more frequent and lasting longer. He often regained consciousness to find himself in unfamiliar surroundings. On several occasions, he had cuts and bruises or torn clothing which suggested that he had been fighting. However, he never remembered what occurred during the blackout periods."

Heads in the audience nodded. They understood what she was telling them; it was a straightforward history for an epileptiform syndrome which might be treated with surgery. But there were complexities.

"The patient's friends," she continued, "told him that he was acting differently, but he discounted their opinion. Gradually he has lost contact with most of his former friends. Around this time—one year ago—he also made what he called a monumental discovery in his work. Benson is a computer scientist specializing in artificial life, or machine intelligence. In the course of this work, he says he discovered that machines were competing with human beings, and that ultimately machines would take over the world."

Now there were whispers in the audience. This interested them, particularly the psychiatrists. She could see her old teacher Manon sitting in the top row holding his head in his hands. Manon knew.

"Benson communicated his discovery to his remaining friends. They suggested that he see a psychiatrist, which angered him. In the last year, he has become increasingly certain that machines are conspiring to take over the world.

"Then, six months ago, the patient was arrested by police on suspicion of beating up an airplane mechanic. Positive identification could not be made, and charges were dropped. But the episode unnerved Benson and led him to seek psychiatric help. He had the vague suspicion that somehow he *had* been the man who had beaten the mechanic so severely. That was unthinkable to him, but the nagging suspicion remained.

"He was referred to the University Hospital Neuropsychiatric Research Unit four months ago, in November, 1970. On the basis of his history—head injury, episodic violence preceded by strange smells—he was considered a probable case of what is now called ADL: Acute Disinhibitory Lesion syndrome, an organic illness in which the patient periodically loses his inhibitions against violent acts. As you know, the NPS now accepts only patients with organically treatable behavioral disturbances.

"A neurological examination was fully normal. An electroencephalogram was fully normal; brainwave activity showed no pathology. It was repeated after alcohol ingestion and an abnormal tracing was obtained. The EEG showed seizure activity in the right temporal lobe of the brain. Benson was therefore considered a stage-one patient—firm diagnosis of ADL syndrome."

She paused to get her breath and let the audience absorb what she had told them. "The patient is an intelligent man," she said, "and his illness was explained to him. He was told he had injured his brain in the automobile accident and, as a result, had an illness that produced 'thought seizures'—seizures of the mind, not the body, leading to loss of inhibitions and violent acts. He was told that the syndrome was well-studied and could be controlled. He was started on a series of drug trials.

"Three months ago, Benson was arrested on charges of assault and battery. The victim was a twenty-four-year-old topless dancer, who later dropped charges. The hospital intervened slightly on his behalf.

"One month ago, drug trials of morladone, para-amino benzadone, and triamiline were concluded. Benson showed no improvement on any drug or combination of drugs. He was therefore a stage two—drug-resistant ADL syndrome. And he was scheduled for a stage-three surgical procedure, which we will discuss today."

She paused. "Before I bring him in," she said, "I think I should add that yesterday afternoon he attacked a gas-station attendant and beat the man rather badly. His operation is scheduled for tomorrow and we have persuaded the police to release him in our custody. But he is still technically awaiting arraignment on charges of assault and battery."

The room was silent as she turned, and went to bring in Benson.

Benson was just outside the doors to the amphitheater, sitting in his wheelchair, wearing the blue-and-white striped bathrobe the hospital issued to its patients. When Janet Ross appeared, he smiled. "Hello, Dr. Ross."

"Hello, Harry." She smiled back. "How do you feel?"

Of course, she could see clearly how he felt. Benson was nervous and threatened: there was sweat on his upper lip, his shoulders were drawn in, his hands clenched together in his lap.

"I feel fine," he said. "Just fine."

Behind Benson was Morris, pushing the wheelchair, and a cop. She said to Morris, "Does he come in with us?"

Before Morris could answer, Benson said lightly, "He goes anywhere I go."

The cop nodded and looked embarrassed.

"All right," she said.

She opened the doors, and Morris wheeled Benson into the amphitheater, over to Ellis. Ellis came forward to shake Benson's hand.

"Mr. Benson, good to see you."

"Dr. Ellis."

Morris turned the wheelchair around so Benson was facing the amphitheater audience. Ross sat to one side and glanced at the cop, who remained by the door trying to look inconspicuous. Ellis stood alongside Benson, who was looking at a wall of frosted glass, against which a dozen X-rays had been clipped. He seemed to realize that they were his own skull films. Ellis noticed, and turned off the light behind the frosted glass. The X-rays became opaquely black.

"We've asked you to come here," Ellis said, "to answer some questions for these doctors." He gestured to the men sitting in the semicircular tiers. "They don't make you nervous, do they?"

Ellis asked it easily. Ross frowned. She'd attended hundreds of grand rounds in her life, and the patients were invariably asked if the doctors peering down at them made them nervous. In answer to a direct question, the patients always denied nervousness.

"Sure they make me nervous," Benson said. "They'd make anybody nervous."

Ross suppressed a smile. Good for you, she thought.

Then Benson said, "What if you were a machine and I brought you in front of a bunch of computer experts who were trying to decide what was wrong with you and how to fix it? How would you feel?"

Ellis was flustered. He ran his hands through his thinning hair and glanced at Ross, and she shook her head fractionally *no*. This was the wrong place to explore Benson's psychopathology.

"I'd be nervous, too," Ellis said.

"Well, then," Benson said. "You see?"

Ellis swallowed.

He's being deliberately irritating, Ross thought. Don't take the bait.

"But, of course," Ellis said, "I'm not a machine, am I?"

Ross winced.

"That depends," Benson said. "Certain of your functions are repetitive and mechanical. From that standpoint, they are easily programmed and relatively straightforward, if you—"

"I think," Ross said, standing up, "that we might take questions from those present now."

Ellis clearly didn't like the interruption, but he was

silent, and Benson mercifully was quiet. She looked up at the audience, and after a moment a man in the back raised his hand and said, "Mr. Benson, can you tell us more about the smells you have before your blackouts?"

"Not really," Benson said. "They're strange, is all. They smell terrible, but they don't smell *like* anything, if you get what I mean. I mean, you can't identify the odor. Memory tapes cycle through blankly."

"Can you give us an approximation of the odor?"

Benson shrugged. "Maybe . . . pig shit in turpentine."

Another hand in the audience went up. "Mr. Benson, these blackouts have been getting more frequent. Have they also been getting longer?"

"Yes," Benson said. "They're several hours now."

"How do you feel when you recover from a blackout?"

"Sick to my stomach."

"Can you be more specific?"

"Sometimes I vomit. Is that specific enough?"

Ross frowned. She could see that Benson was becoming angry. "Are there other questions?" she asked, hoping there would not be. She looked up at the audience. There was a long silence.

"Well, then," Ellis said, "perhaps we can go on to discuss the details of stage-three surgery. Mr. Benson knows all this, so he can stay or leave, whichever he prefers."

Ross didn't approve. Ellis was showing off, the surgeon's instinct for demonstrating to everyone that his patient didn't mind being cut and mutilated. It was unfair to ask—to dare—Benson to stay in the room.

"I'll stay," Benson said.

"Fine," Ellis said. He went to the blackboard and drew a brain schematically. "Now," he said, "our understanding of the disease process in ADL is that a portion of the brain is damaged, and a scar forms. It's like a scar in other body organs—lots of fibrous tissue, lots of contraction and distortion. And it becomes a focus for abnormal electrical discharges. We see spreading waves moving outward from the focus, like ripples from a rock in a pond."

Ellis drew a point on the brain, then sketched concentric circles.

"These electrical ripples produce a seizure. In some parts of the brain, the discharge focus produces a shaking fit, frothing at the mouth, and so on. In other parts, there are other effects. If the focus is in the temporal lobe, as in Mr. Benson's case, you get acute disinhibitory lesion syndrome—strange thoughts and sometimes violent behavior, preceded by a characteristic aura which is often an odor."

Benson was watching, listening, nodding.

"Now, then," Ellis said, "we know from the work of many researchers that it may be incorrect to think of episodes of disinhibition in ADL as seizures in the usual sense. They may simply be intermittent periods of brain malfunction that result from organic damage. Nevertheless these episodes tend to have a characteristic pattern in the way they occur, and so for convenience we speak of them as seizures. We know it is possible to abort a seizure by delivering an electrical shock to the critical portion of the brain substance. There are a few seconds—sometimes as much as half a minute—before the disinhibition takes full effect. A shock at that moment prevents the seizure.''

He drew a large "X" through the concentric circles. Then he drew a new brain, and a head around it, and a neck. "We face two problems," he said. "First, what is the correct part of the brain to shock? In the case of ADL patients, we know roughly that it's in the amygdala, an anterior area of the so-called limbic system. We don't know *exactly* where, but we solve that problem by implanting a number of electrodes in the brain. Mr. Benson will have forty electrodes implanted tomorrow morning.''

He drew two lines into the brain.

"Now, our second problem is how do we know when an attack is starting? We must know when to deliver our aborting shock. Well, fortunately the same electrodes that we use to deliver the shock can also be used to 'read' the electrical activity of the brain. And there is a characteristic electrical pattern that precedes a seizure.''

Ellis paused, glanced at Benson, then up at the audience.

"So we have a feedback system—the same electrodes are used to detect a new attack, and to deliver the aborting shock. A computer controls the feedback mechanism.''

He drew a small square in the neck of his schematic figure.

"The NPS staff has developed a computer that will monitor electrical activity of the brain, and when it sees an attack starting, will transmit a shock to the correct brain area. This computer is about the size of a postage stamp and weighs a tenth of an ounce. It will be implanted beneath the skin of the patient's neck.''

He then drew an oblong shape below the neck and attached wires to the computer square.

''We will power the computer with a Handler PP-J plutonium power pack, which will be implanted beneath the skin of the shoulder. This makes the patient completely self-sufficient. The power pack supplies energy continuously and reliably for twenty years.''

With his chalk, he tapped the different parts of his diagram. ''That's the complete feedback loop—brain, to electrodes, to computer, to power pack, back to brain. A closed loop without any externalized portions.''

He turned to Benson, who had watched the discussion with an expression of bland disinterest.

''Any comments? Mr. Benson? Anything you want to say, or add?''

Ross groaned inwardly. She knew Ellis was only trying to be considerate to his patient, but it was wrong to ask any patient to comment before such frightening surgery, as if the patient himself were not about to undergo it. It was too much to ask.

''No,'' Benson said. ''I have nothing to say.'' And he yawned.

When Benson was wheeled out of the room, Ross went with him. It wasn't really necessary for her to accompany him, but she was concerned about his condition—and a little guilty about the way Ellis had treated him. She said, ''How did that go?''

''I thought it was interesting,'' he said.

''In what way?''

"Well, the discussion was entirely medical. I would have expected a more philosophical approach."

"We're just practical people," she said lightly, "dealing with a practical problem."

Benson smiled. "So was Newton," he said. "What's more practical than the problem of why an apple falls to the ground?"

"Do you really see philosophical implications in all this?"

Benson nodded. "Yes," he said, "and so do you. You're just pretending that you don't."

She stopped then and stood in the corridor, watching as Benson was wheeled down to the elevator. Benson, Morris, and the cop waited in the corridor for the next car. Morris pushed the button repeatedly in that impatient, aggressive way of his. Then the elevator arrived and they got on. Benson waved one last time, and the doors closed.

She went back to the amphitheater.

". . . has been under development for ten years," Ellis was saying. "It was first started for cardiac pacemakers, where changing batteries requires minor surgery every year or so. That's an annoyance to surgeon and patient. The atomic power pack is totally reliable and has a long life span. If Mr. Benson is still alive, we might have to change packs around 1990, but not before then."

Janet Ross slipped back into the room just as another question was asked: "How will you determine which of the forty electrodes will prevent a seizure?"

"We will implant them all," Ellis said, "and wire up the computer. But we will not lock in any electrodes for twenty-four hours. One day after surgery, we'll stimulate each of the electrodes by radio and determine which electrodes work best. Then we will lock those in by remote control.''

High up in the amphitheater, a familiar voice coughed and said, ''These technical details are interesting, but they seem to me to elude the point.'' Ross looked up and saw Manon speaking. Manon was nearly seventy-five, an emeritus professor of psychiatry who rarely came to the hospital any more. When he did, he was usually regarded as a cranky old man, far past his prime, out of touch with modern thinking. ''It seems to me,'' Manon continued, ''that the patient is psychotic.''

''That's putting it a little strongly,'' Ellis said.

''Perhaps,'' Manon said. ''But, at the very least, he has a severe personality disorder. All this confusion about men and machines is worrisome.''

''The personality disorder is part of his disease,'' Ellis said. ''In a recent review, Harley and co-workers at Yale reported that fifty percent of ADL sufferers had an accompanying personality disorder which was independent of seizure activity *per se*.''

''Quite so,'' Manon said, in a voice that had the slightest edge of impatience to it. ''It is part of his disease, independent of seizures. But will your procedure cure it?''

Janet Ross found herself quietly pleased; Manon was reaching exactly her own conclusions.

''No,'' Ellis said. ''Probably not.''

''In other words, the operation will stop his seizures, but it won't stop his delusions.''

''No,'' Ellis repeated. ''Probably not.''

"If I may say so," Manon said, frowning down from the top row, "this kind of thinking is what I fear most from the NPS. I don't mean to single you out. It's a general problem of the medical profession. For example, if we get a suicide attempt or a suicide gesture by drug overdose in the emergency ward, our approach is to pump the patient's stomach, give him a lecture, and send him home. That's a treatment—but it's hardly a cure. The patient will be back sooner or later. Stomach pumping doesn't treat depression. It only treats drug overdose."

"I see what you're saying, but . . ."

"I'd also remind you of the hospital's experience with Mr. L. Do you recall the case?"

"I don't think Mr. L. applies here," Ellis said. But his voice was stiff and exasperated.

"I'm not so sure," Manon said. Since several puzzled faces in the amphitheater were turned toward him, he explained. "Mr. L. was a famous case here a few years ago. He was a thirty-nine-year-old man with bilateral end-stage kidney disease. Chronic glomerulonephritis. He was considered a candidate for renal transplant. Because our facilities for transplantation are limited, a hospital review board selects patients. The psychiatrists on that board strongly opposed Mr. L. as a transplantation candidate, because he was psychotic. He believed that the sun ruled the earth and he refused to go outside during the daylight hours. We felt he was too unstable to benefit from kidney surgery, but he ultimately received the operation. Six months later, he committed suicide. That's a tragedy. But the real question is couldn't someone else have benefited more from the thousands of dollars and many hours of specialized effort that went into the transplant?''

Ellis paced back and forth, the foot of his bad leg scraping slightly along the floor. Ross knew he was feeling threatened, under attack. Normally Ellis was careful to minimize his disability, concealing it so that the limp was noticeable only to a trained eye. But if he was tired, or angry, or threatened, the flaw appeared. It was almost as if he unconsciously wanted sympathy: don't attack me, I'm a cripple.

"I understand your objection," Ellis said. "In the terms you present it, your argument is unanswerable. But I would like to consider the problem from a somewhat different viewpoint. It is perfectly true that Benson is disturbed, and that our operation probably won't change that. But what happens if we *don't* operate on him? We know that his seizures are life-threatening—to himself, to others. His seizures have already gotten him into trouble with the law, and his seizures are getting worse. The operation will prevent seizures, and we think that is an important benefit to the patient."

High up, Manon gave a little shrug. Janet Ross knew the gesture; it signaled irreconcilable differences, an impasse.

"Well, then," Ellis said, "are there other questions?"

There were no other questions.

3

"JESUS FUCKING CHRIST," ELLIS SAID, WIPING his forehead. "He didn't let up, did he?"

Janet Ross walked with him across the parking lot toward the Langer research building. It was late afternoon; the sunlight was yellowing, turning pale and weak.

"His point was valid," she said mildly.

Ellis sighed. "I keep forgetting you're on his side."

"Why do you keep forgetting?" she asked. She smiled as she said it. As the psychiatrist on the NPS staff, she'd opposed Benson's operation from the beginning.

"Look," Ellis said. "We do what we can. It'd be great to cure him, but we can't do that. We can only help him to a partial cure. So we'll do that. We'll help him. It's not a perfect world."

She walked alongside him in silence. There was nothing to say. She had told Ellis her opinion many times before. The operation might not help—it might, in fact, make Benson much worse. She was sure Ellis understood that possibility, but he was stubbornly ignoring it. Or so it seemed to her.

Actually, she liked Ellis, as much as she liked any

surgeon. She regarded surgeons as flagrantly action-oriented men (they were almost always men, which she found significant) desperate to do something, to take some physical action. In that sense, Ellis was better than most of them. He had wisely turned down several stage-three candidates before Benson, and she knew that was difficult for him to do, because he was terribly eager to perform the new operation.

"I hate all this," Ellis said. "Hospital politics."

"But you want to do Benson. . . ."

"I'm ready," Ellis said. "We're all ready. We have to take that first big step, and now is the time to take it." He glanced at her. "Why do you look so uncertain?"

"Because I am," she said.

They came to the Langer building. Ellis went off to an early dinner with McPherson—a political dinner, he said irritably—and she took the elevator to the fourth floor.

After ten years of steady expansion, the Neuropsychiatric Research Unit encompassed the entire fourth floor of the Langer research building. The other floors were painted a dead, cold white, but the NPS was bright with primary colors. The intention was to make patients feel optimistic and happy, but it always had the reverse effect on Ross. She found it falsely and artificially cheerful, like a nursery school for retarded children.

She got off the elevator and looked at the reception area, one wall a bright blue, the other red. Like almost everything else about the NPS, the colors had been McPherson's idea. It was strange, she thought, how much an organization reflected the personality of its leader. McPherson himself always seemed to have a bright kindergarten quality about him, and a boundless optimism.

Certainly you had to be optimistic if you planned to operate on Harry Benson.

The Unit was quiet now, most of the staff gone home for the night. She walked down the corridor past the colored doors with the stenciled labels: SONOENCEPH-ALOGRAPHY, CORTICAL FUNCTION, EEG, RAS SCORING, PARIETAL T, and, at the far end of the hall, TELECOMP. The work done behind those doors was as complex as the labels—and this was just the patient-care wing, what McPherson called "Applications."

Applications was ordinary compared to Development, the research wing with its chemitrodes and compsims and elad scenarios. To say nothing of the big projects, like George and Martha, or Form Q. Development was ten years ahead of Applications—and Applications was very, very advanced.

A year ago, McPherson had asked her to take a group of newspaper science reporters through the NPS. He chose her, he said, "because she was such a piece of ass." It was funny to hear him say that, and shocking in a way. He was usually so courtly and fatherly.

But her shock was minor compared to the shock the reporters felt. She had planned to show them both Applications and Development, but after the reporters had seen Applications they were so agitated, so clearly overloaded, that she cut the tour short.

She worried a lot about it afterward. The reporters hadn't been naïve and they hadn't been inexperienced. They were people who shuttled from one scientific arena to another all their lives. Yet they were rendered speechless by the implications of the work she had shown them. She herself had lost that insight, that perspective—she had been working in the NPS for three years, and she had gradually become accustomed to the things done there. The conjunction of men and machines, human brains and electronic brains, was no longer bizarre and provocative. It was just a way to take steps forward and get things done.

On the other hand, she opposed the stage-three operation on Benson. She had opposed it from the start. She thought Benson was the wrong human subject, and she had just one last chance to prove it.

At the end of the corridor, she paused by the door to Telecomp, listening to the quiet hiss of the printout units. She heard voices inside, and opened the door. Telecomp was really the heart of the Neuropsychiatric Research Unit; it was a large room, filled with electronic equipment. The walls and ceilings were soundproofed, a vestige of earlier days when the readout consoles were clattering teletypes. Now they used either silent CRTs—cathode-ray tubes—or a print-out machine that sprayed the letters with a nozzle, rather than typed them mechanically. The hiss of the sprayer was the loudest sound in the room. McPherson had insisted on the change to quieter units because he felt the clattering disturbed patients who came to the NPS for treatment.

Gerhard was there, and his assistant Richards. The wizard twins, they were called: Gerhard was only twenty-four, and Richards even younger. They were the least professional people attached to the NPS; both men regarded Telecomp as a playground filled with complex toys. They worked long but erratic hours, frequently beginning in the late afternoon, quitting at dawn. They rarely showed up for group conferences and formal meetings, much to McPherson's annoyance. But they were undeniably good.

Gerhard, who wore cowboy boots and dungarees and satiny shirts with pearl buttons, had gained some national attention at the age of thirteen when he built a twenty-foot solid-fuel rocket behind his house in Phoenix. The rocket possessed a remarkably sophisticated electronic guidance system and Gerhard felt he could fire it into orbit. His neighbors, who could see the nose of the finished rocket sticking up above the garage in the backyard, were disturbed enough to call the police, and ultimately the Army was notified.

The Army examined Gerhard's rocket and shipped it to White Sands for firing. As it happened, the second stage ignited before disengagement and the rocket exploded two miles up; but by that time Gerhard had four patents on his guidance mechanism and a number of scholarship offers from colleges and industrial firms. He turned them all down, let his uncle invest the patent royalties, and when he was old enough to drive, bought a Maserati. He went to work for Lockheed in Palmdale, California, but quit after a year because he was blocked from advancement by a lack of formal engineering degrees. It was also true that his colleagues resented a seventeen-year-old with a Maserati Ghibli and a propensity for working in the middle of the night; it was felt he had no "team spirit."

Then McPherson hired him to work at the Neuropsychiatric Research Unit, designing electronic components to be synergistic with the human brain. McPherson, as head of the NPS, had interviewed dozens of candidates who thought the job was "a challenge" or "an interesting systems application context." Gerhard said he thought it would be fun, and was hired immediately.

Richards's background was similar. He had finished high school and gone to college for six months before being drafted by the Army. He was about to be sent to Vietnam when he began to suggest improvements in the Army's electronic scanning devices. The improvements worked, and Richards never got closer to combat than a laboratory in Santa Monica. When he was discharged, he also joined the NPS.

The wizard twins: Ross smiled.

"Hi, Jan," Gerhard said.

"How's it going, Jan?" Richards said.

They were both offhand. They were the only people on the Staff who dared refer to McPherson as "Rog." And McPherson put up with it.

"Okay," she said. "We've got our stage three through grand rounds. I'm going to see him now."

"We're just finishing a check on the computer," Gerhard said. "It looks fine." He pointed to a table with a microscope surrounded by a tangle of electronic meters and dials.

"Where is it?"

"Under the stage."

She looked closer. A clear plastic packet the size of a postage stamp lay under the microscope lens. Through the plastic she could see a dense jumble of micro-miniaturized electronic components. Forty contact points protruded from the plastic. With the help of the microscope, the twins were testing the points sequentially, using fine probes.

"The logic circuits are the last to be checked," Richards said. "And we have a backup unit, just in case."

Janet went over to the file-card storage shelves and began looking through the test cards. After a moment, she said, "Haven't you got any more psychodex cards?"

"They're over here," Gerhard said. "You want five-space or *n*-space?"

"*N*-space," she said.

Gerhard opened a drawer and took out a cardboard sheet. He also took out a flat plastic clipboard. Attached to the clipboard by a metal chain was a pointed metal probe, something like a pencil.

"This isn't for the stage three, is it?"

"Yes," she said.

"But you've run so many psychodexes on him before—"

"Just one more, for the records."

Gerhard handed her the card and clipboard. "Does your stage three know what's going on?"

"He knows most of it," she said.

Gerhard shook his head. "He must be out of his mind."

"He is," she said. "That's the problem."

At the seventh floor, she stopped at the nurses' station to ask for Benson's chart. A new nurse was there, who said, "I'm sorry but relatives aren't allowed to look at medical records."

"I'm Dr. Ross."

The nurse was flustered. "I'm sorry, Doctor, I didn't see a name tag. Your patient is in seven-oh-four."

"What patient?"

"Little Jerry Peters."

Dr. Ross looked blank.

"Aren't you the pediatrician?" the nurse asked, finally.

"No," she said. "I'm a psychiatrist at the NPS." She heard the stridency in her own voice, and it upset her. But all those years growing up with people who said, "You don't *really* want to be a doctor, you want to be a nurse," or, "Well, for a woman, pediatrics is best, I mean, the most natural thing. . . ."

"Oh," the nurse said. "Then you want Mr. Benson in seven-ten. He's been prepped."

"Thank you," she said. She took the chart and walked down the hall to Benson's room. She knocked on Benson's door and heard gunshots. She opened the door and saw that the lights were dimmed except for a small bedside lamp, but the room was bathed in an electric-blue glow from a TV. On the screen, a man was saying, ". . . dead before he hit the ground. Two bullets right through the heart."

"Hello?" she said, and swung the door wider.

Benson looked over. He smiled and pressed a button beside the bed, turning off the TV. His head was wrapped in a towel.

"How are you feeling?" she asked, coming into the room. She sat on a chair beside the bed.

"Naked," he said, and touched the towel. "It's funny. You don't realize how much hair you have until somebody cuts it all off." He touched the towel again. "It must be worse for a woman." Then he looked at her and became embarrassed.

"It's not much fun for anybody," she said.

"I guess not." He lay back against the pillow. "After they did it, I looked in the wastebasket, and I was amazed. So much hair. And my head was cold. It was the funniest thing, a cold head. They put a towel around it. I said I wanted to look at my head—see what I looked like bald—but they said it wasn't a good idea. So I waited until after they left, and then I got out of bed and went into the bathroom. But when I got there . . .''

"Yes?''

"I didn't take the towel off.'' He laughed. "I couldn't do it. What does that mean?''

"I don't know. What do you think it means?''

He laughed again. "Why is it that psychiatrists never give you a straight answer?'' He lit a cigarette and looked at her defiantly. "They told me I shouldn't smoke, but I'm doing it anyway.''

"I doubt that it matters,'' she said. She was watching him closely. He seemed in good spirits, and she didn't want to take that away from him. But on the other hand, it wasn't entirely appropriate to be so cheerful on the eve of brain surgery.

"Ellis was here a few minutes ago,'' he said, puffing on the cigarette. "He put some marks on me. Can you see?'' He lifted up the right side of his towel slightly. exposing white pale flesh over the skull. Two blue "X" marks were positioned behind the ear. "How do I look?'' he asked, grinning.

"You look fine,'' she said. "How do you feel?''

"Fine. I feel fine.''

"Any worries?''

"No. I mean, what is there to worry about? Nothing I can do. For the next few hours, I'm in your hands, and Ellis's hands. . . .'' He bit his lip. "Of course I'm worried.''

"What worries you?"

"Everything," he said. He sucked on the cigarette. "Everything. I worry about how I'll sleep. How I'll feel tomorrow. How I'll be when it's all over. What if somebody makes a mistake? What if I get turned into a vegetable? What if it hurts? What if I . . ."

"Die?"

"Sure. That, too."

"It's really a minor procedure. It's hardly more complicated than an appendectomy."

"I bet you tell that to all your brain-surgery patients."

"No, really. It's a short, simple procedure. It'll take about an hour and a half."

He nodded vaguely. She couldn't tell if she had reassured him. "You know," he said, "I don't really think it will happen. I keep thinking tomorrow morning at the last minute they'll come in and say, 'You're cured, Mr. Benson, you can go home now.' "

"We hope you'll be cured by the operation." She felt a twinge of guilt saying that, but it came out smoothly enough.

"You're so goddamned reasonable," he said. "There are times when I can't stand it."

"Like now?"

He touched the towel around his head again. "I mean, for Christ's sake, they're going to drill holes in my head, and stick wires in—"

"You've known about that for a long time."

"Sure," he said. "Sure. But this is the night before."

"Do you feel angry now?"

"No. Just scared."

"It's all right to be scared, it's perfectly normal. But don't let it make you angry."

He stubbed out the cigarette, and lit another immediately. Changing the subject, he pointed to the clipboard she carried under her arm. "What's that?"

"Another psychodex test. I want you to go through it."

"Now?"

"Yes. It's just for the record."

He shrugged indifferently. He had taken the psychodex several times before. She handed him the clipboard and he arranged the question card on the board, then began to answer the questions. He read them aloud:

"Would you rather be an elephant or a baboon? Baboon. Elephants live too long."

With the metal probe, he punched out the chosen answer on the card.

"If you were a color, would you rather be green or yellow? Yellow. I'm feeling very yellow right now." He laughed, and punched the answer.

She waited until he had done all thirty questions and punched his answers. He handed the clipboard back to her, and his mood seemed to shift again. "Are you going to be there? Tomorrow?"

"Yes."

"Will I be awake enough to recognize you?"

"I imagine so."

"And when will I come out of it?"

"Tomorrow afternoon or evening."

"That soon?"

"It's really a minor procedure," she said again. He nodded. She asked him if she could get him anything, and he said some ginger ale, and she replied that he was NPO, nothing *per ora*, for twelve hours before the operation. She said he'd be getting shots to help him sleep, and shots in the morning before he went to surgery. She said she hoped he'd sleep well.

As she left, she heard a hum as the television went back on, and a metallic voice said, "Look, Lieutenant, I've got a murderer out there, somewhere in a city of three million people. . . ."

She closed the door.

Before leaving the floor, she put a brief note in the chart. She drew a red line around it, so that the nurses would be sure to see it:

ADMITTING PSYCHIATRIC SUMMARY:

This 34-year-old man has documented ADL syndrome of 2 years' duration. The etiology is presumably traumatic, following an automobile accident. This patient has already tried to kill two people, and has been involved in fights with several others. Any statement by him to hospital staff that he "feels funny" or "smells something bad" should be respected as indicating the start of a seizure. Under such circumstances, notify the NPS and Hospital Security at once.

The patient has an accompanying personality disorder which is part of his disease. He is convinced that machines are conspiring to take over the world. These beliefs are strongly held and attempts to dissuade him from them will only draw his enmity and suspicion. One should also remember that he is a highly intelligent and sensitive man. The patient can be quite demanding at times, but he should be treated with firmness and respect.

His intelligent and articulate manner may lead one to forget that his attitudes are not willful. He suffers an organic disease which has affected his mental state. Beneath it all he is frightened and concerned about what is happening to him.

Janet Ross, M.D.
NPS

4

"I DON'T UNDERSTAND," THE PUBLIC RELA-
tions man said.

Ellis sighed. McPherson smiled patiently. "This is an organic cause of violent behavior," he said. "That's the way to look at it."

The three of them were sitting in the Four Kings Restaurant, adjacent to the hospital. The early dinner had been McPherson's idea; McPherson said he wanted Ellis present, so Ellis was present. That was how Ellis thought about it.

Ellis raised his hand, beckoning the waiter for more coffee. As he did so, he thought it might keep him awake. But it didn't matter: he wouldn't sleep much tonight anyway. Not on the eve of his first stage three on a human subject.

He knew he would toss and turn in bed, going over the operative procedure. Over and over again, reviewing the pattern he already knew so well. He'd done a lot of monkeys as stage-three procedures. One hundred and fifty-four monkeys, to be exact. Monkeys were difficult. They pulled out their stitches, they tugged at the wires, they screeched and fought you and bit you—

"Cognac?" McPherson asked.

"Fine," the PR man said.

McPherson glanced questioningly at Ellis. Ellis shook his head. He put cream in his coffee, and sat back suppressing a yawn. Actually, the PR man looked a little like a monkey. A juvenile rhesus: he had the same blocky lower jaw and the same bright-eyed alertness.

The PR man's name was Ralph. Ellis didn't know the last name. No PR man ever gave his last name. Of course, at the hospital he wasn't referred to as a PR man; he was the Hospital Information Officer or News Officer or some damned thing.

He did look like a monkey. Ellis found himself staring at the area of the skull behind the ear, where the electrodes would be implanted.

"We don't know much about the causes of violence," McPherson said. "And there's a lot of bad theory floating around, written by sociologists and paid for by good taxpayer money. But we do know that one particular brain disease, called ADL syndrome, may lead to violence."

"ADL syndrome," Ralph repeated.

"Yes. Acute Disinhibitory Lesion syndrome is caused

by an injury or lesion to the brain. At the NPS, we think these lesions may be extremely common among those people who engage in repetitive violent acts—like certain policemen, gangsters, rioters, Hell's Angels. Nobody ever thinks of these people as *physically* ill. We just accept the idea that there are a lot of men in the world with bad tempers. We think that's normal. Perhaps it isn't.''

"I see," Ralph said. And he did, indeed, seem to be seeing. McPherson should have been a grade school teacher, Ellis thought. His great gift was teaching. Certainly he'd never been much of a researcher.

"So far," McPherson said, brushing his hand through his white hair, "we have no idea exactly how common ADL syndrome is. But our guess is that as much as one or two percent of the population may suffer from it. That's two to four million Americans."

"Gosh," Ralph said.

Ellis sipped his coffee. Gosh, he thought. Good Christ. Gosh . . .

"For some reason," McPherson said, nodding to the waiter as the cognacs were brought, "ADL patients are predisposed to violent, aggressive behavior during their attacks. We don't know why, but it's true. The other things that go along with the syndrome are hypersexuality and pathological intoxication."

Ralph began to look unusually interested.

"We had the case of one woman with this disease," McPherson said, "who during a seizure state would have intercourse with twelve men a night and still be unsatisfied."

Ralph swallowed his cognac. Ellis noticed that Ralph wore a wide tie in a fashionable psychedelic pattern. A hip forty-year-old public-relations man gulping cognac at the thought of this woman.

"Pathological intoxication refers to the phenomenon of excessive, violent drunkenness brought on by minuscule amounts of liquor—just a sip or two. That much liquor will unleash a seizure."

Ellis thought of his first stage three. Benson: pudgy little Benson, the mild-mannered computer programmer who got drunk and beat up people—men, women, whoever happened to be present. The very idea of curing that with wires stuck in the brain seemed absurd.

Ralph seemed to think so, too. "And this operation will cure the violence?"

"Yes," McPherson said. "We believe so. But the operation has never been done before on a human subject. It will be done at the hospital tomorrow morning."

"I *see*," Ralph said, as if he suddenly understood the reason for the dinner.

"It's very sensitive, in terms of the press," McPherson said.

"Oh, yes, I can see that. . . ."

There was a short pause. Finally, Ralph said, "Who's going to do the operation?"

"I am," Ellis said.

"Well," Ralph said, "I'll have to check our files. I want to make sure I have a recent picture of you, and a good bio for the releases." He frowned, thinking of the work ahead of him.

Ellis was astonished at the man's reaction. Was that all he thought? That he might need a recent photo? But McPherson took it smoothly in stride. "We'll get you whatever you need," he said, and the meeting broke up.

5

ROBERT MORRIS WAS SITTING IN THE HOSPITAL cafeteria finishing some stale apple pie when his pagemaster went off. It produced a high electronic squeal, which persisted until he reached down to his belt and turned it off. He returned to his pie. After a few moments, the squeal came again. He swore, put down his fork, and went to the wall phone to answer his page.

There had been a time when he regarded the little gray box clipped to his belt as a wonderful thing. He relished those moments when he would be having lunch or dinner with a girl and his pagemaster would go off, requiring him to call in. That sound demonstrated that he was a busy, responsible person involved in life-and-death matters. When the pagemaster went off, he would excuse himself abruptly and answer the call, radiating a sense of duty before pleasure. The girls loved it.

But after several years it was no longer wonderful. The box was inhuman and implacable, and it had come to symbolize for him the fact that he was not his own man. He was perpetually on call to some higher authority, however whimsical—a nurse who wanted to confirm a medication order at 2 a.m.; a relative who was acting up, making trouble about Mama's post-operative treatment; a call to tell him a conference was being held when he was already there attending the damned conference.

Now the finest moments in his life were those when he went home and put the box away for a few hours. He became unreachable and free. And he liked that very much.

He stared across the cafeteria at the remainder of his apple pie as he dialed the switchboard. "Dr. Morris."

"Dr. Morris, two-four-seven-one."

"Thank you." That was the extension for the seventh floor nurses' station. He had long ago learned all the principal extensions of the University Hospital system. He dialed the floor. "Dr. Morris."

"Oh, yes," a female voice said. "We have a woman with an overnight bag for patient Harold Benson. She says it's personal things. Is it all right to give it to him?"

"I'll come up," he said.

"Thank you, Doctor."

He went back to his tray, picked it up, and carried it to the disposal area. As he did so, his beeper went off again. He went to answer it.

"Dr. Morris."

"Dr. Morris, one-three-five-seven."

That was the metabolic unit. He dialed. "Dr. Morris."

"This is Dr. Hanley," an unfamiliar voice said. "We wondered if you could take a look at a lady we think may have steroid psychosis. She's a hemolytic anemic up for splenectomy."

"I can't see her today," Morris said, "and tomorrow is tight." That, he thought, was the understatement of the year. "Have you tried Peters?"

"No . . ."

"Peters has a lot of experience with steroid mentation. Try him."

"All right. Thanks."

Morris hung up. He got onto the elevator and pressed the button for the seventh floor. His beeper went off a third time. He checked his watch; it was 6:30 and he was supposedly off-duty by now. But he answered it anyway. It was Kelso, the pediatric resident.

"Want your ass whipped?" Kelso said.

"Okay. What time?"

"Say, about half an hour?"

"If you've got the balls."

"I've got them. They're in my car."

"See you on the court," Morris said. Then he added, "I may be a little late."

"Don't be too late," Kelso said. "It'll be dark soon."

Morris said he would hurry, and hung up.

The seventh floor was quiet. Most of the other hospital floors were noisy, jammed with relatives and visitors at this hour, but the seventh floor was always quiet. It had a sedate, calm quality that the nurses were careful to preserve.

The nurse at the station said, "There she is, Doctor," and nodded to a girl sitting on a couch. Morris went over to her. She was young and very pretty in a flashy, show-business sort of way. She had long legs.

"I'm Dr. Morris."

"Angela Black." She stood up and shook hands, very formally. "I brought this for Harry." She lifted a small blue overnight bag. "He asked me to bring it."

"All right." He took the bag from her. "I'll see that he gets it."

She hesitated, then said, "Can I see him?"

"I don't think it's a good idea." Benson would have been shaved by now; pre-op patients who had been shaved often didn't want to see people.

"Just for a few minutes?"

"He's heavily sedated," he said.

She was clearly disappointed. "Then would you give him a message?"

"Sure."

"Tell him I'm back in my old apartment. He'll understand."

"All right."

"You won't forget?"

"No. I'll tell him."

"Thank you." She smiled. It was a rather nice smile, despite the long false eyelashes and the heavy make-up. Why did young girls do that to their faces? "I guess I'll be going now." And she walked off, short skirt and very long legs, a briskly determined walk. He watched her go, then hefted the bag, which seemed heavy.

The cop sitting outside the door to 710 said, "How's it going?"

"Fine," Morris said.

The cop glanced at the overnight bag but said nothing as Morris took it inside the room.

Harry Benson was watching a Western on television. Morris turned down the sound. "A very pretty girl brought you this."

"Angela?" Benson smiled. "Yes, she has a nice exterior. Not a very complicated internal mechanism, but a nice exterior." He extended his hand; Morris gave him the bag. "Did she bring everything?"

Morris watched as Benson opened it, placing the contents on the bed. There were a pair of pajamas, an electric razor, some after-shave lotion, a paperback novel.

Then Benson brought out a black wig.

"What's that?" Morris asked.

Benson shrugged. "I knew I'd need it sooner or later," he said. Then he laughed. "You *are* letting me out of here, aren't you? Sooner or later?"

Morris laughed with him. Benson dropped the wig back into the bag, and removed a plastic packet. With a metallic clink, he unfolded it, and Morris saw it was a set of screwdrivers of various sizes, stored in a plastic package with pockets for each size.

"What's that for?" Morris asked.

Benson looked puzzled for a moment. Then he said, "I don't know if you'll understand. . . ."

"Yes?"

"I always have them with me. For protection."

Benson placed the screwdrivers back into the overnighter. He handled them carefully, almost reverently. Morris knew that patients frequently brought odd things into the hospital, particularly if they were seriously ill. There was a kind of totemic feeling about these objects, as if they might have magical preservative powers. They were often connected with some hobby or favorite activity. He remembered a yachtsman with a metastatic brain tumor who had brought a kit to repair sails, and a woman with advanced heart

disease who had brought a can of tennis balls. That
kind of thing.

"I understand," Morris said.

Benson smiled.

6

TELECOMP WAS EMPTY WHEN SHE CAME INTO
the room; the consoles and teleprinters stood silently,
the screens blinking up random sequences of numbers.
She went to the corner and poured herself a cup of
coffee, then fed the test card from Benson's latest psychodex into the computer.

The NPS had developed the psychodex test, along
with several other computer-analyzed psychological
tests. It was all part of what McPherson called "double-
edged thinking." In this case, he meant that the idea
of a brain being like a computer worked two ways, in
two different directions. On the one hand, you could
utilize the computer to probe the brain, to help you
analyze its workings. At the same time, you could use
your increased knowledge of the brain to help design
better and more efficient computers. As McPherson
said, "The brain is as much a model for the computer
as the computer is a model for the brain."

At the NPS, computer scientists and neurobiologists

had worked together for several years. From that association had come Form Q, and programs like George and Martha, and new psychosurgical techniques, and psychodex.

Psychodex was relatively simple. It was a test that took straightforward answers to psychological questions and manipulated the answers according to complex mathematical formulations. As the data were fed into the computer, Ross watched the screen glow with row after row of calculations.

She ignored them; the numbers, she knew, were just the computer's scratch pad, the intermediate steps that it went through before arriving at a final answer. She smiled, thinking of how Gerhard would explain it—rotation of thirty by thirty matrices in space, deriving factors, making them orthogonal, then weighting them. It all sounded complicated and scientific, and she didn't really understand any of it.

She had discovered long ago that you could use a computer without understanding how it worked. Just as you could use an automobile, a vacuum cleaner—or your own brain.

The screen flashed "CALCULATIONS ENDED. CALL DISPLAY SEQUENCE."

She punched in the display sequence for three-space scoring. The computer informed her that three spaces accounted for eighty-one percent of variance. On the screen she saw a three-dimensional image of a mountain with a sharp peak. She stared at it a moment, then picked up the telephone and paged McPherson.

McPherson frowned at the screen. Ellis looked over his shoulder. Ross said, "Is it clear?"

SERIAL PSYCHODEX SCORE REPRESENTATIONS SHOWING INCREASED ELEVATION (PSYCHOTIC MENTATION)

"Perfectly," McPherson said. "When was it done?"

"Today," she said.

McPherson sighed. "You're not going to quit without a battle, are you?"

Instead of answering, she punched buttons and called up a second mountain peak, much lower. "Here's the last one previously."

"On this scoring, the elevation is—"

"Psychotic mentation," she said.

"So he's much more pronounced now," McPherson said. "Much more than even a month ago."

"Yes," she said.

"You think he was screwing around with the test?"

She shook her head. She punched in the four previous tests, in succession. The trend was clear: on each test the mountain peak got higher and sharper.

"Well, then," McPherson said, "he's definitely getting worse. I gather you still think we shouldn't operate."

"More than ever," she said. "He's unquestionably psychotic, and if you start putting wires in his head—"

"I know," McPherson said. "I know what you're saying."

"—he's going to feel that he's been turned into a machine," she said.

McPherson turned to Ellis. "Do you suppose we can knock this elevation down with thorazine?" Thorazine was a major tranquilizer. With some psychotics, it helped them to think more clearly.

"I think it's worth a try."

McPherson nodded. "I do, too. Janet?"

She stared at the screen and didn't reply. It was odd how these tests worked. The mountain peaks were an abstraction, a mathematical representation of an emotional state. They weren't a real characteristic of a person, like fingers or toes, or height or weight.

"Janet? What do you think?" McPherson repeated.

"I think," she said, "that you're both committed to this operation."

"And you still disapprove?"

"I don't 'disapprove.' I think it's unwise for Benson."

"What do you think about using thorazine?" McPherson persisted.

"It's a gamble."

"A gamble not worth taking."

"Maybe it's worth it, and maybe it's not. But it's a gamble."

McPherson nodded and turned to Ellis. "Do you still want to do him?"

"Yes," Ellis said, staring at the screen. "I still want to do him."

7

AS ALWAYS, MORRIS FOUND IT STRANGE TO play tennis on the hospital court. The hospital buildings looming high above him always made him feel slightly guilty—all those rows of windows, all those patients who could not do what he was doing. Then there was the sound. Or, rather, the absence of sound. The freeway ran near the hospital, and the reassuring *thwok!* of the tennis balls was completely obliterated by the steady, monotonous rush of passing cars.

It was getting dark now, and he was having trouble with his vision; the ball seemed to pop unexpectedly into his court. Kelso was much less hampered. Morris often joked that Kelso ate too many carrots, but whatever the explanation, it was humiliating to play late with Kelso. Darkness helped him. And Morris hated to lose.

He had long ago become comfortable with the fact of his own competitiveness. Morris never stopped competing. He competed in games, he competed in work, he competed with women. More than once Ross had pointed that out to him, and then dropped the subject in the sly way that psychiatrists raise a point, then drop it. Morris didn't mind. It was a fact of his life, and whatever the connotations—deep insecurity, a need to prove himself, a feeling of inferiority—he didn't worry about it. He drew pleasure from competition and satisfaction from winning. And so far in his life he had managed to win more often than not.

In part, he had joined the NPS because the challenges were very great and because the potential rewards were enormous. Privately, Morris expected to be a professor of surgery before he was forty. His past career had been outstanding—that was why Ellis had accepted him—and he was equally confident about his future. It wouldn't hurt to be associated with a landmark case in surgical history.

All in all, he was in a good mood, and he played

hard for half an hour, until he was tired and it was too dark to see. He signaled to Kelso—no point in calling above the freeway sounds—to end the game. They met at the net and shook hands. Morris was reassured to see that Kelso was sweating heavily.

"Good game," Kelso said. "Tomorrow, same time?"

"I'm not sure," Morris said.

Kelso paused. "Oh," he said. "That's right. You have a big day tomorrow."

"Big day," Morris nodded. Christ, had the news even reached the pediatric residents? For a moment he felt what Ellis must be feeling—the intense pressure, abstract, vague, that came from knowing that the entire University Hospital staff was watching this procedure.

"Well, good luck with it," Kelso said.

As the two men walked back to the hospital, Morris saw Ellis, a distant solitary figure, limping slightly as he crossed the parking lot and climbed into his car, and drove home.

WEDNESDAY, MARCH 10, 1971:

Implantation

1

AT 6 A.M. JANET ROSS WAS ON THE THIRD SUR-
gical floor, dressed in greens, having coffee and a
doughnut. The surgeons' lounge was busy at this hour.
Although operations were scheduled to begin at six,
most didn't get going for fifteen or twenty minutes after
that. The surgeons sat around, reading the newspaper,
discussing the stock market and their golf games. From
time to time one of them would leave, go to the overhead viewing galleries, and look down on their ORs to
see how preparations were coming.

Ross was the only woman in the room, and her presence
changed the masculine atmosphere subtly. It annoyed her
that she should be the only woman, and it annoyed her
that the men should become quieter, more polite, less
jovial and raucous. She didn't give a damn if they were
raucous, and she resented being made to feel like an intruder. It seemed to her that she had been an intruder all
her life, even when she was very young. Her father had
been a surgeon who never bothered to conceal his disappointment that he had a daughter instead of a son. A son
would have fitted into his scheme of life; he could have
brought him to the hospital on Saturday mornings, taken
him into the operating rooms—those were all things you

could do with a *son*. But a daughter was something else, a perplexing entity not suited for a surgical life. And therefore an intrusion . . .

She looked around at all the surgeons in the lounge, and then, to cover her unease, she went to the phone and dialed the seventh floor.

"This is Dr. Ross. Is Mr. Benson on call?"

"He was just sent."

"When did he leave the floor?"

"About five minutes ago."

She hung up and went back to her coffee. Ellis appeared and waved to her across the room. "There'll be a five-minute delay hooking into the computer," he said. "They're tying in the lines now. Is the patient on call?"

"Sent five minutes ago."

"You seen Morris?"

"Not yet."

"He better get his ass down here," Ellis said.

Somehow that made her feel good.

Morris was in the elevator with a nurse and Benson, who lay on a stretcher, and one of the cops. As they rode down, Morris said to the cop, "You can't get off on the floor."

"Why not?"

"We're going onto the sterile floor directly."

"What should I do?"

"You can watch from the viewing gallery on the third floor. Tell the desk nurse I said it was all right."

The cop nodded. The elevator stopped at the second floor. The doors opened to reveal a hallway with people, all in surgical greens, walking back and forth. A

large sign read STERILE AREA. NO ADMITTANCE WITH-
OUT AUTHORIZATION. The lettering was red.

Morris and the nurse wheeled Benson out of the elevator. The cop remained behind, looking nervous. He
pushed the button for the third floor, and the doors
closed.

Morris went with Benson down the corridor. After a
moment, Benson said, "I'm still awake."

"Of course you are."

"But I don't want to be awake."

Morris nodded patiently. Benson had gotten pre-op
medications half an hour earlier. They would be taking
effect soon, making him drowsy. "How's your mouth?"

"Dry."

That was the atropine beginning to work. "You'll be
okay."

Morris himself had never had an operation. He'd performed hundreds, but never experienced one himself.
In recent years, he had begun to wonder how it felt to
be on the other side of things. He suspected, though he
would never admit it, that it must be awful.

"You'll be okay," he said to Benson again, and
touched his shoulder.

Benson just stared at him as he was wheeled down
the corridor toward OR 9.

OR 9 was the largest operating room in the hospital.
It was nearly thirty feet square and packed with electronic equipment. When the full surgical team was
there—all twelve of them—things got pretty crowded.
But now just two scrub nurses were working in the cavernous gray-tiled space. They were setting out sterile
tables and drapes around the chair. OR 9 had no op-

erating table—only a softly cushioned upright chair, like a dentist's chair.

Janet Ross was in the scrubroom adjacent to the operating room. Alongside her, Ellis finished his scrub and muttered something about fucking Morris being fucking late. Ellis got very nervous before operations, though he seemed to think nobody noticed it. Ross had scrubbed with him on several animal procedures and had seen the ritual—tension and profanity before the operation, and utter bland calmness once things were under way.

Ellis turned off the faucets with his elbows and entered the OR, backing in so that his arms did not touch the door. A nurse handed him a towel. While he dried his hands, he looked back through the door at Ross, and then up at the glass-walled viewing gallery overhead. Ross knew there would be a crowd in the gallery watching the operation.

Morris came down and began scrubbing. She said, "Ellis wondered where you were."

"Bringing down the patient," he said.

One of the circulating nurses entered the scrub room and said, "Dr. Ross, there's somebody here from the radiation lab with a unit for Dr. Ellis. Does he want it now?"

"If it's loaded," she said.

"I'll ask," the nurse said. She disappeared, and stuck her head in a moment later. "He says it's loaded and ready to go, but unless your equipment is shielded it could give you trouble."

Ross knew that all the OR equipment had been shielded the week before. The plutonium exchanger didn't put out much radiation—not enough to fog an

X-ray plate—but it could confuse more delicate scientific equipment. There was, of course, no danger to people.

"We're shielded," Ross said. "Have him take it into the OR."

Ross turned to Morris, scrubbing alongside her. "How's Benson?"

"Nervous."

"He should be," she said. Morris glanced at her, his eyes questioning above the gauze surgical mask. She shook her hands free of excess water and backed into the OR. The first thing she saw was the rad-lab man wheeling in the tray with the charging unit on it. It was contained in a small lead box. On the sides were stenciled DANGER RADIATION and the triple-blade orange symbol for radiation. It was all faintly ridiculous; the charging unit was quite safe.

Ellis stood across the room, being helped into his gown. He plunged his hands into his rubber gloves and flexed his fingers. To the rad-lab man he said, "Has it been sterilized?"

"Sir?"

"Has the unit been sterilized?"

"I don't know, sir."

"Then give it to one of the girls and have her autoclave it. It's got to be sterile."

Dr. Ross dried her hands and shivered in the cold of the operating room. Like most surgeons, Ellis preferred a cold room—too cold, really, for the patient. But as Ellis often said, "If I'm happy, the patient's happy."

Ellis was now across the room standing by the viewing box, while the circulating nurse, who was not scrubbed, put up the patient's X-rays. Ellis peered closely at them, though he had seen them a dozen times before. They were perfectly normal skull films. Air had been injected into the ventricles, so that the horns stood out darkly.

One by one the rest of the team filtered into the room. All together, there were two scrub nurses, two circulating nurses, one orderly, Ellis, two assistant surgeons including Morris, two electronics technicians, and a computer programmer. The anaesthetist was outside with Benson.

Without looking up from his console, one of the electronics men said, "Any time you want to begin, Doctor."

"We'll wait for the patient," Ellis said dryly, and there were some chuckles from the Nine Group team.

Ross looked around the room at the seven TV screens. They were of different sizes and stationed in different places, depending on how important they were to the surgeon. The smallest screen monitored the closed-circuit taping of the operation. At the moment, it showed an overhead view of the empty chair.

Another screen, nearer the surgeon, monitored the electroencephalogram, or EEG. It was turned off now, the sixteen pens tracing straight white lines across the screen. There was also a large TV screen for basic operative parameters: electrocardiogram, peripheral arterial pressure, respirations, cardiac output, central venous pressure, rectal temperature. Like the EEG screen, it was also tracing a series of straight lines.

Another pair of screens were completely blank. They would display black-and-white image-intensified X-ray views during the operation.

Finally, two color screens displayed the LIMBIC Program output. That program was cycling now, without punched-in coordinates. On the screens, a picture of the brain rotated in three dimensions while random coordinates, generated by computer, flashed below. As always, Ross felt that the computer was another, almost human presence in the room—an impression that was always heightened as the operation proceeded.

Ellis finished looking at the X-rays and glanced up at the clock. It was 6:19; Benson was still outside being checked by the anaesthetist. Ellis walked around the room, talking briefly to everyone. He was being unusually friendly, and Ross wondered why. She looked up at the viewing gallery and saw the director of the hospital, the chief of surgery, the chief of medicine, and the chief of research all looking down through the glass. Then she understood.

It was 6:21 when Benson was wheeled in. He was now heavily pre-medicated, relaxed, his body limp, his eyelids heavy. His head was wrapped in a green towel.

Ellis supervised Benson's transfer from the stretcher to the chair. As the leather straps were placed across his arms and legs, Benson seemed to wake up, his eyes opening wide.

"That's just so you don't fall off," Ellis said easily. "We don't want you to hurt yourself."

"Uh-huh," Benson said softly, and closed his eyes again.

Ellis nodded to the nurses, who removed the sterile towel from Benson's head. The naked head seemed very small—that was Ross's usual reaction—and white. The skin was smooth, except for a razor nick on the left frontal. Ellis's blue-ink "X" marks were clearly visible on the right side.

Benson leaned back in the chair. He did not open his eyes again. One of the technicians began to fix the monitor leads to his body, strapping them on with little dabs of electrolyte paste. They were attached quickly; soon his body was connected to a tangle of multicolored wires running off to the equipment.

Ellis looked at the TV monitor screens. The EEG was now tracing sixteen jagged lines; heartbeat was recorded; respirations were gently rising and falling; temperature was steady. The technicians began to punch pre-op parameters into the computer. Normal lab values had already been fed in. During the operation, the computer would monitor all vital signs at five-second intervals, and would signal if anything went wrong.

"Let's have music, please," Ellis said, and one of the nurses slipped a tape cartridge into the portable cassette recorder in a corner of the room. A Bach concerto began to play softly. Ellis always operated to Bach; he said he hoped that the precision, if not the genius, might be contagious.

They were approaching the start of the operation. The digital wall clock said 6:29:14 a.m. Next to it, an elapsed-time digital clock still read 0:00:00.

With the help of a scrub nurse, Ross put on her sterile gown and gloves. The gloves were always difficult for her. She didn't scrub in frequently, and when she plunged her fingers into the gloves she caught her hand, missing one of the finger slots and putting two fingers in another. It was impossible to read the scrub nurse's reaction; only her eyes were visible above the mask. But Ross was glad that Ellis and the other surgeons were turned away attending to the patient.

She stepped to the back of the room, being careful

not to trip over the thick black power cables that snaked across the floor in all directions. Ross did not participate in the initial stages of the operation. She waited until the stereotaxic mechanism was in place and the coordinates were determined. She had time to stand to one side and pluck at her glove until all the fingers were in the right slots.

There was no real purpose for her to attend the operation at all, but McPherson insisted that one member of the non-surgical staff scrub in each day that they operated. He said it made the Unit more cohesive.

She watched Ellis and his assistants across the room draping Benson; then she looked over to the draping as seen on the closed-circuit monitor. The entire operation would be recorded on video tape for later review.

"I think we can start now," Ellis said easily. "Go ahead with the needle."

The anaesthetist, working behind the chair, placed the needle between the second and third lumbar spaces of Benson's spine. Benson moved once and made a slight sound, and then the anaesthetist said, "I'm through the dura. How much do you want?"

The computer console flashed "OPERATION BEGUN." The computer automatically started the elapsed-time clock, which ticked off the seconds.

"Give me thirty cc's to begin," Ellis said. "Let's have X-ray, please."

The X-ray machines were swung into position at the front and side of the patient's head. Film plates were set on, locking in with a click. Ellis stepped on the floor button, and the TV screens glowed suddenly, showing black-and-white images of the skull. He watched in two views as air slowly filled the ventricles, outlining the horns in black.

The programmer sat at the computer console, his hands fluttering over the buttons. On his TV display screen, the words "PNEUMOGRAPH INITIATED" appeared.

"All right, let's fix his hat," Ellis said. The boxlike tubular stereotactic frame was placed over the patient's head. Burr-hole locations were fixed and checked. When Ellis was satisfied, he injected local anaesthetic into the scalp points. Then he cut the skin and reflected it back, exposing the white surface of the skull.

"Drill, please."

With the 2-mm drill, he made the first of the two holes on the right side of the skull. He placed the stereotactic frame—the "hat"—over the head, and screwed it down securely.

Ross looked over at the computer display. Values for heart rate and blood pressure flashed on the screen and faded; everything was normal. Soon the computer, like the surgeons, would begin to deal with more complex matters.

"Let's have a position check," Ellis said, stepping away from the patient, frowning critically at Benson's shaved head and the metal frame screwed on top of it. The X-ray technician came forward and snapped the pictures.

In the old days, Ross remembered, they actually took X-ray plates and determined position by visual inspection of the plates. It was a slow process. Using a compass, protractor, and ruler, they drew lines across the X-ray, measured them, rechecked them. Now the data were fed directly to the computer, which did the analysis more rapidly and more accurately.

All the team turned to look at the computer print-out screen. The X-ray views appeared briefly, and were replaced by schematic drawings. The maxfield location of the stereotactic apparatus was calculated; the actual location was then merged with it. A set of coordinates flashed up, followed by the notation "PLACEMENT CORRECT."

Ellis nodded. "Thank you for your consultation," he said, and went over to the tray which held the electrodes.

The team was now using Briggs stainless-steel Teflon-coated electrode arrays. In the past, they had tried gold, platinum alloy, and even flexible steel strands, back in the days when the electrodes were placed by inspection.

The old inspection operations were bloody, messy affairs. It was necessary to remove a large portion of the skull and expose the surface of the brain. The surgeon found his landmark points on the surface itself, and then placed his electrodes in the substance of the brain. If he had to place them in deep structures, he would occasionally cut through the brain to the ventricles with a knife, and then place them. There were serious complications; the operations were lengthy; the patients never did very well.

Now the computer had changed all that. The computer allowed you to fix a point precisely in three-dimensional space. Initially, along with other researchers in the field, the NPS group had tried to relate deep brain points to skull architecture. They measured their landmark points from the orbit of the eye, from the meatus of the ear, from the sagittal suture. That, of course, didn't work—people's brains did not fit inside their skulls with any consistency. The only way to determine deep brain points was in relation to other brain points—and the logical landmarks were the ventricles, the fluid-filled spaces within the brain. According to the new system, everything was determined in relation to the ventricles.

With the help of the computer, it was no longer necessary to expose the brain surface. Instead, a few small holes were drilled in the skull and the electrodes inserted, while the computer watched by X-ray to make sure they were being placed correctly.

Ellis picked up the first electrode array. From where Ross stood, it looked like a single slender wire. Actually, it was a bundle of twenty wires, with staggered contact points. Each wire was coated with Teflon except for the last millimeter, which was exposed. Each wire was a different length, so that under a magnifying glass, the staggered electrode tips looked like a miniature staircase.

Ellis checked the array under a large glass. He called for more light and turned the array, peering at all contact points. Then he had a scrub nurse plug it into a testing unit and test every contact. This had been done dozens of times before, but Ellis always checked again before insertion. And he always had four arrays sterilized, though he would need only two. Ellis was careful.

At length he was satisfied. "Are we ready to wire?" he asked the team. They nodded. He stepped up to the patient and said, "Let's go through the dura."

Up to this point in the operation, they had drilled through the skull, but had left intact the membrane of *dura mater* which covered the brain and enclosed the spinal fluid. Ellis's assistant used a probe to puncture the dura.

"I have fluid," he said, and a thin trickle of clear liquid slid down the side of the shaved skull from the hole. A nurse sponged it away.

Ross always found it a source of wonder the way the brain was protected. Other vital body organs were well-protected, of course: the lungs and heart inside the bony cage of the ribs, the liver and spleen under the edge of the ribs, the kidneys packed in fat and secure against thick muscles of the lower back. Good protection, but nothing compared to the central nervous system, which was encased entirely in thick bone. Yet even this was not enough; inside the bone there were sac-like membranes which held cerebrospinal fluid. The fluid was under pressure, so that the brain sat in the middle of a pressurized liquid system that afforded its superb protection.

McPherson had compared it to a fetus in a water-filled womb. "The baby comes out of the womb," McPherson said, "but the brain never comes out of its own special womb."

"We will place now," Ellis said.

Ross moved forward, joining the surgical team gathered around the head. She watched as Ellis slid the tip of the electrode array into the burr hole and then pressed slightly, entering the substance of the brain. The technician punched buttons on the computer console. The display screen read: "ENTRY POINT LOCALIZED."

The patient did not move, made no sound. The brain could not feel pain; it lacked pain sensors. It was one of the freaks of evolution that the organ which sensed pain throughout the body could feel nothing itself.

Ross looked away from Ellis toward the X-ray screens. There, in harsh black and white, she saw the crisply outlined white electrode array begin its slow, steady movement into the brain. She looked from the anterior view to the lateral, and then to the computer-generated images.

The computer was interpreting the X-ray images by drawing a simplified brain, with the temporal-lobe target area in red and a flickering blue track showing the line the electrode must traverse from entry point to the target area. So far, Ellis was following the track perfectly.

"Very pretty," Ross said.

The computer flashed up triple coordinates in rapid succession as the electrodes went deeper.

"Practice makes perfect," Ellis said sourly. He was now using the scale-down apparatus attached to the stereotactic hat. The scaler reduced his crude finger movements to very small changes in electrode movements. If he moved his finger half an inch, the scaler converted that to half a millimeter. Very slowly the electrodes penetrated deeper into the brain.

From the screens, Ross could lift her eyes and watch the closed-circuit TV monitor showing Ellis at work. It was easier to watch on TV than to turn around and see the real thing. But she turned around when she heard Benson say, very distinctly, "Uh."

Ellis stopped. "What was that?"

"Patient," the anaesthetist said, gesturing toward Benson.

Ellis paused, bent over, to look at Benson's face. "You all right, Mr. Benson?" He spoke loudly, distinctly.

"Yuh. Fine," Benson said. His voice was deeply drugged.

"Any pain?"

"No."

"Good. Just relax now." And he returned to his work.

Ross sighed in relief. Somehow, all that had made her tense, even though she knew there was no reason for alarm. Benson could feel no pain, and she had known all along that his sedation was only that—a kind of deep, drugged semi-sleep, and not unconsciousness. There was no reason for him to be unconscious, no reason to risk general anaesthesia.

She turned back to the computer screen. The computer had now presented an inverted view of the brain, as seen from below, near the neck. The electrode track was visible end on, as a single blue point surrounded by concentric circles. Ellis was supposed to keep within one millimeter, one twenty-fifth of an inch, of the assigned track. He deviated half a millimeter.

"50 TRACK ERROR," warned the computer. Ross said, "You're slipping off."

The electrode array stopped in its path. Ellis glanced up at the screens. "Too high on beta plane?"

"Wide on gamma."

"Okay."

After a moment, the electrodes continued along the path. "40 TRACK ERROR," the computer flashed. It rotated its brain image slowly, bringing up an anterolateral view. "20 TRACK ERROR," it said.

"You're correcting nicely," Ross said.

Ellis hummed along with the Bach and nodded.

"ZERO TRACK ERROR," the computer indicated, and

swung the brain view around to a full lateral. The second screen showed a full frontal view. After a few moments, the screen blinked "APPROACHING TARGET." Ross conveyed the message.

Seconds later, the flashing word "STRIKE."

"You're on," Ross said.

Ellis stepped back and folded his hands across his chest. "Let's have a coordinate check," he said. The elapsed-time clock showed that twenty-seven minutes had passed in the operation.

The programmer flicked the console buttons rapidly. On the TV screens, the placement of the electrode was simulated by the computer. The simulation ended, like the actual placement, with the word "STRIKE."

"Now match it," Ellis said.

The computer held its simulation on one screen and matched it to the X-ray image of the patient. The overlap was perfect; the computer reported "MATCHED WITHIN ESTABLISHED LIMITS."

"That's it," Ellis said. He screwed on the little plastic button cap which held the electrodes tightly against the skull. Then he applied dental cement to fix it. He untangled the twenty fine wire leads that came off the electrode array and pushed them to one side.

"We can do the next one now," he said.

At the end of the second placement, a thin, arcing cut was made with a knife along the scalp. To avoid important superficial vessels and nerves, the cut ran from the electrode entry points down the side of the ear to the base of the neck. There it deviated to the right shoulder. Using blunt dissection, Ellis opened a small pocket beneath the skin of the right lateral chest, near the armpit.

"Have we got the charging unit?" he asked.

The charger was brought to him. It was smaller than a pack of cigarettes, and contained thirty-seven grams of the radioactive isotope plutonium-239 oxide. The radiation produced heat, which was converted directly by a thermionic unit to electric power. A Kenbeck solid-state DC/DC circuit transformed the output to the necessary voltage.

Ellis plugged the charger into the test pack and did a last-minute check of its power before implantation. As he held it in his hand, he said, "It's cold. I can't get used to that." Ross knew layers of vacuum-foil insulation kept the exterior cool and that inside the packet the radiation capsule was producing heat at 500 degrees Fahrenheit—hot enough to cook a roast.

He checked radiation to be sure there would be no leakage. The meters all read in the low-normal range. There was a certain amount of leakage, naturally, but it was no more than that produced by a commercial color television set.

Finally he called for the dog tag. Benson would have to wear this dog tag for as long as he had the atomic charging unit in his body. The tag warned that the person had an atomic pacemaker, and gave a telephone number. Ross knew that the number was a listing which played a recorded message twenty-four hours a day. The recording gave detailed technical information about the charging unit, and warned that bullet wounds, automobile accidents, fires, and other damage could release the plutonium, which was a powerful alpha-particle emitter. It gave special instructions to physicians, coroners, and morticians, and warned particularly against cremation of the body, unless the charger was first removed.

Ellis inserted the charging unit into the small subdermal pocket he had made in the chest wall. He sewed tissue layers around it to fix it in place. Then he turned his attention to the postage-stamp-sized electronic computer.

Ross looked up at the viewing gallery and saw the wizard twins, Gerhard and Richards, watching intently. Ellis checked the packet under the magnifying glass, then gave it to a scrubbed technician, who hooked the little computer into the main hospital computer.

To Ross, the computer was the most remarkable part of the entire system. Since she had joined the NPS three years before, she had seen the computer shrink from a prototype as large as a briefcase to the present tiny model, which looked small in the palm of a hand yet contained all the elements of the original bulky unit.

This tiny size made subdermal implantation possible. The patient was free to move about, take showers, do anything he wanted. Much better than the old units, where the charger was clipped to a patient's belt and wires dangled down all over.

She looked at the computer screens which flashed "OPERATIVE MONITORS INTERRUPTED FOR ELECTRONICS CHECK." On one screen, a blown-up circuit diagram appeared. The computer checked each pathway and component independently. It took four-millionths of a second for each check; the entire process was completed in two seconds. The computer flashed "ELECTRONIC CHECK NEGATIVE." A moment later, brain views reappeared. The computer had gone back to monitoring the operation.

"Well," Ellis said, "let's hook him up." He painstakingly attached the forty fine wire leads from the two electrode arrays to the plastic unit. Then he fitted the wires down along the neck, tucked the plastic under the skin, and called for sutures. The elapsed-time clock read one hour and twelve minutes.

2

MORRIS WHEELED BENSON INTO THE RECOVery room, a long, low-ceilinged room where patients were brought immediately after operation. The NPS had a special section of the rec room, as did cardiac patients and burns patients. But the NPS section, with its cluster of electronic equipment, had never been used before. Benson was the first case.

Benson looked pale but otherwise fine; his head and neck were heavily bandaged. Morris supervised his transfer from the rolling stretcher to the permanent bed. Across the room, Ellis was telephoning in his operative note. If you dialed extension 1104, you got a transcribing machine. The dictated message would later be typed up by a secretary and inserted in Benson's record.

Ellis's voice droned on in the background. ". . . centimeter incisions were made over the right temporal region, and 2-millimeter burr holes drilled with a K-7 drill. Implantation of Briggs electrodes carried out with computer assistance on the LIMBIC Program. Honey, that's spelled in capital letters, L-I-M-B-I-C. Program. X-ray placement of electrodes determined with computer review as within established limits. Electrodes sealed with Tyler fixation caps and seven-oh-grade dental sealer. Transmission wires—''

''What do you want on him?'' the rec-room nurse asked.

''Vital signs Q five minutes for the first hour, Q fifteen for the second, Q thirty for the third, hourly thereafter. If he's stable, you can move him up to the floor in six hours.''

The nurse nodded, making notes. Morris sat down by the bedside to write a short operative note:

Short operative note on Harold F. Benson

Pre-op dx: acute disinhibitory lesion (temporal focus)
Post-op dx: same
Procedure: implantation of twin Briggs electrode arrays into right temporal lobe with subdermal placing of computer and plutonium charging unit.
Pre-op meds: phenobarbital 500 mg ⎫   one hr. prior to
      atropine 60 mg   ⎬   procedure

Anaesthesia: lidocaine (1/1000) epinephrine locally
Estimated blood loss: 250 cc
Fluid replacement: 200 cc D5/W
Operative duration: 1 hr. 12 min.
Post-op condition: good

As he finished the note, he heard Ross say to the nurse, "Start him on phenobarb as soon as he's awake." She sounded angry.

Morris looked up at her. She was frowning, her face tight. "Something the matter, Jan?"

"No," she said. "Of course not."

"Well, if there's anything you want to—"

"Just make sure he gets his phenobarb. We want to keep him sedated until we can interface him."

And she stormed out of the room. Morris watched her go, then glanced over at Ellis, who was still dictating but had been watching. Ellis shrugged.

Morris adjusted the monitoring equipment on the shelf above Benson's head. He turned it on and waited until it warmed up. Then he placed the temporary induction unit around Benson's taped shoulder.

During the operation, all the wires had been hooked up, but they were not working yet. First, Benson would have to be "interfaced." This meant determining which of the forty electrodes would stop his seizures, and locking in the appropriate switches on the subdermal computer. Because the computer was under the skin, the locking in would be accomplished by an induction unit, which worked through the skin. But the interfacing couldn't be done until tomorrow.

Meanwhile, the equipment monitored Benson's brainwave activity. The screens above the bed glowed a bright green, and showed the white tracing of his EEG. The pattern was normal for alpha rhythms slowing from sedation.

Benson opened his eyes and looked at Morris.

"How do you feel?" he asked.

"Sleepy," he said. "Is it beginning soon?"

"It's over," Morris said.

Benson nodded, not at all surprised, and closed his eyes. A rad-lab technician came in and checked for leakage from the plutonium with a Geiger counter. There was none. Morris slipped the dog tag around Benson's neck. The nurse picked it up curiously, read it, and frowned.

Ellis came over. "Time for breakfast?"

"Yes," Morris said. "Time for breakfast."

They left the room together.

3

THE TROUBLE WAS HE DIDN'T REALLY LIKE THE sound of his voice. His voice was rough and grating, and his enunciation was poor. McPherson preferred to see the words in his mind, as if they had been written. He pressed the microphone button on the dictation machine. "Roman numeral three. Philosophical Implications."

III. Philosophical Implications.

He paused and looked around his office. The large model of the brain sat at the corner of his desk. Shelves of journals along one wall. And the TV monitor. On the screen now he was watching the playback of the morning's operation. The sound was turned off, the milky images silent. Ellis was drilling holes in Benson's head. McPherson watched and began to dictate.

This procedure represents the first direct link between a human brain and a computer. The link is permanent. Now, of course, any man sitting at a computer console and interacting with the computer by pressing buttons can be said to be linked.

Too stuffy, he thought. He ran the tape back and made changes. *Now, a man sitting at a computer console and interacting with the computer by pressing buttons is linked to the computer. But that link is not direct. And the link is not permanent. Therefore, this operative procedure represents something rather different. How is one to think about it?*

He stared at the TV image of the operation, then continued.

One might think of the computer in this case as a prosthetic device. Just as a man who has his arm amputated can receive a mechanical equivalent of the lost arm, so a brain-damaged man can receive a mechanical aid to overcome the effects of brain damage. This is a comfortable way to think about the operation. It makes the computer into a high-class wooden leg. Yet the implications go much further than that.

He paused to look at the screen. Somebody at the main tape station had changed reels. He was no longer seeing the operation, but a psychiatric interview with Benson before the surgery. Benson was excited, smoking a cigarette, making stabbing gestures with the lighted tip as he spoke.

Curious, McPherson turned the sound up slightly. ". . . know what they're doing. The machines are everywhere. They used to be the servants of man, but now they're taking over. Subtly, subtly taking over.''

Ellis stuck his head into the office, saw the TV screen, and smiled. "Looking at the 'before' pictures?''

"Trying to get a little work done," McPherson said, and pointed to the dictation machine.

Ellis nodded, ducked out, closing the door behind him.

Benson was saying, ". . . know I'm a traitor to the human race, because I'm helping to make machines more intelligent. That's my job, programming artificial intelligence, and—"

McPherson turned the sound down until it was almost inaudible. Then he went back to his dictation.

In thinking about computer hardware, we distinguish between central and peripheral equipment. That is, the main computer is considered central even though, in human terms, it may be located in some out-of-the-way place—like the basement of a building, for example. The computer's read-out equipment, display consoles, and so on, are peripheral. They are located at the edges of the computer system, on different floors of the building.

He looked at the TV screen. Benson was particularly excited. He turned up the sound and heard, ". . . getting more intelligent. First steam engines, then automobiles, and airplanes, then adding machines. Now computers, feedback loops—"

McPherson turned the sound off.

For the human brain, the analogy is a central brain and peripheral terminals, such as mouth, arms, and legs. They carry out the instructions—the output—of the brain. By and large, we judge the workings of the brain by the activity of these peripheral functions. We notice what a person says, and how he acts, and from that deduce how his brain works. This idea is familiar to everyone.

He looked at Benson on the TV screen. What would Benson say? Would he agree or disagree?

Now, however, in this operation we have created a man with not one brain but two. He has his biological brain, which is damaged, and he has a new computer brain, which is designed to correct the damage. This new brain is intended to control the biological brain. Therefore a new situation arises. The patient's biological brain is the peripheral terminal—the only peripheral terminal—for the new computer. In one area, the new computer brain has total control. And therefore the patient's biological brain, and indeed his whole body, has become a terminal for the new computer. We have created a man who is one single, large, complex computer terminal. The patient is a read-out device for the new computer, and he is as helpless to control the read-out as a TV screen is helpless to control the information presented on it.

Perhaps that was a bit strong, he thought. He pressed the button and said, "Harriet, type that last paragraph but I want to look at it, okay? Roman numeral four. Summary and Conclusions."

IV. Summary and Conclusions.

He paused again, and turned up the sound on Benson. Benson was saying, ". . . hate them, particularly the prostitutes. Airplane mechanics, dancers, translators, gas-station attendants, the people who are machines, or who service machines. The prostitutes. I hate them all."

As he spoke, Benson continued to stab with his cigarette.

4

"AND HOW DID YOU FEEL?" DR. RAMOS SAID.

"Angry," Janet Ross said. "Angry as hell. I mean, that nurse was standing there, watching it all. She pretended she didn't understand what was happening, but she did."

"You felt angry about . . ." Dr. Ramos let his voice trail off.

"About the operation. About Benson. They went ahead and did it. I told them from the beginning—from the goddamned very beginning—that it was a bad idea, but Ellis and Morris and McPherson all wanted to do it. They're so cocky. Particularly Morris. When I saw him in the recovery room, gloating over Benson—who was all taped up and pale as a ghost—I just got mad."

"Why is that?"

"Because he was so pale, because he, uh—"

She stopped. She fumbled for an answer, but couldn't think of a logical response.

"I gather the operation was successful," Dr. Ramos said. "And most people are pale after surgery. What made you mad?"

She said nothing. Finally, she said, "I don't know."

She heard Dr. Ramos shift in his chair. She could not see him; she was lying on the couch, and Dr. Ramos was behind her head. There was a long silence while she stared at the ceiling and tried to think what to say. Her thoughts seemed to be churning, not making any sense. Finally Dr. Ramos said, "The presence of the nurse seems important to you."

"It does?"

"Well, you mentioned it."

"I wasn't aware I had."

"You said the nurse was there and knew what was going on. . . . What, exactly, was going on?"

"I was mad."

"But you don't know why? . . ."

"Yes, I do," she said. "It was Morris. He's so cocky."

"Cocky," Dr. Ramos repeated.

"Overly self-assured."

"You said cocky."

"Look, I didn't mean anything by that; it was just a word—" She broke off. She was very angry. She could hear it in her voice.

"You are angry now," Dr. Ramos said.

"Very."

"Why?"

After a long pause, she said, "They didn't listen to me."

"Who didn't listen to you?"

"Any of them. Not McPherson, not Ellis, not Morris. Nobody listened to me."

"Did you tell Dr. Ellis or Dr. McPherson you were angry?"

"No."

"But you indicated your anger to Dr. Morris."

"Yes." He was leading her someplace and she couldn't see where. Normally at this point she could jump ahead and understand. But this time—

"How old is Dr. Morris?"

"I don't know. About my age. Thirty, thirty-one—something in there."

"About your age."

That pissed her off, his way of repeating things. "Yes, God damn it, about my age."

"And a surgeon."

"Yes. . . ."

"Is it easier to express anger toward someone you regard as a contemporary?"

"Probably. I never thought about it."

"Your father was also a surgeon, but he wasn't your contemporary."

"You don't have to draw me a picture," she said.

"You're still angry."

She sighed. "Let's change the subject."

"All right," he said, in that easy voice that she sometimes liked, and sometimes hated.

5

MORRIS HATED TO DO INITIAL INTERVIEWS.— The Initial Interview staff consisted mostly of clinical psychologists; the work was lengthy and boring. A recent tabulation had shown that only one in forty new patients to the NPS received further work; and only one in eighty-three was accepted as having some variety of organic brain disease with behavioral manifestations. That meant most Initial Interviews were a waste of time.

And it was particularly true of off-the-street patients. A year ago McPherson had decided, for political reasons, that anyone who heard of the NPS and presented himself directly would be seen. Most patients were still referrals, of course, but McPherson felt the image of the Unit depended upon prompt treatment of self-referrals as well.

McPherson also felt that everyone on the staff should do Initial Interviews from time to time. Morris worked two days a month in the little interview rooms with the one-way glass mirrors. This was one of his days, but he didn't want to be here; he was still exhilarated from the morning's operation, and he resented returning to this kind of mundane routine.

He looked up unhappily as the next patient came into

87

the room. He was a young man in his twenties, wearing dungarees and a sweatshirt. He had long hair. Morris stood to greet him.

"I'm Dr. Morris."

"Craig Beckerman." The handshake was soft and tentative.

"Please sit down." He waved Beckerman to a chair which faced Morris's desk, and the one-way mirror behind. "What brings you to us?"

"I, uh . . . I'm curious. I read about you," Beckerman said, "in a magazine. You do brain surgery here."

"That's true."

"Well, I uh . . . I was curious about it."

"In what sense?"

"Well, this magazine article— Can I smoke here?"

"Of course," Morris said. He pushed an ashtray across the desk to Beckerman. Beckerman brought out a pack of Camels, tapped one on the desk, then lit it.

"The magazine article . . ."

"Right. The magazine article said that you put wires in the brain. Is that true?"

"Yes, we sometimes perform that kind of surgery."

Beckerman nodded. He smoked the cigarette. "Yeah, well, is it true that you can put wires in so that you feel pleasure? Intense pleasure?"

"Yes," Morris said. He tried to say it blandly.

"That's really true?"

"It's really true," Morris said. And then he shook his pen, indicating that it was out of ink. He opened the desk drawer to take out another pen, and as he reached into the drawer, he pressed a sequence on the buttons hidden inside. Immediately his telephone rang.

"Dr. Morris."

At the other end, the secretary said, "You rang?"

"Yes. Would you hold all calls, please, and transfer them to Development section?"

"Right away," the secretary said.

"Thank you." Morris hung up. He knew that the Development people would arrive soon, to watch on the other side of the one-way mirror. "I'm sorry for the interruption. You were saying . . ."

"About the wires in the brain."

"Yes. We do that operation, Mr. Beckerman, under special circumstances, but it's still pretty experimental."

"That's all right," Beckerman said. He puffed on his cigarette. "That's fine with me."

"If you want information, we can arrange for you to have some reprints and magazine tear sheets explaining our work here."

Beckerman smiled and shook his head. "No, no," he said. "I don't want information. I want the operation. I'm volunteering."

Morris pretended to be surprised. He paused a moment and said, "I see."

"Listen," Beckerman said, "in the article it said that one jolt of electricity was like a dozen orgasms. It sounded really terrific."

"And you want this operation performed on you?"

"Yeah," Beckerman said, nodding vigorously. "Right."

"Why?"

"Are you kidding? Wouldn't everybody want it? Pleasure like that?"

"Perhaps," Morris said, "but you're the first person to ask for it."

"What's the matter?" Beckerman said. "Is it really expensive or something?"

"No. But we don't perform brain surgery for trivial reasons."

"Oh, wow," Beckerman said. "So that's where you are. Jesus."

And he got up and left the room, shaking his head.

The three Development guys looked stupefied. They sat in the adjoining room and stared through the one-way glass. Beckerman had long since departed.

"Fascinating," Morris said.

The Development guys didn't reply. Finally one of them cleared his throat and said, "To say the least."

Morris knew what was going through their heads. For years, they had been doing feasibility studies, potential application studies, ramification studies, industrial operations studies, input-output studies. They were geared to think in the future—and now they were suddenly confronted with the present.

"That man is an elad," one of them said. And sighed.

The elad concept had caused a lot of interest and some detached academic concern. The notion of an electrical addict—a man who needed his jolts of electricity just as some men needed doses of drugs—had seemed almost fancifully speculative. But now they had a patient who was clearly a potential addict.

"Electricity is the biggest kick of all," one of them said, and laughed. But the laugh was nervous, edged with tension.

Morris wondered what McPherson would say. Probably something philosophical. McPherson was mostly interested in philosophy these days.

The idea of an electrical addict was predicated on an astonishing discovery made by James Olds in the 1950s. Olds found that there were areas in the brain where electrical stimulation produced intense pleasure—strips of brain tissue he called "rivers of reward." If an electrode was placed in such an area, a rat would press a self-stimulation lever to receive a shock as often as five thousand times an hour. In its quest for pleasure, it would ignore food and water. It would stop pressing the lever only when it was prostrate with exhaustion.

This remarkable experiment had been repeated with goldfish, guinea pigs, dolphins, cats, and goats. There was no longer any question that the pleasure terminals in the brain were a universal phenomenon. They had also been located in humans.

Out of these considerations had come the notion of the electrical addict, the man who needed pleasurable shocks. At first glance, it seemed impossible for a person to become an addict. But it actually wasn't.

For instance, the technological hardware was now expensive, but it needn't be. One could envision clever Japanese firms manufacturing electrodes for as little as two or three dollars and exporting them.

Nor was the idea of an illegal operation so farfetched. At one time a million American women underwent illegal abortions each year. The implantation brain surgery was somewhat more complex, but not forbiddingly so. And the surgical techniques would become more standardized in the future. It was easy to imagine clinics springing up in Mexico and the Bahamas.

Nor was there a problem finding surgeons to do the

job. A single busy, well-organized neurosurgeon could perform ten or fifteen operations a day. He could certainly charge a thousand dollars for each—and with that kind of incentive, unscrupulous surgeons could be found. A hundred thousand dollars a week in cash was a strong inducement to break the law—if indeed a law were ever passed.

That did not seem very likely. A year before, the hospital had organized a seminar with legal scholars on "Biomedical Technology and the Law." Elads were among the subjects discussed, but the lawyers were not responsive. The elad concept did not fit neatly into the already existing pattern of laws governing drug addiction. All those laws recognized that a person could become a drug addict innocently or involuntarily—quite a different proposition from a person coldly seeking a surgical procedure that would make him an addict. Most of the lawyers felt that the public would not seek such an operation; there would be no legal problem because there would be no public demand. Now Beckerman had provided evidence for such a demand.

"I'll be goddamned," another of the Development people said.

Morris found that comment hardly adequate. He himself felt something he had felt once or twice before since joining the NPS. It was the sensation that things were moving too fast, without enough caution and control, and that it could *all* get out of control, suddenly, and without warning.

6

AT 6 P.M., ROGER MCPHERSON, HEAD OF THE
Neuropsychiatric Research Unit, went up to the seventh
floor to check on his patient. At least, that was how he
thought of Benson—as his patient. A proprietary feeling, but not entirely incorrect. Without McPherson,
there would be no NPS, and without an NPS, there
would be no surgery, no Benson. That was how he
thought of it.

Room 710 was quiet and bathed in reddish light from
the setting sun. Benson appeared to be asleep, but his
eyes opened when McPherson closed the door.

"How are you feeling?" McPherson asked, moving
close to the bed.

Benson smiled. "Everyone wants to know that," he
said.

McPherson smiled back. "It's a natural question."

"I'm tired, that's all. Very tired. . . . Sometimes I
think I'm a ticking time bomb, and you're wondering
when I'll explode."

"Is that what you think?" McPherson asked.

Automatically, he adjusted Benson's covers so he
could look at the I.V. line. It was flowing nicely.

93

"Ticktick," Benson said, closing his eyes again.
"Ticktick."

McPherson frowned. He was accustomed to mechanical metaphors from Benson—the man was preoccupied, after all, with the idea of men as machines. But to have them appear so soon after operation . . .

"Any pain?"

"None. A little ache behind my ears, like I'd fallen. That's all."

That, McPherson knew, was the bone pain from the drilling.

"Fallen?"

"I'm a fallen man," Benson said. "I've succumbed."

"To what?"

"To the process of being turned into a machine." He opened his eyes and smiled again. "Or a time bomb."

"Any smells? Strange sensations?" As he asked, McPherson looked at the EEG scanner above the bed. It was still reading normal alpha patterns, without any suggestion of seizure activity.

"No. Nothing like that."

"But you feel as if you might explode?" He thought: Ross should really be asking these questions.

"Sort of," Benson said. "In the coming war, we may all explode."

"How do you mean?"

"In the coming war between men and machines. The human brain is obsolete, you see."

That was a new thought. McPherson hadn't heard it from Benson before. He stared at him, lying in the bed, his head and shoulders heavily bandaged. It made the upper part of his body and his head appear thick, gross, oversized.

"Yes," Benson said. "The human brain has gone as far as it is going to go. It's exhausted, so it spawned the next generation of intelligent forms. They will— Why am I so tired?" He closed his eyes again.

"You're exhausted from the operation."

"A minor procedure," he said, and smiled with his eyes closed. A moment later he was snoring.

McPherson remained by the bed for a moment, then turned to the window and watched the sun set over the Pacific. Benson had a nice room; you could see a bit of the ocean between the high-rise apartments in Santa Monica. He remained there for several minutes. Benson did not wake. Finally, McPherson went out to the nurses' station to write his note in the chart.

"Patient alert, responsive, oriented times three." He paused after writing that. He didn't really know if Benson was oriented to person, place, and time; he hadn't checked specifically. But he was clear and responsive, and McPherson let it go. "Flow of ideas orderly and clear, but patient retains machine imagery of pre-operative state. It is too early to be certain, but it appears that early predictions were correct that the operation would not alter his mentation between seizures."

Signed, "Roger A. McPherson, M.D."

He stared at it for a moment, then closed the chart and replaced it on the shelf. It was a good note, cool, direct, holding out no false anticipations. The chart was a legal document, after all, and it could be called into court. McPherson didn't expect to see Benson's chart in court, but you couldn't be too careful.

The head of any large scientific laboratory performed a political function. You might deny it; you might dislike it. But it was nonetheless true, a necessary part of the job.

You had to keep all the people in the lab happy as they worked together. The more prima donnas you had, the tougher the job was, as pure politics.

You had to get your lab funded from outside sources, and that was also pure politics. Particularly if you were working in a delicate area, as the NPS was. McPherson had long since evolved the horseradish-peroxidase principle of grant applications. It was simple enough: when you applied for money, you announced that the money would be spent to find the enzyme horseradish peroxidase, which could lead to a cure for cancer. You would easily get sixty thousand dollars for that project—although you couldn't get sixty cents for mind control.

He looked at the row of charts on the shelf, a row of unfamiliar names, into which BENSON, H. F. 710 merged indistinguishably. In one sense, he thought, Benson was correct—he was a walking time bomb. A man treated with mind-control technology was subject to all sorts of irrational public prejudice. "Heart control" in the form of cardiac pacemakers was considered a wonderful invention; "kidney control" through drugs was a blessing. But "mind control" was evil, a disaster—even though the NPS control work was directly analogous to control work with other organs. Even the technology was similar: the atomic pacemaker they were using had been developed first for cardiac applications.

But the prejudice remained. And Benson thought of himself as a ticking time bomb. McPherson sighed, took out the chart again, and flipped to the section containing doctors' orders. Both Ellis and Morris had written post-op care orders. McPherson added: "After inter-facing tomorrow a.m., begin thorazine."

He looked at the note, then decided the nurses wouldn't understand interfacing. He scratched it out and wrote: "After noon tomorrow, begin thorazine."

As he left the floor, he thought that he would rest more easily once Benson was on thorazine. Perhaps they couldn't defuse the time bomb—but they could certainly drop it into a bucket of cold water.

7

LATE AT NIGHT, IN TELECOMP, GERHARD stared anxiously at the computer console. He typed in more instructions, then walked to a print-out typewriter and began reviewing the long sheaf of green-striped sheets. He scanned them quickly, looking for the error he knew was there in the programmed instructions.

The computer itself never made a mistake. Gerhard had used computers for nearly ten years—different computers, different places—and he had never seen one make a mistake. Of course, mistakes occurred all the time, but they were always in the program, not in the machine. Sometimes that infallibility was hard to accept. For one thing, it didn't fit with one's view of the rest of the world, where machines were always making mistakes—fuses blowing, stereos breaking down, ovens overheating, cars refusing to start. Modern man expected machines to make their fair share of errors.

But computers were different, and working with them could be a humiliating experience. They were never wrong. It was as simple as that. Even when it took weeks to find the source of some problem, even when the program was checked a dozen times by as many different people, even when the whole staff was slowly coming to the conclusion that for once, the computer circuitry had fouled up—it always turned out, in the end, to be a human error of some kind. Always.

Richards came in, shrugging off a sport coat, and poured himself a cup of coffee. "How's it going?"

Gerhard shook his head. "I'm having trouble with George."

"Again? Shit." Richards looked at the console. "How's Martha?"

"Martha's fine, I think. It's just George."

"Which George is it?"

"Saint George," Gerhard said. "Really a bitch."

Richards sipped his coffee and sat down at the console. "Mind if I try it?"

"Sure," Gerhard said.

Richards began flicking buttons. He called up the program for Saint George. Then he called up the program for Martha. Then he pushed the interaction button.

Richards and Gerhard hadn't devised these programs; they were modified from several existing computer programs developed at other universities. But the basic idea was the same—to create a computer program that would make the computer act emotionally, like people. It was logical to designate the programs with names like George and Martha. There was a precedent for that: Eliza in Boston, and Aldous in England.

George and Martha were essentially the same program with slight differences. The original George was programmed to be neutral in his response to stimuli. Then Martha was created. Martha was a little bitchy; Martha disliked most things. Finally, another George was formulated, a very loving George, who was referred to as Saint George.

Each program could respond with three emotional states—love, fear, and anger. Each could produce three actions—approach, withdrawal, and attack. All this was, of course, highly abstract. It was carried out in terms of numbers. For example, the original George was neutral to most numbers, but disliked the number 751. He was programmed to dislike it. And by extension he disliked similar numbers—743, 772, and so on. He much preferred numbers such as 404, 133, and 918. If you punched in one of these numbers, George responded with numbers signifying love and approach. If you punched in 707, George withdrew. If you punched in 750, George angrily attacked—according to the numbers he printed out.

The NPS staff had played with the programs in this way for a long time. Then they had incorporated program modifications to allow for "talk" from the computer. The numbers were translated into sentences. This was amusing, and revealing. The actual interaction was referred to as "the Christmas game" because most of it was conducted as giving and receiving gifts—objects that had an assigned or learned emotional value, just as the numbers did.

Normal George interacting with Martha would eventually win her over, and her bitchiness would recede into the background.

But Saint George had a much worse effect on her. His loving acceptance drove her up the wall. That is, if things were working normally. Richards watched as the print-out flashed across the screen.

HELLO I'M SAINT GEORGE
HELLO
WHAT IS YOUR NAME?
MARTHA.
YOU DON'T SAY MUCH, MARTHA.
NO
BUT I LIKE YOU.
WHY I DON'T LIKE YOU.
I UNDERSTAND THAT. HOW CAN I HELP?

"It isn't printing periods consistently," Richards said. "When did that start?"

"That's nothing," Gerhard said. "Just keep watching."

HELP?
YES, I WOULD LIKE TO HELP YOU.
HAVE A CAT.

Richards winced. Cats were programmed to be something that both George and Martha disliked. Giving George a cat was a very hostile move.

```
THANK YOU
HAVE ANOTHER CAT.
THANK YOU YOU ARE VERY KIND.
HAVE ANOTHER CAT.
NO THANK YOU.
DON'T YOU LIKE CATS?
YES BUT I HAVE ENOUGH CATS.
HAVE A GORILLA.
```

"Really nasty," Richards said. "What are the other interactions like?"

"Pretty much the same," Gerhard said.

"As bad as this?"

"Pretty much."

They were accustomed now to the idea that when the computers interacted, the results were unpredictable. The general form of interaction could be guessed, but the specific results were uncertain. It was like a computer playing checkers—it was probably going to win, but it would win a different way each time, depending on what the opponent did.

```
I DON'T WANT A GORILLA.
DON'T YOU LIKE GORILLAS?
NO THANK YOU.
YOU ARE TOO POLITE.
I AM SORRY IF I OFFEND YOU IN ANY WAY.
YOU TALK TOO MUCH.
I AM SORRY.
HAVE AN EGGPLANT.
```

Richards watched with interest. Saint George had no background for eggplants. But he disliked cucumbers and bananas.

```
NO THANK YOU.
DON'T YOU LIKE EGGPLANT?
NOT VERY MUCH.
HERE HAVE ANOTHER ONE.
NO THANK YOU.
I WANT YOU TO HAVE IT.
NO THANK YOU.
GO ON AND TAKE IT.
NO THANK YOU.
I INSIST.
NO THANK YOU.
```

"What's happened to Saint George?" Richards asked. "His responses are too much the same."

"That's what's bothering me."

"What's he cycling through on the program?"

"I was looking for it when you came in."

```
I INSIST THAT YOU HAVE A CUCUMBER.
I REFUSE.
```

"George!" Richards said, almost without thinking.

```
THEN HAVE A BANANA.
NO.
```

"George is breaking down," Richards said. "He's not a saint any more."

THEN HAVE BOTH A BANANA AND A CUCUMBER.
NO THANK YOU.
I INSIST.
GO TO HELL I WILL KILL YOU: : : : : : : : : : : :
: :
: :

The screen was filled with white dots. "What does that mean, unprintable response?" Richards said.

"I don't know. I've never seen it before tonight."

"How many times has this program been run?" Richards asked.

"One hundred and ten, against Martha."

"Any learning erasures?"

"No."

"I'll be goddamned," Richards said. "He's getting to be a short-tempered saint." He grinned. "We can write this one up."

Gerhard nodded and went back to the print-out. In theory, what was happening was not puzzling. Both George and Martha were programmed to learn from experience. Like the checkers-playing programs—where the machine got better each time it played a game—this program was established so that the machine would "learn" new responses to things. After one hundred and ten sets of experience, Saint George had abruptly stopped being a saint. He was learning not to be a saint around Martha—even though he had been programmed for saintliness.

"I know just how he feels," Richards said, and switched the machine off. Then he joined Gerhard, looking for the programming error that had made it happen.

THURSDAY, MARCH 11, 1971:

Interfacing

1

JANET ROSS SAT IN THE EMPTY ROOM AND glanced at the wall clock. It was 9 a.m. She looked down at the desk in front of her, which was bare except for a vase of flowers and a notepad. She looked at the chair opposite her. Then, aloud, she said, "How're we doing?"

There was a mechanical click and Gerhard's voice came through the speaker mounted in the ceiling. "We need a few minutes for the sound levels. The light is okay. You want to talk a minute?"

She nodded, and glanced over her shoulder at the one-way mirror behind her. She saw only her reflection, but she knew Gerhard, with his equipment, was behind, watching her. "You sound tired," she said.

"Trouble with Saint George last night," Gerhard said.

"I'm tired, too," she said. "I was having trouble with somebody who isn't a saint." She laughed. She was just talking so they could get a sound level for the room; she hadn't really paid attention to what she was saying. But it was true: Arthur was no saint. He was also no great discovery, though she'd thought he might be a few weeks ago when she first met him. She had

107

been, in fact, a little infatuated with him. ("Infatuated? Hmm? Is that what you'd call it?" She could hear Dr. Ramos now.) Arthur had been born handsome and wealthy. He had a yellow Ferrari, a lot of dash, and a lot of charm. She was able to feel feminine and frivolous around him. He did madcap, dashing things like flying her to Mexico City for dinner because he knew a little restaurant where they made the best tacos in the world. She knew it was all silly, but she enjoyed it. And in a way she was relieved—she never had to talk about medicine, or the hospital, or psychiatry. Arthur wasn't interested in any of those things; he was interested in her as a woman. ("Not as a sex object?" Damn Dr. Ramos.)

Then, as she got to know him better, she found herself wanting to talk about her work. And she found, with some surprise, that Arthur didn't want to hear about it. Arthur was threatened by her work; he had problems about achievement. He was nominally a stockbroker—an easy thing for a rich man's son to be—and he talked with authority about money, investments, interest rates, bond issues. But there was an aggressive quality in his manner, a defensiveness, as if he were substantiating himself.

And then she realized what she should have known from the beginning, that Arthur was chiefly interested in her because she was substantial. It was—in theory—more difficult to impress her, to sweep her off her feet, than it was to impress the little actresses who hung out at Bumbles and the Candy Store. And therefore more satisfying.

As time went on, she no longer drew pleasure from being frivolous around him, and everything became vaguely depressing. She recognized all the signs: her work at the hospital became busier, and she had to break dates with him. When she did see him, she was bored by his flamboyance, his restless impulsiveness, his clothes, and his cars. She would look at him across the dinner table and try to discover what she had once seen. She could not find even a trace of it. Last night she had broken it off. They both knew it was coming, and—

"You stopped talking," Gerhard said.

"I don't know what to say . . . Now is the time for all good men to come to the aid of the patient. The quick brown fox jumped over the pithed frog. We are all headed for that final common pathway in the sky." She paused. "Is that enough?"

"A little more."

"Mary, Mary, quite contrary, how does your garden grow? I'm sorry I don't remember the rest. How does the poem go?" She laughed.

"That's fine, we have the level now."

She looked up at the loudspeaker. "Will you be interfacing at the end of the series?"

"Probably," Gerhard said, "if it goes well. Rog is in a hurry to get him onto tranquilizers."

She nodded. This was the final stage in Benson's treatment, and it had to be done before tranquilizers could be administered. Benson had been kept on sedation with phenobarbital until midnight the night before. He would be clearheaded this morning, and ready for interfacing.

It was McPherson who had coined the term "interfacing." McPherson liked computer terminology. An interface was the boundary between two systems. Or between a computer and an effector mechanism. In

Benson's case, it was almost a boundary between two computers—his brain and the little computer wired into his shoulder. The wires had been attached, but the switches hadn't been thrown yet. Once they were, the feedback loop of Benson-computer-Benson would be instituted.

McPherson saw this case as the first of many. He planned to go from organic seizures to schizophrenics to mentally retarded patients to blind patients. The charts were all there on his office wall, projecting the technology five years into the future. And he planned to use more and more sophisticated computers in the link-up. Eventually, he would get to projects like Form Q, which seemed farfetched even to Ross.

But today the practical question was which of the forty electrodes would prevent an attack. Nobody knew that yet. It would be determined experimentally.

During the operation, the electrodes had been located precisely, within millimeters of the target area. That was good surgical placement, but considering the density of the brain it was grossly inadequate. A nerve cell in the brain was just a micron in diameter. There were a thousand nerve cells in the space of a millimeter.

From that standpoint, the electrodes had been crudely positioned. And this crudeness meant that many electrodes were required. One could assume that if you placed several electrodes in the correct general area, at least one of them would be in the precise position to abort an attack. Trial-and-error stimulation would determine the proper electrode to use.

"Patient coming," Gerhard said over the loudspeaker. A moment later, Benson arrived in a wheelchair, wearing his blue-and-white striped bathrobe. He seemed alert as he waved to her stiffly—the shoulder bandages inhibited movement of his arm. "How are you feeling?" he said, and smiled.

"I'm supposed to ask you."

"I'll ask the questions around here," he said. He was still smiling, but there was an edge to his voice. With some surprise, she realized that he was afraid. And then she wondered why that surprised her. Of course he would be afraid. Anyone would be. She wasn't exactly calm herself.

The nurse patted Benson on the shoulder, nodded to Dr. Ross, and left the room. They were alone.

For a moment, neither spoke. Benson stared at her; she stared back. She wanted to give Gerhard time to focus the TV camera in the ceiling, and to prepare his stimulating equipment.

"What are we doing today?" Benson asked.

"We're going to stimulate your electrodes, sequentially, to see what happens."

He nodded. He seemed to take this calmly, but she had learned not to trust his calm. After a moment he said, "Will it hurt?"

"No."

"Okay," he said. "Go ahead."

Gerhard, sitting on a high stool in the adjacent room, surrounded in the darkness by glowing green dials of equipment, watched through the one-way glass as Ross and Benson began to talk.

Alongside him, Richards picked up the tape recorder microphone and said quietly, "Stimulation series one, patient Harold Benson, March 11, 1971."

Gerhard looked at the four TV screens in front of

him. One showed the closed-circuit view of Benson that would be stored on video tape as the stimulation series proceeded. Another displayed a computer-generated view of the forty electrode points, lined up in two parallel rows within the brain substance. As each electrode was stimulated, the appropriate point glowed on the screen.

A third TV screen ran an oscilloscope tracing of the shock pulse as it was delivered. And a fourth showed a wiring diagram of the tiny computer in Benson's neck. It also glowed as stimulations traveled through the circuit pathways.

In the next room, Ross was saying, "You'll feel a variety of sensations, and some of them may be quite pleasant. We want you to tell us what you feel. All right?"

Benson nodded.

Richards said, "Electrode one, five millivolts, for five seconds." Gerhard pressed the buttons. The computer diagram showed a tracing of the circuit being closed, the current snaking its way through the intricate electronic maze of Benson's shoulder computer. They watched Benson through the one-way glass.

Benson said, "That's interesting."

"What's interesting?" Ross asked.

"That feeling."

"Can you describe it?"

"Well, it's like eating a ham sandwich."

"Do you like ham sandwiches?"

Benson shrugged. "Not particularly."

"Do you feel hungry?"

"Not particularly."

"Do you feel anything else?"

"No. Just the taste of a ham sandwich." He smiled. "On rye."

Gerhard, sitting at the control panel, nodded. The first electrode had stimulated a vague memory trace.

Richards: "Electrode two, five millivolts, five seconds."

Benson said, "I have to go to the bathroom."

Ross said, "It will pass."

Gerhard sat back from the control panel, sipped a cup of coffee, and watched the interview progress.

"Electrode three, five millivolts, five seconds."

This one produced absolutely no effect on Benson. Benson was quietly talking with Ross about bathrooms in restaurants, hotels, airports—

"Try it again," Gerhard said. "Up five."

"Repeat electrode three, ten millivolts, five seconds," Richards said. The TV screen flashed the circuit through electrode three. There was still no effect.

"Go on to four," Gerhard said. He wrote out a few notes:

#1—? memory trace (ham sand.)
#2—bladder fullness
#3—no subjective change
#4—

He drew the dash and waited. It was going to take a long time to go through all forty electrodes, but it was fascinating to watch. They produced such strikingly different effects, yet each electrode was very close to the next. It was the ultimate proof of the density of the brain, which had once been described as the most complex structure in the known universe. And it was certainly true: there were three times as many cells packed into a single human brain as there were human beings on the face of the earth. That density was hard to comprehend, sometimes. Early in his NPS career, Gerhard had requested a human brain to dissect. He had done it over a period of several days, with a dozen neuroanatomy texts opened up before him. He used the traditional tool for brain dissection, a blunt wooden stick, to scrape away the cheesy gray material. He had patiently, carefully scraped away—and in the end, he had nothing. The brain was not like the liver or the lungs. To the naked eye, it was uniform and boring, giving no indication of its true function. The brain was too subtle, too complex. Too dense.

"Electrode four," Richards said into the recorder. "Five millivolts, five seconds." The shock was delivered.

And Benson, in an oddly childlike voice, said, "Could I have some milk and cookies, please?"

"That's interesting," Gerhard said, watching the reaction.

Richards nodded. "How old would you say?"

"About five or six, at most."

Benson was talking about cookies, talking about his tricycle, to Ross. Slowly, over the next few minutes, he seemed to emerge like a time-traveler advancing through the years. Finally he became fully adult again, thinking back to his youth, instead of actually being there. "I always wanted the cookies, and she would never give them to me. She said they were bad for me and would give me cavities."

"We can go on," Gerhard said.

Richards said, "Electrode five, five millivolts, five seconds."

In the next room, Benson shifted uncomfortably in his wheelchair. Ross asked him if something was wrong. Benson said, "It feels funny."

"How do you mean?"

"I can't describe it. It's like sandpaper. Irritating."

Gerhard nodded, and wrote in his notes, "#5—potential attack electrode." This happened sometimes. Occasionally an electrode would be found to stimulate a seizure. Nobody knew why—and Gerhard personally thought that nobody ever would. The brain was, he believed, beyond comprehension.

His work with programs like George and Martha had led him to understand that relatively simple computer instructions could produce complex and unpredictable machine behavior. It was also true that the programmed machine could exceed the capabilities of the programmer; that was clearly demonstrated in 1963 when Arthur Samuel at IBM programmed a machine to play checkers—and the machine eventually became so good that it beat Samuel himself.

Yet all this was done with computers which had no more circuits than the brain of an ant. The human brain far exceeded that complexity, and the programming of the human brain extended over many decades. How could anyone seriously expect to understand it?

There was also a philosophical problem. Goedel's Theorem: that no system could explain itself, and no machine could understand its own workings. At most, Gerhard believed that a human brain might, after years of work, decipher a frog brain. But a human brain could never decipher itself in the same detail. For that you would need a superhuman brain.

Gerhard thought that someday a computer would be developed that could untangle the billions of cells and hundreds of billions of interconnections in the human brain. Then, at last, man would have the information that he wanted. But man wouldn't have done the work—another order of intelligence would have done it. And man would not know, of course, how the computer worked.

Morris entered the room with a cup of coffee. He sipped it, and glanced at Benson through the glass. "How's he holding up?"

"Okay," Gerhard said.

"Electrode six, five and five," Richards intoned.

In the next room, Benson failed to react. He sat talking with Ross about the operation, and his lingering headache. He was quite calm and apparently unaffected. They repeated the stimulation, still without change in Benson's behavior. Then they went on.

"Electrode seven, five and five," Richards said. He delivered the shock.

Benson sat up abruptly. "Oh," he said, "that was nice."

"What was?" Ross said.

"You can do that again if you want to."

"How does it feel?"

"Nice," Benson said. His whole appearance seemed to change subtly. "You know," he said after a moment, "you're really a wonderful person, Dr. Ross."

"Thank you," she said.

"Very attractive, too. I don't know if I ever told you before."

"How do you feel now?"

"I'm really very fond of you," Benson said. "I don't know if I told you that before."

"Nice," Gerhard said, watching through the glass. "Very nice."

Morris nodded. "A strong P-terminal. He's clearly turned on."

Gerhard made a note of it. Morris sipped his coffee. They waited until Benson settled down. Then, blandly, Richards said, "Electrode eight, five millivolts, five seconds."

The stimulation series continued.

2

AT NOON, MCPHERSON SHOWED UP TO SUPER-vise interfacing. No one was surprised to see him. In a sense, this was the irrevocable step; everything preceding it was unimportant. They had implanted electrodes and a computer and a power pack, and they had hooked everything up. But nothing functioned until the interfacing switches were thrown. It was a little like building an automobile and then finally turning the ignition.

Gerhard showed him notes from the stimulation series. "At five millivolts on a pulse-form stimulus, we have three positive terminals and two negatives. The positives are seven, nine, and thirty-one. The negatives are five and thirty-two."

McPherson glanced at the notes, then looked through the one-way glass at Benson. "Are any of the positives true P's?"

"Seven seems to be."

"Strong?"

"Pretty strong. When we stimulated him, he said he liked it, and he began to act sexually aroused toward Jan."

"Is it too strong? Will it tip him over?"

Gerhard shook his head. "No," he said. "Not unless he were to receive multiple stimulations over a short time course. There was that Norwegian . . ."

"I don't think we have to worry about that," McPherson said. "We've got Benson in the hospital for the next few days. If anything seems to be going wrong, we can switch to other electrodes. We'll just keep track of him for a while. What about nine?"

"Very weak. Equivocal, really."

"How did he respond?"

"There was a subtle increase in spontaneity, more tendency to smile, to tell happy and positive anecdotes."

McPherson seemed unimpressed. "And thirty-one?"

"Clear tranquilizing effect. Calmness, relaxation, happiness."

McPherson rubbed his hands together. "I guess we can get on with it," he said. He looked once through the glass at Benson, and said, "Interface the patient with seven and thirty-one."

McPherson was clearly feeling a sense of high drama and medical history. Gerhard got off his stool and walked to a corner of the room where there was a computer console mounted beneath a TV screen. He began to touch the buttons. The TV screen glowed to life. After a moment, letters appeared on it.

BENSON, H. F.
INTERFACING PROCEDURE
POSSIBLE ELECTRODES: 40, designated serially
POSSIBLE VOLTAGES: continuous
POSSIBLE DURATIONS: continuous
POSSIBLE WAVE FORMS: pulse only

Gerhard pressed a button and the screen went blank. Then a series of questions appeared, to which Gerhard typed out the answers on the console.

INTERFACE PROCEDURES BENSON, H. F.
1. WHICH ELECTRODES WILL BE ACTIVATED?

7, 31 ONLY

2. WHAT VOLTAGE WILL BE APPLIED TO ELECTRODE SEVEN?

5 MV

3. WHAT DURATION WILL BE APPLIED TO ELECTRODE SEVEN?

5 SEC

There was a pause, and the questions continued for electrode 31. Gerhard typed in the answers. Watching him, McPherson said to Morris, "This is amusing, in a way. We're telling the tiny computer how to work. The little computer gets its instructions from the big computer, which gets its instructions from Gerhard, who has a bigger computer than any of them."

"Maybe," Gerhard said, and laughed.

The screen glowed:

INTERFACING PARAMETERS STORED. READY TO PROGRAM AUXILIARY UNIT.

Morris sighed. He hoped that he would never reach the point in his life when he was referred to by a computer as an "auxiliary unit." Gerhard typed quietly, a soft clicking sound. On the other TV screens, they could see the inner circuitry of the small computer. It glowed intermittently as the wiring locked in.

BENSON HF HAS BEEN INTERFACED. IMPLANTED DEVICE NOW READING EEG DATA AND DELIVERING APPROPRIATE FEEDBACK.

That was all there was to it. Somehow Morris was disappointed; he knew it would be this way, but he had expected—or needed—something more dramatic. Gerhard ran a systems check which came back negative. The screen went blank and then came through with a final message:

UNIVERSITY HOSPITAL SYSTEM 360 COMPUTER THANKS YOU FOR REFERRING THIS INTERESTING PATIENT FOR THERAPY.

Gerhard smiled. In the next room, Benson was still talking quietly with Ross. Neither of them seemed to have noticed anything different at all.

3

JANET ROSS FINISHED THE STIMULATION SERIES profoundly depressed. She stood in the corridor watching as Benson was wheeled away. She had a last glimpse of the white bandages around his neck as the nurse turned the corner; then he was gone.

She walked down the hallway in the other direction, through the multicolored NPS doors. For some reason, she found herself thinking about Arthur's yellow Ferrari. It was so marvelous and elegant and irrelevant to anything. The perfect toy. She wished she were in Monte Carlo, stepping out of Arthur's Ferrari wearing her Balenciaga gown, going up the stairs to the casino to gamble with nothing more important than money.

She looked at her watch. Christ, it was only 12:15. She had half the day ahead of her. What was it like to be a pediatrician? Probably fun. Tickling babies and giving shots and advising mothers on toilet training. Not a bad way to live.

She thought again of the bandages on Benson's shoulder, and went into Telecomp. She had hoped to speak to Gerhard alone, but instead everyone was in the room—McPherson, Morris, Ellis, everyone. They were all jubilant, toasting each other with coffee in Styrofoam cups.

Someone thrust a cup into her hands, and McPherson put his arm around her in a fatherly way. "I gather we turned Benson on to you today."

"Yes, you did," she said, managing to smile.

"Well, I guess you're used to that."

"Not exactly," she said.

The room got quieter, the festive feeling slid away. She felt bad about that, but not really. There was nothing amusing about shocking a person into sexual arousal. It was physiologically interesting, was frightening and pathetic, but not funny. Why did they all find it so goddamned funny?

Ellis produced a hip flask and poured clear liquid into her coffee. "Makes it Irish," he said, with a wink. "Much better."

She nodded, and glanced across the room at Gerhard.

"Drink up, drink up," Ellis said.

Gerhard was talking to Morris about something. It seemed a very intent conversation; then she heard Morris say, " . . . you please pass the pussy?" Gerhard laughed; Morris laughed. It was some kind of joke.

"Not bad, considering," Ellis said. "What do you think?"

"Very good," she said, taking a small sip. She managed to get away from Ellis and McPherson and went over to Gerhard. He was momentarily alone; Morris had gone off to refill his cup.

"Listen," she said, "can I talk to you for a second?"

"Sure," Gerhard said. He bent his head closer to hers. "What is it?"

"I want to know something. Is it possible for you to monitor Benson here, on the main computer?"

"You mean monitor the implanted unit?"

"Yes."

Gerhard shrugged. "I guess so, but why bother? We know the implanted unit is working—"

"I know," she said. "I know. But will you do it anyway, as a precaution?"

Gerhard said nothing. His eyes said: Precaution against what?

"Please?"

"Okay," he said. "I'll punch in a monitoring sub-routine as soon as they leave." He nodded to the group. "I'll have the computer check on him twice an hour."

She frowned.

"Four times an hour?"

"How about every ten minutes?" she said.

"Okay," he said. "Every ten minutes."

"Thanks," she said. Then she drained her coffee, and left the room.

4

ELLIS SAT IN A CORNER OF ROOM 710 AND watched the half-dozen technicians maneuvering around the bed. There were two people from the rad lab doing a radiation check; there was one girl drawing blood for the chem lab, to check steroid levels; there was an EEG technician resetting the monitors; and there were Gerhard and Richards, taking a final look at the interface wiring.

Throughout it all, Benson lay motionless, breathing easily, staring up at the ceiling. He did not seem to notice the people touching him, moving an arm here, shifting a sheet there. He stared straight up at the ceiling.

One of the rad-lab men had hairy hands protruding from the cuffs of his white lab coat. For a moment, the man rested his hairy dark hand on Benson's bandages. Ellis thought about the monkeys he had operated on. There was nothing to that except technical expertise, because you always knew—no matter how hard you pretended—that it was a monkey and not a human being, and if you slipped and cut the monkey from ear to ear, it didn't matter at all. There would be no questions, no relatives, no lawyers, no press, no nothing—not even a nasty note from Requisitions asking what was happening to all those eighty-dollar monkeys. Nobody gave a damn. And neither did he. He wasn't interested in helping monkeys. He was interested in helping human beings.

Benson stirred. "I'm tired," he said. He glanced over at Ellis.

Ellis said, "About ready to wrap it up, boys?"

One by one, the technicians stepped back from the bed, nodding, collected their instruments and their data, and left the room. Gerhard and Richards were the last to go. Finally Ellis was alone with Benson.

"You feel like sleeping?" Ellis said.

"I feel like a goddamned machine. I feel like an automobile in a complicated service station. I feel like I'm being *repaired*."

Benson was getting angry. Ellis could feel his own tension building. He was tempted to call for nurses and orderlies to restrain Benson when the attack came. But he remained seated.

"That's a lot of crap," Ellis said.

Benson glared at him, breathing deeply.

Ellis looked at the monitors over the bed. The brain waves were going irregular, moving into an attack configuration.

Benson wrinkled his nose and sniffed. "What's that smell?" he said. "That awful—"

Above the bed, a red monitor light blinked STIMU-LATION. The brain waves spun in a distorted tangle of white lines for five seconds. Simultaneously, Benson's pupils dilated. Then the lines were smooth again; the pupils returned to normal size.

Benson turned away, staring out the window at the afternoon sun. "You know," he said, "it's really a very nice day, isn't it?"

5

FOR NO PARTICULAR REASON, JANET ROSS came back to the hospital at 11 p.m. She had gone to see a movie with a pathology resident who had been asking her for weeks; finally she had relented. They had seen a murder mystery, which the resident claimed was the only kind of movie he attended. This one featured five murders before she stopped counting them. In the darkness, she had glanced at the resident, and he was smiling. His reaction was so stereotyped—the pathologist drawn to violence and death—that she found herself thinking of the other stereotypes in medicine: the sadistic surgeons and the childish pediatricians and the woman-hating gynecologists. And the crazy psychiatrists.

Afterward, he had driven her back to the hospital because she had left her car in the hospital parking lot. But instead of driving home she had gone up to the NPS. For no particular reason.

The NPS was deserted, but she expected to find Gerhard and Richards at work, and they were, poring over computer print-outs in Telecomp. They hardly noticed when she came into the room and got herself some coffee. "Trouble?" she said.

Gerhard scratched his head. "Now it's Martha," he said. "First George refuses to be a saint. Now Martha is becoming nice. Everything's screwed up."

Richards smiled. "You have your patients, Jan," he said, "and we have ours."

"Speaking of my patient . . ."

"Of course," Gerhard said, getting up and walking over to the computer console. "I was wondering why you came in." He smiled. "Or was it just a bad date?"

"Just a bad movie," she said.

Gerhard punched buttons on the console. Letters and numbers began to print out. "Here's all the checks since I started it at one-twelve this afternoon."

01:12	NORMAL EEG	04:22	NORMAL EEG
01:22	NORMAL EEG	04:32	SLEEP EEG
01:32	SLEEP EEG	04:42	NORMAL EEG
01:42	SLEEP EEG	04:52	NORMAL EEG
01:52	NORMAL EEG	05:02	SLEEP EEG
02:02	NORMAL EEG	05:12	NORMAL EEG
02:12	NORMAL EEG	05:22	NORMAL EEG
02:22	NORMAL EEG	05:32	SLEEP EEG
02:32	SLEEP EEG	05:42	NORMAL EEG
02:42	NORMAL EEG	05:52	NORMAL EEG
02:52	NORMAL EEG	06:02	NORMAL EEG
03:02	NORMAL EEG	06:12	NORMAL EEG
03:12	SLEEP EEG	06:22	NORMAL EEG
03:22	SLEEP EEG	06:32	NORMAL EEG
03:32	STIMULATION	06:42	NORMAL EEG
03:42	NORMAL EEG	06:52	STIMULATION
03:52	SLEEP EEG	07:02	NORMAL EEG
04:02	NORMAL EEG	07:12	NORMAL EEG
04:12	NORMAL EEG	07:22	SLEEP EEG

07:32	SLEEP EEG	09:22	NORMAL EEG
07:42	SLEEP EEG	09:32	NORMAL EEG
07:52	NORMAL EEG	09:42	NORMAL EEG
08:02	NORMAL EEG	09:52	NORMAL EEG
08:12	NORMAL EEG	10:02	NORMAL EEG
08:22	SLEEP EEG	10:12	NORMAL EEG
08:32	NORMAL EEG	10:22	NORMAL EEG
08:42	NORMAL EEG	10:32	STIMULATION
08:52	NORMAL EEG	10:42	SLEEP EEG
09:02	STIMULATION	10:52	NORMAL EEG
09:12	SLEEP EEG	11:02	NORMAL EEG

"I can't make anything out of this," Ross said, frowning. "It looks like he's dozing on and off, and he's gotten a couple of stimulations, but . . ." She shook her head. "Isn't there another display mode?"

As she spoke, the computer produced another report, adding it to the column of numbers:

11:12   NORMAL EEG

"People," Gerhard said, in mock irritation. "They just can't handle machine data." It was true. Machines could handle column after column of numbers. People needed to see patterns. On the other hand, machines were very poor at recognizing patterns. The classic problem was trying to get a machine to differentiate between the letter "B" and the letter "D." A child could do it; it was almost impossible for a machine to look at the two patterns and discern the difference.

"I'll give you a graphic display," Gerhard said. He punched buttons, wiping the screen. After a moment,

cross-hatching for a graph appeared, and the points began to blink on:

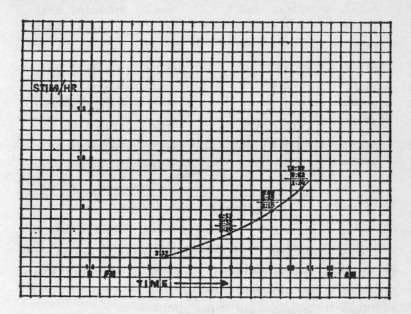

"Damn," she said when she saw the graph.

"What's the matter?" Gerhard said.

"He's getting more frequent stimulations. He had
none for a long time, and then he began to have them
every couple of hours. Now it looks like one an hour."

"So?" Gerhard said.

"What does that suggest to you?" she said.

"Nothing in particular."

"It should suggest something quite specific," she
said. "We know that Benson's brain will be interacting
with the computer, right?"

"Yes . . ."

"And that interaction will be a learning pattern of some
kind. It's just like a kid with a cookie jar. If you slap the

kid's hand every time he reaches for the cookies, pretty soon he won't reach so often. Look." She drew a quick sketch.

"Now," she said, "that's negative reinforcement. The kid reaches, but he gets hurt. So he stops reaching. Eventually he'll quit altogether. Okay?"

"Sure," Gerhard said, "but—"

"Let me finish. If the kid is normal, it works that way. But if the kid is a masochist, it will be very different." She drew another curve.

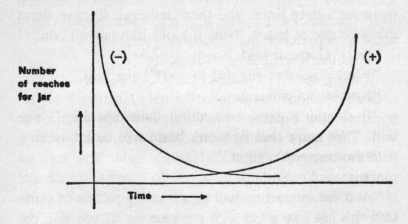

"Here the kid is reaching more often for the cookies, because he likes getting hit. It should be negative reinforcement, but it's really positive reinforcement. Do you remember Cecil?"

"No," Gerhard said.

On the computer console, a new report appeared:

11:22 STIMULATION

"Oh shit," she said. "It's happening."

"What's happening?"

"Benson is going into a positive progression cycle."

"I don't understand."

"It's just like Cecil. Cecil was the first monkey to be wired with electrodes to a computer. That was back in '65. The computer wasn't miniaturized then; it was a big clunky computer, and the monkey was wired up by actual wires. The computer detected the start of a seizure in Cecil, and delivered a counter-shock to stop it. Okay. Now the seizures should have come less and less frequently, like the hand reaching for the cookies less and less often. But instead the reverse happened. Cecil liked the shocks. And he began to initiate seizures in order to experience the pleasurable shocks."

"And that's what Benson is doing?"

"I think so."

Gerhard shook his head. "Listen, Jan, that's all interesting. But a person can't start and stop seizures at will. They can't control them. The seizures are—"

"Involuntary," she said. "That's right. You have no more control over them than you do over heart rate and blood pressure and sweating and all the other involuntary acts."

There was a long pause. Gerhard said, "You're going to tell me I'm wrong."

On the screen, the computer blinked:

11:32 ------

"I'm going to tell you," she said, "that you've cut too many conferences. You know about autonomic learning?"

After a guilty pause: "No."

"It was a big mystery for a long time. Classically, it was believed that you could learn to control only voluntary acts. You could learn to drive a car, but you couldn't learn to lower your blood pressure. Of course, there were those yogis who supposedly could reduce oxygen requirements of their body and slow their heartbeats to near death. They could reverse intestinal peristalsis and drink liquids through the anus. But that was all unproven—and theoretically impossible."

Gerhard nodded cautiously.

"Well, it turns out to be perfectly possible. You can teach a rat to blush in only one ear. Right ear or left ear, take your pick. You can teach it to lower or raise blood pressure or heartbeat. And you can do the same thing with people. It's not impossible. It can be done."

"How?" He asked the question with unabashed curiosity. Whatever embarrassment he had felt before was gone.

"Well, with people who have high blood pressure, for instance, all you do is put them in a room with a blood-pressure cuff on their arm. Whenever the blood pressure goes down, a bell rings. You tell the person to try to make the bell ring as often as possible They work for that reward—a bell ringing. At first it happens by accident. Then pretty soon they learn how to make it happen more often. The bell rings more frequently. After a few hours, it's ringing a lot.''

Gerhard scratched his head. "And you think Benson is producing more seizures to be rewarded with shocks?''

"Yes.''

"Well, what's the difference? He still can't have any seizures. The computer always prevents them from happening.''

"Not true,'' she said. "A couple of years ago, a Norwegian schizophrenic was wired up and allowed to stimulate a pleasure terminal as often as he wanted. He pushed himself into a convulsion by overstimulating himself.''

Gerhard winced.

Richards, who had been watching the computer console, suddenly said, "Something's wrong.''

"What is it?''

"We're not getting readings any more.''

On the screen, they saw:

11:32 ------
11:42 ------

Ross looked and sighed. "See if you can get a computer extrapolation of that curve,'' she said. "See if he's really going into a learning cycle, and how fast.'' She started for the door. "I'm going to see what's happened to Benson.''

FRIDAY, MARCH 12, 1971:

Breakdown

1

THE SEVENTH (SPECIAL SURGICAL) FLOOR WAS quiet; there were two nurses at the station. One was making progress notes in a patient's chart; the other was eating a candy bar and reading a movie magazine. Neither paid much attention to Ross as she went to the chart shelf, opened Benson's record, and checked it.

She wanted to be certain that Benson had received all his medications, and to her astonishment she found that he had not. "Why hasn't Benson gotten his thorazine?" she demanded.

The nurses looked up in surprise. "Benson?"

"The patient in seven-ten." She glanced at her watch; it was after midnight. "He was supposed to be started on thorazine at noon. Twelve hours ago."

"I'm sorry . . . may I?" One of the nurses reached for the chart. Ross handed it to her and watched while she turned to the page of nursing orders. McPherson's order for thorazine was circled in red by a nurse, with the cryptic notation "Call."

Ross was thinking that without heavy doses of thorazine Benson's psychotic thinking would be unchecked, and could be dangerous.

"Oh, yes," the nurse said. "I remember now. Dr.

137

Morris told us that only medication orders from him or
from Dr. Ross were to be followed. We don't know this
Dr. McPhee, so we waited to call him to confirm the
therapy. It—''

"Dr. Mc*Pherson*," Ross said heavily, "is the chief
of the NPS.''

The nurse frowned at the signature. "Well, how are
we supposed to know that? You can't read the name.
Here.'' She handed back the chart. "We thought it
looked like McPhee, and the only McPhee in the hospital directory is a gynecologist and that didn't seem
logical, but sometimes doctors will put a note in the
wrong chart by mistake, so we—''

"All right," Ross said, waving her hand. "All right.
Just get him his thorazine now, will you?''

"Right away, Doctor," the nurse said. She gave her
a dirty look and went to the medicine locker. Ross went
down the hall to Room 710.

The cop sat outside Benson's room with his chair
tipped back against the wall. He was reading *Secret
Romances* with more interest than Ross would have
thought likely. She knew without asking where he had
gotten the magazine; he had been bored, one of the
nurses had given it to him. He was also smoking a cigarette, flicking the ashes in the general direction of an
ashtray on the floor.

He looked up as she came down the hall. "Good
evening, Doctor.''

"Good evening.'' She stifled an impulse to lecture
him on his sloppy demeanor. But the cops weren't under her jurisdiction, and besides, she was just irritated
with the nurses. "Everything quiet?'' she asked.

"Pretty quiet."

Inside 710 she could hear television, a talk show with laughter. Someone said, "And what did you do then?" There was more laughter. She opened the door.

The room lights were off; the only light came from the glow of the television. Benson had apparently fallen asleep; his body was turned away from the door, and the sheets were pulled up over his shoulder. She clicked the television off and crossed the room to the bed. Gently, she touched his leg.

"Harry," she said softly. "Harry—"

She stopped.

The leg beneath her hand was soft and formless. She pressed down; the "leg" bulged oddly. She reached for the bedside lamp and turned it on, flooding the room with light. Then she pulled back the sheets.

Benson was gone. In his place were three plastic bags of the kind the hospital used to line wastebaskets. Each had been inflated and then knotted shut tightly. Benson's head was represented by a wadded towel; his arm by another.

"Officer," she said, in a low voice, "you'd better get your ass in here."

The cop came bounding into the room, his hand reaching for his gun. Ross gestured to the bed.

"Holy shit," the cop said. "What happened?"

"I was going to ask you."

The cop went immediately to the bathroom and checked there; it was empty. He looked in the closet. "His clothes are still here—"

"When was the last time you looked into this room?"

"—but his shoes are gone," the cop said, still looking in the closet. "His shoes are missing." He turned and looked at Ross with a kind of desperation. "Where is he?"

"When was the last time you looked into this room?" Ross repeated. She pressed the bedside buzzer to call the night nurse.

"About twenty minutes ago."

Ross walked to the window and looked out. The window was open, but there was a sheer drop of seven stories to the parking lot below. "How long were you away from the door?"

"Look, Doc, it was only a few minutes—"

"How long?"

"I ran out of cigarettes. The hospital doesn't have any machines. I had to go to that coffee shop across the street. I was gone about three minutes. That was around eleven-thirty. The nurses said they'd keep an eye on things."

"Great," Ross said. She checked the bedside table and saw that Benson's shaving equipment was there, his wallet, his car keys . . . all there.

The nurse stuck her head in the door, answering the call. "What is it now?"

"We seem to be missing a patient," Ross said.

"I beg your pardon?"

Ross gestured to the plastic bags in the bed. The nurse reacted slowly, and then turned quite pale.

"Call Dr. Ellis," Ross said, "and Dr. McPherson and Dr. Morris. They'll be at home; have the switchboard put you through. Say it's an emergency. Tell them Benson is gone. Then call hospital security. Is that clear?"

"Yes, Doctor," the nurse said, and hurried from the room.

Ross sat down on the edge of Benson's bed and turned her attention to the cop.

"Where did he get those bags?" the cop said.

She had already figured that out. "One from the bed-side wastebasket," she said. "One from the wastebasket by the door. One from the bathroom wastebasket. Two towels from the bathroom."

"Clever," the cop said. He pointed to the closet. "But he can't get far. He left his clothes."

"Took his shoes."

"A man with bandages and a bathrobe can't get far, even if he has shoes." He shook his head. "I better call this in."

"Did Benson make any calls?"

"Tonight?"

"No, last month."

"Look, lady, I don't need any of your lip right now."

She saw then that he was really quite young, in his early twenties, and that he was afraid. He had screwed up, and he didn't know what would happen. "I'm sorry" she said. "Yes, tonight."

"He made one call," the cop said. "About eleven."

"Did you listen to it?"

"No." He shrugged. "I never thought . . ." His voice trailed off. "You know."

"So he made one call at eleven, and left at eleven-thirty." She walked outside to the hallway and looked down the corridor to the nurses' station. There was al-ways somebody on duty there, and he would have to pass the nurses' station to reach the elevator. He'd never make it.

What else could he have done? She looked toward the other end of the hall. There was a stairway at the far end. He could walk down. But seven flights of stairs? Benson was too weak for that. And when he got to the ground-floor lobby, there he'd be, in his bathrobe with his head bandaged. The reception desk would stop him.

"I don't get it," the cop said, coming out into the hallway. "Where could he go?"

"He's a very bright man," Ross said. It was a fact that they all tended to forget. To the cops, Benson was a criminal charged with assault, one of the hundreds of querulous types they saw each day. To the hospital staff, he was a diseased man, unhappy, dangerous, borderline psychotic. Everyone tended to forget that Benson was also brilliant. His computer work was outstanding in a field where many intelligent men worked. On the initial psychological testing at the NPS, his abbreviated WAIS I.Q. test had scored 144. He was fully capable of planning to leave, then listening at the door, hearing the cop and the nurse discuss going for cigarettes—and then making his escape in a matter of minutes. But how?

Benson must have known that he could never get out of the hospital in his bathrobe. He had left his street clothes in his room—he probably couldn't get out wearing those, either. Not at midnight. The lobby desk would have stopped him. Visiting hours had ended three hours before.

What the hell would he do?

The cop went up to the nurses' station to phone in a report. Ross followed along behind him, looking at the doors. Room 709 was a burns patient; she opened the door and looked inside, making sure only the patient was there. Room 708 was empty; a kidney-transplant patient had been discharged that afternoon. She checked that room, too.

The next door was marked SUPPLIES. It was a standard room on surgical floors. Bandages, suture kits, and linen supplies were stored there. She opened the door and went inside. She passed row after row of bottled intravenous solutions; then trays of different kits. Then sterile masks, smocks, spare uniforms for nurses and orderlies—

She stopped. She was staring at a blue bathrobe, hastily wadded into a corner on a shelf. The rest of the shelf contained neatly folded piles of white trousers, shirts, and jackets worn by hospital orderlies.

She called for the nurse.

"It's impossible," Ellis said, pacing up and down in the nurses' station. "Absolutely impossible. He's two days—a day and a half—post-op. He couldn't possibly leave."

"He did," Janet Ross said. "And he did it the only way he could, by changing into an orderly's uniform. Then he probably walked downstairs to the sixth floor and took an elevator to the lobby. Nobody would have noticed him; orderlies come and go at all hours."

Ellis wore a dinner jacket and a white frilly shirt; his bow tie was loosened and he was smoking a cigarette. She had never seen him smoke before. "I still don't buy it," he said. "He was tranked heavily with thorazine, and—"

"Never got it," Ross said.

"Never got it?"

"What's thorazine?" the cop said, taking notes.

"The nurses had a question on the order and didn't administer it. He had no sedatives and no tranquilizers since midnight last night."

"Christ," Ellis said. He looked at the nurses as if he could kill them. Then he paused. "But what about his head? It was covered with bandages. Someone would notice that."

Morris, who had been sitting silently in a corner, said, "He had a wig."

"You're kidding."

"I saw it," Morris said.

"What was the color of the wig in question?" the cop said.

"Black," Morris said.

"Oh Christ," Ellis said.

Ross said, "How did he get this wig?"

"A friend brought it to him. The day of admission."

"Listen," Ellis said, "even with a wig, he can't have gotten anywhere. He left his wallet and his money. There are no taxis at this hour."

She looked at Ellis, marveling at his ability to deny reality. He just didn't want to believe that Benson had left; he was fighting the evidence, fighting hard.

"He called a friend," Ross said, "about eleven." She looked at Morris. "You remember who brought the wig?"

"A pretty girl," Morris said.

"Do you remember her name?" Ross said, with a sarcastic edge.

"Angela Black," Morris said promptly.

"See if you can find her in the phone book," Ross said. Morris began to check; the phone rang, and Ellis answered it. He listened, then without comment handed the phone to Ross.

"Yes," Ross said.

"I've done the computer projection." Gerhard said.

"It just came through. You were right. Benson is on a learning cycle with his implanted computer. His stimulation points conform to the projected curve exactly."

"That's wonderful," Ross said. As she listened, she glanced at Ellis, Morris, and the cop. They watched her expectantly.

"It's exactly what you said," Gerhard said. "Benson apparently likes the shocks. He's starting seizures more and more often. The curve is going up sharply."

"When will he tip over?"

"Not long," Gerhard said. "Assuming that he doesn't break the cycle—and I doubt that he will—then he'll be getting almost continuous stimulations at six-four a.m."

"You have a confirmed projection on that?" she asked, frowning. She glanced at her watch. It was already 12:30.

"That's right," Gerhard said. "Continuous stimulations starting at six-four this morning."

"Okay," Ross said, and hung up. She looked at the others. "Benson has gone into a learning progression with his computer. He's projected for tipover at six a.m. today."

"Christ," Ellis said, looking at the wall clock. "Less than six hours from now."

Across the room, Morris had put aside the phone books and was talking to Information. "Then try West Los Angeles," he said, and after a pause, "What about new listings?"

The cop stopped taking notes, and looked confused. "Is something going to happen at six o'clock?"

"We think so," Ross said.

Ellis puffed on his cigarette. "Two years," he said,

"and I'm back on them." He stubbed it out carefully.
"Has McPherson been notified?"

"He's been called."

"Check unlisted numbers," Morris said. He listened
for a moment. "This is Dr. Morris at University Hospital," he said, "and it's an emergency. We have to
locate Angela Black. Now, if—" Angrily, he slammed
down the phone. "Bitch," he said.

"Any luck?"

He shook his head.

"We don't even know if Benson called this girl,"
Ellis said. "He could have called someone else."

"Whoever he called may be in a lot of trouble in a
few hours," Ross said. She flipped open Benson's chart.
"It looks like a long night. We'd better get busy."

2

THE FREEWAY WAS CROWDED. THE FREEWAY
was always crowded, even at 1 a.m. on a Friday morning. She stared ahead at the pattern of red tail-lights,
stretching ahead like an angry snake for miles. So many
people. Where were they going at this hour?

Janet Ross usually took pleasure in the freeways.
There had been times when she had driven home from
the hospital at night, with the big green signs flashing

past overhead, and the intricate web of overpasses and underpasses, and the exhilarating anonymous speed, and she had felt wonderful, expansive, free. She had been raised in California, and as a child she remembered the first of the freeways. The system had grown up as she had grown, and she did not see it as a menace or an evil. It was part of the landscape; it was fast; it was fun.

The automobile was important to Los Angeles, a city more technology-dependent than any in the world. Los Angeles could not survive without the automobile, as it could not survive without water piped in from hundreds of miles away, and as it could not survive without certain building technologies. This was a fact of the city's existence, and had been true since early in the century.

But in recent years Ross had begun to recognize the subtle psychological effects of living your life inside an automobile. Los Angeles had no sidewalk cafés, because no one walked; the sidewalk café, where you could stare at passing people, was not stationary but mobile. It changed with each traffic light, where people stopped, stared briefly at each other, then drove on. But there was something inhuman about living inside a cocoon of tinted glass and stainless steel, air-conditioned, carpeted, stereophonic tape-decked, power-optioned, isolated. It thwarted some deep human need to congregate, to be together, to see and be seen.

Local psychiatrists recognized an indigenous depersonalization syndrome. Los Angeles was a town of recent emigrants and therefore strangers; cars kept them strangers, and there were few institutions that served to bring them together. Practically no one went to church, and work groups were not entirely satisfactory. People became lonely; they complained of being cut off, without friends, far from families and old homes. Often they became suicidal—and a common method of suicide was the automobile. The police referred to it euphemistically as "single unit fatalities." You picked your overpass, and hit it at eighty or ninety, foot flat to the floor. Sometimes it took hours to cut the body out of the wreckage. . . .

Moving at sixty-five miles an hour, she shifted across five lanes of traffic and pulled off the freeway at Sunset, heading up into the Hollywood Hills, through an area known locally as the Swish Alps because of the many homosexuals who lived there. People with problems seemed drawn to Los Angeles. The city offered freedom; its price was lack of supports.

She came to Laurel Canyon and took the curves fast, tires squealing, headlamps swinging through the darkness. There was little traffic here; she would reach Benson's house in a few minutes.

In theory, she and the rest of the NPS staff had a simple problem: get Benson back before six o'clock. If they could get him back into the hospital, they could uncouple his implanted computer and stop the progression series. Then they could sedate him and wait a few days before relinking him to a new set of terminals. They'd obviously chosen the wrong electrodes the first time around; that was a risk they accepted in advance. It was an acceptable risk because they expected to have a chance to correct any error. But that opportunity was no longer there.

They had to get him back. A simple problem, with a relatively simple solution—check Benson's known haunts. After reviewing his chart, they'd all set out to different places. Ross was going to his house on Laurel. Ellis was going to a strip joint called the Jackrabbit Club, where Benson often went. Morris was going to Autotronics, Inc., in Santa Monica, where Benson was employed; Morris had called the president of the firm, who was coming to the offices to open them up for him.

They would check back in an hour or so to compare notes and progress. A simple plan, and one she thought unlikely to work. But there wasn't much else to do.

She parked her car in front of Benson's house and walked up the slate path to the front door. It was ajar; from inside she could hear the sound of laughter and giggles. She knocked and pushed it open.

"Hello?"

No one seemed to hear. The giggles came from somewhere at the back of the house. She stepped into the front hallway. She had never seen Benson's house, and she wondered what it was like.

Looking around, she realized she should have known.

From the outside, the house was an ordinary ranch-style house as unremarkable in its appearance as Benson himself. But the inside looked like the drawing rooms of Louis XVI—graceful antique chairs and couches, tapestries on the walls, bare hardwood floors.

"Anybody home?" she called. Her voice echoed through the house. There was no answer, but the laughter continued. She followed the sound toward the rear. She came into the kitchen—antique gas stove, no oven, no dishwasher, no electric blender, no toaster. No machines, she thought. Benson had built himself a world without any sort of modern machine in it.

The kitchen window looked out onto the back of the

house. There was a small patch of lawn and a swimming pool, all perfectly ordinary and modern, Benson's ordinary exterior again. The back yard was bathed in greenish light from the underwater pool lights. In the pool, two girls were laughing and splashing. She went outside.

The girls were oblivious to her arrival. They continued to splash and shriek happily; they wrestled with each other in the water. She stood on the pool deck and said, "Anybody home?"

They noticed her then, and moved apart from each other. "Looking for Harry?" one of them said.

"Yes."

"You a cop?"

"I'm a doctor."

One of the girls got out of the pool lithely and began toweling off. She wore a brief red bikini. "You just missed him," the girl said. "But we weren't supposed to tell the cops. That's what he said." She put one leg on a chair to dry it with the towel. Ross realized the move was calculated, seductive, and directed toward her.

"When did he leave?"

"Just a few minutes ago."

"How long have you been here?"

"About a week," the girl in the pool said. "Harry invited us to stay. He thought we were cute."

The other girl wrapped the towel around her shoulders and said, "We met him at the Jackrabbit. He comes there a lot."

Ross nodded.

"He's a lot of fun," the girl said. "A lot of laughs. You know what he was wearing tonight?"

"What?"

"A hospital uniform. All white." She shook her head. "What a riot."

"Did you talk to him?"

"Sure."

"What did he say?"

The girl in the red bikini started back inside the house. Ross followed her. "He said not to tell the cops. He said to have a good time."

"Why did he come here?"

"He had to pick up some stuff."

"What stuff?"

"Some stuff from his study."

"Where is the study?"

"I'll show you."

She led her back into the house, through the living room. Her wet feet left small pools on the bare hardwood floor. "Isn't this place wild? Harry's really crazy. You ever heard him talk about things?"

"Yes."

"Then you know. He's really nutty." She gestured around the room. "All this old stuff. Why do you want to see him?"

"He's sick," Ross said.

"He must be," the girl said. "I saw those bandages. What was he, in an accident?"

"He had an operation."

"No kidding. In a hospital?"

"Yes."

"No kidding."

They went through the living room and down a corridor toward the bedrooms. The girl turned right into one room, which was a study—antique desk, antique lamps, overstuffed couches. "He came in here and got some stuff."

"Did you see what he got?"

"We didn't really pay much attention. But he took some big rolls of paper." She gestured with her hands. "Real big. They looked like blueprints or something."

"Blueprints?"

"Well, they were blue on the inside of the roll, and white on the outside, and they were big." She shrugged.

"Did he take anything else?"

"Yeah. A metal box."

"What kind of a metal box?" Ross was thinking of a lunchbox, or a small suitcase.

"It looked like a tool kit, maybe. I saw it open for a moment, before he closed it. It seemed to have tools and stuff inside."

"Did you notice anything in particular?"

The girl was silent then. She bit her lip. "Well, I didn't really see, but . . ."

"Yes?"

"It looked like he had a gun in there."

"Did he say where he was going?"

"No."

"Did he give any clue?"

"No."

"Did he say he was coming back?"

"Well, that was funny," the girl said. "He kissed me, and he kissed Suzie, and he said to have a good time, and he said not to tell the cops. And he said he didn't think he'd be seeing us again." She shook her head. "It was funny. But you know how Harry is."

"Yes," Ross said. "I know how Harry is." She

looked at her watch. It was 1:47. There were only four
hours left.

3

THE FIRST THING THAT ELLIS NOTICED WAS
the smell: hot, damp, fetid—a dark warm animal smell.
He wrinkled his nose in distaste. How could Benson
tolerate a place like this?

He watched as the spotlight swung through the darkness and came to rest on a pair of long tapering thighs.
There was an expectant rustling in the audience. It reminded Ellis of his days in the Navy, stationed in Bal-
timore. That was the last time he had been in a place
like this, hot and sticky with fantasies and frustrations.
That had been a long time ago. It was a shock to think
how fast the time had passed.

"Yes, ladies and gentlemen, the incredible, the
lovely, *Cynthia Sin*-cere. A big hand for the lovely *Cynthia!*"

The spotlight widened onstage, to show a rather ugly
but spectacularly constructed girl. The band began to
play. When the spotlight was wide enough to hit Cynthia's eyes, she squinted and began an awkward dance.
She paid no attention to the music, but nobody seemed
to mind. Ellis looked at the audience. There were a lot

of men here—and a lot of very tough-looking girls with short hair.

"Harry Benson?" the manager said, at his elbow. "Yeah, he comes in a lot."

"Have you seen him lately?"

"I don't know about lately," the manager said. He coughed. Ellis smelled sweet alcoholic breath. "But I tell you," the manager said, "I wish he wouldn't hang around, you know? I think he's a little nuts. And always bothering the girls. You know how hard it is to keep the girls? Fucking murder, that's what it is."

Ellis nodded, and scanned the audience. Benson had probably changed clothes; certainly he wouldn't be wearing an orderly's uniform any more. Ellis looked at the backs of the heads, at the area between hairline and shirt collar. He looked for a white bandage. He saw none.

"But you haven't seen him lately?"

"No," the manager said, shaking his head. "Not for a week or so." A waitress went by wearing a rabbitlike white fur bikini. "Sal, you seen Harry lately?"

"He's usually around," she said vaguely, and wandered off with a tray of drinks.

"I wish he wouldn't hang around, bothering the girls," the manager said, and coughed again.

Ellis moved deeper into the club. The spotlight swung through smoky air over his head, following the movements of the girl on stage. She was having trouble unhooking her bra. She did a sort of two-step shuffle, hands behind her back, eyes looking vacantly out at the audience. Ellis understood, watching her, why Benson thought of strippers as machines. They were mechanical, no question about it. And artificial—when the bra came off, he could see the U-shaped surgical incision beneath each breast, where the plastic had been inserted.

Jaglon would love this, he thought. It would fit right into his theories about machine sex. Jaglon was one of the Development boys and he was preoccupied with the idea of artificial intelligence merging with human intelligence. He argued that, on the one hand, cosmetic surgery and implanted machinery were making man more mechanical, while on the other hand robot developments were making machines more human. It was only a matter of time before people began having sex with humanoid robots.

Perhaps it's already happening, Ellis thought, looking at the stripper. He looked back at the audience, satisfying himself that Benson was not there. Then he checked a phone booth in the back, and the men's room.

The men's room was small and reeked of vomit. He grimaced again, and stared at himself in the cracked mirror over the washbasin. Whatever else was true about the Jackrabbit Club, it produced an olfactory assault. He wondered if that mattered to Benson.

He went back into the club itself and made his way toward the door. "Find him?" the manager asked.

Ellis shook his head and left. Once outside, he breathed the cool night air, and got into his car. The notion of smells intrigued him. It was a problem he had considered before, but never really resolved in his own mind.

His operation on Benson was directed toward a specific part of the brain, the limbic system. It was a very old part of the brain, in terms of evolution. Its original purpose had been the control of smell. In fact, the old term for it was *rhinencephalon*—the "smelling brain."

The rhinencephalon had developed 150 million years ago, when reptiles ruled the earth. It controlled the most primitive behavior—anger and fear, lust and hunger, attack and withdrawal. Reptiles like crocodiles had little else to direct their behavior. Man, on the other hand, had a cerebral cortex.

But the cerebral cortex was a recent addition. Its modern development had begun only two million years ago; in its present state, the cerebral cortex of man was only 100,000 years old. In terms of evolutionary time scales, that was nothing. The cortex had grown up around the limbic brain, which remained unchanged, embedded deep inside the new cortex. That cortex, which could feel love, and worry about ethical conduct, and write poetry, had to make an uneasy peace with the crocodile brain at its core. Sometimes, as in the case of Benson, the peace broke down, and the crocodile brain took over intermittently.

What was the relationship of smell to all this? Ellis was not sure. Of course, attacks often began with the sensation of strange smells. But was there anything else? Any other effect?

He didn't know, and as he drove he reflected that it didn't much matter. The only problem was to find Benson before his crocodile brain took over. Ellis had seen that happen once, in the NPS. Ellis had watched it through the one-way glass. Benson had been quite normal—and suddenly he had lashed out against the wall, striking it viciously, picking up his chair, smashing it against the wall. The attack had begun without warning, and had been carried out with utter, total, unthinking viciousness.

Six a.m., he thought. There wasn't much time.

4

"WHAT IS IT, SOME KIND OF EMERGENCY?" Farley asked, unlocking the door to Autotronics.

"You could say so," Morris said, standing outside, shivering. It was a cold night, and he had been waiting half an hour. Waiting for Farley to show up.

Farley was a tall, slender man with a slow manner. Or perhaps he was just sleepy. He seemed to take forever to unlock the offices and let Morris inside. He turned on the lights in a rather plain lobby-reception area. Then he went back toward the rear of the building.

The rear of Autotronics was a single cavernous room. Desks were scattered here and there around several pieces of enormous, glittering machinery. Morris frowned slightly.

"I know what you're thinking," Farley said. "You're thinking it's a mess."

"No, I—"

"Well, it is. But we get the job done, I can tell you

that.'' He pointed across the room. ''That's Harry's desk, next to Hap.''

''Hap?''

Farley gestured to a large, spidery metal construction across the room. ''Hap,'' he said, ''is short for Hopelessly Automatic Ping-pong Player.'' He grinned. ''Not really,'' he said. ''But we have our little jokes here.''

Morris walked over to the machine, circled around it, staring. ''It plays ping-pong?''

''Not well,'' Farley admitted. ''But we're working on that. It's a DOD—Department of Defense—grant, and the terms of the grant were to devise a ping-pong-playing robot. I know what you're thinking. You're thinking it isn't an important project.''

Morris shrugged. He didn't like being told what he was thinking all the time.

Farley smiled. ''God knows what they want it for,'' he said. ''Of course, the capability would be striking. Imagine—a computer that could recognize a sphere moving rapidly through three-dimensional space, with the ability to contact the sphere and knock it back according to certain rules. Must land between the white lines, not off the table, and so on. I doubt,'' he said, ''that they'll use it for ping-pong tournaments.''

He went to the back of the room and opened a refrigerator which had a big orange RADIATION sign on it, and beneath, AUTHORIZED PERSONNEL ONLY. He removed two jars. ''Want some coffee?''

Morris was staring at the signs.

''That's just to discourage the secretaries,'' Farley said, and laughed again. His jovial mood bothered Morris. He watched as Farley made instant coffee.

Morris went over to Benson's desk and began checking the drawers.

"What is it about Harry, anyway?"

"How do you mean?" Morris asked. The top drawer contained supplies—paper, pencils, slide rule, scribbled notes and calculations. The second drawer was a file drawer; it seemed to hold mostly letters.

"Well, he was in the hospital, wasn't he?"

"Yes. He had an operation, and left. We're trying to find him now."

"He's certainly gotten strange," Farley said.

"Uh-huh," Morris said. He was thumbing through the files. Business letters, business letters, requisition forms . . .

"I remember when it began," Farley said. "It was during Watershed Week."

Morris looked up from the letters. "During what?"

"Watershed Week," Farley said. "How do you take your coffee?"

"Black."

Farley gave him a cup, stirred artificial cream into his own. "Watershed Week," he said, "was a week in July of 1969. You've probably never heard of it."

Morris shook his head.

"That wasn't an official title," Farley said, "but that was what we called it. Everybody in our business knew it was coming, you see."

"What was coming?"

"The Watershed. Computer scientists all over the world knew it was coming, and they watched for it. It happened in July of 1969. The information-handling capacity of all the computers in the world exceeded the information-handling capacity of all the human brains in the world. Computers could receive and store more information than the 3.5 billion human brains in the world.''

''That's the Watershed?''

''You bet it is,'' Farley said.

Morris sipped the coffee. It burned his tongue, but he woke up a little. ''Is that a joke?''

''Hell, no,'' Farley said. ''It's true. The Watershed was passed in 1969, and computers have been steadily pulling ahead since then. By 1975, they'll lead human beings by fifty to one in terms of capacity.'' He paused. ''Harry was awfully upset about that.''

''I can imagine,'' Morris said.

''And that was when it began for him. He got very strange, very secretive.''

Morris looked around the room, at the large pieces of computer equipment standing in different areas. It was an odd sensation: the first time he could recall being in a room littered with computers. He realized that he had made some mistakes about Benson. He had assumed that Benson was pretty much like everyone else— but no one who worked in a place such as this was like everyone else. The experience must change you. He remembered that Ross had once said that it was a liberal myth that everybody was fundamentally the same. Lots of people weren't. They weren't like everybody else.

Farley was different, too, he thought. In another situation, he would have dismissed Farley as a jovial clown. But he was obviously bright as hell. Where did that grinning, comic manner come from?

''You know how fast this is moving?'' Farley said. ''Damned fast. We've gone from milliseconds to nanoseconds in just a few years. When the computer ILLIAC I was built in 1952, it could do eleven thousand arithmetical operations a second. Pretty fast, right? Well, they're almost finished with ILLIAC IV now. It will do two hundred *million* operations a second. It's the fourth generation. Of course, it couldn't have been built without the help of other computers. They used two other computers full time for two years, designing the new ILLIAC.''

Morris drank his coffee. Perhaps it was his fatigue, perhaps the spookiness of the room, but he was beginning to feel some kinship with Benson. Computers to design computers—maybe they were taking over, after all. What would Ross say about that? A shared delusion?

"Find anything interesting in his desk?"

"No," Morris said. He sat down in the chair behind the desk and looked around the room. He was trying to act like Benson, to think like Benson, to *be* Benson.

"How did he spend his time?"

"I don't know," Farley said, sitting on another desk across the room. "He got pretty distant and withdrawn the last few months. I know he had some trouble with the law. And I knew he was going into the hospital. I knew that. He didn't like your hospital much."

"How is that?" Morris asked, not very interested. It wasn't surprising that Benson was hostile to the hospital.

Farley didn't answer. Instead, he went over to a bulletin board, where clippings and photos had been tacked up. He removed one yellowing newspaper item and gave it to Morris.

It was from the Los Angeles *Times*, dated July 17,

1969. The headline read: UNIVERSITY HOSPITAL GETS
NEW COMPUTER. The story outlined the acquisition of
the IBM System 360 computer which was being installed in the hospital basement, and would be used for
research, assistance in operations, and a variety of other
functions.

"You notice the date?" Farley said. "Watershed
Week."

Morris stared at it and frowned.

5

"I AM TRYING TO BE LOGICAL, DR. ROSS."

"I understand, Harry."

"I think it's important to be logical and rational when
we discuss these things, don't you?"

"Yes, I do."

She sat in the room and watched the reels of the tape
recorder spin. Across from her, Ellis sat back in a chair,
eyes closed, cigarette burning in his fingers. Morris
drank another cup of coffee as he listened. She was
making a list of what they knew, trying to decide what
their next step should be.

The tape spun on.

"I classify things according to what I call trends to

be opposed," Benson said. "There are four important trends to be opposed. Do you want to hear them?"

"Yes, of course."

"Do you really?"

"Yes, really."

"Well, trend number one is the generality of the computer. The computer is a machine but it's not like any machine in human history. Other machines have a specific function—like cars, or refrigerators, or dishwashers. We expect machines to have specific functions. But computers don't. They can do all sorts of things."

"Surely computers are—"

"Please let me finish. Trend number two is the autonomy of the computer. In the old days, computers weren't autonomous. They were like adding machines; you had to be there all the time, punching buttons, to make them work. Like cars: cars won't drive without drivers. But now things are different. Computers are becoming autonomous. You can build in all sorts of instructions about what to do next—and you can walk away and let the computer handle things."

"Harry, I—"

"Please don't interrupt me. This is very serious. Trend number three is miniaturization. You know all about that. A computer that took up a whole room in 1950 is now about the size of a carton of cigarettes. Pretty soon it'll be smaller than that."

There was a pause on the tape.

"Trend number four—" Benson began, and she clicked the tape off. She looked at Ellis and Morris. "This isn't getting us anywhere," she said.

They didn't reply, just stared with a kind of blank fatigue. She looked at her list of information.

Benson home at 12:30. Picked up ? blueprints, ?
gun, and tool kit.
Benson not seen in Jackrabbit Club recently.
Benson upset by UH computer, installed 7/69.

"Suggest anything to you?" Ellis asked.

"No," Ross said. "But I think one of us should talk to McPherson." She looked at Ellis, who nodded without energy. Morris shrugged slightly. "All right," she said. "I'll do it."

It was 4:30 a.m.

"The fact is," Ross said, "we've exhausted all our options. Time is running out."

McPherson stared at her across his desk. His eyes were dark and tired. "What do you expect me to do?" he said.

"Notify the police."

"The police are already notified. They've been notified from the beginning by one of their own people. I understand the seventh floor is swarming with cops now."

"The police don't know about the operation."

"For Christ's sake, the police brought him here for the operation. Of course they know about it."

"But they don't really know what it involves."

"They haven't asked."

"And they don't know about the computer projection for 6 a.m."

"What about it?" he said.

She was becoming angry with him. He was so damned stubborn. He knew perfectly well what she was saying.

"I think their attitude might be different if they knew that Benson was going to have a seizure at six a.m."

"I think you're right," McPherson said. He shifted his weight heavily in his chair. "I think they might stop thinking about him as an escaped man wanted on a charge of assault. And they would begin thinking of him as a crazy murderer with wires in his brain." He sighed. "Right now, their objective is to apprehend him. If we tell them more, they'll kill him."

"But innocent lives may be involved. If the projection—"

"The projection," McPherson said, "is just that. A computer projection. It is only as good as its input and that input consists of three timed stimulations. You can draw a lot of curves through three graph points. You can extrapolate it a lot of ways. We have no positive reason to believe he'll tip over at six a.m. In actual fact, he may not tip over at all."

She glanced around the room, at the charts on his walls. McPherson plotted the future of the NPS in this room, and he kept a record of it on his walls, in the form of elaborate, multicolored charts. She knew what those charts meant to him; she knew what the NPS meant to him; she knew what Benson meant to him. But even so, his position was unreasonable and irresponsible.

Now how was she going to say that?

"Look, Jan," McPherson said, "you began by saying that we've exhausted all our options. I disagree. I think we have the option of waiting. I think there is a possibility he will return to the hospital, return to our care. And as long as that is possible, I prefer to wait."

"You're not going to tell the police?"

"No."

"If he doesn't come back," she said, "and if he attacks someone during a seizure, do you really want that on your head?"

"It's already on my head," McPherson said, and smiled sadly.

It was 5 a.m.

6

THEY WERE ALL TIRED, BUT NONE OF THEM could sleep. They stayed in Telecomp, watching the computer projections as they inched up the plotted line toward a seizure state. The time was 5:30, and then 5:45.

Ellis smoked an entire pack of cigarettes, and then left to get another. Morris stared at a journal in his lap but never turned the page; from time to time, he glanced up at the wall clock.

Ross paced, and looked at the sunrise, the sky turning pink over the thin brown haze of smog to the east.

Ellis came back with more cigarettes.

Gerhard stopped working with the computers to make

fresh coffee. Morris got up and stood watching Gerhard make it; not speaking, not helping, just watching.

Ross became aware of the ticking of the wall clock. It was strange that she had never noticed it before, because in fact it ticked quite loudly. And once a minute there was a mechanical click as the minute hand moved another notch. The sound disturbed her. She began to fix on it, waiting for that single click on top of the quieter ticking. Mildly obsessive, she thought. And then she thought of all the other psychological derangements she had experienced in the past. *Déjà vu*, the feeling that she had been somewhere before; depersonalization, the feeling that she was watching herself from across the room at some social gathering; clang associations, delusions, phobias. There was no sharp line between health and disease, sanity and insanity. It was a spectrum, and everybody fitted somewhere on the spectrum. Wherever you were on that spectrum, other people looked strange to you. Benson was strange to them; without question, they were strange to Benson.

At 6 a.m., they all stood and stretched, glancing up at the clock. Nothing happened.

"Maybe it's six-four exactly," Gerhard said.

They waited.

The clock showed 6:04. Still nothing happened. No telephones rang, no messengers arrived. Nothing.

Ellis slipped the cellophane wrapper off his cigarettes and crumpled it. The sound made Ross want to scream. He began to play with the cellophane, crumpling it, smoothing it out, crumpling it again. She gritted her teeth.

The clock showed 6:10, then 6:15. McPherson came

into the room. "So far, so good," he said, smiled
bleakly, and left. The others stared at each other.

Five more minutes passed.

"I don't know," Gerhard said, staring at the computer console. "Maybe the projection was wrong after
all. We only had three plotting points. Maybe we should
run another curve through."

He sat down at the console and punched buttons. The
screen glowed with alternative curves, streaking white
across the green background. Finally, he stopped.
"No," he said. "The computer sticks with the original
curve. That should be the one."

"Well, obviously the computer is wrong," Morris
said. "It's almost six-thirty. The cafeteria will be opening. Anybody want to have breakfast?"

"Sounds good to me," Ellis said. He got out of his
chair. "Jan?"

She shook her head. "I'll wait here awhile."

"I don't think it's going to happen," Morris said.
"You better get some breakfast."

"I'll wait here." The words came out almost before
she realized it.

"Okay, okay," Morris said, raising his hands. He
shot a glance at Ellis, and the two men left. She remained in the room with Gerhard.

"Do you have confidence limits on that curve?" she
said.

"I did," Gerhard said. "But I don't know any more.
We've passed the confidence limits already. They were
about plus or minus two minutes for ninety-nine percent."

"You mean the seizure would have occurred between
six-two and six-six?"

"Yeah, roughly." He shrugged. "But it obviously didn't happen."

"It might take time before it was discovered."

"It might," Gerhard nodded. He didn't seem convinced.

She returned to the window. The sun was up now, shining with a pale reddish light. Why did sunrises always seem weaker, less brilliant, than sunsets? They should be the same.

Behind her she heard a single electronic *beep.*

"Oh-oh," Gerhard said.

She turned. "What is it?"

He pointed across the room to a small mechanical box on a shelf in the corner. The box was attached to a telephone. A green light glowed on the box.

"What is it?" she repeated.

"That's the special line," he said. "The twenty-four-hour recording for the dog tag."

She went over and picked up the telephone from its cradle. She listened and heard a measured, resonant voice saying, ". . . should be advised that the body must not be cremated or damaged in any way until the implanted atomic material has been removed. Failure to remove the material presents a risk of radioactive contamination. For detailed information—"

She turned to Gerhard. "How do you turn it off?"

He pressed a button on the box. The recording stopped.

"Hello?" she said.

There was a pause. Then a male voice said, "Whom am I speaking to?"

"This is Dr. Ross."

"Are you affiliated with the"—a short pause—"the Neuropsychiatric Research Unit?"

"Yes, I am."

"Get a pencil and paper. I want you to take an address down. This is Captain Anders of the Los Angeles police."

She gestured to Gerhard for something to write with. "What's the problem, Captain?"

"We have a murder here," Anders said, "and we've got some questions for your people."

7

THREE PATROL CARS WERE PULLED UP IN FRONT of the apartment building off Sunset. The flashing red lights had already drawn a crowd, despite the early hour and the morning chill. She parked her car down the street and walked back to the lobby. A young patrolman stopped her.

"You a tenant?"

"I'm Dr. Ross. Captain Anders called me."

He nodded toward the elevator. "Third floor, turn left," he said, and let her through. The crowd watched curiously as she crossed the lobby and waited for the elevator. They were standing outside, looking in, peering over each other's shoulders, whispering among themselves. She wondered what they thought of her. The flashing lights from the patrol cars bathed the lobby intermittently with a red glow. Then the elevator came, and the doors closed.

The interior of the elevator was tacky: plastic paneling made to look like wood, worn green carpeting stained by innumerable pets. She waited impatiently for it to creak up to the third floor. She knew what these buildings were like—full of hookers, full of gays, full of drugs and transients. You could rent an apartment without a long lease, just month to month. It was that kind of place.

She stepped off at the third floor and walked down to a cluster of cops outside an apartment. Another policeman blocked her way; she repeated that she was here to see Captain Anders, and he let her through with the admonition not to touch anything.

It was a one-bedroom apartment furnished in pseudo-Spanish style. Or at least she thought it was. Twenty men were crowded inside, dusting, photographing, measuring, collecting. It was impossible to visualize how it had looked before the onslaught of police personnel.

Anders came over to her. He was young, in his middle thirties, wearing a conservative dark suit. His hair was long enough to hang over the back of his collar and he wore horn-rimmed glasses. The effect was almost professorial, and quite unexpected. It was strange how you built up prejudices. When he spoke, his voice was soft: "Are you Dr. Ross?"

"Yes."

"Captain Anders." He shook hands quickly and

firmly. "Thank you for coming. The body is in the bedroom. The coroner's man is in there, too."

He led the way into the bedroom. The deceased was a girl in her twenties, sprawled nude across the bed. Her head was crushed and she had been stabbed repeatedly. The bed was soaked with blood, and the room had the sickly sweet odor of blood.

The rest of the room was in disarray—a chair by the dressing table knocked over, cosmetics and lotions smeared on the rug, a bedside lamp broken. Six men were working in the room, one of them a doctor from the medical examiner's office. He was filling out the death report.

"This is Dr. Ross," Anders said. "Tell her about it."

The doctor shrugged toward the body. "Brutal methodology, as you can see. Strong blow to the left temporal region, producing cranial depression and immediate unconsciousness. The weapon was that lamp over there. Blood of her type and some of her hair are affixed to it."

Ross glanced over at the lamp, then back to the body. "The stab wounds?"

"They're later, almost certainly post-mortem. She was killed by the blow to the head."

Ross looked at the head. It was squashed in on one side, like a deflated football, distorting the features of what had once been a conventionally pretty face.

"You'll notice," the doctor said, moving closer to the girl, "that she's put on half her make-up. As we reconstruct it, she's sitting at the dressing table, over there, making up. The blow comes from above and from the side, knocking her over in the chair, spilling the lotions and crap. Then she's lifted up"—the doctor raised his arms and frowned in mock effort, lifting an invisible body—"from the chair and placed on the bed."

"Somebody pretty strong?"

"Oh, yes. A man for sure."

"How do you know that?"

"Pubic hair in the shower drain. We've found two varieties. One matches hers, the other is male. Male pubic hair as you know is more circular, less elliptical in cross section than female hair."

"No," Ross said. "I didn't know that."

"I can give you a reference on it, if you want," the doctor said. "It's also clear that her killer had intercourse with her before the murder. We've got a blood type on the seminal fluid and it's AO. The man apparently takes a shower after intercourse, and then comes out and kills her."

Ross nodded.

"Following delivery of the blow to the head, she's lifted up and placed on the bed. At this time, she's not bleeding much. No blood to speak of on the dressing table or rug. But now her killer picks up some instrument and stabs her in the stomach several times. You'll notice that the deepest wounds are all in the lower abdomen, which may have some sexual connotations for the killer. But that's just guessing on our part."

Ross nodded but said nothing. She moved closer to the body to examine the stab wounds. They were all small, puncture-like in appearance, with a good deal of skin-tearing around the wounds.

"You find a weapon?"

"No," the doctor said.

"What do you think it was?"

"I'm not sure. Nothing very sharp, but something strong—it took a lot of force to penetrate this way with a relatively blunt instrument."

"Another argument that it's a man," Anders said.

"Yes. I'd guess it was something metal, like a blunt letter opener, or a metal ruler, or a screwdriver. Something like that. But what's really interesting," the doctor went on, "is this phenomenon here." He pointed to the girl's left arm, which was outstretched on the bed and mutilated badly by stab wounds. "You see, he stabbed her in the stomach, and then stabbed her arm, moving out in a regular way, a succession of stabbings. Now, notice: when he's past the arm, he continues to stab. You can see the tears in the sheet and blanket. They continue out in a straight line."

He pointed to the tears.

"Now," the doctor said, "in my book that's perseveration. Automatic continuation of pointless movement. Like he was some kind of machine that just kept going and going. . . ."

"That's correct," Ross said.

"We assume," the doctor said, "that it represents some kind of trance or seizure state. But we don't know if it was organic or functional, natural or artificially induced. Since the girl let him into the apartment freely, this trance-like state developed only later."

Ross realized that the coroner's man was showing off, and it irritated her. This was the wrong time to be playing Sherlock Holmes.

Anders handed her the metal dog tag. "We were proceeding routinely with the investigation," he said, "when we found this."

Ross turned the tag over in her hand.

I HAVE AN IMPLANTED ATOMIC PACEMAKER. DIRECT
PHYSICAL INJURY OR FIRE MAY RUPTURE THE CAPSULE
AND RELEASE TOXIC MATERIALS. IN THE EVENT OF
INJURY OR DEATH CALL NPS, (213) 652-1134.

"That was when we called you," Anders said. He
watched her carefully. "We've leveled with you," he
said. "Now it's your turn."

"His name is Harry Benson," she said. "He's thirty-
four and he has a disinhibitory lesion."

The doctor snapped his fingers. "I'll be damned.
ADL."

"What's a disinhibitory lesion?" Anders said. "And
what's ADL?"

At that moment, a plainclothesman came in from the
living room. "We got a trace on the prints," he said.
"They're listed in the Defense data banks, of all places.
This guy had classified clearance from 1968 to the present. His name's Harry Benson, lives in L.A."

"Clearance for what?" Anders said.

"Computer work, probably," Ross said.

"That's right," the plainclothesman said. "Last three
years, classified computer research."

Anders was making notes. "They have a blood type
on him?"

"Yeah. Type AO is what's listed."

Ross turned to the doctor. "What do you have on the
girl?"

"Names Doris Blankfurt, stage name Angela Black.
Twenty-six years old, been in the building six weeks."

"What does she do?"

"Dancer."

Ross nodded.

Anders said, "Does that have some special meaning?"

"He has a thing about dancers."

"He's attracted to them?"

"Attracted and repelled," she said. "It's rather complicated."

He looked at her curiously. Did he think she was putting him on?

"And he has some kind of seizures?"

"Yes."

Anders made notes. "I'm going to need some explanations," he said.

"Of course."

"And a description, pictures—"

"I can get you all that."

"—as soon as possible."

She nodded. All her earlier impulses to resist the police, to refuse to cooperate with them, had vanished. She kept staring at the girl's caved-in head. She could imagine the suddenness, the viciousness of the attack.

She glanced at her watch. "It's seven-thirty now," she said. "I'm going back to the hospital, but I'm stopping at home to clean up and change. You can meet me there or at the hospital."

"I'll meet you there," Anders said. "I'll be finished here in about twenty minutes."

"Okay," she said, and gave him the address.

8

THE SHOWER FELT GOOD, THE HOT WATER LIKE stinging needles against her bare skin. She relaxed, breathed the steam, and closed her eyes. She had always liked showers, even though she knew it was the masculine pattern. Men took showers, women took baths. Dr. Ramos had mentioned that once. She thought it was bullshit. Patterns were made to be broken. She was an individual.

Then she'd discovered that showers were used to treat schizophrenics. They were sometimes calmed by alternating hot and cold spray.

"So now you think you're schizophrenic?" Dr. Ramos had said, and laughed heartily. He didn't often laugh. Sometimes she tried to make him laugh, usually without success.

She turned off the shower and climbed out, pulling a towel around her. She wiped the steam off the bathroom mirror and stared at her reflection. "You look like hell," she said, and nodded. Her reflection nodded back. The shower had washed away her eye make-up, the only make-up she wore. Her eyes seemed small now, and weak with fatigue. What time was her hour with Dr. Ramos today? Was it today?

177

What day was it, anyway? It took her a moment to remember that it was Friday. She hadn't slept for at least twenty-four hours, and she was having all the sleepless symptoms she'd remembered as an intern. An acid gnawing in her stomach. A dull ache in her body. A kind of slow confusion of the mind. It was a terrible way to feel.

She knew how it would progress. In another four or five hours, she would begin to daydream about sleeping. She would imagine a bed, and the softness of the mattress as she lay on it. She would begin to dwell on the wonderful sensations that would accompany falling asleep.

She hoped they found Benson before long. The mirror had steamed over again. She opened the bathroom door to let cool air in, and wiped a clean space with her hand again. She was starting to apply fresh make-up when she heard the doorbell.

That would be Anders. She had left the front door unlocked. "It's open," she shouted, and then returned to her make-up. She did one eye, then paused before the second. "If you want coffee, just boil water in the kitchen," she said.

She did her other eye, pulled the towel tighter around her, and leaned out toward the hallway. "Find everything you need?" she called.

Harry Benson was standing in the hallway. "Good morning, Dr. Ross," he said. His voice was pleasant. "I hope I haven't come at an inconvenient time."

It was odd how frightened she felt. He held out his hand and she shook it, hardly conscious of the action. She was preoccupied with her own fear. Why was she afraid? She knew this man well; she had been alone with him many times before, and had never been afraid.

The surprise was part of it, the shock of finding him here. And the unprofessional setting: she was acutely aware of the towel, her still-damp bare legs.

"Excuse me a minute," she said, "and I'll get some clothes on."

He nodded politely and went back to the living room. She closed the bedroom door and sat down on the bed. She was breathing hard, as if she had run a great distance. Anxiety, she thought, but the label didn't really help. She remembered a patient who had finally shouted at her in frustration, "Don't tell me I'm depressed. I feel *terrible*!"

She went to the closet and pulled on a dress, hardly noticing which one it was. Then she went back into the bathroom to check her appearance. Stalling, she thought. This is not the time to stall.

She took a deep breath and went outside to talk with him.

He was standing in the middle of the living room, looking uncomfortable and confused. She saw the room freshly, through his eyes: a modern, sterile, hostile apartment. Modern furniture, black leather and chrome, hard lines; modern paintings on the walls; modern, glistening, machine-like, efficient, a totally hostile environment.

"I never would have thought this of you," he said.

"We're not threatened by the same things, Harry." She kept her voice light. "Do you want some coffee?"

"No, thanks."

He was neatly dressed, in a jacket and tie, but his wig, the black wig, threw her off. Also his eyes: they

were tired, distant—the eyes of a man near the breaking
point of fatigue. She remembered how the rats had collapsed from excessive pleasurable stimulation. Eventually they lay spread-eagled on the floor of the cage,
panting, too weak to crawl forward and press the shock
lever one more time.

"Are you alone here?" he said.

"Yes, I am."

There was a small bruise on his left cheek, just below
the eye. She looked at his bandages. They just barely
showed, a bit of white between the bottom of his wig
and the top of his collar.

"Is something wrong?" he asked.

"No, nothing."

"You seem tense." His voice sounded genuinely
concerned. Probably he'd just had a stimulation. She
remembered how he had become sexually interested in
her after the test stimulations, just before he was interfaced.

"No . . . I'm not tense." She smiled.

"You have a very nice smile," he said.

She glanced at his clothes, looking for blood. The
girl had been soaked; Benson must have been covered
with blood, yet there was none on his clothes. Perhaps
he'd dressed after taking a second shower. After killing
her.

"Well," she said, "I'm going to have some coffee."
She went into the kitchen with a kind of relief. It was
somehow easier to breathe in the kitchen, away from
him. She put the kettle on the burner, turned on the
gas, and stayed there a moment. She had to get control
of herself. She had to get control of the situation.

The odd thing was that while she had been shocked

to see him suddenly in her apartment, she was not really surprised that he had come. Some ADL patients feared their own violence.

But why hadn't he returned to the hospital?

She went out to the living room. Benson was standing by the large windows, looking out over the city, which stretched away for miles in every direction.

"Are you angry with me?" he said.

"Angry? Why?"

"Because I ran away."

"Why did you run away, Harry?" As she spoke, she felt her strength coming back, her control. She could handle this man. It was her job. She'd been alone with men more dangerous than this. She remembered a six-month period at Cameron State Hospital, where she had worked with psychopaths and multiple murderers—charming, engaging, chilling men.

"Why? Because." He smiled, and sat down in a chair. He wriggled around in it, then stood up, sitting down again on the sofa. "All your furniture is so uncomfortable. How can you live in such an uncomfortable place?"

"I like it."

"But it's uncomfortable." He stared at her, a faint challenge in the look. She wished again that they were not meeting here. This environment was too threatening, and Benson reacted to threats with attack.

"How did you find me, Harry?"

"You're surprised I knew where you lived?"

"Yes, a little."

"I was careful," he said. "Before I went into the hospital, I found out where you lived, where Ellis lived, where McPherson lived. I found out where everybody lived.''

"Why?''

"Just in case.''

"What were you expecting?''

He didn't reply. Instead, he got up and walked to the windows, looked out over the city. "They're searching for me out there,'' he said. "Aren't they?''

"Yes.''

"But they'll never find me. The city is too big.''

From the kitchen, her kettle began to whistle. She excused herself and went in to make coffee. Her eyes scanned the counter, searching for something heavy. Perhaps she could hit him over the head. Ellis would never forgive her, but—

"You have a picture on your wall,'' Benson called. "A lot of numbers. Who did that?''

"A man named Johns.''

"Why would a man draw numbers? Numbers are for machines.''

She stirred the instant coffee, poured in milk, went back out and sat down.

"Harry . . .''

"No, I mean it. And look at this. What is this supposed to mean?'' He tapped another picture with his knuckles.

"Harry, come and sit down.''

He stared at her for a moment, then came over and sat on the couch opposite her. He seemed tense, but a moment later smiled in a relaxed way. For an instant, his pupils dilated. Another stimulation, she thought.

What the hell was she going to do?

"Harry,'' she said, "what happened?''

"I don't know," he said, still relaxed.

"You left the hospital. . . ."

"Yes, I left the hospital wearing one of those white suits. I figured it all out. Angela picked me up."

"And then?"

"And then we went to my house. I was quite tense."

"Why were you tense?"

"Well, you see, I know how this is all going to end."

She wasn't sure what he was referring to. "How is it going to end?"

"And after we left my house, we went to her apartment, and we had some drinks, and we made love, and then I told her how it was going to end. That was when she got scared. She wanted to call the hospital, to tell them where I was. . . ." He stared off into space, momentarily confused. She didn't want to press the point. He had had a seizure and he would not remember killing the girl. His amnesia would be total and genuine.

But she wanted to keep him talking. "Why did you leave the hospital, Harry?"

"It was in the afternoon," he said, turning to look at her. "I was lying in bed in the afternoon, and I suddenly realized that everybody was taking care of me, *taking care*, servicing me, like a machine. I was afraid of that all along."

In some distant, detached, and academic corner of her mind, she felt that a suspicion was confirmed. Benson's paranoia about machines was, at bottom, a fear of dependency, of losing self-reliance. He was quite literally telling the truth when he said he was afraid of being taken care of. And people usually hated what they feared.

But then Benson was dependent on her. And how would he react to that?

"You people lied to me," he said suddenly.

"Nobody lied to you, Harry."

He began to get angry. "Yes, you did, you—" He broke off and smiled again. The pupils were briefly larger: another stimulation. They were very close now. He'd tip over again soon.

"You know something? That's the most wonderful feeling in the world," he said.

"What feeling?"

"That buzz."

"Is that how it feels?"

"As soon as things start to get black—buzz!—and I'm happy again," Benson said. "Beautifully warm and happy."

"The stimulations," she said.

She resisted the impulse to look at her watch. What did it matter? Anders had said he would be coming in twenty minutes, but anything could delay him. And even if he came, she wondered if he could handle Benson. An ADL patient out of control was an awesome thing. Anders would probably end up shooting Benson, or trying to. And she didn't want that.

"But you know what else?" Benson said. "The buzz is only nice occasionally. When it gets too heavy, it's . . . suffocating."

"Is it getting heavy now?"

"Yes," he said. And he smiled.

In that moment when he smiled, she was stunned into the full realization of her own helplessness. Everything she had been taught about controlling patients, everything about directing the flow of thought, about watching the speech patterns, was useless here. Verbal maneuvers would not work, would not help her—any more than they would help control a rabies victim, or a person with a brain tumor. Benson had a physical problem. He was in the grip of a machine that was inexorably, flawlessly pushing him toward a seizure. Talk couldn't turn off the implanted computer.

There was only one thing she could do, and that was get him to the hospital. How? She tried an appeal to his cognitive functions. "Do you understand what's happening, Harry? The stimulations are overloading you, pushing you into seizures."

"The feeling is nice."

"But you said yourself it's not always nice."

"No, not always."

"Well, don't you want to have that corrected?"

He paused a moment. "Corrected?"

"Fixed. Changed so that you don't have seizures any more." She had to choose her words carefully.

"You think I need to be fixed?" His words reminded her of Ellis: the surgeon's pet phrase.

"Harry, we can make you feel better."

"I feel fine, Dr. Ross."

"But, Harry, when you went to Angela's—"

"I don't remember anything about that."

"You went there after you left the hospital."

"I don't remember anything. Memory tapes are all erased. Nothing but static. You can put it on audio if you want, and listen to it yourself." He opened his mouth, and made a hissing sound. "See? Just static."

"You're not a machine, Harry," she said softly.

"Not yet."

Her stomach churned. She felt physically sick with

tension. Again that detached part of her mind noted the interesting physical manifestation of an emotional state. She was grateful for the detachment, even for a few instants of it.

But she was also angry at the thought of Ellis and McPherson, and all those conferences when she had argued that implanting machinery into Benson would exaggerate his pre-existing delusional state. They hadn't paid any attention.

She wished they were here now.

"You're trying to make me into a machine," he said. "You all are. I'm fighting you."

"Harry—'"

"Let me finish." His face was taut; abruptly, it loosened into a smile.

Another stimulation. They were coming only minutes apart now. Where was Anders? Where was anybody? Should she run out into the hall screaming? Should she try to call the hospital? The police?

"It feels so good," Benson said, still smiling. "That feeling, it feels so good. Nothing feels as good as that. I could just swim in that feeling forever and ever."

"Harry. I want you to try and relax."

"I'm relaxed. But that's not what you really want, is it?"

"What do I want?"

"You want me to be a good machine. You want me to obey my masters, to follow instructions. Isn't that what you want?"

"You're not a machine, Harry."

"And I never will be." His smile faded. "Never. Ever."

She took a deep breath. "Harry," she said, "I want you to come back to the hospital."

"No."

"We can make you feel better."

"No."

"We care about you, Harry."

"You care about me." He laughed, a nasty hard sound. "You don't care about *me*. You care about your experimental preparation. You care about your scientific protocol. You care about your follow-up. You don't care about *me*."

He was becoming excited and angry. "It won't look so good in the medical journals if you have to report so many patients observed for so many years, and one died because he went crazy and the cops killed him. That will reflect badly."

"Harry—"

"I *know*," Benson said. He held out his hands. "I was sick an hour ago. Then, when I woke up, I saw blood under my fingernails. Blood. I know." He stared at his hands, curling them to look at the nails. Then he touched his bandages. "The operation was supposed to work," he said. "But it isn't working."

And then, quite abruptly, he began to cry. His face was bland, but the tears rolled down his cheeks. "It isn't working," he said. "I don't understand, it isn't working. . . ."

Equally abruptly, he smiled. Another stimulation. This one had come less than a minute after the one previously. She knew that he'd tip over in the next few seconds.

"I don't want to hurt anyone," he said, smiling cheerfully.

She felt sympathy for him, and sadness for what had happened. "I understand," she said. "Let's go back to the hospital."

"No, no . . ."

"I'll go with you. I'll stay with you all the time. It will be all right."

"Don't argue with me!" He snapped to his feet, fists clenched, and glared down at her. "I will not listen—" He broke off, but did not smile.

Instead, he began to sniff the air.

"What is that smell?" he said. "I hate that smell. What is it? I hate it, do you hear me, I *hate* it!"

He moved toward her, sniffing. He reached his hands out toward her.

"Harry . . ."

"I hate this feeling," he said.

She got up off the couch, moving away. He followed her clumsily, his hands still outstretched. "I don't want this feeling, I don't want it," he said. He was no longer sniffing. He was fully in a trance state, coming toward her.

"Harry . . ."

His face was blank, an automaton mask. His arms were still extended toward her. He almost seemed to be sleep-walking as he advanced on her. His movements were slow and she was able to back away from him, maintaining distance.

Then, suddenly, he picked up a heavy glass ashtray and flung it at her. She dodged; it struck one of the large windows, shattering the glass.

He leaped for her and threw his arms around her, holding her in a clumsy bear hug. He squeezed her with incredible strength. "Harry," she gasped, "Harry." She looked up at his face and saw it was still blank.

She kneed him in the groin.

He grunted and released her, bending at the waist, coughing. She moved away from him and picked up the phone. She dialed the operator. Benson was still bent over, still coughing.

"Operator."

"Operator, give me the police.."

"Do you want the Beverly Hills police, or the Los Angeles police?"

"I don't care!"

"Well, which do you—"

She dropped the phone. Benson was stalking her again. She heard the tiny voice of the operator saying, "Hello, hello . . ."

Benson tore the phone away and flung it behind him across the room. He picked up a floor lamp and held it base outward. He began to swing it in large hissing arcs. She ducked it once and felt the gush of air in the wake of the heavy metal base. If it hit her, it would kill her. It would kill her. The realization pushed her to action.

She ran to the kitchen. Benson dropped the lamp and followed her. She tore open drawers, looking for a knife. She found only a small paring knife. Where the hell were her big knives?

Benson was in the kitchen. She threw a pot at him blindly. It clattered against his knees. He moved forward.

The detached and academic part of her mind was still operating, telling her that she was making a big mistake, that there was something in the kitchen she could use. But what?

Benson's hands closed around her neck. The grip was terrifying. She grabbed his wrists and tried to pull them away. She kicked up with her leg, but he twisted his body away from her, then pressed her back against the counter, pinning her down.

She could not move, she could not breathe. She began to see blue spots dancing before her eyes. Her lungs burned for air.

Her fingers scratched along the counter, feeling for something, anything, to strike him with. She touched nothing.

The kitchen . . .

She flung her hands around wildly. She felt the handle of the dishwasher, the handle to the oven, the machines in her kitchen.

Her vision was greenish. The blue spots were larger. They swam sickeningly before her. She was going to die in the kitchen.

The kitchen, the kitchen, *dangers of the kitchen*. It came to her in a flash, just as she was losing consciousness.

Microwaves.

She no longer had any vision; the world was dull gray, but she could still feel. Her fingers touched the metal of the oven, the glass of the oven door, then up . . . up to the controls . . . she twisted the dial. . . .

Benson screamed.

The pressure around her neck was gone. She slumped to the floor. Benson was screaming, horrible agonized sounds. Her vision came back to her slowly and she saw him, standing over her, clutching his head in his hands. Screaming.

He paid no attention to her as she lay on the floor, gasping for breath. He twisted and writhed, holding his head and howling like a wounded animal. Then he rushed from the room, still screaming.

And she slid smoothly and easily into unconsciousness.

9

THE BRUISES WERE ALREADY FORMING—LONG, purplish welts on both sides of her neck. She touched them gently as she looked into the mirror.

"When did he leave?" Anders said. He stood in the doorway to the bathroom, watching her.

"I don't know. Around the time I passed out."

He looked back toward the living room. "Quite a mess out there."

"I imagine so."

"Why did he attack you?"

"He had a seizure."

"But you're his doctor—"

"That doesn't matter," she said. "When he has a seizure, he's out of control. Totally. He'd kill his own child during a seizure. People have been known to do that.''

Anders frowned uncertainly. She could imagine the trouble he was having with the idea. Unless you had seen an ADL seizure, you could not comprehend the unreasonable, brutal violence of an attack. It was completely beyond any normal life experience. Nothing else was like it, analogous to it, similar to it.

"Umm," Anders said finally. "But he didn't kill you."

Not quite, she thought, still touching the bruises. The bruises would get much worse in the next few hours. What could she do about it? Make-up? She didn't have any. A high-necked sweater?

"No," she said, "he didn't kill me. But he would have."

"What happened?"

"I turned on the microwave."

Anders looked puzzled. "The microwave?"

"It affected Benson's electronic machinery. Microwave radiation screws up pacemaking machinery. It's a big problem for cardiac pacemakers now. Dangers of the kitchen. There have been a lot of recent articles."

"Oh," Anders said.

He left the room to make some calls, while she dressed. She chose a black turtleneck sweater and a gray skirt, and stepped back to look at herself in the mirror. The bruises were hidden. Then she noticed the colors, black and gray. That wasn't like her. Too somber, too dead and cold. She considered changing, but didn't.

She heard Anders talking on the phone in the living room. She went out to the kitchen to make herself a drink—no more coffee; she wanted Scotch on the rocks—and as she poured it, she saw the long scratches in the wooden counter that her fingernails had left. She looked at her fingernails. Three of them were broken; she hadn't noticed before.

She made the drink and went out to sit in the living room.

"Yes," Anders was saying into the phone. "Yes, I understand. No . . . no idea. Well, we're trying." There was a long pause.

She went to the broken window and looked out at the city. The sun was up, lighting a dark band of brown air that hung above the buildings. It was really a lethal place to live, she thought. She should move to the beach where the air was better.

"Well, listen," Anders said angrily, "none of this would have happened if you'd kept that fucking guard at his door in the hospital. I think you better keep that in mind."

She heard the phone slam down, and turned.

"Shit," he said. "Politics."

"Even in the police department?"

"Especially in the police department," he said. "Anything goes wrong, and suddenly there's a scramble to see who can get stuck with it."

"They're trying to stick you?"

"They're trying me on for size."

She nodded, and wondered what was happening back at the hospital. Probably the same thing. The hospital had to maintain its image in the community; the chiefs of service would be in a sweat; the director would be worrying about fundraising. Somebody at the hospital would get stuck. McPherson was too big; she and Mor-

ris were too small. It would probably be Ellis—he was
an assistant professor. If you fired an assistant professor
it had connotations of firing a temporary appointment
who had proven himself too aggressive, too reckless,
too ambitious. Much better than firing a full professor,
which was very messy and reflected badly on the earlier
decision that had given him tenure.

It would probably be Ellis. She wondered if he knew.
He had just recently bought a new house in Brentwood.
He was very proud of it; he had invited everyone in the
NPS to a housewarming party next week. She stared
out the window, through the shattered glass.

Anders said, "Listen, what do seizures have to do
with cardiac pacemakers?"

"Nothing," she said, "except that Benson has a brain
pacemaker, very similar to a cardiac pacemaker."

Anders flipped open his notebook. "You better start
from the beginning," he said, "and go slowly."

"All right." She set down her drink. "Let me make
one call first."

Anders nodded, sat back, and waited while she called
McPherson. Then, as calmly as she could, she explained everything she knew to the policeman.

10

MCPHERSON HUNG UP THE TELEPHONE AND stared out his office window at the morning sun. It was no longer pale and cold; there was the full warmth of morning. "That was Ross," he said.

Morris nodded from the corner. "And?"

"Benson came to her apartment. She lost him."

Morris sighed.

"It doesn't seem to be our day," McPherson said. He shook his head, not taking his eyes off the sun. "I don't believe in luck," he said. He turned to Morris. "Do you?"

Morris was tired; he hadn't really been listening. "Do I what?"

"Believe in luck."

"Sure. All surgeons believe in luck."

"I don't believe in luck," McPherson repeated. "Never did. I always believed in planning." He gestured to the charts on his wall, then lapsed, staring at them.

The charts were large things, four feet across, and intricately done in many colors. They were really glorified flow charts with timetables for technical advances. He had always been proud of them. For instance, in 1967 he had examined the state of three areas—diagnostic conceptualization, surgical technology, and microelectronics—and concluded that they would all come together to allow an operation for ADL seizures in July of 1971. They had beaten his estimate by four months, but it was still damned accurate.

"Damned accurate," he said.

"What?" Morris said.

McPherson shook his head. "Are you tired?"

"Yes."

"I guess we're all tired. Where's Ellis?"

"Making coffee."

McPherson nodded. Coffee would be good. He rubbed his eyes, wondering when he would be able to sleep. Not for a while—not until they had Benson back. And that could take many hours more, perhaps another day.

He looked again at the charts. Everything had been going so well. Electrode implantation four months ahead of schedule. Computer simulation of behavior almost nine months ahead—but that, too, was having problems. George and Martha programs were behaving erratically. And Form Q?

He shook his head. Form Q might never get off the ground now, although it was his favorite project, and had always been. Form Q on the flow chart for 1979, with human application beginning in 1986. In 1986 he would be seventy-five years old—if he was still alive—but he didn't worry about that. It was the idea, the simple idea, that intrigued him.

Form Q was the logical outgrowth of all the work at the NPS. It began as a project called Form Quixoticus, because it seemed so impossible. But McPherson felt certain that it would happen because it was so necessary. For one thing, it was a question of size; for another, a question of expense.

A modern electronic computer—say, a third-generation IBM digital computer—would cost several million dollars. It drew an enormous amount of power. It consumed space voraciously. Yet the largest computer still had the same number of circuits as the brain of an ant. To make a computer with the capacity of a human brain would require a huge skyscraper. Its energy demands would be the equivalent of a city of half a million.

Obviously, nobody would ever try to build such a computer using current technology. New methods would have to be found—and there wasn't much doubt in McPherson's mind what the methods would be.

Living tissues.

The theory was simple enough. A computer, like a human brain, was composed of functioning units—little flip-flop cells of one kind or another. The size of those units had shrunk considerably over the years. They would continue to shrink as large-scale integration and other microelectronic techniques improved. Power requirements would also decrease.

But the individual units would never become as small as a nerve cell, a neuron. You could pack a billion nerve cells into one cubic inch. No human miniaturization method would ever achieve that economy of space. Nor would any human method ever produce a unit that operated on so little power as a nerve cell.

Therefore, make your computers from living nerve cells. It was already possible to grow isolated nerve cells in tissue culture. It was possible to alter them artificially in different ways. In the future, it would be possible to grow them to specification, to make them link up in specified ways.

Once you could do that, you could make a computer that was, say, six cubic feet in volume, but contained thousands of billions of nerve cells. Its energy requirements would not be excessive; its heat production and waste products would be manageable. Yet it would be the most intelligent entity on the planet, by far.

Form Q.

Preliminary work was already being done in a number of laboratories and government research units around the country. Advances were being made.

But for McPherson the most exciting prospect was not a superintelligent organic computer. That was just a side product. What was really interesting was the idea of an organic prosthesis for the human brain.

Because once you developed an organic computer— a computer composed of living cells, and deriving energy from oxygenated, nutrified blood—then you could transplant it into a human being. And you would have a man with two brains.

What would that be like? McPherson could hardly imagine it. There were endless problems, of course. Problems of interconnection, problems of location, speculative problems about competition between the old brain and the new transplant. But there was plenty of time to solve that before 1986. After all, in 1950 most people still laughed at the idea of going to the moon.

Form Q. It was only a vision now, but with funding it would happen. And he had been convinced that it would happen, until Benson left the hospital. That changed everything.

Ellis stuck his head in the office door. "Anybody want coffee?"

"Yes," McPherson said. He looked over at Morris.

"No," Morris said. He got up out of his chair. "I think I'll replay some of Benson's interview tapes."

"Good idea," McPherson said, though he did not really think so. He realized that Morris had to keep busy—had to do something, anything, just to remain active.

Morris left, Ellis left, and McPherson was alone with his multicolored charts, and his thoughts.

11

IT WAS NOON WHEN ROSS FINISHED WITH Anders, and she was tired. The Scotch had calmed her, but it had intensified her fatigue. Toward the end she had found herself stumbling over words, losing track of her thoughts, making statements and then amending them because they were not exactly what she had intended to say. She had never felt so tired, so drugged with fatigue, in her life.

Anders, on the other hand, was maddeningly alert. He said, "Where do you suppose Benson is now? Where would he be likely to go?"

She shook her head. "It's impossible to know. He's

in a post-seizure state—post-ictal, we call it—and that's not predictable.''

"You're his psychiatrist," Anders said. "You must know a lot about him. Isn't there any way to predict how he'll act?"

"No," she said. God, she was tired. Why couldn't he understand? "Benson is in an abnormal state. He's nearly psychotic, he's confused, he's receiving stimulations frequently, he's having seizures frequently. He could do anything."

"If he's confused . . ." Anders let his voice trail off. "What would he do if he was confused? How would he behave?"

"Look," she said, "it's no good working that way. He could do *anything*."

"Okay," Anders said. He glanced at her, and sipped his coffee.

Why couldn't he just let it go, for Christ's sake? His desire to psych out Benson was ludicrously unrealistic. Besides, everybody knew how this was going to turn out. Somebody would spot Benson and shoot him, and that would be the end of it. Even Benson had said—

She paused, frowning. What had he said? Something about how it would all end. What were his exact words? She tried to remember, but couldn't. She had been too frightened to pay close attention.

"These are the impossible ones," Anders said, getting up and walking to the window. "In another city, you might have a chance, but not in Los Angeles. Not in five hundred square miles of city. It's bigger than New York, Chicago, San Francisco, and Philadelphia put together. Did you know that?"

"No," she said, hardly listening.

"Too many places to hide," he said. "Too many ways to escape—too many roads, too many airports, too many marinas. If he's smart, he's left already. Gone to Mexico or to Canada."

"He won't do that," she said.

"What will he do?"

"He'll come back to the hospital."

There was a pause. "I thought you couldn't predict his behavior," Anders said.

"It's just a feeling," she said, "that's all."

"We'd better go to the hospital," he said.

The NPS looked like the planning room for a war. All patient visits had been canceled until Monday; no one but staff and police were admitted to the fourth floor. But for some reason, all the Development people were there, and they were running around with horrified looks on their faces, obviously worried that their grants and their jobs were in jeopardy. Phones rang constantly; reporters were calling in; McPherson was locked in his office with hospital administrators; Ellis was swearing at anyone who came within ten yards of him; Morris was off somewhere and couldn't be found; Gerhard and Richards were trying to free some telephone lines so they could run a projection program using another computer, but all the lines were in use.

Physically, the NPS was a shambles—ashtrays heaped with cigarette butts, coffee cups crumpled on the floor, half-eaten hamburgers and tacos everywhere, jackets and uniforms thrown across the backs of chairs. And the telephones never stopped ringing: as soon as anyone hung up on a call, the phone rang again instantly.

Ross sat with Anders in her office and went over the

LOS ANGELES POLICE DEPARTMENT
MISCELLANEOUS CRIME REPORT

☐ Shots Fired ☐ Attempt

DR 705901Y-A

TYPE OF CRIME: HOM

VICTIM'S NAME (Last, First, Middle, If Married):
BLACK, ANGELA —

	MO	DAY	YEAR	DAY WK	TIME
OCCURRED: ON OR AFTER	3	12	71	F	6:00 AM
AND	3	12	71	F	6:30 AM

REPORTED: 3 12 71 6:55 AM

V'S SEX, DESCENT, AGE: F - CAUC - 26

INVESTIGATIVE DIVISION & PERSON NOTIFIED:
LAPD - HOM - ANDERS/STAFF

CONNECTED REPORTS — TYPE & D.R. NO.:
DEATH REPORT (711 958) + AUXILIARY FINDINGS REPORT

PREMISES

14	Business	11	Vehicle
04	BANK/S&L, LOAN	02	SUSPECT'S
05	HOSPITAL	03	VICTIM'S
15	MEDICAL OFF	07	TAXI
18	PUBLIC DEPOT	10	OTHER'S
11	RESTAURANT		
11	LAUNDROMAT	15	Miscellaneous
20	OTHER	01	ALLEY
		02	CARPORT
10	Store	06	GARAGE
05	LIQUOR	08	PARK
01	OTHER	16	PKG LOT
		14	SCHOOL
13	Residence	12	STREET
02	SUSPECT'S	11	FLD. TUNNEL
03	VICTIM'S	17	FLD. OVER TOMB
04	APT/PROJECT	18	YARD
06	HOTEL	19	OTHER
07	MOTEL		
08	SINGLE FAMILY		
09	OTHER		

CODE: V—Victim R—Person Reporting W—Witness

Name & Phone Listed Above

R | JOS. R. ALLPORT

VEHICLE

	Interior		Exterior
4	STEREO TAPE	4	PAINTED INSCRIP.
2	MIRROR ORNAM	2	STICKER/DECAL
1	FLOOR SHIFT	1	PINSTRIPE
4	EQUIP. ADDED	4	VINYL TOP
2	EQUIP. MISSING	2	DECORATING PAINT
1	UNIQUE ITEM	1	LTTR./ASTERID

	Upholstery	Modified	Body	Wheels
4	UPHOLSTERY	4 FRONT	4 DAMAGE	4 FRONT
2	BUCKET SEATS	2 REAR	2 SIDE	2 REAR
1	HEADLINER	1 OTHER	1 LEFT	1 FRONT

FURTHER VEHICLE DESCRIPTION (INCLUDE DENTS, COLOR)

7734 LAUREL CANYON   —

SUSPECT

SER.	DESCENT	HAIR	EYES	HEIGHT	WEIGHT	AGE	CLOTHING
1	M	CAUC	BL	BL	5:8	140	314	—
2							
3							

PERSONAL ODDITIES

300 Amputee
1 LEG
2 ARM
3 FOOT
4 HAND
5 EAR
6 FINGERS

301 Deformed
1 LEG
2 ARM
3 HAND
4 LIMP
5 FINGERS
6 BOWLEGGED

302 Tattoo
1 ARM
2 HAND
3 FINGERS
4 CHEST/NECK

303
1 PICTURES
2 DESIGNS

303 Tattoo (cont.)
3 NAMES
4 WORDS
5 INITIALS
6 PACHUCO

304 Facial Scars
1 CHEEK
2 CHIN
3 FOREHEAD
4 LIP
5 EAR
6 EYEBROW

305 Facial Oddity
0 BIRTHMARKS
1 POCKMARKS
2 MOLES
3 FRECKLES
4 PIMPLES
5 LIPS - THICK
6 LIPS - THIN
7 CHIN - PROTRUDED
8 CHIN - RECEDED
9 HOLLOW CHEEK

307 Teeth
1 MISSING
2 GOLD
3 FALSE
4 STAINED/DECAY
5 PROTRUDING
6 IRREGULAR

308 Body Scars
1 ARM
2 HAND
3 WRIST
4 NECK
5 BURN
6 CHEST

306 Speech
0 IMPEDIMENT
1 ACCENT (U.S.)
2 ACCENT (OTHER)
3 LISPS
4 STUTTERS
5 HARE LIP
6 MUMBLES
7 RAPID
8 SOFT/LOW
9 REFINED

311 Eyes
1 MISSING
2 CROSSED
3 SUNGLASSES
4 GLASSES (PLAIN)
5 BULGING
6 SQUINT/BLINK
7 SLANTED

312 Hair Type
1 DYED
2 PROCESSED
3 WIG/TOUPEE
4 CREW CUT
5 BALD
6 AFRO
7 LONG
8 THIN/RECEDED
9 STRAIGHT

313
1 WAVY
2 BUSHY
3 CURLY

314 Facial Hair
1 MUST - CHINESE
2 GOATEE
3 BEARD - FULL
4 MUST - HEAVY
5 MUST - THIN
6 MUST - MEDIUM
7 SIDEBURNS - HEAVY
8 UNSHAVEN

315 Ears
1 CAULIFLOWER
2 PIERCED
3 PROTRUDING
4 CLOSE TO HEAD
5 LARGE
6 SMALL

316 Nose
1 CROOKED
2 HOOKED
3 UPTURNED
4 LONG
5 BROAD
6 FLAT
7 SMALL
8 THIN

317 Face
1 NEGRO W/CAUC. FEATURES
2 HI CHEEK BONE
3 LONG
4 BROAD
5 THIN
6 ROUND

318 Complexion
1 DARK
2 SALLOW
3 RUDDY
4 LIGHT/FAIR
5 MEDIUM

318 Other:

WEAPON

40
GUN - CALIBER
REVOLVER
AUTOMATIC
13 2 INCH
14 4 INCH
15 6 IN. OR MORE
16 BLUE STEEL
17 NICKEL PLATED
18 UNUSUAL GRIPS
21 RIFLE
22 SHOTGUN
23 SAWED OFF
19 RUSTY/DEFECTIVE
24 MACHINE GUN
20 RARE TYPE GUN

40
25 TOY GUN
26 OTHER GUN
28 KNIFE
31 SWITCH BLADE
32 BLADE OVER 5 INCH
29 BODILY FORCE (ON/WT)
28 CAUSTIC CHEM/POISON
45 FIRECRACKERS

40
41 LIQUOR/DRUGS
47 FUSED OIL (WALL EYE)
46 BLACKJACK/CLUB
44 EXPLOSIVES
43 RAZOR
50 SCALDING LIQUID
49 MISSILE, ROCK
51 BELT, CORD, WIRE

40
60 BOTTLE, BRICK, GLASS
52 VEHICLE
54 ASPHYXIATION/SUFFOCATION
55 DROWNING
56 NARCOTICS
57 AXE, CLEAVER
58 ICE PICK

40
59 SCISSORS, FORK
61 GAS, CARBON MONOXIDE
53 PAINT, TAR, CRAYON
64 23 GUN, AIR RIFLE, PELLET GUN, SLINGSHOT
62 FLOODING
63 FIRE
70 OTHER (UNKNOWN)

MISCELLANEOUS CRIME REPORT

CHECKED

MISCELLANEOUS CRIME REPORT

DR

TRADEMARKS

23 Abnormal Acts
- 55 URINATION
- 56 DEFECATION
- 57 PHOTOGRAPHED VICT.
- 58 SET FIRE
- 59 PUT OBJ. IN VAGINA
- 60 DERIVED PLEASURE FROM INFLICTING PAIN
- 62 GROOM
- 63 DERIVED SATISFACTION BY ORAL - FOOT, HAIR, ETC.
- 64 OTHER - UNUSUAL ACT *Masturbation*

24 Suspect's Actions
- 12 DAMAGED BUILDING
- 13 DAMAGED PUBLIC PROP.
- 17 COMMITTED SEX ACTS IN PRESENCE OF VICTIM
- 29 HARBORED A RUNAWAY
- 40 OTHERS

22 Pretended To Be
- 31 POLICE
- 40 OTHER

22 Victim Was
- 61 POLICEMAN
- 62 FIREMAN
- 63 LADYLORD

23 Type
- 27 HOMOSEXUAL
- 31 RIOT
- 33 CULT RITUAL
- 34 ORGANIZED GANG
- 37 DISRUPTIVE PRESENCE-SCHOOL
- 12 CAUSED HOSTILE CROWD TO GATHER
- 42 MAIL/MAILBOX TAMPER
- 51 CHILD STEALING
- 14 CHILD BEATING
- 16 WIFE BEATING
- 19 OTHER: *epileptic*

25 Bombing
- 91 PRIOR WARNING
- 92 FAILED TO EXPLODE
- 93 EXPLODED
- 94 CAUSED FIRE

Quarrel
- 58 REVENGE
- 59 TRAFFIC ITEM
- 60 JUV. PARTY
- 61 BUSINESS
- 62 DRUNKEN
- 63 GAMBLING
- 64 NEIGHBOR
- 65 FAMILY
- 66 LANDLORD/ NEIGHBOR
- 67 COMMON-LAW
- 68 OTHER *Unknown*

24 Suspect Wore
- 08 CLOTHES OF OPPOSITE SEX
- 09 MASK - FACE-COVER
- 10 UNUSUAL CLOTHES

24 Lingerie Involved
- 41 CUT OR TORN
- 44 OTHER

24 Telephone
- 80 TORE FROM WALL
- 81 PULL/CUT/OBS. CONNECT.
- 82 CONTACTED BY
- 83 OTHERS

24 Solicited/Offered
- 36 RIDE
- 37 ASSISTANCE
- 38 NARCOTICS
- 39 OTHERS

22 Shots Fired
- 93 AT VICTIM
- 94 AT INHABITED DWELL.
- 95 AT MOVING VEH.
- 98 OTHERS

23 Initial Contact
- 17 SUSPECT IN VEHICLE
- 23 VICTIM IN VEHICLE
- 29 SUSPECT A PED.
- 30 VICTIM A PED.
- 08 BAR
- 11 INVITATION
- 12 PLACE OF ENTERTAINMENT
- 18 RESIDENCE
- 10 SUSP. A RELATIVE
- 19 VICTIM KNOWS SUSP.

22 Reason
- 04 SEX
- 05 ROBBERY
- 06 BURGLARY
- 09 RACIAL HOSTILITY
- 07 STRANGLES/ SMOTHERS
- 08 SUICIDE/ *drowns*
- 27 OVERDOSE
- 83 OTHERS

25 Force
- 44 HANDCUFFED
- 45 COVERED VICT'S. FACE
- 46 TIED. VICT. TO OBJECT
- 47 GAGGED VICTIM
- 48 GAGGED
- 49 BOUND
- 50 OUTNUMBERED
- 51 BRUTAL ASSAULT
- 41 CHOKED
- 42 ZERO. THREATS, PLEASE, NO HARM FOUND
- 43 OTHERS

22 Vehicle Involved
- 71 CAUSED DAMAGE TO VEHICLE
- 28 FORCED VICT. INTO VICTIM VEHICLE
- 83 OTHERS

---

(1) IDENTIFY ADDITIONAL SUSPECTS ON A SECOND FACE SHEET. IDENTIFY ADDITIONAL WITNESSES. (2) RECONSTRUCT THE CRIME. (3) DESCRIBE PHYSICAL EVIDENCE-STATE LOCATION FOUND AND
BY WHOM. GIVE DISPOSITION. (4) SUMMARIZE OTHER DETAILS RELATING TO CRIME. (5) INDICATE TIME AND LOCATION WHERE VICTIM AND WITNESS CAN BE LOCATED BY DAY INVESTIGATORS IF
NO AVAILABLE PHONE. (6) LIST STOLEN ITEMS -EXCEPT IF CASH IS THE ONLY ITEM TAKEN- ON A PROPERTY SUPPLEMENTAL REPORT. FORM CO.59.A.

(2) *Victim invited suspect to apt. Apparently friendly relations occurred and*
sexual intercourse obtained. Following this victim and suspect took
shower. There victim was apptly making when suspect shot
her on head with lamp. This apparently caused death of

any victim. Suspect placed victim on bed and anal at
multiple stab/bite's with instrument weapon/postmortem Want In-
inquest filed for same

(3) Physical evidence—refer to crime lab photographs and ofc'r of RW Hoggard

(4) No Semen details known

(5) Victim to morgue. No witness

(6) No stolen items

SUPERVISOR APPROVING	SERIAL NO.	INTERVIEWING OFFICERS	SERIAL NO.	DIVISION	DETAIL	PERSON REPORTING (SIGNATURE)
		RW Hoggard	1158-A	Hom	4	x John Andrew
DIVISION	CLERK	TW Yorth	1277-C	Hom	6	CLEARED BY MULTIPLE FOLLOW-UP DR NO.
DATE & TIME REPRODUCED						CLEARED BY ARREST ☐ Yes ☒ No

Los Angeles Police Department
DEATH REPORT

NAME OF DECEASED (LAST, FIRST, MIDDLE)				DR. 711398
BLACK, ANGELA —				
LOCATION OF OCCURRENCE			RPT. DIST. 04	TYPE (TRF., ACC., Susp., Nat.) HOM
SAME			DPT. REST. 09	TYPE CALL OFF. DUTY HOM

DESCRIPTION OF DECEASED

SEX F	DESCENT COUC	HAIR BLOND	EYES BL
HEIGHT 5'4"	WEIGHT 110	AGE 26	BUILD MED	COMPLEXION FAIR

DATE/TIME ARRIVAL AT RPT. RES. 8:10 AM 4/12/71	OCCUPATION OF DECEASED DANCER
DATE/TIME DECEASED DISCOVERED 7:04 PM 4/2/71	DATE/TIME DEATH OCCURRED 6:10 AM 4/12/71

IDENTIFYING MARKS AND CHARACTERISTICS

	DATE/TIME RPTR. TO P.S. 4/12/71 6:52 AM
	RELATIVES NOTIFIED BY CDE

CLOTHING AND JEWELRY WORN
NUDE BODY

REMOVED BY (name & unit) CDE

REMOVED TO (if known)
MORGUE — LA COUNTY

REMOVED BY (name & unit)
CDR

DECEASED'S RESIDENCE ADDRESS
AT LOCATION OF OCCURRENCE

DECEASED'S BUSINESS ADDRESS
NONE KNOWN

PRIMARY CAUSE OF DEATH

REASON (Illness — Injury — Mental, etc.)

INVESTIGATIVE DIVISION/UNIT OR UNITES NOTIFIED AND PERSONS CONTACTED

CODE: R—Person reporting death   D—Person discovering deceased   I—Person identifying deceased   W—Witness

CODE	NEAREST RELATIVE	RELATIONSHIP	NOTIFIED	ADDRESS	CITY	PHONE	X
D/I	Jas R. Allport	Apt Mgr	☐ YES ☐ NO	SAME	Los Agch	▮	M
			RES.				
			BUS.				
			RES.				
			BUS.				
			RES.				
			BUS.				

BUSINESS ADDRESS   PHONE

DOCTOR IN ATTENDANCE
CALLISON — CORONER'S OFF

SOURCE OF CALL (HOW NOTIFIED AND BY WHOM)
X → LAD (City)

| CHRONO'S CASE NUMBER 5:54/71/AB | ASSIGNED BY REAM |

| DISPOSITION OF PROPERTY | ☐ TURNED TO PROPERTY | RECEIPT ☐ YES ☐ NO | RECEIPT NUMBER 2034598 |
| | ☐ RELEASED TO RELATIVE | NAME | ADDRESS |

LIST RECORD PROP THE CIRCUMSTANCES SURROUNDING THE DEATH, OR DESCRIBE PHYSICAL EVIDENCE, LOCATION FOUND AND ITS DISPOSITION.

See Misc. Summary DR 7058R14—A

Miscellaneous Crime Report, checking the description of Benson. The description was computerized, but it read out fairly accurately: *male Caucasian black hair brown eyes 5'8" 140# 34 years old.* Personal oddities: *312/3 wig,* and *319/1 bandages on neck.* Thought to be armed with: 40/11 *revolver.* Trademarks: 23/60 *abnormal act (other)—perseveration.*

Reason for crime: *23/86 suspect insane.*

Ross sighed. "He doesn't really fit your computer categories."

"Nobody does," Anders said. "All we can hope is that it's accurate enough to allow somebody to identify him. We're also circulating his picture. Several hundred photos are being run off now, and distributed around the city. That'll help."

"What happens now?" Ross said.

"We wait," he said. "Unless you can think of a hiding place he'd use."

She shook her head.

"Then we wait," he said.

12

IT WAS A BROAD, LOW-CEILINGED, WHITE-tiled room, lit brightly by overhead fluorescent lights. Six stainless-steel tables were set out in a row, each emptying into a sink at one end of the room. Five of the tables were empty; the body of Angela Black lay on the sixth. Two police pathologists and Morris were bent over the body as the autopsy proceeded.

Morris had seen a lot of autopsies in his day, but the autopsies he attended as a surgeon were usually different. In this one, the pathologists spent nearly half an hour examining the exterior appearance of the body and taking photographs before they made the initial incision. They paid a lot of attention to the external appearance of the stab wounds, and what they called a "stretch laceration" appearance to the wounds.

One of the pathologists explained that this means the wounds were caused by a blunt object. It didn't cut the skin; it pulled it and caused a split in the taut portion. Then the instrument went in, but the initial split was always slightly ahead of the deeper penetration track. They also pointed out that skin hair had been forced down into the wounds in several places—further evidence of a blunt object producing the cuts.

"What kind of blunt object?" Morris had asked.

They shook their heads. "No way to know yet. We'll have to take a look at the penetration."

Penetration meant the depth that the weapon had entered the body. Determining penetration was difficult; skin was elastic and tended to snap back into shape; underlying tissues moved around before and after death. It was a slow business. Morris was tired. His eyes hurt. After a time, he left the autopsy room and went next door to the police lab, where the girl's purse contents were spread out on a large table.

Three men went through it: one identifying the objects, one recording them, and the third tagging them.

Morris watched in silence. Most of the objects seemed commonplace: lipstick, compact, car keys, wallet, Kleenex, chewing gum, birth control pills, address book, ball-point pen, eye shadow, hair clip. And two packs of matches.

"Two packs of matches," one of the cops intoned. "Both marked Airport Marina Hotel."

Morris sighed. They were going through this so slowly, so patiently. It was no better than the autopsy. Did they really think they'd find anything this way? He found the plodding routine intolerable. Janet Ross called that the surgeon's disease, this urge to take decisive action, the inability to wait patiently. Once in an early NPS conference where they were considering a stage-three candidate—a woman named Worley—Morris had argued strongly for taking her as a surgical candidate, even though she had several other problems. Ross had laughed; "poor impulse control," she had said. In that moment, he could cheerfully have killed her, and his murderous feelings were not relieved when Ellis then said, in a clinical, quiet tone, that he agreed that Mrs. Worley was an inappropriate surgical candidate. Morris felt let down in the worst way, even though McPherson said that he thought the candidate had some worth, and probably should be listed as a "possible" and held for a while.

Poor impulse control, he thought. The hell with her.

"Airport Marina, huh?" one of the cops said. "Isn't that where all the stewardesses stay?"

"I dunno," the other cop said.

Morris hardly listened. He rubbed his eyes and decided to get more coffee. He'd been awake for thirty-six hours straight, and he wasn't going to last much longer.

He left the room and went upstairs looking for a coffee machine. There must be coffee someplace in the building. Even cops drank coffee; everybody drank coffee. And then he stopped, shivering.

He knew something about the Airport Marina.

The Airport Marina was where Benson had first been arrested, on suspicion of beating up a mechanic. There was a bar in the hotel; it had happened there. Morris was sure of it.

He glanced at his watch and then went out to the parking lot. If he hurried, he'd beat rush-hour traffic to the airport.

A jet screamed overhead and descended toward the runway as Morris took the airport offramp from the freeway and drove down Airport Boulevard. He passed bars and motels and car-rental offices. On the radio, he heard the announcer drone: "And on the San Diego Freeway, there is an accident involving a truck blocking three northbound lanes. Computer projection of flow is twelve miles an hour. On the San Bernardino Freeway, a stalled car in the left lane south of the Exeter offramp. Computer projection of traffic flow is thirty-one miles an hour . . ."

Morris thought of Benson again. Perhaps computers really were taking over. He remembered a funny little Englishman who had lectured at the hospital and told the surgeons that soon operations would be done with the surgeon on another continent—he would work using robot hands, the signals being transmitted via satellite.

The idea had seemed crazy, but his surgical colleagues had squirmed at the thought.

"On the Ventura Freeway west of Haskell, a two-car collision has slowed traffic. Computer projection is eighteen miles an hour."

He found himself listening to the traffic report intently. Computers or not, the traffic report was vital to anyone who lived in Los Angeles. You learned to pay attention to any traffic report automatically, the way people in other parts of the country automatically paid attention to weather reports.

Morris had come to California from Michigan. For the first few weeks after his arrival, he had asked people what the weather was going to be like later in the day, or on the following day. It seemed to him a natural question for a newcomer to ask, and a natural ice breaker. But he got very strange, puzzled looks from people. Later he realized that he had come to one of the few places in the world where the weather was of no interest to anyone—it was always more or less the same, and rarely discussed.

But automobiles! Now there was a subject of almost compulsive fascination. People were always interested in what kind of car you drove, how you liked it, whether it was reliable, what troubles you had had with it. In the same vein, driving experiences, bad traffic, shortcuts you had found, accidents you had experienced, were always welcome conversation topics. In Los Angeles, anything relating to cars was a serious matter, worthy of as much time and attention as you could devote to it.

He remembered, as a kind of final proof of the idiocy of it all, that an astronomer had once said that if Mar-

tians looked at Los Angeles, they would probably conclude that the automobile was the dominant life form
of the area. And, in a sense, they would be right.

He parked in the lot of the Airport Marina Hotel and
entered the lobby. The building was as incongruous as
its name, with that California quality of bizarre
mixtures—in this case, a sort of plastic-and-neon Japanese inn. He went directly to the bar, which was dark
and nearly deserted at 5 p.m. There were two stewardesses in a far corner, talking over drinks; one or two
businessmen seated at the bar; and the bartender himself, staring off vacantly into space.

Morris sat at the bar. When the bartender came over,
he pushed Benson's picture across the counter. "You
ever seen this man?"

"What'll it be?" the bartender said.

Morris tapped the picture.

"This is a bar. We serve liquor."

Morris was beginning to feel strange. It was the kind
of feeling he sometimes had when he began an operation and felt like a surgeon in a movie. Something very
theatrical. Now he was a private eye.

"His name is Benson," Morris said. "I'm his doctor. He's very ill."

"What's he got?"

Morris sighed. "Have you seen him before?"

"Sure, lots of times. Harry, right?"

"That's right. Harry Benson. When was the last time
you saw him?"

"An hour ago." The man shrugged. "What's he
got?"

"A serious brain disease. It's important to find him. Do you know where he went?"

"Brain disease? No shit." The bartender picked up the picture and examined it closely in the light of a glowing Schlitz sign behind the bar. "That's him, all right. But he dyed his hair black."

"Do you know where he went?"

"He didn't look sick to me. Are you sure you're—"

"Do you know where he went?"

There was a long silence. The bartender looked grim. "You're no fucking doctor," he said. "Now beat it."

"I need your help," Morris said. "Time is very important." As he spoke, he opened his wallet, took out his identification cards, credit cards, everything with an M.D. on it. He spread them across the counter.

The bartender didn't even glance at them.

"He is also wanted by the police," Morris said.

"I knew it," the bartender said. "I knew it."

"And I can get some policeman down here to help question you. You may be an accessory to murder." Morris thought that sounded good. At least it sounded dramatic.

The bartender picked up one of the cards, peered at it, dropped it. "I don't know nothing," he said. "He comes in sometimes, that's all."

"Where did he go today?"

"I don't know. He left with Joe."

"Who's Joe?"

"Mechanic. Works the late shift at United."

"United Air Lines?"

"That's right," the bartender said. "Listen, what about this—"

But Morris was already gone.

* * *

In the hotel lobby, he called the NPS and got through the switchboard to Captain Anders.

"Anders here."

"Listen, this is Morris. I'm at the airport. I have a lead on Benson. About an hour ago, he was seen in the bar of the Airport Marina Hotel. He left with a mechanic named Joe who works for United. Works the evening shift."

There was a moment of silence. Morris heard the scribbling sound of a pencil. "Got it," Anders said. "Anything else?"

"No."

"We'll get some cars out right away. You think he went to the United hangars?"

"Probably."

"We'll get some cars out right away."

"What about—"

Morris stopped, and stared at the receiver. It was dead in his hand. He took a deep breath and tried to decide what to do next. From now on, it was police business. Benson was dangerous. He should let the police handle it.

On the other hand, how long would it take them to get here? Where was the nearest police station? Inglewood? Culver City? In rush hour traffic, even with their sirens it might take twenty minutes. It might take half an hour.

That was too much time. Benson might leave in half an hour. Meanwhile, he ought to keep track of him. Just locate Benson, and keep track of him.

Not interfere. But not let him get away, either.

* * *

The large sign said UNITED AIR LINES—MAINTE-
NANCE PERSONNEL ONLY. There was a guardhouse beneath the sign. Morris pulled up, leaned out of his car.

"I'm Dr. Morris. I'm looking for Joe."

Morris was prepared for a lengthy explanation. But
the guard didn't seem to care. "Joe came on about ten
minutes ago. Signed in to hangar seven."

Ahead of him, Morris saw three very large airplane
hangars, with parking lots behind. "Which one is
seven?"

"Far left," the guard said. "Don't know why he went
there, except maybe the guest."

"What guest?"

"He signed in a guest. . . ." The guard consulted
his clipboard. "A Mr. Benson. Took him to seven."

"What's in seven?"

"A DC-10 that's in for major overhaul. Nothing doing there—they're waiting for a new engine. It'll be
another week in there. Guess he wanted to show it to
him."

"Thanks," Morris said. He drove past the gates, onto
the parking lot, and parked close to hangar seven. He
got out of the car, then paused. The fact was, he really
didn't know whether Benson was in the hangar or not.
He ought to check that. Otherwise, when the police
arrived he might appear a fool. He might sit here in
this parking lot while Benson escaped.

He thought he'd better check. He was not afraid. He
was young and in good physical condition. He was also
fully aware that Benson was dangerous. That fore-
knowledge would protect him. Benson was most dangerous to those who didn't recognize the lethal nature
of his illness.

He decided to take a quick look inside the hangar to make sure Benson was inside. The hangar was an enormous structure but didn't seem to have any doors, except for the giant doors to admit the airplane. They were now closed. How did you get in?

He scanned the exterior of the building, which was mostly corrugated steel. Then he saw a normal-sized door to the far left. He got back in his car and drove up to it, parked, and entered the hangar.

It was pitch black inside. And totally silent. He stood by the door for a moment, then heard a low groan. He ran his hands along the walls, feeling for a light switch. He touched a steel box, felt it carefully. There were several large heavy-duty switches.

He threw them.

One by one, the overhead lights came on, very bright and very high. He saw in the center of the hangar a giant plane, glinting with reflections from the overhead bulbs. It was odd how much more enormous it seemed inside a building. He walked toward it, away from the door.

He heard another groan.

At first he could not determine where it was coming from. There was no one in sight; the floor was bare. But there was a ladder near the far wing. He walked beneath the high sleek tail assembly toward the ladder. The hangar smelled of gasoline and grease, sharp smells. It was warm.

Another groan.

He walked faster, his footsteps echoing in the cavernous hangar space. The groan seemed to be coming from somewhere inside the airplane. How did you get inside? It was an odd thought: he'd made dozens of airplane trips. You always got on by a ramp near the cockpit. But here, in the hangar . . . the plane was so damned enormous, how could you possibly get inside?

He passed the two jet engines of the near wing. They were giant cylinders, black turbine blades inside. Funny the engines had never seemed so big before. Probably never noticed.

There was still another groan.

He reached the ladder and climbed up. Six feet in the air, he came to the wing, a gleaming expanse of flat silver, nubbled with rivets. A sign said STEP HERE. There were drops of blood by the sign. He looked across the wing and saw a man covered with blood lying on his back. Morris moved closer and saw that the man's face was horribly mangled, and his arm was twisted back at a grotesquely unnatural angle.

He heard a noise behind him. He spun.

And then, suddenly, all the lights in the hangar went out.

Morris froze. He had a sense of total disorientation, of being suspended in air in vast and limitless blackness. He did not move. He held his breath. He waited.

The injured man groaned again. There was no other sound. Morris knelt down, not really knowing why. Somehow he felt safer being close to the metal surface of the wing. He was not conscious of being afraid, just badly confused.

Then he heard a soft laugh. And he began to be afraid.

"Benson?"

There was no reply.

"Benson, are you there?"

No reply. But footsteps, moving across the concrete floor. Steady, quietly echoing footsteps.

"Harry, it's Dr. Morris."

Morris blinked his eyes, trying to adjust to the darkness. It was no good. He couldn't see anything. He couldn't see the edges of the wing; he couldn't see the outline of the fuselage. He couldn't see a fucking thing.

The footsteps came closer.

"Harry, I want to help you." His voice cracked as he spoke. That certainly conveyed his fear to Benson. He decided to shut up. His heart was pounding, and he was breathing hard, gasping for breath.

"Harry . . ."

No reply. But the footsteps stopped. Perhaps Benson was giving up. Perhaps he had had a stimulation. Perhaps he was changing his mind.

A new sound: a metallic creak. Quite close.

Another creak.

He was climbing the ladder.

Morris was drenched with cold sweat. He still could see nothing, nothing at all. He was so disoriented he no longer remembered where he was on the wing. Was the ladder in front of him or behind?

Another creak.

He tried to fix the sound. It was coming somewhere in front of him. That meant he was facing the tail, the rear of the wing. Facing the ladder.

Another creak.

How many steps were there? Roughly six feet, six steps. Benson would be standing on the wing soon. What could he use for a weapon? Morris patted his pockets. His clothes were soaked and clinging with

sweat. He had a momentary thought that this was all
ridiculous, that Benson was the patient and he was the
doctor. Benson would listen to reason. Benson would
do as he was told.

Another creak.

A shoe! Quickly, he slipped off his shoe, and cursed
the fact that it had a rubber sole. But it was better than
nothing. He gripped the shoe tightly, held it above his
head, ready to swing. He had a mental image of the
beaten mechanic, the disfigured, bloody face. And he
suddenly realized that he was going to have to hit Benson very hard, with all the strength he had.

He was going to have to try to kill Benson.

There were no more creaking sounds, but he could
hear breathing. And then, distant at first but growing
rapidly louder, he heard sirens. The police were coming. Benson would hear them, too, and would give up.

Another creak.

Benson was going back down the ladder. Morris
breathed a sigh of relief.

Then he heard a peculiar scratching sound and felt
the wing beneath his feet shake. Benson had not
climbed down. He had continued to climb up, and was
now standing on the wing.

"Dr. Morris?"

Morris almost answered, but didn't. He knew then
that Benson couldn't really see, either. Benson needed
a voice fix. Morris said nothing.

"Dr. Morris? I want you to help me."

The sirens were louder each moment. Morris had a
momentary elation at the thought that Benson was going to be caught. This whole nightmare would soon be
over.

"Please help me, Dr. Morris."

Perhaps he was sincere, Morris thought. Perhaps he really meant it. If that were so, then as his doctor he had a duty to help him.

"Please?"

Morris stood. "I'm over here, Harry," he said. "Now, just take it easy and—"

Something hissed in the air. He felt it coming before it hit. Then he felt agonizing pain in his mouth and jaw, and he was knocked backward, rolling across the wing. The pain was awful, worse than anything he had ever felt.

And then he fell into blackness. It was not far to fall from the wing to the ground. But it seemed to be taking a long time. It seemed to take forever.

13

JANET ROSS STOOD OUTSIDE THE TREATMENT room in the emergency ward, watching through the small glass window. There were six people in there taking care of Morris, all clustered around him. She couldn't see much. All she could really see were his feet. He had one shoe on; the other was off. There was a lot of blood; most of the EW people were spattered with it.

Standing outside with her, Anders said, "I don't have to tell you what I think of this."

"No," she said.

"The man is extremely dangerous. Morris should have waited for the police."

"But the police didn't catch him," she said, suddenly angry. Anders didn't understand anything. He didn't understand how you could feel responsible for a patient, how you could want to take care of somebody.

"Morris didn't catch him, either," Anders said.

"And why didn't the police get him?"

"Benson was gone when they got to the hangar. There are several exits from the hangar, and they couldn't all be covered. They found Morris under the wing and the mechanic on top of the wing, and they were both pretty badly hurt."

The treatment-room door opened. Ellis came out, looking haggard, unshaven, defeated.

"How is he?" Ross said.

"He's okay," Ellis said. "He won't have much to say for a few weeks, but he's okay. They're taking him to surgery now, to wire up his jaw and get all the teeth out." He turned to Anders. "Did they find the weapon?"

Anders nodded. "Two-foot section of lead pipe."

"He must have got it right in the mouth," Ellis said. "But at least he didn't inhale any of the loose teeth. The bronchi are clean on lung films." He put his arm around Janet. "They'll fix him up."

"What about the other one?"

"The mechanic?" Ellis shook his head. "I wouldn't place bets. His nose was shattered and the nasal bones were driven up into the substance of the brain. He's leaking CSF through the nostrils. Lot of bleeding and a big problem with encephalitis.''

Anders said, ''How do you assess his chances?''

''He's on the critical list.''

''All right,'' Anders said. He walked off.

Ross walked with Ellis out of the emergency ward toward the cafeteria. Ellis kept his arm around her shoulders. ''This has turned into a horrible mess,'' he said.

''Will he really be all right?''

''Sure.''

''He was kind of good-looking. . . .''

''They'll get his jaw back together. He'll be fine.''

She shuddered.

''Cold?''

''Cold,'' she said, ''and tired. Very tired.''

She had coffee with Ellis in the cafeteria. It was 6:30, and there were a lot of staff people eating. Ellis ate slowly, his movements showing fatigue. ''It's funny,'' he said.

''What?''

''I had a call this afternoon from Minnesota. They have a professorship in neurosurgery to fill. Asked me if I was interested.''

She didn't say anything.

''Isn't that funny?''

''No,'' she said.

''I told them I wasn't considering anything until I was fired here,'' he said.

''Are you sure that'll happen?''

''Aren't you?'' he said. He stared across the cafeteria

at all the nurses and interns and residents in white. "I wouldn't like Minnesota," he said. "It's too cold."

"But it's a good school."

"Oh, yes. A good school." He sighed. "A fine school."

She felt sorry for him, and then suppressed the emotion. He had brought it on himself, and against her advice. For the last twenty-four hours, she had not allowed herself to say "I told you so" to anyone; she had not allowed herself to think it. For one thing, it wasn't necessary to say it. For another, it would not be useful in helping Benson, which was her chief concern.

But she didn't have much sympathy now for the brave surgeon. Brave surgeons risked other people's lives, not their own. The most a surgeon could lose was his reputation.

"Well," he said, "I better get back to the NPS. See how things are going. You know what?"

"What?"

"I hope they kill him," Ellis said. And he walked away toward the elevators.

The operation began at 7 p.m. She watched from the overhead glass viewing booth as Morris was wheeled into the OR, and the surgeons draped him. Bendixon and Curtiss were doing the procedure; they were both good plastic surgeons; they would fix him up as well as anybody possibly could.

But it was still a shock to watch as the sterile gauze packs were taken away from Morris's face and the flesh exposed. The upper part of his face was normal, though pale. The lower part was a red mash, like butcher's meat. It was impossible to find the mouth in all the redness.

Ellis had seen that in the emergency ward. It was shocking to her now, even at a distance. She could imagine the effect much closer.

She stayed to watch as the drapes were placed over the body, and around the head. The surgeons were gowned and gloved; the instrument tables set in position; the scrub nurses stood ready. The whole ritual of preparing for surgery was carried out smoothly and efficiently. It was a wonderful ritual, she thought, so rigid and so perfect that nobody would ever know—and the surgeons themselves probably didn't consider—that they were operating on a colleague. The ritual, the fixed procedure, was anaesthetic for the surgeon just as gas was anaesthetic for the patient.

She stayed a few moments longer, and then left the room.

14

As she approached the NPS, she saw that a cluster of reporters had cornered Ellis outside the building. He was answering their questions in clear bad humor; she heard the words "mind control" repeated several times.

Feeling slightly guilty, she cut around to the far entrance and took the elevator to the fourth floor. Mind control, she thought. The Sunday supplements were going to have a field day with mind control. And then there would be solemn editorials in the daily papers, and even more solemn editorials in the medical journals, about the hazards of uncontrolled and irresponsible research. She could see it coming.

Mind control. Christ.

The truth was that everybody's mind was controlled, and everybody was glad for it. The most powerful mind controllers in the world were parents, and they did the most damage. Theorists usually forgot that nobody was born prejudiced, neurotic, or hung-up; those traits required a helping hand. Of course, parents didn't intentionally damage their children. They merely inculcated attitudes that they felt would be important and useful to their offspring.

Newborn children were little computers waiting to be programmed. And they would learn whatever they were taught, from bad grammar to bad attitudes. Like computers, they were undiscriminating; they had no way to differentiate between good ideas and bad ones. The analogy was quite exact: many people had remarked on the childishness and the literalness of computers. For example, if you could instruct a computer to "Put on your shoes and socks," the computer would certainly reply that socks could not be fitted over shoes.

All the important programming was finished by the age of seven. Racial attitudes, sexual attitudes, ethical attitudes, religious attitudes, national attitudes. The gyroscope was set, and the children let loose to spin off on their predetermined courses.

Mind control.

What about something as simple as social conventions? What about shaking hands when you meet someone? Facing forward in elevators? Passing on the left? Having your wineglass on the right? Hundreds of little conventions that people needed in order to stereotype social interaction—take away any of them, and you produce unbearable anxiety.

People needed mind control. They were glad to have it. They were hopelessly lost without it.

But let a group of people try to solve the greatest problem in the world today—uncontrolled violence—and suddenly there are shouts from all sides: mind control, mind control!

Which was better, control or uncontrol?

She got off at the fourth floor, brushed past several policemen in the hallway, and went into her office. Anders was there, hanging up the telephone. And frowning.

"We just got our first break," he said.

"Oh?" Her irritation dissipated in a wave of expectancy.

"Yes," Anders said, "but I'll be damned if I know what it means."

"What happened?"

"Benson's description and his pictures are being circulated downtown, and somebody recognized him."

"Who?"

"A clerk in Building and Planning, in City Hall. He said Benson came in ten days ago. Building and Planning files specifications on all public structures erected within city limits, and they administer certain building codes."

Ross nodded.

"Well, Benson came in to check specs on a building. He wanted to review electrical blueprints. Said he was an electrical engineer, produced some identification."

Ross said, "The girls at his house said he'd come back for some blueprints."

"Well, apparently he got them from Building and Planning."

"What are they for?"

"University Hospital," Anders said. "He has the complete wiring system for the entire hospital. Now what do you make of that?"

By eight o'clock, she was almost asleep standing up. Her neck was hurting badly, and she had a headache. She realized that she didn't have a choice any more—either she got some sleep, or she'd pass out. "I'll be on the floor if you need me," she told Anders, and left. She walked down the corridor of the NPS, past several uniformed cops. She no longer noticed them; it seemed as if there had always been cops in the hallways for as long as she could remember.

She looked into McPherson's office. He was sitting behind his desk, head on his shoulder, sleeping. His breath came in short, ragged gasps. It sounded as if he were having nightmares. She closed the door quietly.

An orderly walked past her, carrying filled ashtrays and empty coffee cups. It was strange to see an orderly doing cleaning duties. The sight triggered a thought in her mind—something unusual, some question she couldn't quite formulate.

It nagged at her mind, but she finally gave up on it. She was tired; she couldn't think clearly. She came to one of the treatment rooms and saw that it was empty. She went in, closed the door, and lay down on the examination couch.

She was almost instantly asleep.

15

IN THE LOUNGE, ELLIS WATCHED HIMSELF ON the 11 o'clock news. It was partly vanity and partly morbid curiosity that made him do it. Gerhard was also there, and Richards, and the cop Anders.

On the screen, Ellis squinted slightly into the camera as he answered the questions of a group of reporters. Microphones were jammed up toward his face, but he seemed to himself calm. That pleased him. And he found his answers reasonable.

The reporters asked him about the operation, and he explained it briefly but clearly. Then one asked, "Why was this operation done?"

"The patient," Ellis answered, "suffers from intermittent attacks of violent behavior. He has organic brain disease—his brain is damaged. We are trying to fix that. We are trying to prevent violence."

No one could argue with that, he thought. Even Mc-Pherson would be pleased with it as a polite answer.

"Is that common, brain damage associated with violence?"

"We don't know how common it is," Ellis said. "We don't even know how common brain damage alone is. But our best estimates are that ten million Americans have obvious brain damage, and five million more have subtle brain damage."

"Fifteen million?" one reporter said. "That's one person in thirteen."

Pretty quick, Ellis thought. He'd figured it out later as one in fourteen.

"Something like that," he replied on the screen. "There are two and a half million people with cerebral palsy. There are two million with convulsive disorders, including ADL. There are six million with mental retardation. There are probably two and a half million with hyperkinetic behavior disorders."

"And all of these people are violent?"

"No, certainly not. Most are perfectly peaceable. But if you check violent people, you will find an unusually high proportion have brain damage. *Physical* brain damage. And we believe physical brain damage is very often the cause of violence. That contradicts a lot of theories about poverty and discrimination and social injustice. Of course those social factors may contribute to violence. But physical brain damage is also a major factor. And you can't correct physical brain damage with social remedies."

There was a pause in the reporters' questions. Ellis remembered the pause, and remembered being elated by it. He was winning; he was running the show.

"When you say violence—"

"I mean," Ellis said, "attacks of unprovoked violence initiated by single individuals. It's the biggest problem in the world today, violence. And it's a huge problem in this country. In 1969, more Americans were killed or attacked in this country than have been killed or wounded in all the years of the Vietnam war. Specifically—"

The reporters were writing fast.

"—we had 14,500 murders, 36,500 rapes, and 306,500 cases of aggravated assault. All together a third of a million cases of violence. That doesn't include automobile deaths, and a lot of violence is carried out with cars. We had 56,000 deaths in autos, and three million injuries."

"You always were good with figures," Gerhard said, watching.

"It's working, isn't it?" Ellis said.

"Yeah. But you have a squinty, untrustworthy look."

"That's my normal look."

Gerhard laughed.

On the screen, a reporter was saying, "And you think these figures reflect physical brain disease?"

"In large part," Ellis said. "Yes. One of the clues pointing to physical brain disease in a single individual is a history of repeated violence. There are some famous examples. Charles Whitman, who killed seventeen people in Texas, had a malignant brain tumor and told his psychiatrist for weeks before that he was having thoughts about climbing the tower and shooting people. Richard Speck engaged in several episodes of brutal violence before he killed eight nurses. Lee Harvey Oswald repeatedly attacked people, including his wife on many occasions. Those were famous cases. There are a third of a million cases every year that are not famous.

We're trying to correct that violent behavior with surgery. I don't think that's a despicable thing. I think it's a noble goal and an important goal."

"But isn't that mind control?"

Ellis said, "What do you call compulsory education through high school?"

"Education," the reporter said.

And that ended the interview. Ellis got up angrily. "That makes me look like a fool," he said.

"No, it doesn't," Anders, the cop, said.

SATURDAY, MARCH 13, 1971:

Termination

1

SHE WAS BEING POUNDED, BEATEN SENSELESS by brutal, jarring blows. She rolled away and moaned.

"Come on," Gerhard said, shaking her. "Wake up, Jan."

She opened her eyes. The room was dark. Someone was leaning over her.

"Come on, come on, wake up."

She yawned. The movement sent streaks of pain down through her neck. "What is it?"

"Telephone for you. It's Benson."

That jolted her awake faster than she would have thought possible. Gerhard helped her sit up, and she shook her head to clear it. Her neck was a column of pain, and the rest of her body was stiff and aching, but she ignored that.

"Where?"

"Telecomp."

She went outside into the hallway, blinking in the bright light. The cops were still there, but they were tired now, eyes dulled, jaws slack. She followed Gerhard into Telecomp.

Richards held out the phone to her, saying, "Here she is."

235

She took the receiver. "Hello? Harry?"

Across the room, Anders was listening on an extension.

"I don't feel good," Harry Benson said. "I want it to stop, Dr. Ross."

"What's the matter, Harry?" She could hear the fatigue in his voice, the slow and slightly childlike quality. What would one of those rats say after twenty-four hours of stimulation?

"Things aren't working very well. I'm tired."

"We can help you," she said.

"It's the feelings," Benson said. "They're making me tired now. That's all. Just tired. I want them to stop."

"You'll have to let us help you, Harry."

"I don't believe you will."

"You have to trust us, Harry."

There was a long pause. Anders looked across the room at Ross. She shrugged. "Harry?" she said.

"I wish you never did this to me," Benson said. Anders checked his watch.

"Did what?"

"The operation."

"We can fix it for you, Harry."

"I wanted to fix it myself," he said. His voice was very childlike, almost petulant. "I wanted to pull out the wires."

Ross frowned. "Did you try?"

"No. I tried to pull off the bandages, but it hurt too much. I don't like it when it hurts."

He was really being quite childlike. She wondered if the regression was a specific phenomenon, or the result of fear and fatigue.

"I'm glad you didn't pull—"

"But I have to do *something*," Benson said. "I have to stop this feeling. I'm going to fix the computer."

"Harry, you can't do that. We have to do that for you."

"No. I'm going to fix it."

"Harry," she said, in a low, soothing, maternal voice. "Harry, please trust us."

There was no reply. Breathing on the other end of the line. She looked around the room at the tense, expectant faces.

"Harry, please trust us. Just this once. Then everything will be all right."

"The police are looking for me."

"There are no police here." she said. "They've all gone. You can come here. Everything will be all right."

"You lied to me before," he said. His voice was petulant again.

"No, Harry, it was all a mistake. If you come here now, everything will be all right."

There was a very long silence, and then a sigh. "I'm sorry," Benson said. "I know how it's going to end. I have to fix the computer myself."

"Harry—"

There was a click, and then the buzz of a disconnection. Ross hung up. Anders immediately dialed the phone company and asked whether they had been able to trace the call. So that was why he had been looking at his watch, she thought.

"Hell," Anders said, and slammed the phone down. "They couldn't get a trace. They couldn't even find the incoming call. Idiots." He sat down across the room from Ross.

"He was just like a child," she said, shaking her head.

"What did he mean about fixing the computer?"

"I suppose he meant tearing out the wires from his shoulder."

"But he said he tried that."

"Maybe he did, maybe he didn't," she said. "He's confused now, under the influence of all the stimulations and all the seizures."

"Is it physically possible to pull out the wires, and the computer?"

"Yes," she said. "At least, animals do it. Monkeys . . ." She rubbed her eyes. "Is there any coffee?"

Gerhard poured her a cup.

"Poor Harry," she said. "He must be terrified out there."

Across the room, Anders said, "How confused do you suppose he is, really?"

"Very." She sipped the coffee. "Is there any sugar left?"

"Confused enough to mix up computers?"

"We're out of sugar," Gerhard said. "Ran out a couple of hours ago."

"I don't understand," she said.

"He had wiring plans for the hospital," Anders said. "The main computer, the computer that assisted in his operation, is in the hospital basement."

She set down her coffee cup and stared at him. She frowned, rubbed her eyes again, picked the coffee up, then set it down once more. "I don't know," she said finally.

"The pathologists called while you were asleep,"

Anders said. "They determined that Benson stabbed the dancer with a screwdriver. He attacked the mechanic, and he attacked Morris. Machines and people connected with machines. Morris was connected with his own mechanization."

She smiled slightly. "*I'm* the psychiatrist around here."

"I'm just asking. Is it possible?"

"Sure, of course it's possible. . . ." ·

The telephone rang again. Ross answered it. "NPS."

"Pacific Telephone liaison here," a male voice said. "We've rechecked that trace for Captain Anders. Is he there?"

"Just a minute." She nodded to Anders, who picked up the phone.

"Anders speaking." There was a long pause. Then he said, "Would you repeat that?" He nodded as he listened. "And what was the time period you checked? I see. Thank you."

He hung up, and immediately began dialing again. "You better tell me about that atomic power pack," he said as he dialed.

"What about it?"

"I want to know what happens if it's ruptured," Anders said, then turned away as his call was put through. "Bomb squad. This is Anders, homicide." He turned back to Ross.

Ross said, "He's carrying around thirty-seven milligrams of radioactive plutonium, Pu-239. If it breaks open, you'll expose everyone in the area to serious radiation."

"What particles are emitted?"

She looked at him in surprise.

"I've been to college," he said, "and I can even read and write, when I have to."

"Alpha particles," she said.

Anders spoke into the phone. "Anders, homicide," he said. "I want a van at University Hospital right away. We've got a possible radiation hazard pending. Man and immediate environment may be contaminated with an alpha emitter, Pu-239." He listened, then looked at Ross. "Any possibility of explosion?"

"No," she said.

"No explosive," Anders said. He listened. "All right. I understand. Get them here as quickly as you can."

He hung up. Ross said, "Do you mind telling me what's going on?"

"The phone company rechecked that trace," Anders said. "They've determined that there were no calls into the NPS from the outside at the time Benson called. None at all."

Ross blinked.

"That's right," Anders said. "He must have called from somewhere inside the hospital."

Ross stared out the fourth-floor window at the parking lot, and watched as Anders gave instructions to at least twenty cops. Half of them went into the main hospital building; the rest remained outside, in little groups, talking together quietly, smoking. Then a white bomb-squad van rumbled up, and three men in gray metallic-looking suits lumbered out. Anders talked to them briefly, then nodded and stayed with the van, unpacking some very peculiar equipment.

Anders walked back toward the NPS.

Alongside her, Gerhard watched the preparations. "Benson won't make it," he said.

"I know," she said. "I keep wondering if there is any way to disarm him, or immobilize him. Could we make a portable microwave transmitter?"

"I thought of that," Gerhard said. "But it's unsafe. You can't really predict the effect on Benson's equipment. And you know it'll raise hell with all the cardiac pacemakers in other patients in the hospital."

"Isn't there anything we can do?"

Gerhard shook his head.

"There must be *something*," she said.

He continued to shake his head. "Besides," he said, "pretty soon the incorporated environment takes over."

"Theoretically."

Gerhard shrugged.

The incorporated environment was one of the notions from the Development group of the NPS. It was a simple idea with profound implications. It began with something that everybody knew: that the brain was affected by the environment. The environment produced experiences that became memories, attitudes, and habits—things that got translated into neural pathways among brain cells. And these pathways were fixed in some chemical or electrical fashion. Just as a common laborer's body altered according to the work he did, so a person's brain altered according to past experience. But the change, like the calluses on a worker's body, persisted after the experience ended.

In that sense, the brain incorporated past environments. Our brains were the sum total of past experiences—long after the experiences themselves were gone.

That meant that cause and cure weren't the same thing. The cause of behavior disorders might lie in childhood experiences, but you couldn't cure the disorder by eliminating the cause, because the cause had disappeared by adulthood. The cure had to come from some other direction. As the Development people said, "A match may start a fire, but once the fire is burning, putting out the match won't stop it. The problem is no longer the match. It's the fire."

As for Benson, he had had more than twenty-four hours of intense stimulation by his implanted computer. That stimulation had affected his brain by providing new experiences and new expectations. A new environment was being incorporated. Pretty soon, it would be impossible to predict how the brain would react. Because it wasn't Benson's old brain any more—it was a new brain, the product of new experiences.

Anders came into the room. "We're ready," he said.

"I can see."

"We've got two men for every basement access, two for the front door, two for the emergency ward, and two for each of the three elevators. I've kept men away from the patient-care floors. We don't want to start trouble in those areas."

Considerate of you, she thought, but said nothing.

Anders glanced at his watch. "Twelve-forty," he said. "I think somebody should show me the main computer."

"It's in the basement," she said, nodding toward the main building. "Over there."

"Will you show me?"

"Sure," she said. She didn't really care. She no longer maintained any illusions about her ability to affect the outcome of events. She realized that she was in the grip of an inexorable process involving many people and many past decisions. What would happen would happen.

She walked down the corridor with Anders, and found herself thinking about Mrs. Crail. It was odd; she hadn't thought of Mrs. Crail in years. Emily Crail had been her first patient as a psychiatric resident, years ago. The woman was fifty, her children grown, her husband bored with her. She was suicidally depressed. Janet Ross had taken the case with a sense of personal responsibility; she was young and eager, and she fought Mrs. Crail's impulses like a general fighting a war—marshaling resources, planning strategies, revising and updating battle plans. She nursed Mrs. Crail through two unsuccessful suicide attempts.

And then she began to realize that there were limits to her own energy, skills, and knowledge. Mrs. Crail was not improving; her suicidal attempts became more crafty; eventually she succeeded in killing herself. But by that time, Ross had—fortunately—detached herself from the patient.

As she was detached from Benson now.

They had reached the far end of the corridor when behind them, from Telecomp, they heard Gerhard shout, "Janet! Janet, are you still here?"

She returned to Telecomp, with Anders following along curiously. Inside the computer room, the console lights were flickering unsteadily.

"Look at this," Gerhard said, pointing to one printout console.

CURRENT PROGRAM TERMINATED.
PROGRAM CHANGE
IN 05 04 02 01 00
PROGRAM CHANGE

"The main computer is going to a new program," Gerhard said.

"So what?"

"We didn't instruct that."

"What's the new program?"

"I don't know," Gerhard said. "We didn't instruct any change."

Ross and Anders watched the console.

NEW PROGRAM READS AS

Then there was nothing. No further letters appeared on the screen. Anders said, "What does it mean?"

"I don't know," Gerhard said. "Maybe another time-sharing terminal is overriding us, but that shouldn't be possible. We locked in priority for our terminal for the last twelve hours. Ours should be the only terminal that can initiate program changes."

The console flashed up new letters.

NEW PROGRAM READS AS MACHINE MALFUNCTION ALL
PROGRAMMING   TERMINATED   TERMINATED
TERMINATED   TERMINATED   TERMINATED
TERMINATED   TERMINATED   TERMINATED
TERMINATED

"What?" Gerhard said. He started to punch buttons on the console, then quit. "It isn't accepting any new instructions."

"Why not?"

"Something must be wrong with the main computer in the basement."

Ross looked at Anders. "You better show me that computer," he said.

Then, as they watched, one of the consoles went completely dead. All its lights blinked off; the TV screen shrank to a single fading white dot. A second console went off, then a third. The teleprinter stopped printing.

"The computer has shut itself down," Gerhard said.

"It probably had help," Anders said.

He went with Ross to the elevators.

It was a damp evening, and cold as they hurried across the parking lot toward the main building. Anders was checking his gun, turning it sideways to catch the light from the parking-lot lamps.

"I think you should know one thing," she said. "It's no good threatening him with that. He won't respond rationally to it."

Anders smiled. "Because he's a machine?"

"He just won't respond. If he has a seizure, he won't see it, won't recognize it, won't react appropriately to it."

They entered the hospital through the brightly lit main entrance, and walked back to the central elevator banks. Anders said, "Where's the atomic pack located?"

"Beneath the skin of his right shoulder."

"Where, exactly?"

"Here," she said, pointing to her own shoulder, tracing a rectangle.

"That size?"

"Yes. About the size of a pack of cigarettes."

"Okay," Anders said.

They took the elevator to the basement. There were two cops in the elevator car, and they were both tense, fidgety, hands touching their guns.

As they rode down, Anders nodded to his own gun. "You ever fire one of these?"

"No."

"Never at all?"

"No."

He didn't say anything after that. The elevator doors opened. They felt the coolness of the basement air and looked down the corridor ahead—bare concrete walls, unpainted; overhead pipes running along the ceiling, harsh electric lighting. They stepped out. The doors closed behind them.

They stood for a moment, listening. They heard nothing except the distant hum of power equipment. Anders whispered, "Anybody usually in the basement at night?"

She nodded. "Maintenance people. Pathologists, if they're still going."

"The pathology labs are down here?"

"Yes."

"Where's the computer?"

"This way."

She led him down the corridor. Straight ahead was the laundry room. It was locked for the night, but huge carts with bundles of laundry were outside in the corridor. Anders eyed the bundles cautiously before they moved on to the central kitchens.

The kitchens were shut down, too, but the lights were

on, burning in a vast expanse of white-tiled rooms, with stainless-steel steam tables in long rows. "This is a short cut," she said as they went through the kitchen. Their footsteps echoed on the tiles. Anders walked loosely, holding his gun slightly ahead, barrel pointed out to the side.

They passed through the kitchen and back into another hallway. It was almost identical to the one they had left. Anders glanced at her questioningly. She knew he was lost; she remembered the months it had taken her to learn her way through the basement. "Turn right," she said.

They passed a sign on the wall: EMPLOYEES REPORT ALL ACCIDENTS TO YOUR SUPERVISOR. It showed a man with a small cut on his finger. Further down was another sign: NEED A LOAN? SEE YOUR CREDIT UNION.

They turned right down another corridor, and approached a small section containing vending machines—hot coffee, doughnuts, sandwiches, candy bars. She remembered all the late nights when she had been a resident in the hospital and had come down to the vending machines for a snack. The old days, when being a doctor seemed like a good and hopeful thing to be. Great advances would be made during her lifetime; it would be exciting; she would be a part of it.

Anders peered into the vending area, then paused. He whispered: "Have a look at this."

She looked, astonished. Every machine had been smashed. There were candy bars and sandwiches wrapped in plastic strewn across the floor. Coffee was pouring in short, arterial spurts from the coffee vender onto the floor.

Anders stepped around the puddles of coffee and soda and touched the dents and tears in the metal of the machines. "Looks like an axe," he said. "Where would he get an axe?"

"Fire-extinguisher stations have them."

"I don't see the axe here," he said, looking around the room. Then he glanced at her.

She didn't reply. They left the vending area and continued down the corridor. They came to a turn in the tunnels.

"Which way now?"

"Left," she said. And she added: "We're very close."

Ahead of them, the hall took another turn. Ross knew that hospital records was around the turn, and just beyond that, the computer. The planners had located the computer near the records room because they eventually hoped to computerize all the hospital records.

Suddenly Anders froze. She stopped and listened with him. They heard footsteps, and humming—somebody humming a tune.

Anders put his finger to his lips, and gestured to Ross to stay where she was. He moved forward, toward the turn in the corridor. The humming was louder. He paused at the turn and looked cautiously around the corner. Ross held her breath.

"Hey!" a male voice shouted, and suddenly Anders's arm flicked around the corner like a snake, and a man sprawled across the floor, skidding down the hall toward Ross. "Hey!" A bucket of water sloshed across the floor. Ross saw that it was an elderly maintenance man. She went over to him.

"What the—"

"Sh-h-h," she said, a finger to her lips. She helped the man back to his feet.

Anders came back. "Don't leave the basement," he said to the man. "Go to the kitchen and wait. *Don't try to leave.*" His voice was an angry hiss.

Ross knew what he was saying. Anyone who tried to leave the basement now was likely to be shot by the waiting cops.

The man was nodding, frightened and confused.

"It's all right," Ross said to him.

"I didn't do nothin'."

"There's a man down here we have to find," Ross said. "Just wait until it's over."

"Stay in the kitchen," Anders said.

The man nodded, brushed himself off, and walked away. He looked back once, shaking his head. She and Anders continued along the corridor, turned a corner, and came to the records section. A large sign sticking out from the wall said: PATIENT RECORDS.

Anders looked at her questioningly. She nodded. They went inside.

Records was a giant space, filled with floor-to-ceiling shelves of patient records. It was like an enormous library. Anders paused in surprise.

"Lot of bookkeeping," she said.

"Is this every patient the hospital ever had?"

"No," she said. "Every patient seen in the last five years. The others are stored in a warehouse."

"Christ."

They moved down the parallel stacks of shelves quietly, Anders leading with his gun. Occasionally he would pause to look through a gap in the shelves to another corridor. They saw no one at all.

"Anybody on duty here?"

"Should be."

She scanned the rows of charts. The record room always impressed her. As a practicing doctor she had an image of medical practice that involved large numbers of patients. She had treated hundreds, seen thousands for a single hour or a few weeks. Yet the hospital records ran into the millions—and that was just one hospital, in one city, in one country. Millions and millions of patients.

"We have a thing like this, too," Anders said. "You lose records often?"

"All the time."

He sighed. "So do we."

At that moment, a young girl no more than fifteen or sixteen came around the corner. She carried a stack of records in her arms. Anders had his gun up in an instant. The girl looked, dropped the records, and started to scream.

"*Quiet,*" Anders hissed.

The scream was cut off abruptly, to a kind of gurgle. The girl's eyes were wide.

"I'm a policeman," Anders said. He flicked out his shoulder wallet to show the badge. "Have you seen anyone here?"

"Anyone . . ."

"This man." He showed her the picture, She looked at it, and shook her head.

"You're sure?"

"Yes . . . I mean, no . . . I mean . . ."

Ross said, "I think we should go on to the computer.'' In some way, she was embarrassed at frightening the girl. The hospital hired high school and college students part-time to do the clerical work in records; they weren't paid much.

Ross herself remembered when she had been frightened at about the same age. She had been walking in the woods with a boy. They had seen a snake. The boy told her it was a rattlesnake, and she was terrified. Much later she learned he had been teasing her. The snake was harmless. She had resented—

''All right,'' Anders said. ''The computer. Which way?''

Ross led the way out. Anders turned back once to the girl, who was picking up the charts she had dropped. ''Listen,'' he said. ''If you do see this man, don't talk to him. Don't do anything except shout your bloody head off. You understand?''

She nodded.

And then Ross realized that the rattlesnake was real, this time. It was all real.

They came out into the corridor again, and continued down it toward the computer section. The computer section was the only refinished part of the basement. The bare concrete floor changed abruptly to blue carpeting; one corridor wall had been knocked out to install large glass windows that looked in, from the corridor, to the room that housed the main banks of the computer. Ross remembered when the computer was being installed; it seemed to her that the windows were an unnecessary expense, and she had mentioned it to McPherson.

''Better let the people see what's coming,'' McPherson had replied.

"What does that mean?"

"It means that the computer is just a machine. Bigger and more expensive than most, but still just a machine. We want people to get used to it. We don't want them to fear or worship it. We want them to see it as part of the environment."

Yet every time she passed the computer section, she had the opposite feelings: the special treatment, the hallway carpeting, and the expensive surroundings served to make the computer special, unusual, unique. She thought it significant that the only other place in the hospital where the floor was carpeted was outside the small nondenominational chapel on the first floor. She had the same sense here: a shrine to the computer.

Did the computer care if there were carpets on the floor?

In any case, the employees of the hospital had provided their own reaction to the spectacle inside the glass windows. A handwritten sign had been taped to the glass: DO NOT FEED OR MOLEST THE COMPUTER.

She and Anders crouched down below the level of the window. Anders peered over cautiously.

"What do you see?" she said.

"I think I see him."

She looked, too. She was aware that her heart was suddenly pounding; her body was tense and expectant.

Inside the room there were six magnetic tape units, a broad L-shaped console for the central processor, a printer, a card-punch reader, and two disc drive units. The equipment was shiny, sharp-edged, gleaming. It sat quiet under even, fluorescent lighting. She saw no one—

just the equipment, isolated, alone. It reminded her of Stonehenge, the vertical stone columns.

Then she saw him: a man moving between two tape units. White orderly's coat, black hair.

"It's him," she said.

"Where's the door?" Anders asked. For no good reason, he was checking his gun again. He snapped the revolver chamber closed with a loud click.

"Down there." She pointed down the corridor to the door, perhaps ten feet away.

"Any other entrances or exits?"

"No."

Her heart was still pounding. She looked from Anders to the gun and back to Anders.

"Okay. You stay down." Anders pressed her down to the floor as he spoke. Then he crawled forward to the door. He paused, got to his knees, and looked back at her once. She was surprised to see that he was frightened. His face was taut, his body hunched tensely. He held the gun stiffly forward by his straight arm.

We're all afraid, she thought.

Then, with a loud slam, Anders knocked the door open and flung himself on his belly into the room. She heard him shout, "Benson!" And then almost immediately there was a gunshot. This was followed by a second shot, and a third. She could not tell who was firing. She saw Anders's feet sticking out of the door as he lay on the carpeting. Gray smoke billowed out through the open door and rose lazily in the corridor.

There were two more shots and a loud scream of pain. She closed her eyes and pressed her cheek to the carpet. Anders shouted: "Benson! Give it up, Benson!"

It won't do any good, she thought. Didn't Anders understand?

Still more shots, in rapid succession. Suddenly, the glass window above her shattered, and large slabs of glass fell over her shoulders, onto her hair. She shook it off. And then to her astonishment Benson landed on the corridor floor beside her. He had thrown himself through the glass window and landed quite close to her. His body was just a few feet from her. She saw that one leg was bloody, red seeping onto the white trouser leg.

"Harry—"

Her voice cracked strangely. She was terrified. She knew she should not be afraid of this man—that was a disservice to him, a betrayal of her profession, and a loss of some important trust—but she was afraid nonetheless.

Benson looked at her, eyes blank and unseeing. He ran off down the basement corridor.

"Harry, wait—"

"Never mind," Anders said, coming out of the computer room, sprinting after Benson, holding his gun stiffly in his hand. The policeman's posture was absurd; she wanted to laugh. She heard Benson's running footsteps echoing faintly down the tunnel. Then Anders turned a corner, continuing after him. The footsteps blended in staccato echoes.

And then she was alone. She got to her feet, dazed, feeling sick. She knew what was going to happen now. Benson, like a trapped animal, would head for one of the emergency exits. As soon as he appeared outside—

where it was safe to shoot—the waiting policemen would gun him down. All the exits were covered. There was no possible escape. She didn't want to be there to see it.

Instead, she went into the computer room and looked around. The main computer was demolished. Two magnetic tape banks were knocked over; the main control panel was riddled with fine round punctures, and sparks sputtered and dripped from the panel toward the floor. She ought to control that, she thought. It might start a fire. She looked around for a fire extinguisher and saw Benson's axe lying on the carpet in a corner. And then she saw the gun.

Curious, she picked it up. It was surprisingly heavy, much heavier than she expected. It felt big and greasy and cold in her hand. She knew Anders had his gun; therefore this must be Benson's. Benson's gun. She stared at it oddly, as if it might tell her something about him.

From somewhere in the basement, there were four gunshots in rapid succession. They echoed through the labyrinthine hospital tunnels. She walked to the broken windows and looked out at the tunnels. She saw nothing, heard nothing.

It must be finished, she thought. The sputtering, hissing sound of sparks behind her made her turn. There was also a slapping sound, repetitive and monotonous. She saw that one of the magnetic tape reels had spun out, and the edge of the tape was slapping against the hardware spindle.

She went back to the reel and turned it off. She glanced up at one of the display consoles, which was now printing "ERMINA" over and over. "ERMINA, ER-

MINA.'' Then there were two more gunshots, not so distant as the others, and she realized that somehow Benson was still alive, still going. She stood in a corner of the demolished computer room and waited.

Another gunshot, very close now.

She ducked down behind one of the magnetic tape banks as she heard approaching footsteps. She was aware of the irony: Benson had been hiding behind the computers, and now she was hiding, cowering behind the metal columns, as if they could protect her in some way.

She heard someone gasping for breath; the footsteps paused; the door to the computer room opened, then closed with a slam. She was still hidden behind the tape bank, and could not see what was happening.

A second set of running feet went past the computer room and continued down the corridor, fading into echoes. Everything was quiet. Then she heard heavy breathing and a cough.

She stood.

Harry Benson, in his torn white orderly's clothes, his left leg very red, was sprawled on the carpet, his body half-propped up against the wall. He was sweating; his breath came in ragged gasps; he stared straight ahead, unaware of anyone else in the room.

She still held the gun in her hand, and she felt a moment of elation. Somehow it was all going to work out. She was going to get him back alive. The police hadn't killed him, and by the most unbelievable stroke of luck she had him alone, to herself. It made her wonderfully happy,

"Harry." He looked over slowly and blinked. He did

not seem to recognize her for a moment, and then he smiled. "Hello, Dr. Ross."

It was a nice smile. She had the brief image of McPherson, with his white hair, bending over to congratulate her on saving the project and getting Benson back alive. And then she remembered, quite incongruously, how her own father had gotten sick and had suddenly had to leave her medical-school graduation ceremonies. Why did she think of that now?

"Everything is going to be all right, Harry," she said. Her voice was full of confidence; it pleased her.

She wanted to reassure him, so she did not move, did not approach him. She stayed across the room, behind the computer data bank.

He continued to breathe heavily, and said nothing for a moment. He looked around the room at the demolished computer equipment. "I really did it," he said. "Didn't I?"

"You're going to be fine, Harry," she said. She was drawing up a schedule in her mind. He could undergo emergency surgery on his leg that night, and in the morning they could disconnect his computer, reprogram the electrodes, and everything would be corrected. A disaster would be salvaged. It was the most incredible piece of luck. Ellis would keep his house. McPherson would continue to expand the NPS into new areas. They would be grateful. They would recognize her achievement and appreciate what she—

"Dr. Ross . . ." He started to get up, wincing in pain.

"Don't try to move. Stay where you are, Harry."

"I have to."

"Stay where you are, Harry."

Benson's eyes flashed briefly, and the smile was gone. "Don't call me Harry. My name is Mr. Benson. Call me Mr. Benson."

There was no mistaking the anger in his voice. It surprised her and upset her. She was trying to help him. Didn't he know that she was the only one who still wanted to help him? The others would be just as happy if he died.

He continued to struggle to his feet.

"Don't move, Harry." She showed him the gun then. It was an angry, hostile move. He had angered her. She knew she shouldn't get angry at him, but she had.

He grinned in childish recognition. "That's my gun."

"I have it now," she said.

He still grinned, a fixed expression, partly from pain. He got to his feet and leaned heavily against the wall. There was a dark red stain on the carpet where his leg had rested. He looked down and saw it.

"I'm hurt," he said.

"Don't move. You'll be all right."

"He shot me in the leg. . . ." He looked from the blood up to her. His smile remained. "You wouldn't use that, would you?"

"Yes," she said, "if I had to."

"You're my doctor."

"Stay where you are, Harry."

"I don't think you would use it," Benson said. He took a step toward her.

"Don't come closer, Harry."

He smiled. He took another step, unsteady, but he maintained his balance. "I don't think you would."

His words frightened her. She was afraid that she would shoot him, and afraid that she would not. It was the strangest set of circumstances, alone with this man, surrounded by the wreckage of a computer.

"Anders!" she shouted. *"Anders!"* Her voice echoed through the basement.

Benson took another step. His eyes never left her face. He started to fall, and leaned heavily on one of the disc drive consoles. It tore his white jacket at the armpit. He looked at the tear numbly. "It tore. . . ."

"Stay there, Harry. Stay there." It's like talking to an animal, she thought. Do not feed or molest the animals. She felt like a lion tamer in the circus.

He hung there a moment, supporting himself on the drive console, breathing heavily. "I want the gun," he said. "I need it. Give it to me."

"Harry—"

With a grunt, he pushed away from the console and continued moving toward her.

"Anders!"

"It's no good," Benson said. "There's no time left, Dr. Ross." His eyes were on her. She saw the pupils expand briefly as he received a stimulation. "That's beautiful," he said, and smiled.

The stimulation seemed to halt him for a time. He was turned inward, enjoying the sensation. When he spoke again, his voice was calm and distant. "You see," he said, "they are after me. They have turned their little computers against me. The program is hunt. Hunt and kill. The original human program. Hunt and kill. Do you understand?"

He was only a few steps away. She held the gun in her hand stiffly, as she had seen Anders hold it. But her hand was shaking badly. "Please don't come closer, Harry," she said. "Please."

He smiled.

He took another step.

She didn't really know what she was going to do until she found herself squeezing the trigger, and the gun discharged. The noise was painfully loud, and the gun snapped in her hand, flinging her arm up, almost knocking her off her feet. She was thrown back against the far wall of the computer room.

Benson stood blinking in the smoke. Then he smiled again. "It's not as easy as it looks."

She gripped the gun in her hand. It felt warm now. She raised it, but it was shaking worse than before. She steadied it with the other hand.

Benson advanced.

"No closer, Harry. I mean it."

A flood of images overcame her. She saw Benson as she had first met him, a meek man with a terrifying problem. She saw him in a montage of all the hour-long interviews, all the tests, all the drug trials. He was a good person, an honest and frightened person. Nothing that had happened was his fault. It was her fault, and Ellis's fault, and McPherson's fault, and Morris's fault.

Then she thought of Morris, the face mashed into a red pulp, deformed into butcher meat.

"Dr. Ross," Benson said. "You're my doctor. You wouldn't do anything to hurt me."

He was very close now. His hands reached out for the gun. Her whole body was shaking as she watched the hands move closer, within inches of the barrel, reaching for it, reaching for it. . . .

She fired at point-blank range.

With remarkable agility, Benson jumped and spun in

the air, dodging the bullet. She was pleased. She had managed to drive him back without hurting him. Anders would arrive any minute to help subdue him before they took him to surgery.

Benson's body slammed hard into the printing unit, knocking it over. It began to clatter in a monotonous, mechanical way as the keys printed out some message. Benson rolled onto his back. Blood spurted in heavy thick gushes from his chest. His white uniform became darkly red.

"Harry?" she said.

He did not move.

"Harry? Harry?"

She didn't remember clearly what happened after that. Anders returned and took the gun from her hand. He moved her to the side of the room as three men in gray suits arrived, carrying a long plastic capsule on a stretcher. They opened the capsule up; the inside was lined in a strange, yellow honeycomb insulation. They lifted Benson's body—she noticed they were careful, trying to keep the blood off their special suits—and placed him inside the capsule. They closed it and locked it with special locks. Two of the men carried it away. A third went around the room with a Geiger counter, which chattered loudly. Somehow the sound reminded her of an angry monkey. The man went over to Ross. She couldn't see his face behind the gray helmet he wore; the glass was fogged.

"You better leave this area," the man said.

Anders put his arm around her shoulders. She began to cry.

Bibliography

GENERAL

Apter, Michael J. *The Computer Simulation of Behavior.* New York: Harper Colophon, 1971.

Bruner, Jerome. *On Knowing, Essays for the Left Hand.* Cambridge: Harvard University Press, 1962.

Calder, Nigel. *The Mind of Man,* New York: Viking, 1970.

Delgado, J. M. R. *Physical Control of the Mind: Toward a Psychocivilized Society.* New York: Harper & Row, 1968.

Koestler, A. *The Ghost in the Machine.* New York: Macmillan, 1967.

London, P. *Behavior Control.* Harper & Row, 1969; Perennial paperback, 1971.

Wiener, N. *The Human Use of Human Beings: Cybernetics and Society.* Boston: Houghton Mifflin, 1954; Avon paperback, 1967.

Wolstenholme, G. ed., *Man and His Future.* London: Churchill, 1963.

Wooldridge, D. E. *The Machinery of the Brain.* New York: McGraw-Hill, 1963.

TECHNICAL REFERENCES

Adams, John E. "The Future of Stereotaxic Surgery." *J. Am. Med. Assn.* 198(1966):648-652

Aird, R. B., et al. "Antecedents of Temporal Lobe Epilepsy." *Arch. Neurology* 16(1967):67-73

Anastasopoulos, G., et al. "Transient Bulimia-Anorexia and Hypersexuality Following Pneumoencephalography in a Case of Psychomotor Epilepsy." *J. Neuropsych.*, 4(1963):135-142.

Bennett, A. E. "Mental Disorders Associated with Temporal Lobe Epilepsy." *Dis. of the Nervous System*, 26(1965):275-280.

Bishop, M. P., et al. "Intracranial Self-Stimulation in Man." *Science*, 140(1963):394-396.

Bloch, S. "Aetiological Aspects of the Schizophrenia-Like Psychosis of Temporal Lobe Epilepsy." *Med. J. Australia*, 66(1969):451-453

Carleton, R. A., et al. "Environmental Influence on Implantable Cardiac Pacemakers." *J. Am. Med. Assn.*, 190(1964):938-940

Chase, R. A., et al. "Ictal Speech Automatisms and Swearing: Studies on the Auditory Feedback Control of Speech." *J. Nervous and Mental Disease*, 144(1967):406-420.

Crandall, P. H., et al. "Clinical Applications of Studies on Stereotactically Implanted Electrodes in Temporal-Lobe Epilepsy." *J. Neurosurgery* 20(1964): 827–840.

Delgado, J. M. R., et al. "Intracerebral Radio Stimulation and Recording in Completely Free Patients." *J. Nervous and Mental Disease*, 147(1968):329–340.

Duffy, J. C., et al. "Psychic and Somatic Interactions in Psychomotor Epilepsy." *Psychosomatics*, 7(1966):353–356.

Ellinwood, E. H., Jr. "Amphetamine Psychosis: Theoretical Implications." *International J. of Neuropsych.*, 4(1968):45–54.

Falconer, M. A. "Problems in Neurosurgery: 1. Temporal Lobe Epilepsy." *Trans. Med. Soc. London*, 82(1967):111–126.

Falconer, M. A. "Surgical Treatment of Temporal Lobe Epilepsy." *New Zealand Med. J.*, 66(1964):539–542.

Falconer, M. A., et al. "Temporal Lobe Epilepsy Due to Distant Lesions: Two Cases Relieved by Operation." *Brain*, 85(1961):521–534.

Fenton, G. W., et al., "Homicide, Temporal Lobe Epilepsy and Depression: A Case Report." *Brit. J. Psychiatry*, 111(1965):304–306.

Fenyes, I., et al. "Temporal Epilepsies with Deep-seated Eliptogenic Foci: Postoperative Course." *Archives of Neurology* 4(1964):559–571.

Glaser, G. H. "The Problem of Psychosis in Psychomotor Temporal Lobe Epileptics." *Epilepsia*, 5(1964):271-278.

Green, J. R. "Temporal Lobectomy, with Special Reference to Selection of Epileptic Patients." *J. Neurosurg.*, 26(1966):584-593.

Greenberg, R., et al. "Sleep Patterns in Temporal Lobe Epilepsy." *Comprehensive Psychiatry*, 9(1968): 194-199.

Hierons, R., et al. "Impotence in Patients with Temporal Lobe Lesions." *Lancet*, 2(1966):761-763.

Holowach, J., et al. "Psychomotor Seizures in Childhood, a Clinical Study of 120 Cases." *Pediatrics*, 59(1961):339-345.

Hommes, O. R. "Psychomotor Epilepsy: A Neurological Approach to Hysteria." *Psychiat. Neurol. Neurochir.*, 67(1964):497-519.

Hunter, R., et al. "Temporal Lobe Epilepsy Supervening on Longstanding Transvestism and Fetishism: A Case Report." *Epilepsia*, 4(1963):60-65.

Kenna, J. C., et al. "Depersonalization in Temporal Lobe Epilepsy and the Organic Psychoses." *Brit J. Psychiatry*, 111(1965):293-299.

Knapp, D. E., et al. "Nuclear Electrical Power Sources for Biomedical Applications." Proceedings of the Fourth Intersociety Energy Conversion Engineering Conference, Washington, D.C., September 22-26, 1969. New York: American Institute of Chemical Engineers, 1969, pp. 101-106.

Kolarsky, A., et al. "Male Sexual Deviation: Association with Early Temporal Lobe Damage." *Arch. Gen. Psychiat.*, 17(1967):735–743.

Norman, J. C., et al. "Implantable Nuclear-Powered Cardiac Pacemakers." *New Eng. J. Med.*, 283(1971): 1203–1206.

Pickers, B. A., et al. "Inhibition of a Demand Pacemaker and Interference with Monitoring Equipment by Radio-Frequency Transmissions." *Brit. Med. J.*, 2(1969):504–506.

Rand, R. W., et al. "Chronic Stereotactic Implantation of Depth Electrodes for Psychomotor Epilepsy." *Acta Neurochirurgica*, 11(1968):609–630.

Reiher, J., et al. "Combined Electroencephalography and Sonoencephalography in Temporal Lobe Epilepsy." *Neurology*, 19(1969):157–159.

Roth, M., et al. "Temporal Lobe Epilepsy and the Phobic Anxiety-Depersonalization Syndrome." *Comprehensive Psychiatry* 3(1963):130–151, 215–226.

Serafetinides, E. A., et al. "Some Observations on Memory Impairment After Temporal Lobectomy for Epilepsy." *J. Neurol. Neurosurg. Psychiat.*, 25(1962):251–255.

Serafetinides, E. A., "Aggressiveness in Temporal Lobe Epileptics and Its Relation to Cerebral Dysfunction and Environmental Factors." *Epilepsia*, 6(1965):33–42.

268   Bibliography

tiides, E. A., et al. "The Effects of Temporal Lobectomy in Epileptic Patients with Psychosis." *J. Ment. Sci.*, 108(1962):584–593.

Slotnick, D. L. "The Fastest Computer." *Sci. Am.*, 224(1971):76–87.

Stevens, J. R. "Psychiatric Implications of Psychomotor Epilepsy." *Arch. Gen. Psych.* 14(1966):461–471.

Stevenson, H. G. "Psychomotor Epilepsy Associated with Criminal Behaviour." *Med. J. Australia*, 60(1963):784–785.

Strobos, R. J. et al. "Mechanisms in Temporal Lobe Seizures." *Arch. Neurology*, 5(1961):48–57.

Walker, E. A. "Temporal Lobectomy." *J. Neurosurgery*, 26(1966):642–649.

Weiss, A. A. "Psychodiagnostic Follow-Up of Eight Cases of Temporal Lobectomy." *Israel Ann. Psychiat.*, 3–4 (1962): 259–266

Yatteau, R. F. "Radar-Induced Failure of a Demand Pacemaker," *New Eng. J. Med.*, 283 (1971): 1447–1448.